Tyler Anne Snell live in South Alabama with her same-named husband, their artist kiddo, four mini 'lions' and a burning desire to meet Kurt Russell. Her superpowers include binge-watching TV and herding cats. When she isn't writing thrilling mysteries and romance, she's reading everything she can get her hands on. How she gets through each day starts and ends with a big cup of coffee. Visit her at tylerannesnell.com

Having written over ninety novels, **Tara Taylor Quinn** is a *USA TODAY* bestselling author with more than seven million copies sold. She is known for delivering intense, emotional fiction. Tara is a past president of Romance Writers of America and a seven-time RITA® Award finalist. She has also appeared on TV across America, including CBS Sunday Morning.

RETRACING THE INVESTIGATION

TYLER ANNE SNELL

COLTON COUNTDOWN

TARA TAYLOR QUINN

MILLS & BOON

First Published in Great Britain 2022
by Mills & Boon, an imprint of HarperCollins*Publishers* Ltd
1 London Bridge Street, London, SE1 9GF

www.harpercollins.co.uk

HarperCollins*Publishers*
1st Floor, Watermarque Building,
Ringsend Road, Dublin 4, Ireland

Retracing the Investigation © 2022 Tyler Anne Snell
Colton Countdown © 2022 Harlequin Enterprises ULC

Special thanks and acknowledgement are given to Tara Taylor Quinn for her contribution to *The Coltons of Colorado* series.

ISBN: 978-0-263-30347-6

0622

MIX
Paper from
responsible sources
FSC™ C007454
FSC
www.fsc.org

This book is produced from independently certified FSC™ paper to ensure responsible forest management.

For more information visit: www.harpercollins.co.uk/green

Printed and Bound in Spain using 100% Renewable electricity at CPI Black Print, Barcelona

RETRACING THE INVESTIGATION

TYLER ANNE SNELL

This book is for Ashley Parr. You're the best dang social worker in the world, and without your guidance and compassion helping us through a wild ride, this book would have still been a thought in my head. Thank you for making us a family.

Prologue

Annie McHale's disappearance was the beginning of the end for Kelby Creek. They hadn't known it then. Not when the town helped searched for the teen, not when the ransom demand came in proving her kidnapping, not when Annie's godfather, the former Sheriff Barkley from five years ago, took over to help. Not even when the ambush at the park happened.

Not even when Helen Murphy died on her picnic blanket during that ambush waiting for her husband to arrive, caught in the cross fire.

It was only after an FBI agent, Jacqueline—Jackie—Ortega, went missing while looking for Annie that people started to suspect something bad was coming.

And when the sheriff and mayor were arrested for orchestrating Annie's kidnapping?

Most knew it was over for normal in Kelby Creek.

For the holdouts, they lost hope when widespread corruption was revealed to have been festering throughout their town for years, while no one had been the wiser.

Five years later and Jones Murphy, a widower since Helen's death, was wiser.

He drove the long way round to his father's home instead of the shortcut through downtown. His father's truck bed was filled with boxes that Jones had dumped into the family storage unit after he'd come back to town with his five-year-old daughter, Bonnie. Coming back to Kelby Creek had been hard enough. Living with his father was proving trickier than he'd originally thought it would be. Ted Murphy was a man who dabbled in multiple hobbies. Hobbies that took up so much space that trips to the storage unit to pack things away and to get his and Bonnie's belongings to the house had become normal since being back.

Not exactly how Jones had expected his homecoming to look. Then again, he hadn't expected to be in Kelby Creek again.

Jones took the extra five minutes of the longer drive to list all the things he had to do in the coming week. Bonnie was starting kindergarten and he had to meet the teachers and principal. His father also needed to start physical therapy for his knee now that the surgery was done. Then there was Bonnie's room. He wanted to paint it Almost Pink, the same color her bedroom had been in every place they'd lived in the last five years. The same color her nursery had been even before she'd been born.

"It's light and warm and feels just rosy enough for a girl who's going to be light and warm, too," Helen had told him, pregnant belly still growing. "And couldn't we all use a little of both?"

Jones tightened his hand on the steering wheel at the memory.

He always tightened when he had to remember that his wife was exactly that.

A memory.

He gritted his teeth and couldn't help but feel an anger in him as he pulled into the drive of his childhood home. Seeing Bonnie would help the anger, but the ache that followed would linger. It always did.

Jones cut the engine and realized the house for sale next door had two vehicles parked in its drive. Both were empty.

All six-five of Jones made his way to and through the front door in seconds. He saw his father's crutches first and his father second. The man and woman sitting across from him on the couch came next.

"I knew he wouldn't be long," his father said to his guests. He looked at Jones. "You have some company, son."

Jones had kept in contact with absolutely no one other than his father after he and Bonnie had left Kelby Creek. But that didn't mean he didn't recognize the man who stood first.

He was older, had grayed and had survived a heart attack during an exceptionally dangerous investigation according to the news a while ago. He'd also been Jones's boss for a short time.

"Brutus Chamblin."

The woman at his side was younger, had a long braid and a severe look. Jones had never met her, but he realized who she was quickly enough.

"Blake Bennet," he added.

She gave a deep nod.

Jones didn't understand why either was at his father's house, but Brutus wasn't a man to beat around the bush.

"You think we can talk outside for a sec?" he asked. "Won't take long."

Jones was ready to say no but his dad was quicker at the draw.

"Best to do it out on the back porch since Bonnie is still napping. Y'all can walk out through the door in the kitchen."

Brutus and Blake didn't wait for an okay from Jones. It put him on edge even more when they did as his dad said and headed to the back porch. Once outside, they faced Jones, but he spoke first.

"When the former and current sheriffs of Kelby Creek come calling, it can't be good."

Brutus, the former and most beloved sheriff in the history of Kelby Creek, cracked a smile. Blake, the current sheriff, had a less-warm reaction.

"We're not here because of trouble or anything sordid," Brutus said. "In fact, we're here in a very opposite capacity." The older man shared a look with Blake. Her posture was already straight, but it seemed to stiffen a bit more as she lifted her chin to meet his gaze.

"No one but us and a few others know this, but I'm leaving my position as sheriff," she began. "My sister passed and I'm taking custody of my niece and nephew, and to make it a little easier on them, I'm moving back to Georgia."

Jones was surprised, but offered his sympathy first.

"I'm sorry for your loss," he said. Blake nodded. She didn't continue, so Jones went with surprise next. He looked to Brutus. "Do you want me to suggest someone for sheriff? You know I haven't been around in years. I mean, I've kept up with the news, but I haven't been on duty with more than half of this new department."

Brutus and Blake shared another look. It should have tipped off Jones.

"We're not asking for suggestions," Blake explained.

Brutus cleared his throat. His smile went serious when he spoke next.

"We're here because we want you to run for sheriff."

Jones blinked a few times because he was sure he hadn't heard him right.

"You've got to be kidding me," he replied.

They were, in fact, not kidding him.

"The job of sheriff is the last piece, Jones," Brutus said. "The department is different, a whole helluva lot different than when you left. It needs a permanent head of the table."

Before he could respond, there was another look between Brutus and Blake.

This time she spoke.

"And we don't just need you to be sheriff. We need you to reinvestigate the Annie McHale kidnapping."

"What do you mean 'reinvestigate'?" Jones asked.

Brutus turned and took a seat at one of the two rocking chairs on the porch. Blake wordlessly followed and stood next to him.

Brutus motioned to the other chair.

"Boy, have we got a story to tell you."

Jones could have said no. He could have asked them to leave. He could have cussed them for even suggesting he ever go back to the department. That he go back and investigate the one case that broke the town, that shattered so many lives and that took Helen's along with it.

Yet, Jones found himself sitting all the same.

"You have one minute."

CASSANDRA WEST DIDN'T typically go to a bar when she was at home. That went doubly so for when she was on the road. Yet, there she was at the hotel bar, a few hours from home, trying not to cry into her drink.

June Smith, her friend and co-teacher, had told her it was more than okay to stay an extra day and just *be*. It was, after all, what should have been her wedding anniversary. It wasn't Cassandra's fault that it coincided with their conference ending.

Yet, there she was, alone at the hotel bar, when she should have been home in her bed crying.

Changing locations wasn't helping her heart. Neither was the wine she was drinking.

It wasn't until a man sat next to her and ordered a beer with the heaviest sigh she'd ever heard that she wondered how the few other patrons viewed her. And it wasn't until that same man turned her way that Cassandra realized her poker face was as disastrous as a spilled can of glitter.

"Been a day, huh?"

Cassandra was glad there was a stool between them. If there hadn't been she would have craned her head all the way back to see the man.

He was tall.

Extremely tall.

And handsome.

Even in the dim bar light, she could see that.

"It has," she agreed amicably.

The man let that lie and Cassandra ran her finger across her glass. The burgeoning tears, thankfully, stayed right where they were. Yet the silence now bothered her. As if the giant man had blown a hole into the darkness and now she had to fill it.

Or maybe that was her personality trying to claw its way back to the surface.

Or maybe it was simply because on any given week-day, she was in a conversation, or twelve, with several small children.

"I don't think people come to hotel bars unless they've been having one," she said after a moment. "A day, that is." She looked around them with a self-deprecating smile. "Or maybe they're tired from whatever work conference or travel they're doing and drinking from the minifridge is just too expensive."

The man smirked at that statement.

"Then there's how expensive room service is," he said.

"I took one look at how much a sandwich ran for and decided it was time to close the menu."

Cassandra agreed.

"I was lucky enough to get a food allowance for my work thing and it still was ridiculous. My coworkers and I spent one night at McDonald's to save some money."

It was a pleasant, nothing conversation.

But it felt nice.

"Are you here for work?" she asked, surprising herself. "I heard there was an accountants' type of get-together starting tomorrow."

The man didn't look like an accountant, but sometimes she was told she didn't look like an elementary school teacher. Mostly because when she didn't have to be at school, her outfits ran more formal. Sometimes it was a nice change of pace to wear a pencil skirt versus a sundress with a cardigan that had rainbow patches all over it.

"I am but I'm not," the man answered. The bartender delivered his drink. He explained before she could decide if she was going to follow up with that. "I'm trying to decide if I should take a job or not. To do that I decided to give myself some time to think without distractions. Hence, getting a hotel room even though I have a perfectly good home I could be at."

"According to my friend, sometimes you just need somewhere you can just be and usually that's easier at a place like this."

The man chuckled.

"I guess it makes sense. I'll have to remind myself of that, though, when the bill comes in." He stretched out his hand to her. "I'm Jones."

Cassandra wished she had more time to marvel at how large his hand was around hers as she shook it. Instead, she was quick.

"Cassandra—a woman with a friend who sounds like a fortune-cookie writer."

He laughed again. This time, though, his gaze seemed to linger on her.

It made something in Cassandra shift.

It also brought on a slight blush.

She tried to distract herself from it.

"So this job—what was your gut reaction to the offer? Or are you a pro-and-con-list kind of guy instead of only listening to your instincts?"

Jones ran a thumb across his jaw and sighed again.

"Well, the problem is I'm an instincts guy who still likes making lists. My gut reaction was to turn the job down but also to take it. My list had the same amount of pros and cons."

"Which means as of right now you should and shouldn't take it."

He nodded.

Cassandra swiveled in her seat so she could face him. She thought about his predicament for a little bit, trying to stay respectful of his privacy. To an extent.

"Have you ever seen the show *Friends*?"

The question seemed to catch the man off guard. He answered all the same.

"Some of it as reruns, but I couldn't name the characters off even with a gun to my head."

Cassandra smiled.

"Well, there's something one of the characters does to try and figure out how they're really feeling. It's a game. I ask quick questions and you give quick answers. No time to pause and think. Just answer. It might help you push you over your indecision?"

Jones made a face, but then turned on his stool so he was finally open to her.

"At this point what would it hurt to try?"

Cassandra put down her drink and used her hands, palms up, for each option. Given her profession of dealing with little kids all of the time, she was always using her hands when she spoke.

"Ready?"

Jones smiled. "Ready."

Cassandra didn't skip a beat. "Red or blue?" she started.

"Blue," he said immediately.

"Cats or dogs?"

"Dogs."

"The moon landing was faked, yes or no?"

"No."

"Alabama or Auburn?"

"Alabama."

"Beer or whiskey?"

"Beer."

"Rain or shine?"

"Rain."

"Do you want this job, yes or no?"

"Yes."

The answer was as quick as the rest, if not quicker.

Cassandra watched as Jones's eyes widened. Then his expression melted into an easy smile.

She joined in.

"I don't know about your pro-and-con list but I think your instincts want you to take the job," she said. "But that's just my opinion and, I should note, I don't even know what job it was you were offered, so I can't take responsibility if you take it and it doesn't work out."

Jones was back to smirking.

"I'm not about to blame someone who just ended my day-long turmoil of indecision." He took a sip of his drink. Cassandra mirrored him. She half expected them to slip back into silence, but Jones didn't let them. "In fact, maybe I can repay you by buying you dinner? Someplace that's more reasonably priced than the minifridge, of course."

Cassandra didn't normally drink at unfamiliar bars. Even less so did she accept dinner invites from men she met in them.

Yet...there was something about the man that stuck.

Or maybe your heart hurts and he's managed to make you forget that for a few minutes.

Cassandra wasn't sure what her reasons were for saying yes, but she did.

Had she known that their dinner would turn into one amazing night spent back in her room, she might have hesitated.

But, in the moment, all she said was "I won't say no to that."

Chapter One

Ray Cooke was two steps from the side of a bridge that if he fell from, would surely make his bad day that much worse.

Jones saw the man as he got out of his father's truck, but he let his new chief deputy walk up to him before he made his way to Ray's side.

"What's he going on about?" Jones asked his right-hand man.

Carlos Park had been a part of the Dawn County Sheriff's Department since before The Flood, a series of events that started with Annie McHale's kidnapping and snowballed into a corruption case involving her godfather, Sheriff Barkley, and the mayor, both of whom had played a major role in the crime. It was why trust had been so low in town every day since, but people like Carlos and his team were trying to earn it back. If Carlos stayed long enough, Jones suspected he'd be the next sheriff down the road. Now he looked close to rolling his eyes at good ol' Ray Cooke, one of their frequent flyers at the jail.

"He's drunk as a skunk and talking about his lady again," Carlos said with a heavy dose of "same song and dance" in his tone. "She went off with Trevor, he thinks, and Ray's trying to take out his frustration by yelling at any and all cars driving through. Lucky for him it's piss early and the only car he yelled at was Millie's, and she knows how to handle herself."

It had been seven months since Jones had been asked to run for sheriff. He'd done that, been elected and had those months to get his feet wet, so to speak.

Now he knew that Millie was the wife of their lead detective, Foster Lovett, and given their history, she could, in fact, hold her own. Just as he now knew that Ray Cooke didn't listen to reason when he was being belligerent. He only responded to something bigger and scarier than him.

"It's just like scaring a bear off the trail by making yourself seem larger and louder," Kathryn Juliet, one of their detectives, had instructed when Jones had been on his way to his first Ray Cooke experience. "Last time Howie went, she actually waved her arms a little to make herself seem bigger. It worked."

Jones wasn't about to wave his arms. He didn't have to. Ray might have been six feet tall, but Jones was well over that.

"All right, you head on to the department. I got this," Jones said to Carlos at his cruiser.

"How about I just make the first call I need to make today in my car," Carlos offered instead. "Ray might be harmless but better safe than sorry."

Before The Flood, Jones might have shooed the man away without a second thought, but he no longer trusted his gut on who was or wasn't harmless anymore. He'd made that mistake before with trusting Sheriff Barkley and everyone else who had become a part of the corruption. That was even accounting for Annie McHale's specific investigation, something Jones was itching to get back to instead of dealing with Ray and his women troubles.

"All right," Jones conceded. "This won't take but a minute."

Ray Cooke was standing on the road side of the bridge's

concrete railing. Though there was nothing too mighty about the structure. It was just made to keep cars off the creek water that rose too high in the rain. Given it was more of a trickle than a creek beneath the bridge, it wasn't all that worrisome if Ray tried to flee over its edge. He'd drop maybe four feet, get a little wet and limp along until they got him.

Maybe that's why he'd picked this bridge and not one of the others in town that had a good amount of water beneath them.

Ray liked pretending he had control, that he had options.

He didn't. At least, none of them good.

Jones approached the man and looped his thumbs between his belt and pants. Ray took a moment to really look at Jones before he went on the defensive, putting his arms across his chest and holding his chin high.

"Well, look who got the sheriff out to see him," Ray sneered. "Must be rating pretty high to get that kinda treatment."

Jones held in his sigh.

"Morning, Ray," he greeted. "Been a minute."

Ray was a younger man who looked like he'd probably been a good quarterback in high school. Square shoulders, wide arms, could run at a decent clip. Wasn't too big, wasn't too thin. But after his glory days were over, he'd softened for whatever reason.

He looked like he was "hunched against the wind," as Jones's dad liked to say.

But troubles or no, Ray couldn't keep doing what he was doing. One day he was going to cause trouble he couldn't take back and that was something that no one wanted.

Ray wasn't done sneering. He made a show of looking Jones up and down.

"There wasn't no need for you to come on out." He nodded to Carlos's cruiser. "No need for any of you. I wasn't doing nothing."

"You were barking at cars, Ray," Jones responded. "That's not nothing, especially when you follow it up by running into the road. Someone could have been hurt, or worse, you included."

Ray scoffed, shook his head enough to cross his eyes a moment and set his jaw like a man who wasn't going to make the next few minutes easy.

"No one can take a joke in this town. That's all it was. Me being funny. But *no*, ain't you or anyone at that box of nothings going to see that." He pointed out at Jones but his eyes went to the sheriff's star on his breast pocket. "That badge don't mean a thing. Just something to keep crumbs off of your shirt."

Jones kept his relaxed stance. This was tame talk compared to some other verbal altercations he'd had during his career before The Flood.

"It also looks nice in pictures," Jones said with a small smile. "Not to mention makes me responsible for keeping everyone as safe as I can. So why don't you let me give you a ride home and you can sleep off last night there?"

Because of his experiences with Ray in the last few months, Jones expected the man to hesitate before relenting with a nod. But, for whatever reason, this Monday morning, Ray was proud.

He stuck out his chest and gave Jones a stare that would have stung had Ray been serious. When he spoke it was snake-in-the-grass deceptive.

"A badge didn't help save your wife—what makes you think this one can save any of us?"

Jones had nerves of steel, body strength near it and could shut his mouth like a vault when needed.

But Ray's pride and the words that followed had taken a bite out of Jones. A surprisingly harsh one.

Which made him want to bite right on back.

Jones unhooked his thumbs from his belt and slowly started toward the smaller man.

And Ray *was* small.

Lightweight in body, heavyweight in mind.

He wasn't so sure of his words the closer Jones got. That much was clear.

"You get two options, Ray Cooke," Jones growled. "You either call the one taxi in this whole town and get going in it, or you accept my more-than-nice offer to give you a ride and you shut your mouth until I drop you at your front door. Do you understand?"

Ray had to raise his chin to keep eye contact. He'd gone awfully still for a man keen on slinging pointed comments.

Jones leaned into the quiet.

"Do you understand me?" he repeated. "Or do I need to rephrase the options?"

Ray finally broke.

His eyes hit the ground, his arms went limp at his sides.

"Could you call me up the cab? I got enough to get home."

Jones took a moment but nodded into his rising anger. He called the only transportation that ran in town and, when the driver heard it was the sheriff, he arrived promptly.

The anger was still there as Jones watched Ray get in.

It was still there when the taillights disappeared in the distance.

It would probably be there all day, if Jones was being honest with himself.

Mostly, because it was true.

"You good?" Carlos asked with genuine concern. That concern turned to object sympathy. "Ray has a way of getting under the skin sometimes. No matter what he says, it's just coming from a place of regret from his own life choices. Once, my girl—my friend Amanda—overheard him say at the bar that he wishes he'd never gotten back together with Lottie the first time. Said he should have left to go to college instead. Left all the bad behind."

Jones sighed, pushing that anger in him far enough away to deal with later.

"I still wish he wouldn't bark at cars, though."

Carlos agreed.

"I'm heading back to the department now to talk to Kenneth about the cold-case task force's progress on another cold case. Last night, Lily—Detective Howard, I mean—and Kenneth were pretty dang close to figuring something out. I don't think they knew what, but I've seen them almost work miracles, so I bet they've got something now. You heading there or working out-of-office today?"

Jones had a folder in his truck, beneath the passenger seat. He had copies of it at work, but it was there so he could disappear into it no matter where he was.

Today he wanted to do it around town and not behind his desk.

"I have to check up on some things. Then I'll be back in."

Carlos nodded. He might have been second-in-command, but he didn't need a play-by-play on what Jones was doing. He knew, even if he didn't know the hourly details of it.

"Good luck, Sheriff."

Jones's mind stuck on the title *Sheriff*. It still felt off to him. A shoe that fit but only with the perfect sock.

He didn't mind it but he didn't love it yet, either.

"You, too."

Jones watched Carlos drive off. He didn't immediately follow.

Fall was being kind to Kelby Creek. Cool enough for him to keep his jacket handy, not cold enough to keep his heavy one zipped up. It also had the sky dancing between hazy, orange and clear. The rain would come, sure, but the menace behind their summer storms had lessened.

There was a calmness in fall.

That calm only lasted a few moments in Jones's chest.

He needed to decide where to go next.

The McHale Manor, or to talk to the gardener next door.

Maybe you should play the question game, he thought with an equal level of seriousness and amusement.

It had, after all, worked out for him last time.

He'd run for sheriff and won.

He'd found a new purpose in an old pain.

He'd spent the night with a beautiful woman.

The same woman who had suggested they treat their time together as something wonderful but something brief.

"Some things are beautiful because they end," she'd said. "Let's keep this beautiful."

Jones had been surprised at the suggestion, but maybe not so much at his agreeing to it.

Maybe it was the way she'd said it, or maybe she'd been right.

Sometimes it was better to end things the right way than have them ended for you.

Still, as Jones hopped into his truck and took in the autumn sky one more time, he couldn't help his mind going back to the memory of her laugh, her smile, the way he'd forgotten for a while that he had a hole in him.

Then Jones shook his head and turned over the engine.

Best not to lose sleep over someone he'd likely never see again.

CASSANDRA WAS STARING down the barrel of a paper-towel roll and right into the eye of Keith McGibbon. She was tense; he was smiling. She could move, run, or at the very least hit the cardboard away, but in her experience that would only set off Keith.

And if she'd learned anything in the last three months, it was that you didn't openly antagonize a kindergartener who had a handful of glitter balled up in his hand.

"Let's take a calming breath, Keith," she said.

Keith had turned six over the weekend, and today they'd thrown him a little party at lunch. An hour later, the candy from the festivities was obviously still spiking his energy level and exhausting hers.

And tricky.

Keith was going through a phase where he pretended to be a pirate at every turn. Normally it was harmless, but somehow he'd found his way to the glitter stash and it was Cassandra who would pay the price if she didn't get through to him.

"Pirates don't throw glitter," she added matter-of-factly. "It goes against their code."

Keith lowered his pretend periscope.

"The pirate code?"

Cassandra didn't break eye contact.

"Yes, sir! Pirates have a code, one they always live by," she said. "Throwing glitter at people goes against that because once glitter gets into something it doesn't get out. That's why glitter is only ever used in art class and for crafting."

Keith seemed to consider that.

Behind him at one of the learning stations, her colleague, June, eyed the interaction with clear concern. And very apparent relief that it wasn't her. They, like most kindergarten teachers, had a running joke about how powerfully awful glitter was. No matter how far you stayed away from it, it followed you home, got into your best clothes and somehow, sometimes could be found in your hair even if you hadn't been around a jar of it in days.

If Keith decided to forsake her last-second addition to the imaginary pirate code, Cassandra was sure she'd be sporting that glitter until the day she retired.

Luckily, though, Keith's loyalty to his pirate lifestyle won out. Slowly he lifted his hand to her, palm up.

Cassandra was fast. She gently guided it and him to the trash can by the classroom door.

"The pirates thank you," she told him as the devil dust showered down into the plastic bag.

Once the threat was gone, Keith returned to his station under the extra watchful eye of June. Cassandra went back to her independent-play kids and, before she knew it, the clock hit two thirty.

"I'll take the kids to car pool since I almost cost you a nice dress," June said with a laugh after the class had lined up. Her eyes flitted down. "Plus, you have to be a little tired. You've been on your feet all day."

Cassandra rolled her eyes.

"The offer to take the kids, I'll accept. Thinking I can't stand an extra half hour just because I have some added weight, I'll deny."

June laughed and Cassandra smiled at the chorus of goodbyes from their students.

It wasn't until all were out of sight that Cassandra did take a seat behind her desk. She was tired, but it had nothing to do with standing all day and everything to do with the protruding belly that was taking up room beneath her maternity dress.

"'You probably won't show that much until closer to

your due date,'" she mockingly said to herself, repeating her doctor's words. "'Since this is your first baby and all.'"

Cassandra snorted.

Even at six and a half months, she was undeniably round and pregnant.

Kelby Creek Elementary went from chaos to quiet as the clock inched past three. June returned after car-pool duty and collected her things before saying goodbye. Cassandra was going through her lesson plan and the next day's activities when a custodial worker moved through their classroom, and on to the rest of the kindergarten wing of the school. Then the quiet seemed loud, and Cassandra realized it was time to go.

She loaded her purse with things she didn't need and made her way to the heart of the school. Instead of cutting to her left to go out to the car-pool pickup and the front doors, though, she paused by the wall of windows that showed the playground in the back.

Mrs. Letterman, the oldest on staff at Kelby Creek Elementary, looked defeated next to the jungle gym. She was on extended day duty. Today there were only two kids left.

Cassandra sighed when she saw Keith among the two. She nixed her plan to go home and walked out to Mrs. Letterman with a smile.

"These two the only ones left?"

Mrs. Letterman nodded.

Keith looked up and the girl he was playing with turned. She wasn't Cassandra's student, but she knew her name was Bonnie. Her dark curls were as wild as her personality. Which was probably why Mrs. Letterman looked particularly tired.

She'd been assigned extended day with two of the most energetic kindergarteners this side of the Mississippi.

Cassandra laughed as Bonnie gave a war cry that was instantly repeated by Keith.

"How about I take over and you head out?" Cassandra offered to Mrs. Letterman. Before the older woman could politely refuse, Cassandra lifted her hand in a stop motion. "Let me do this before my maternity leave sneaks up on us and leaves everyone one teacher down. I really don't mind."

Mrs. Letterman only hesitated a little.

"Keith said his grown-up runs late sometimes and Bonnie's grandfather called and said he was having car trouble, but her dad is going to be here any minute. Coach Rich is in his office still. Let him know when you head out."

Mrs. Letterman left like the world was chasing her. Quite deceptive for her age.

Cassandra set down her bag, then put one hand on her belly and one on the bar closest to her on the gym. Keith was grinning from ear-to-ear at her.

"We're walking the planks," he told her, pride in his voice. "Bonnie said she has a wooden leg."

"That must make swimming a bit harder, huh?" Cassandra asked Bonnie, who was standing next to the jungle gym and not beneath it like her crew member.

But her attention wasn't on Cassandra. It wasn't on Keith, either.

Instead, Bonnie was wide-eyed, her focus past both of them and in the direction of the fence that faced the faculty parking lot, where the buses turned around after picking up and dropping off kids. It was also where parents could sign out their kids from extended day.

Yet, when Cassandra turned, she didn't recognize the man at the gate.

Keith was only allowed to be picked up by his foster mom and social worker, both women. Definitely not the man.

Cassandra directed her question to Bonnie, but didn't break eye contact with the stranger.

"Bonnie, is that your dad?"

Bonnie took a small step back.

The man went through the gate, a hundred or so yards away from them.

"No." Bonnie's voice had gone as quiet as the playground around them.

The hair on the back of Cassandra's neck stood.

She kept her voice low when she spoke next.

"Keith, come grab my hand."

Bless the boy—he listened. A second later his sticky hand was in hers.

The man seemed to get faster at the move. He wasn't smiling. Not even a little.

"Bonnie," Cassandra continued, "I need you to run as fast as you can to the doors. Right *now*."

Bless Bonnie—she was just as good a listener.

Chapter Two

The man was tall and slender. Unflinching.

His clothes were normal in their everyday appearance—a button-up shirt and jeans. He had golden hair that curled a little and a few creases along his forehead that made it hard for her to place his age. If there was a weapon on him, it was hidden. And, if there was a reason he gave chase the moment Cassandra ran with the children, he didn't voice it.

No "Hey, sorry I startled y'all. This is just a big ol' misunderstanding."

No "It's okay. I'm here for a valid reason that has nothing to do with ill intent."

The man was as quiet as a statue.

One that would have no doubt reached them had Cassandra not thrown the lock on the door as soon as the three of them were through.

The man slammed into it, but didn't make a noise when the door didn't give.

"This is an emergency," Bonnie said from behind Cassandra. "We need to call my dad!"

Cassandra pictured her phone in the bottom of her purse. The same purse she'd left on the ground next to the jungle gym. Had she known some strange man would be running after them, Cassandra wouldn't have put it down at all.

"The front office has a phone we can—"

Cassandra's attempt at a quick plan and providing reassurance was dashed. The man took two steps back and squatted. He was as quick at scooping up one of the painted rocks as he was at rearing back and throwing it.

Cassandra jumped back, taking Keith and pushing Bonnie with her, just as the rock collided with the glass top of the door.

The pumpkin shape on the rock was cute.

The way the glass turned into a spiderweb of cracks made her stomach drop below her feet.

"Come on!"

Cassandra pulled the kids toward the center of the school. Several hallways fed into the main hub before branching off into the front end, where the office, cafeteria and front pickup area were. She had every intention of going to the office, hoping Mrs. Letterman had dallied and could call for help ASAP, but the sickening sound of glass shattering made her plan of getting to a phone go off the rails.

When the back door made an awful noise opening over the broken glass, Cassandra went with a plan that would hopefully get them to some doors that weren't so easily broken into.

She took a turn that almost made Keith lose his footing and soon all three were in the elementary school's library.

"Be quiet," she whispered to the kids.

To their utter credit, they kept on listening to her, even when she took them right into the stacks.

Kelby Creek Elementary's library wasn't the biggest space in the school, but it was mighty all its own. Seven rows of bookcases created four long aisles that ended at a square of open space at the back corner. Cassandra ushered both children toward that corner, mind already on the door that said Employees Only behind it. That door led to the storage room that connected to the back of the teachers' lounge. For as long as Cassandra had been teaching at the school, neither the storage room nor its connecting door had been locked.

But the teacher's lounge *could* be locked when inside.

It didn't have a landline but if she could make sure the children were safe inside, Cassandra could bolt to the office and hope it was open so she could make a call. Each classroom had a landline, but everyone locked up before they left for the day.

Where was the custodian?

Had she already left?

What about Coach Rich?

There was a clattering behind them.

The door flung open.

Cassandra took the kids along to the right and stopped between two of the aisles. Bonnie was fastened to her back, Keith to her front. She didn't want to, but Cassandra put her hand over the boy's mouth. He was a talker when the going was good; she didn't know how he would be in a situation like this.

Footfalls moved outside of the shelves. The man was searching the desk and the reader area of the room first.

It was a small blessing.

One that gave Cassandra hope.

She tapped Bonnie's arm and slowly slid her hand off Keith's mouth. Cassandra took both of them by the hand again and kept going to her earlier destination.

The Employees Only sign was a beacon of light.

Keith and Bonnie were wide-eyed as the door opened. Everyone was blessedly quiet and still, the door included.

Cassandra pushed the kids inside and shut the door behind them with more concentration than she'd ever had. It was a soft close.

"Keep going," she whispered to the children, nodding toward the other side of the room.

For as long as she lived, Cassandra would never forget how beautifully calm the two were. Quiet but terrified, and following her instructions while someone came after them. Most adults would have already folded.

Not them.

They were pirates.

Bonnie made it to the next door first. Her hands went around the knob as Cassandra was already mentally slamming the door behind them and locking it tight. Yet, when Bonnie turned nothing happened.

Cassandra's blood went cold. Bonnie tried again before she could get there. The door still wasn't opening.

Cassandra moved her aside and hoped the six-year-old had been clumsy at the attempt.

But, she hadn't.

The door that was never locked was locked.

"What do we do?" Keith's voice broke into the quiet.

Cassandra touched her belly, trying to think of a back-up plan. She looked around the room with new, terrified eyes.

The storage room wasn't the only one in the school and wasn't at all big. There was nowhere to hide and not enough space to get around someone standing in the doorway.

Did the man have a weapon?

Would he try to hurt them?

Take them?

Why was he here?

What could he want?

Cassandra didn't have time to do anything but cycle through her questions in a hurried mess.

The door they'd come in from opened.

Cassandra whirled around and pushed Keith behind her in the process. The man paused his strides to take in the scene.

No one spoke for a moment.

Cassandra then broke the quiet.

"Leave them here and I'll go with you," she said, voice even and firm. It surprised even herself.

Not as much as the man's response, though.

He didn't smile but he certainly didn't frown.

"No," he said. "I don't want you."

That was it.

Those were the magic words.

The ice in Cassandra's veins went to boiling quick.

The man wanted the kids.

The man was about to get her.

Cassandra went into full guardian mode. She let go of the children's hands and was standing still one second, and running at the man the next.

The element of surprise proved useful.

He took a few steps back and out the doorway.

Cassandra didn't stop. She threw her hands out and pushed into his chest as hard as she could.

The man yelled out, stumbling at the contact.

Cassandra kept the attack going.

She grabbed two fistfuls of his shirt and tried to sling him into the closest bookshelf.

The move gave her a half of what she wanted.

He didn't hit the shelf, but he did fall.

"Bonnie! Keith! Run!"

Whatever calm Cassandra had been possessing turned into a bark of a demand. But, again, the kids listened.

Bonnie ran out of the storage room pulling Keith along with her as Cassandra grabbed for the closest book from a shelf. Cassandra felt the whoosh of air as they went past her.

They weren't the only ones who were fast.

The man got up to his feet quickly.

Cassandra hit him in the face with an early readers chapter book.

It wasn't hard enough for him to go down again, but it was hard enough to tick him off. He made an awful noise and lunged forward.

Cassandra yelled in surprise and got a taste of her own medicine. He hit her shoulders hard, but before she could fall, one of his hands went to her hair.

She yelled out again as pain lit up her scalp. On reflex, she went to grab his wrist but he yanked her downward. With one hand going to cradle her stomach, she managed to hit the ground with her hip instead.

The man released his hold but Cassandra saw his eyes.

He was going to hurt her, and now that she was on the ground beneath him, all he had to do was hit or kick her and he would do just that.

Cassandra moved her arm over her stomach and readied to try and defend herself as best she could, when something happened that made both of them jump.

The fire alarm went off.

And then a book hit the man's hip.

Cassandra turned just as another book was launched through the air.

Keith was already reaching for another from the shelf closest.

"Run," Cassandra yelled out, but all Keith did was try and hit the man again.

And the man didn't appreciate it one bit.

He went for Keith.

Cassandra kicked out but missed his feet.

She yelled out to the boy to run again, but Keith froze. Cassandra's adrenaline was nothing but a flood raging through her body.

She scrambled to her feet just as the man grabbed Keith.

The boy yelled, and so did Cassandra.

She needed to end the fight.

She needed to stop the man.

Now.

JONES LEFT THE sheriff's department cussing, but managed not to speed on his way to the elementary school. It wasn't his dad's fault that his truck's engine had up and died. It also wasn't the first time Bonnie had gone to extended day when plans had changed at the last minute. Still, Jones hated the idea of Bonnie looking out for her grandpa and instead getting shuffled to the playground to wait when he didn't come.

It's why Jones wanted to get there fast.

Waiting for someone you love and them not showing up hurt, even when you knew the reason behind it.

So Jones parked in the school lot and jumped out, still wearing his badge and his holster, with his service weapon tucked inside. His feet hit the asphalt and then the sidewalk to the playground gate before he thought about putting the weapon in the car. But that thought stalled as quick as spit when Jones realized he was staring out at an empty playground.

Well, not completely.

The jungle gym, Bonnie's favorite piece of equipment, was unoccupied in the middle of the space. Next to it was a bag.

Not just any bag—it was a purse on the ground.

Jones looked back at the parking lot. Three cars. He burned all three into memory and opened the gate.

No one called out to him as he moved across the grass and sand to the purse. One glance down showed an adult-size shoe print and at least two pairs of kids' feet. They trailed up to the doors leading back into the school.

Jones felt adrenaline spike and rage through his system as he looked at those doors.

One was shut.

The other had its glass absolutely shattered.

Jones went for his phone at his hip, his other hand hovering over his gun. Before he could move, something else made the world around him take on a more menacing feel.

The fire alarm started blaring through the school.

He threw open the back door and crunched his way over the broken glass into the hallway.

It was as eerie as it was concerning.

There was no one around. Just the strobe lights of the alarm and its loud warning.

Jones put his hand on the butt of his gun.

He almost drew it when a sudden burst of movement caught his eye deeper in the school.

His heart burst with relief when he saw that it was a little girl.

His little girl.

"Bonnie!"

Chapter Three

With wild dark hair and eyes that were exactly her mother's, Bonnie locked in on him and he knew in an instant that something *was* terribly wrong.

She was terrified.

"Dad," she yelled out, running full speed at him.

However, instead of colliding into him, she skidded to a stop a foot away.

Her hands were so small as they waved backward and then pointed.

"There's a man hurting Miss West!"

Her voice was small but confident.

Jones believed her in an instant.

"Just one man?" Jones took his cell phone out and handed it to her as Bonnie nodded. "Call 911 and tell them where we are and we need help. Tell them your name. Can you do that?"

Jones knew Bonnie could. He'd done several emergency drills with her from toddler age to the present. He knew how dangerous the world was and he'd wanted to make sure Bonnie was as prepared as a small child could be, including how to use any phone to call for help.

"Yeah, I can," she exclaimed.

Jones couldn't take her with him. It was too risky. They'd done drills similar to this before. Hiding when needed, running when needed too. Jones also knew the rough layout of the school. He pointed in the direction of the older students' bathrooms.

"Go hide in one of the bathroom stalls and do it," Jones ordered. "Be quiet until I come back."

Jones watched his daughter nod and then was off to where she'd pointed.

He might not know what the situation was, who Miss West was, or why the man was causing trouble, but Jones knew one thing for sure.

He was about to put a stop to it right now.

He heard noises from an open door, the sounds of scuffling and worse. Jones hadn't been in the elementary library before, but he didn't need a breakdown of the layout to see what needed to happen as soon as he rushed inside.

"Let go!"

There was a man and woman in between two of the bookshelves near the back of the room. Jones couldn't see either of their faces because of their positions, but he could make out that the man had his arms around a boy between them.

And, while Bonnie was only six, Jones trusted his daughter's plea.

Miss West was being attacked by the man.

Which meant the man was the problem.

Jones kept the element of surprise as he closed the gap between him and the fighting. Miss West surely wasn't making the man's life easier. She heaved a book through the air and hit his shoulder. Then she threw out a punch that didn't land, though it did make the man take a step back to avoid it.

The boy in his arms didn't stick to the movement. He flailed out and toward the teacher just as she grabbed at his shirt. The whole exchange took less than thirty seconds, but it was just enough time to give Jones the perfect lead-in.

He focused solely on the man and bellowed out.

"Sheriff's department—stop where you are!"

The man spun around. His eyes were wide with surprise and panic. He was tall but he wasn't Jones tall, and the best he could guess, the man hadn't counted on him showing up. Jones started to repeat himself but the man's apparent fight response turned to flight just as quickly.

He lunged forward and directly at the boy and teacher, but instead of grabbing for them, he pushed them down and ran past them as they hit the floor.

"You okay?" Jones yelled out to them, already moving.

He saw the woman nod out of his peripheral vision as he sped up.

It was clear that the man hadn't been in the library before, either. He ran clumsily and turned into a dead end made up of bookshelves.

"Stop and put your hands up right now," Jones said, blocking his escape. He went to tap his badge but the man decided to be bold again.

Instead of putting his hands up in surrender, the intruder turned and pushed the bookshelf with all that he had. And, since they were in a public school and not some high-end library, that bookshelf did a mighty fine job of giving up.

Books hit the floor before the metal made it over onto the gray, rug-covered tile.

It was a nasty noise. The boy behind him in the stacks yelled. His attacker scurried over the fallen bookshelf. It opened up his escape route to the study side of the library.

Well, at least it gave him the illusion that he had a chance to leave.

"All right," Jones growled out. "We're not going to keep doing this."

He backtracked through the stacks and used his long strides to his advantage. The culprit made it to the door a second after Jones.

It was then, in the man's infinite wisdom, that he tried to go back to fighting.

He balled his fist and swung out hard. Had Jones been a smaller man, the hit might have landed with some heft.

Instead, it gave Jones the opening he needed to dole out his own punishment.

The man yelled out as Jones leveled him with a solid hit along his jaw.

He went slack right after.

Jones said a little cuss under his breath as he pulled his pair of cuffs from the back of his belt. It was easy work securing them on the man's wrists, and even easier work to confirm he was unconscious due to the punch.

That hadn't been Jones's intent, but given where they were and what the man had seemingly been up to, maybe it was best he take a little time-out.

Finally, when Jones was sure the threat was neutralized, he was able to really check on the boy and Miss West.

Both had made their way to their feet and both were staring at him with wide eyes.

He looked to the boy first. He was crying, but there were no obvious wounds. He was scared but not hurt. Miss West had her hands on his shoulders, steadying him. It seemed the only reason he might not have been completely breaking down. That, and shock.

Jones was relieved.

Then he was abruptly shocked himself.

For the first time since coming into the library, Jones was able to look at Miss West. *Really* look. Not a passing, calculated glance to get the bare facts.

A true *look* at her.

She might not have been Bonnie's teacher, but Jones absolutely knew her.

"Cassandra?"

The woman he thought about every time he sat down behind his desk or caught his badge's reflection in the mirror.

The woman who had helped him decide on a different future than the one he was planning.

The woman he'd spent one hell of a night with before they'd agreed to part ways with no more than the fond memories they'd shared.

That decision he'd often regretted in the last several months, but they'd only exchanged first names.

But now, there she was.

Cassandra West, apparently.

Teacher at his daughter's school.

And she was, without a doubt, just as surprised to see him.

"Jones?" she asked.

He might have answered—or asked several questions all at once—had the boy not moved aside so he could turn to see Cassandra better. But he did and that's when Jones saw all of her.

Not only was Cassandra in Kelby Creek, at his daughter's school, and standing no more than a few feet from him, but she was also pregnant.

"Dad?" All thoughts screamed to a halt as Bonnie's voice yelled out from behind him. "Can I come in now?"

Jones cut eye contact with Cassandra and found his little girl standing uncertainly in the doorway. Her gaze had fallen to the man beneath him.

It sobered him.

It didn't matter right now that Cassandra was in Kelby Creek.

It only mattered why the man was.

BONNIE RAN IN and there wasn't much time between her coming back into the library and another man of the law running in, too.

Marco Rossi, a deputy sheriff, came in quickly with his badge, looking concerned. He took in the scene with grave attention. He focused on Jones next.

"What do you need from me, Sheriff?"

Cassandra, who believed herself to be in some kind of shock, was shaken a little at that revelation. Just as she had been to hear Bonnie call Jones "Dad."

Jones wasn't just in Kelby Creek, he was the sheriff of it.

Before Cassandra could come to terms with that realization, the man who had attacked them started to stir. Keith went back to her side in a flash. Bonnie backtracked to Cassandra, too, taking one of her hands. Cassandra had the other one on her stomach.

"Let's get him out of here," Jones answered after a quick look at Bonnie, her and Keith. "Your cruiser outside, Rossi?"

Marco shook his head.

"We just came from car pool here about twenty minutes ago," he said. "All I had time to do was drop off the kids and turn back around. Sterling's close though. He should be here any second."

Jones nodded and hoisted the man up. His head lolled to the side, but his feet found the ground easily enough. Bonnie tightened her hold on Cassandra's hand. It was like her father felt her anxiety flare. His focus went to her.

"Bonnie, you and your friend stay here with Miss West and Deputy Rossi here. I'll be back in a jiffy."

Marco took the order with a nod, and Bonnie said okay. Cassandra, still feeling like she was in some bizarre dream, took an uncertain step forward.

"Jones... I mean, Sheriff?" she said.

Jones's perfect warm eyes—the same eyes she'd stared into longingly during their one night together—met hers and Cassandra almost became speechless.

After their time together at the hotel, Cassandra had wished they hadn't made the rule of just being passing ships in the night. Sure, she wasn't looking for a relationship and it seemed the man had had a lot on his mind with not a lot of room for any other thoughts or people. Yet, when Cassandra had made it home to her bed the next night, she'd looked at the pillow next to her and wished Jones had been there.

If not kissing, talking, and even if not talking, just being there.

Because that's what their time together had been like. Brief but poignant. Small talk that felt whole. Intimacy even without the details of their lives. Details that would have complicated their already complicated lives.

Details that would have let them know they were headed home to the same exact zip code.

But that night of longing had turned into regret, anger and then acceptance that the man named Jones might never cross her path again. That her luck in love and life would never be that good.

Then, to prove to her that nothing worked out the way she ever planned, she'd realized her period hadn't shown.

When she found out that she was pregnant and Jones was the only man she'd been with since Ryan?

Well, she'd fallen right out of acceptance and gone to anger and grief.

She'd always wanted kids but she'd never thought she'd be a single parent. And what about what Jones wanted?

That thought had haunted her as the months went by and her stomach, and their baby, grew.

Only June knew who the father was, and even so she hadn't known him, just the name.

"You could hire a private eye to try and find him," June had suggested once she'd made it to her third trimester. "You know, see who he really is before you tell him you're expecting. Maybe even wait until Kiddo is born to feel him out in person before you bring him into your lives."

It had been good advice Cassandra had often thought about taking.

Yet, every time she did, she'd think of Ryan.

She'd think of the wedding she never had.

She'd think of her luck.

Then she'd decide to think about it all again later.

But, now?

Now that Jones was in front of her?

Now that she saw his badge?

It didn't feel real.

So Cassandra stayed in the present.

She pushed back her shoulders and made sure her voice was strong and even, so as not to frighten the children anymore.

"Keith's grown-ups might show up," she said. "Lila Shaw or Renee Parr. Coach Rich might also be in the gym still, but I'm not sure. Other than that the school should be empty."

Jones, in all of his massive glory, nodded.

Then it was like he put on a mask. Or, really, a face of concentration unlike any Cassandra had seen him wear during their night of passion as strangers in a hotel room.

"I'll keep a lookout," he told her. "Thanks."

Cassandra nodded.

It felt wholly inadequate.

"No problem."

She watched him go, pulling the unknown man along

with him. Marco, as directed, stayed. Keith pressed his body weight into Cassandra's leg. Bonnie kept Cassandra's hand.

She contemplated how strange life was, to be holding the sheriff's daughter's hand while also carrying his son.

Chapter Four

There was a lot going on, but almost none of it provided Jones with any answers that made a whole lot of sense.

"It takes some stones to go after children on the playground," Carlos said to Jones as they watched a cruiser leaving the school. "I never thought Bill a man to do anything like that."

Jones and Kelby Creek transplant Marco hadn't recognized Bill Burrows, the man who'd had the absolute gall to chase Jones's daughter, but Carlos and Sterling had been quick to identify him. Bill had gone to school with Sterling when they were young. He currently resided with his uncle in the Community Garden Trailer Park near the town limits.

He had no children attending Kelby Creek Elementary.

He had no relationship with any of the staff.

He had no reason to do what he had done.

"No one knows every part of a man," Jones said, arms crossed over his chest and watching as another cruiser left. "Everyone in Kelby Creek was given the horrible kindness of learning that after Annie McHale was taken."

Jones let out a sigh that went from spine to belly. An approaching truck from the other end of the parking lot was coming in hot. Carlos tensed for a second.

"I didn't know how long this was going to take so Dad

grabbed the neighbor's car to come get Bonnie," he explained before the question was asked.

Jones's father had never been a man to hold back an apology, just as he had never been a man known to give one that he shouldn't. Yet, Jones saw in his father's body language, as soon as he parked and jumped out of the car, that the older man was riddled with misplaced guilt and heading fast to singing sorry.

Jones didn't want to hear it so he met his father between the school's front pavilion and the parking lot, and stopped him before he started.

"There's no way in the world that you could have known what was going to happen today," Jones said, forcing his posture to relax a little. "The only blame that's getting placed is squarely on the shoulders of some man named Bill Burrows."

His father didn't like being talked at about what he should or shouldn't be feeling—a trait Jones had more than inherited—and took to the defensive fast.

"I've known for two whole months that that dang truck of mine needed to get seen about. Had I gone and done it, Bonnie would have already been home with me." He shook his head, in full-on self-loathing mode. A feeling that Jones was also well-versed in.

Jones started to point out, once again, that his father wasn't to blame, but the door to the school opened farther behind them. They turned to see Bonnie run out, and Jones's father met Bonnie in his own little jog. He crouched down and threw his arms around her in one fluid motion.

Behind her, Jones noted the boy named Keith, his foster mother and Cassandra.

Cassandra West.

Miss Cassandra West.

Miss "Unforgettable and Pregnant" Cassandra West.

Jones let his eyes take her in for a long moment. Her attention was on the conversation with Keith's foster mother, giving him an opening to stare.

She was beautiful, breathtakingly so.

That was true from the moment Jones had seen her to the moment he'd really taken her in while in the library.

Now, though, it was a different look. At the hotel she'd been dressed up, chic. Fashion-forward, at least several steps in front of where Jones was. Her hair had been done neat, and even her eyes, which had captivated him, had a crispness. An edge that he guessed came from experience. What experience that was hadn't mattered then, at the bar, out at dinner, or between the sheets. He wasn't supposed to see her again, after all.

But here she was, wearing a colorful dress with wild, full hair and a streak of glitter across her belly.

Her pregnant belly.

He hadn't had the time to run the numbers between their encounter and today, but when his late wife had been pregnant with Bonnie and showing like Cassandra, she'd been about ready to pop.

Did that mean Cassandra had been pregnant already when they'd met?

Or was Cassandra pregnant because of their meeting?

"Dad! I didn't get in trouble for the fire alarm!"

Bonnie's eager voice broke through his internal questions. He needed to talk to Cassandra, one way or the other, but he wasn't going to jump the line.

Jones put on a smile and joined his father and daughter.

"Nope, you didn't," he said to her. "In this situation pulling the fire alarm was a very good thing, even if there was no fire."

Bonnie beamed as Keith and his mother met them, Cassandra trailing behind. She'd become the unofficial liaison to the group, since no one could get a hold of the principal, vice principal, or superintendent. Coach Rich, the only other person still on the school grounds, was inside talking to one of the firemen who had responded. He seemed more miffed that he'd missed out on the action, rather than that the action had happened at all.

"Is there anything else I need to do before we go?" Keith's foster mom asked. Carlos had been the one to address her earlier.

Carlos gave Jones a quick look. He nodded, but before she could move along, he handed her a business card.

"Millie Lovett contracts with the sheriff's department and helps kids deal with certain stressful situations like today. It's free of charge and DHR-approved in most cases. Just give her a ring."

She didn't look like she was going to make the call, but she took the card all the same.

The little boy started to follow her but Cassandra took his hand. She lowered herself to meet his gaze, careful of her stomach.

"And if you don't end up talking to the nice Mrs. Foster, you can always talk to me," she said to the boy. Jones suspected, though, that her tone was meant for his grown-up. She smiled and tapped the spot over her heart twice. "Pirate's code—I'll always listen."

Jones quirked an eyebrow at that statement, but the boy obviously understood. His voice was a little tearful but he held her gaze when he answered.

"Pirate's code."

His foster mother led him away and Cassandra took a little time standing. She was chewing on a thought and spit it out with a dollop of quiet.

"Mrs. Shaw is a good woman but she's…got a lot on her plate."

Jones, his father and Carlos let that sit. Then it was time to move along. Carlos went back inside to finish up and Jones's father took Bonnie's hand. He promised her a stop to get ice cream, something that made Jones laugh.

"This time don't bother saying you're getting one for me and saving it," he said. "We all know you two just split my cone the second y'all get home."

Bonnie "Miss Sweet Tooth" Murphy put on her most mischievous grin.

It warmed Jones's heart.

Just as much as it almost shattered it.

What had Bill Burrows been up to?

What would have happened had Cassandra not been as fast on her feet?

The woman in question was smiling politely at them. Jones realized, belatedly, he should have introduced them all. At least Cassandra to his father. Apparently, she already knew his daughter.

Instead, he hugged Bonnie and promised his dad he'd be home when he was finished.

Cassandra didn't speak for a moment as they watched them get into the car.

When she did, her voice had taken on yet another pitch. It was soft and this time ever so warm.

"You know, Bonnie did some quick thinking with that fire alarm. Six-year-old me might have kept running."

Jones smiled at that.

"I think some kids thrive under pressure, even when they're scared. Look at that boy, Keith. Bonnie said he refused to leave you and went back to try and help. That's a kid who loves his teacher."

A rose tint went across Cassandra's cheeks.

"It's pirate code. You don't leave your friends behind." She laughed. "Then again, I made that code for our school trip to the aquarium, so he'd be more inclined to want to stay with his field-trip buddy."

Jones wanted to know more about where this pirate code had originated, but what they weren't talking about was too hard to ignore. Cassandra was quickest to the punch.

"So." She motioned to his badge. "This is the job you were considering? Sheriff?"

Jones nodded.

"It was."

"Well, I have to say I'm glad for it." She glanced at the school. It wasn't lost on Jones that he'd been wearing the badge Cassandra had helped him decide to put on while trying to save her.

"This is definitely feeling like a full-circle moment," he responded.

She laughed. There were nerves in it. She ran a hand over her belly. There was no ring on her finger.

Did that mean…?

"So I guess neither one of us did mention that we were from Kelby Creek. That might have changed some things." Cassandra rubbed her belly again. Was it his imagination, or had her eyes gone to his hand, too?

She took a notable deep breath in.

Then notable hesitation.

"Do you think we could talk later?" she added. "Like maybe not at my work or, uh, a crime scene?"

Jones, who had been waiting for her to say something else, nodded.

He took care not to stare down at her pregnant stomach.

"Is tonight too soon? We could grab some food. My place, or maybe Crisp's?"

Jones resisted the urge to make a joke about minibars costing too much, a reference to their first meeting. But that version of him—flying solo in a hotel to think about the future—had been more carefree. A lot more so than the man with the badge standing in front of her now.

He couldn't be that man who had made her laugh at the hotel bar.

Not when he was standing guard over his family and the town. Not when it was Kelby Creek.

"Crisp's sounds great," Cassandra responded quickly. "I can meet you there at seven?"

"Sounds good to me."

She went back to smiling but there was something weighing it down.

Then again, she'd just been through a lot.

Cassandra started to walk away but Jones gently took her elbow. She stopped in her tracks and met his gaze with eyes that seemed to glow. Jones let her go.

"Thank you, again, for what you did today," he said from the bottom of his heart. "You fought to keep the kids safe. You did good. Really good."

Cassandra's voice went back to soft.

"I had no other choice." She shrugged. "Pirate's code."

Jones wanted to say more, wanted to keep talking, but her words coincided with Carlos coming back out of the school and calling to him.

With one last look, Jones and Cassandra parted ways.

"This is the woman? The woman?"

Hours later and Jones's father was handing his son his jacket at his truck and trying, and failing, to keep his curiosity in check.

"Minifridge-joke woman?" his dad added when Jones didn't instantly answer.

He shrugged into his jacket and sighed.

His father was the only person who knew about his time with Cassandra, from their game at the bar to the reason he'd missed his early check-out time. It wasn't that Jones and his father shared every detail about their lives, but not telling someone about Cassandra somehow felt wrong. It might have felt like a dream but he wasn't about to let it be forgotten.

So he'd shared the information. All of it.

Just as he'd keyed his dad into Cassandra's surprise occupation and location in relation to him.

Then he'd had to ask him to babysit Bonnie while Jones went to their more relaxed reunion.

What Jones hadn't expected was his father to get so excited about it all.

"Yes, it's minifridge-joke woman," he finally confirmed, starting his truck so it could warm up. Kelby Creek was only getting colder at night now. "But maybe let's stick with calling her Cassandra."

His dad crossed his arms over his chest and shook his head in disbelief.

"You drove out to that hotel a good four hours away from here and just happened to meet someone who broke through that metal cage around you and now she's teaching Bonnie at Kelby Creek Elementary? If that doesn't make you feel all squiggly inside, I don't know what will."

Jones rolled his eyes. There was a fine line between answering his dad with a yes or no, and diving into feelings about being squiggly or not. He got into the truck.

"She isn't Bonnie's teacher. She's Bonnie adjacent in a way. She's a kindergarten teacher but not Bonnie's."

His father gave a dismissive snort.

"The same woman you've been pining for all these months was holding your daughter's hand a few hours ago, protecting her. That's something wild and you know it, son."

He did know it but that was neither here nor there right now.

"See you in a few hours," Jones said, slowly shutting his door. "Tell Bonnie I'll come in and check on her when I'm back."

The door closing was a satisfying noise. Seeing his dad now roll his eyes was a bonus.

Kelby Creek at night when it was cold was something else. Something nice. Never a true fan of the cold, Jones nevertheless rolled down the window a little just to feel the cool against his face.

Or, he realized, maybe it was less about feeling the cold as it was trying to calm himself down.

He wouldn't call what he felt squiggly but he wouldn't say that his stomach wasn't a little knotted in nerves.

Nerves that were split, at that.

Jones glanced at the passenger seat and the folder he knew that was under it.

A breakdown of Annie McHale's last day in public was detailed in his own handwriting inside. Notes he'd been taking at his desk when his father had called in about his car trouble. Notes he'd been still thinking about when he'd parked at the elementary school.

The first week that he'd been able to start his investigation into Annie's case and his daughter had been involved in an attack with still no clear motive?

Some chance meetings were a happy coincidence.

This, though?

Jones didn't like this one bit.

Chapter Five

Crisp's Kitchen hadn't changed at all since it had opened when Jones was a kid. Sure, it had changed hands, but the simple decorations and furniture were the same as the printed menus and radio station playing softly from the kitchen.

Yet Crisp's could do a lot of things with the little it had.

The same place where they had their Sunday afternoon family dinners now felt wholly intimate. The lights were warmer, softer, and there were only a few people seated. As Jones walked in he turned his attention to a beautiful woman wearing a long-sleeved dress and smiling.

Jones didn't have to check his watch to know he wasn't late. In fact, he'd planned on coming early and had.

Apparently he hadn't come early enough.

Cassandra didn't get up to greet him, but waved a hand at the seat across from her. She laughed.

"Yes, I got here very early," she said as a greeting. It got a smile out of him. "And, yes, that's one of my things that I do. I arrive early, way earlier than anyone ever should." She raised her hands in mock defense. "It's something I've been working on."

Jones sat down and moved his legs into just the right spot so his knees wouldn't hit the table. This was something he'd practiced after his last growth spurt as a teenager. Being so tall often had small annoyances like that to deal with.

"I can't say anything, I'm up with the sun," he said. "That's more speaking to Bonnie training me quick that babies, toddlers and especially six-year-olds don't believe in sleeping in."

Cassandra's smile straightened out.

"How is Bonnie? Today is going to give me nightmares, can't imagine it on a kiddo."

After finishing up at the school, Jones had let Carlos convince him to go home instead of back to work. He was glad for the push. Part of him wanted to tear apart Bill Burrows's motive and plan, but a bigger part wanted to eat ice cream with his daughter and make sure she was okay.

"We watched her favorite cartoons together and then had a good talk about people doing bad things and emergencies. I'm sure something will crop up about it all, but I'm going to get her in with Millie next week since she has some time in her schedule then. I know you don't teach her directly but I'm thinking you might have noticed that Bonnie is a bit...free-spirited."

He never meant Bonnie's wild streak as an insult, so he made sure to laugh at the last part. It was easy considering Cassandra was already nodding.

"I know at the big Family Picnic party a while back she had to be coaxed down from the big kid jungle gym after climbing to the top and, uh, howling like a wolf."

This time that got Jones. A belly laugh shook him and vibrated into the table.

"That would be on me and my dad. We might have watched a movie where a man turned into a werewolf and climbed on top of a roof and howled to signal his pack." He shrugged. "It was some B-rated horror movie Dad and

I were watching and we realized that she was not, in fact, asleep on the couch when it was through."

"Sponges," Cassandra said knowingly. "Children, especially at that age, are dang sponges and soak up anything and everything adults don't want them to."

Jones agreed to that as a waitress came. Deputy Marigold's ex-mother-in-law, Nan. Marigold had made no small show of letting him know that if he wanted a good meal he shouldn't bring up how beloved she was within the department. Marigold had been trying to be funny, of course, but her partner, Sterling, had made sure they all knew it was true. If you wanted a good meal at Crisp's, you didn't mention Marigold's name unless you wanted scowling, grumping and general anger.

"She'll retire one day soon," Marigold had said in the break room when they were talking about lunch spots. "And the day after that happens I'll buy everyone something good."

Today wasn't that day and Nan was in a fine mood. She nodded to Jones.

"Sheriff, been a stretch since you've come in," she said in greeting. "I was starting to think you didn't like us anymore."

Jones put on his most, he hoped, charming smile.

"It's nothing on this place, Nan. I've just been under piles of work, is all. Best I've been eating is whatever Dad has in the fridge for leftovers, and you know him—he's all about the power of a good sandwich."

Nan, who was in her upper sixties, had known his father since they were both in their thirties.

"It's been a longer stretch since I've seen Ted." She placed her pad on the table, giving up the illusion that she was going to take anything but gossip before she wrote down their order. A look of concern pulled at her brow.

"How's he doing, by the way? I heard his knee surgery went okay but there were some issues."

The easiest way to get out of gossip was to simply go through it. Jones kept with the facts.

"Yes, ma'am, the surgery went fine. It was the pain meds that are supposed to help manage the aftermath that we had some issues with. We found out he was allergic and had to stick with the normal over-the-counter meds. He managed fine, though. Still a little stiff at times but he's been off the crutches for months."

Nan nodded and put a hand to her chest as if she had been there through it.

"Bless his heart." Nan surprised him by reaching out to touch his hand. She went full-on staring when she continued. "And bless *your* heart for coming back to take care of that old fool. I know how hard that must've been. Coming back."

Jones wasn't in a pleasant, polite mood anymore. He felt his smile tighten. He gave one nod. He didn't enjoy being blunt about not wanting to talk about his past.

But he would.

Nan opened her mouth and Jones knew she was about to go right for the jugular.

"I'm so sorry but could I go ahead and order, Nan?" Both Jones and the older woman turned. Cassandra gave her an apologetic smile. "I've just been craving your delicious burger and fries all dang day and I don't think I can go without them much longer. In fact, could I just go ahead and order a cup of sweet tea with that, too? You know how I love your sweet tea."

Nan, clearly miffed at being interrupted, had no choice but to meet the sweet with her own sweet. She slid her writing pad back into her hand.

"Oh, of course, darlin'. I know all about cravings. Let me stop gabbing and get you going. What about you, Sheriff?"

"I'll actually take the same, but a coffee, black, instead of the tea."

Nan nodded, and didn't write anything down.

"I'll get y'all in and be back in a jiffy with your drinks."

Jones and Cassandra thanked her, and then Jones gave another thanks to Cassandra for the save when the older woman was gone. She waved her hand dismissively.

"Nan has a way of digging in on things she has no business digging in on," Cassandra responded. "Her family might make a mean burger, but that's no reason to tell her your whole life story every time you sit down."

Jones leaned back a little. He already felt more relaxed now that Nan was gone. Or, maybe it had to do with his current company. During their night together Jones had felt, for the first time in a long time, lighter.

"You seem to know the routine here pretty good. How long have you lived in Kelby Creek, if you don't mind my asking?"

"Oh, I don't mind." Cassandra waved her hand in another dismissive move. Jones noticed she used her hands to talk a lot, more than most. He wondered now if that had to do with her being a teacher. It was probably easier to get kids to listen when you used your hands to grab their attention.

"I've been here for three years, four in December," she continued. "It's crazy that it's been that long, though sometimes it feels like I've been here forever." She laughed.

Jones didn't.

If she had only been in town for almost four years then she'd missed what had happened. She'd missed the corruption and the town falling apart. She'd missed Annie's kidnapping. She'd missed him packing up Bonnie and all of their things and driving as fast as he could away from Kelby Creek, not once looking in the rearview.

She'd missed his world crumbling all because of a picnic blanket.

He could have told her that, asked her about what she knew of The Flood, but instead he was genuinely curious as to why she'd chosen their town.

"I have to say, Kelby Creek isn't usually a destination people strive to visit, let alone move to. Is there a particular reason you picked it? Do you have any kin here?"

Cassandra's smile faltered. It was a brief thing but one that resonated hard in Jones's chest. He was ready to take back his question but she beat him to the answer before he could.

"No, I'm not from here." She was quiet but not so much that she was whispering. "My fiancé lived here for a few years and said it was a good place to start over. When I was looking for my own new start, I saw the job opening at the elementary school and, well, it seemed like a sign."

Jones raised an eyebrow at *fiancé*, even though he hadn't meant it to. Once again he glanced to see her bare ring finger. Was she married now? Engaged? Was she not wearing a ring because she was pregnant?

Helen's fingers had started to swell while she was carrying Bonnie. She'd ditched her wedding band during the second trimester.

Had Cassandra done the same?

Jones was about to rephrase his original question to try and get an answer without outright prodding.

Cassandra, once again, was quick to explain herself without the question.

"He passed away a few weeks before our wedding," she continued. "A car accident. No pain, just didn't make it." Her smile turned watery. Jones knew the feeling all too well.

He reached across the table and placed his hand over one of hers.

"I'm sorry." It wasn't enough—he knew that, too—but he couldn't just say nothing.

Cassandra took her other hand and patted his twice. When she was done, Jones pulled his back. Though the urge to keep it there was tugging at him.

"Thanks," she said. "I just never really know how to refer to him. Some people around here know him as my ex without all of the sad details. Sometimes that's easier than dealing with those who like to take other people's sad stories and spread them for something to talk about."

Jones could have brought up Helen then. Told Cassandra about what had happened at the park that day. Told her about how he'd gone from a new father to a single dad within the space of a few breaths.

Yet, he hesitated.

They both knew loss and he'd never take that from her or discount it because it was different from his, but there was something nasty about the way Helen had gone.

Daggers of salt in a wound torn open so wide you couldn't even see the other side.

Jones froze, wanting to talk about it but unable to muster the energy.

"Not saying the words, doesn't make it any less real, son," his dad had told him during one of his long stays when Bonnie was a baby. "The pain just sits and hollows you out, even when you're not looking."

That was the thing, though.

Jones wasn't keeping quiet about Helen's death because he was in denial. He didn't talk about that horrible day because of one thing and one thing only.

Guilt.

Ravenous, bottomless, dragging, smothering guilt.

That's why Jones couldn't tell Cassandra now about what had happened then.

He didn't want to show that guilt to someone openly showing him their grief.

It wasn't fair to her.

Or her unborn child, cradled inside of her and the only question he'd needed answered since the moment he saw her at the school.

"Speaking of people who seem to enjoy other people's troubles."

Cassandra had put on a smile that Jones now recognized as practiced politeness. He followed her gaze to Nan, who was bustling over to their table with their drinks. The second she put them down she was looking at Jones with noticeable annoyance.

"I know this isn't proper of me but Jimmy is in the back and is asking to talk to you, Sheriff. I told him it's not good manners or business to go after you before you've even had the time to drink a drop, but he's insisting something awful."

Jones shared a look with Cassandra.

"Tell him I have business hours or, at least, that he can wait until I'm done eating with my companion here."

Nan rolled her eyes.

"Wish I could convince him to listen to me for once, but not a thing in the world I can do to shut him up other than to say I tried. I even told him he could come out here himself but he got all squirrely. Said he doesn't want the rest of the guests here to see him bothering you. Me, though? He has no problem bothering in public."

Under normal circumstances Jones would have told

Jimmy "too dang bad," but there was his curiosity keeping the impulse back.

Jimmy was Nan's younger brother and not at all a fan of the Dawn County Sheriff's Department. His dislike, though, hadn't come from The Flood, but was from his younger years as a frequent flyer at the county jail. If he wasn't in cuffs for possession or disorderly, he was behind bars for assault or public intoxication. Sure, he'd found his own redemption after a short stint in prison when he was in his twenties, but now he was a man in his midfifties who was king at holding grudges against any and all law enforcement. The fact that he wanted to talk to someone with a badge was surprising.

The fact that he wanted to talk to the sheriff was downright wild.

Jones shared another look with Cassandra.

She used her hands to talk along with her when she spoke.

"Go on, I promise I don't mind," she said. "I was thinking about checking in with Keith again to make sure he was doing okay."

Jones pushed back his chair.

"You sure?"

Cassandra nodded.

"Go on," she repeated.

Jones didn't like it, but he soon was knocking at the office door at the back of the building. He'd only been inside of the office once when he was a teen. When Jimmy opened the door, however, it was like stepping into a time capsule. Everything was old, dated. Weathered, worn.

Even Jimmy, who was gray and worried.

He didn't beat around the bush after letting in Jones.

"You grabbed Bill from the school today, but did he have anything with him?"

Jones knew that the story of what happened at the school had already been teased on the social-media account of the local news, but none of the names had been released. Still, Jones wasn't surprised the details had traveled fast.

"You know I can't talk about ongoing investigations, Jimmy. Those are the rules."

Jimmy shook his head. Jones saw urgency and aggression in the movement.

"I don't care about no rules, I just want to know if you found his bomb or not."

That was a surprise.

"What do you mean, his bomb?"

Jimmy was as expressive as Cassandra, but with a whole heap of worry added in.

"The other night at the bar he got to talking and said he knew how to make a bomb from his time in the military and could use it to get this town out of the past and into something new if he really wanted to. We thought he was just talking to talk—he's like that, you know?—but then I heard about him attacking kids at the school and, well, I got that bad feeling. The one in your gut that tells you to get going."

Jones already had his phone out.

"If it was him today, and I'm not saying it was, there was nothing recovered on him or his car. Same with his house." Carlos had led those searches, along with Detective Lovett.

But that wasn't sitting right with Jimmy. He shook his head again.

"If he ever made anything it would have been with Miles, his ex's son," he said. "Miles idolizes him and is old enough to drive. He'd do whatever that man asked him to do and I can't seem to find him anywhere. That's what scares me, Sheriff. If Bill wasn't just talking and y'all didn't find anything, then what if that boy got talked into something worse than attacking kids on the playground?"

The last headshake was one of complete anxiety.

Jones felt it transfer through the man's final words.

"All I know is, if I was you, Jones, I'd want to find that boy before he found you and yours."

Lila Shaw, Keith's foster mother, said that Keith had been fine all night until when it was time to get ready for bed.

"He's in his room, quiet as a mouse, but won't lie down. I'm about to try and talk to him. Maybe read something to distract him," Lila said on the phone. Cassandra told her that she thought that was a good idea.

"Maybe stay away from pirate books, if you can. We talked a lot about the pirate code earlier and it might trigger him."

Lila seemed confused by the directive, but agreed to read the book her former foster child had left with her about space travel.

Keith would like that and hopefully get some sleep, Cassandra thought. If not, she'd be loving on him extra the next day just in case.

The conversation ended there. It had been quick.

But not as quick as Jones, and the man who must have been Jimmy, who came out of the back and hurried toward the table.

"I'm so sorry, Cassandra," Jones said, cell phone in his hand. "But I have something urgent that I need to see to. Can I call you later?"

He was stressed. Tenfold. It could be seen in the crease

above his brow, the flare of his nostrils and how his posture had gone from casual and relaxed to stiff.

Something was happening.

And it put anxiety into her veins.

"Yeah, sure," she said. "Go ahead."

Jones didn't prod her again to make sure she was okay with it. One second he was there, the next he and Jimmy were bustling out.

It happened so quickly that Cassandra didn't realize she'd never given her phone number to Jones until he was already gone.

Disappointment mixed with and an exhaustion that had become familiar since she'd seen those two red lines on her pregnancy test.

Nan appeared at her side, flustered.

"Your food's ready. Jimmy said it's on the house. Do you still want it?"

Her earlier sweetness had dried up. Nan was confused and worried, too. That didn't mean Cassandra wanted to stay.

"Could I have it in a to-go box, please?" she asked. "My back is starting to ache and I wouldn't mind stretching out."

Nan nodded absently and was back before Cassandra could collect herself.

"Have a good one," she told the older lady.

Nan smiled, then pulled out her cell phone. She was staring at it when Cassandra was walking to the front doors.

Kelby Creek was cold tonight.

Cassandra breathed in air that cooled her lungs and calmed her soul. She had a jacket in her car, but had been too hot to wear it earlier. Too nervous at seeing Jones and telling him some news that was going to rock his world.

A world that, apparently, was already rocking.

Nan being passive-aggressive as she'd tried to pry into his homecoming hadn't been missed by Cassandra. Neither were Jones's several looks at her pregnant stomach.

He wanted to ask who the father was, as much as she was worried about telling him it was him.

Cassandra still didn't know if Jones was married, if he was seeing someone, if his interest in being a father only extended to Bonnie.

Though, whatever his situation was, it didn't change Cassandra's.

She was going to be a mom to a little boy she hadn't yet thought of a name for and she was as nervous as she was excited to meet him.

How Jones wanted to factor into that didn't change her feelings on her son.

But what if Jones does want to be a family? What if he wants your son all to himself? Joint custody? Marriage and a house with a white picket fence? What if he wants nothing to do with us at all?

These were questions Cassandra hadn't had to answer before since she hadn't known where in the world Jones might be.

Now?

Now she could see him in the car-pool pickup line, or at the grocery store, or in line at the bank.

Their time together at the hotel had felt like a dream.

Now the consequences of that night were about to bring them to a new reality.

And it terrified Cassandra because she had no idea what she hoped Jones wanted.

"At least now we have another night to stress over it," she told her pregnant belly once she was behind the wheel of her car. "I hope you're ready for burgers, fries and ice cream, baby boy. Because that's on the menu as soon as we get home."

Cassandra pulled out of the parking lot and was surprised to pass Jimmy standing next to a car, talking expressively on his phone. She had thought he was going someplace with Jones, but maybe he couldn't because he wasn't the law. That got Cassandra wondering about what could have been that urgent as she made her way toward Wayne's Road.

She lived in the neighborhood of Holly Oak and the quickest way across town without going through a ton of lights and four-way stops was Wayne's Road. It was relatively scenic but had enough lighting that taking it at night didn't feel like a total gamble on safety.

And then there was Cassandra's thing about driving.

If she could avoid as many drivers as possible, she tried.

Cassandra passed by a stretch of woods on one side, an open field on the other. The stars were in full bloom and the spaces between the streetlights were wide enough to see them.

It was nice for a bit, all things considered.

Even when she saw the taillights, she was glad to only see the one set.

Though, they were disappearing fast in the distance.

Too fast.

Cassandra slowed down. Something wasn't quite right. There was fog around the edge of the bridge up ahead. She peered through the windshield, squinting since the nearest lights were yards behind her.

The bridge was old, with guardrails made of metal and wood. While the creek that wound its way through town was narrow in parts, this spot let the waterway breathe and stretch, was not so much wide as deep.

Cassandra slowed the closer she got.

Then she pulled onto the grass shoulder, right above the slope down to the creek bed.

Part of the guardrail was gone and the fog was definitely not fog.

It was smoke.

Cassandra flung open her door and ran onto the bridge. The smoke was coming out of the truck that was currently sinking down into the water below.

A truck whose doors and windows were shut.

Whoever was driving was still inside.

"Hold on!"

Cassandra didn't know if her voice carried below or not, since the drop was at least ten feet down, but she didn't stand still to check.

She'd prepared for this.

She knew what to do.

Cassandra ran back to her car and opened the center console. She grabbed what she needed, put it in her pocket and swiped her phone as she maneuvered down the sloped grass. Her call to 911 was fast and efficient.

She knew more than most that time mattered in these situations. Seconds were precious.

She wasn't going to waste hers.

"A truck ran off of the bridge on Wayne's Road. It's going underwater," she yelled as soon as the dispatcher answered. "I think someone is still inside."

The grass was slick, or maybe she had more adrenaline in her than she realized.

Either way, Cassandra made it to the water's edge and pulled out her pocket-size flashlight, her legs shaking.

Dispatch started talking but Cassandra was focused on

her beam of light as it skated across the front of the truck being covered by the water. When the beam landed on the driver, she found her words quickly.

"Oh, my God, it's Jones," she yelled into the phone. "It's Sheriff Murphy!"

PAIN.

In his head and along his right leg.

Jones reasoned it probably hurt more at the moment of the collision than it did when he'd regained consciousness, but seeing as he'd also been knocked clean out, there was no way to tell.

He just groaned as he rejoined the land of the living and had a hard time placing where he was and why he was there in the first place.

There had been the school, then ice cream with Bonnie, then Cassandra…

Then Billy.

Which had led to Jones getting all the information he could about Miles before peeling out of the parking lot in the direction of his house.

But why was Jones…?

The truck around him shuddered. He realized belatedly that he wasn't on the road anymore. He was tilted, downward. But he was moving.

Jones heard a splash. Then he felt the familiar sway that he'd only ever experienced on a boat.

Finally, the rest of the details surrounding his new reality pieced together.

He'd been run off of the Wayne's Road Bridge. Meaning he was now in a truck that was in creek water deep enough to drown him, if he didn't get going.

Jones went to his seat belt as water slapped against his window. In his time as deputy, he'd seen a car go off into water not as deep as the spot he was in. The only reason the man had been able to get out when he did was because his door had already been open before water pressure had sealed it shut. Jones had had no idea he was about to go for a swim, or else he would have done the same. Now he tried to open the door and it didn't do a thing. He went to the power window next. The lights went out as the engine drowned. The button under his finger did nothing.

Jones unbuckled his seat belt and reached over for his cell phone. It wasn't there and he didn't have time to find it. He was going to have to break his window or else risk not being able to escape when the vehicle went to the bottom of the creek.

He went for his gun next, deciding to go ahead and use that to get out. Yet, as was his luck tonight, he remembered it was stashed in his holder in the glove compartment. The locked glove compartment.

Jones fumbled for his keys but knew he'd lost his opening to do what he needed to do.

The water was rising.

Bonnie came to the front of his mind like a slap to the face. Then his father.

Then—

"Jones!" He thought he'd imagined it or manifested it somehow. A muffled voice, there at his window. He turned to see that voice wasn't just a figment of his imagination, but was coming from a woman treading water next to his door.

Not just any woman.

Cassandra put one hand on the truck to keep her steady. She had something in her other hand. It was orange and small, but she reared her arm back, ready to use it.

"Cover your eyes!"

Jones didn't have time to ask why. He shielded his

eyes just as a *tink* sounded against the window. That *tink* sounded one more time before something new gave way.

Glass.

Breaking.

Cassandra had one of those car-escape tools. Ones meant to break windows in an emergency.

Jones could have kissed her when he felt some glass land on his lap.

He might have done it if water hadn't come in, too.

"Hurry!" Cassandra was yelling but had done the main job. Now she used her little orange hammer to clear away the rest of the glass.

Jones undid his belt and started to make his way out of the window, when the water finally got its fingers all the way around the car.

Instead of slowly sinking, he went from seeing Cassandra and the night sky to being underwater.

He was pushed against his seat and soaked.

But he wasn't trapped anymore.

Cassandra had seen to that.

SHE HAD NEVER been the greatest of swimmers and she wasn't sure how long she could safely hold her breath while pregnant, but Cassandra plugged her nose and knew she had to try.

She took a deep breath and felt her muscles move as she readied to dive when something touched her arm.

The yell that escaped her was partially filled with water.

It didn't stop Cassandra from saying his name when Jones broke the surface right next to her.

"Are you okay?" she asked, bobbing up and down.

Jones answered by putting his arm around her waist. He pulled her along with him as he swam them a few feet over to the shallow part of the creek. Despite finding their footing, he kept her close to him until they were out of the water. He let her go and touched his head, wincing.

There was blood.

Cassandra's worry started to climb again, but Jones was all eyes on her.

"Are *you* okay?"

Cassandra was.

She knew she was.

All she'd done was swim a little, use her emergency tool a little more and then tread water.

She was *fine* physically.

But, man, her emotions were rough.

The blood on his head, his completely soaked clothes, the image of him not moving in the driver's seat…?

What if Cassandra hadn't been there?

Would he have made it out?

Or would he have died, at the bottom of the creek, never knowing…?

It was all too much and Cassandra did the only thing that she could think of in the moment.

"He's yours," she blurted out. Her hands went to her stomach. "The baby. He's yours."

The sound of a siren whirled in the distance.

Jones's eyes stayed right on her.

Chapter Seven

"I—I was going to tell you earlier, but I was trying to wait for the right moment." Cassandra motioned generally around them. "I know this wasn't it, but I—I had to make sure you knew."

Jones, bless him, didn't ask if she was sure. Though, he did have one question.

"Did you say a boy?"

Cassandra's heart melted a little.

"Yes. A boy."

Jones took a step forward, face still impassive. The sirens had become louder. He stopped and looked to the road.

"Is your car up there?"

Cassandra's heart fell a little at that, even though she knew it wasn't the time to talk about their baby or their future.

"Yeah. Flashers on, too. And my phone is, uh, somewhere over there and should still be on with Dispatch." Cassandra pointed to the spot she'd dropped her phone after seeing Jones with his eyes closed. She figured she'd already told them all of the pertinent information they needed to know. Sheriff unconscious in a sinking truck next to Wayne's Road Bridge.

"Come on." Jones took her hand and led her to her

dropped phone before taking them both back up the slope of grass that led to the road. He was cold, she realized, as she was shivering. They both must have looked like something wild when a cruiser pulled up behind her car.

A man she didn't recognize jumped out of the driver's seat, while a man she did, Sterling Costner, tore out of the passenger side. His signature cowboy hat was missing and he was actively stripping out of his coat when his eyes landed on them.

"Sheriff!" It was two syllables but it did a fine job of conveying absolute relief and confusion. "What's going on?"

Cassandra hadn't had time to wonder how Jones had made it into the creek, just that he had been there, but now she tilted up a curious chin to his answer.

"I was burning rubber to Miles's house when a car came out of nowhere. Slammed into my side. Hit my head somewhere between that and the water."

The other deputy ran to the bridge and looked over its edge.

"The truck's gone," Jones added. "Only reason I'm above water is because Miss West here thinks quicker than most people blink." He glanced back at the cruiser. "You got a blanket in there?"

Sterling nodded and rushed off, returning in a few seconds with a heavy coverlet that Jones draped over her shoulders. She accepted it with a quick thanks.

"I got a bead on the car. A silver or beige Taurus. I couldn't tell with the lighting. Front left headlight was out."

"I saw a car speeding off that way when I came up and saw the bridge." Cassandra pointed ahead of them.

The other deputy backtracked. More sirens sounded in the distance.

"Want in, or want to stay?" The question was to Jones.

Of course it was—he was the sheriff. Still, Cassandra felt a ping of panic at the choice. First of all, Jones was hurt. Blood was clearly at his hairline and he'd already admitted to losing consciousness.

Not to mention, both of them were soaked in the cold.

"Go ahead. I'm staying here."

Jones's words were heavy and final.

Sterling didn't follow up. He was back to the cruiser in a flash.

"EMT is en route. Marigold should be pulling up right before them," he called over the hood of the car. "Foster is on Miles."

Jones nodded and together they watched the car speed off.

"Do you think it was an accident?" Cassandra shivered as she said the words. Jones took her hand again and walked her to her car. He opened the door and cranked the engine. She didn't understand why until he reached inside and fiddled with the air-conditioner controls. More aptly, the heat. Cassandra heard it click on.

Jones stood straight again. He'd been thinking of his answer.

"No," he said simply.

"But why? Why would someone do that? Because you're sheriff?"

At this, he stood in front of her and looped one hand inside of her coat under the blanket. She could feel the weight of him against her. It was comforting and distracting all at once.

"I've been sheriff for months now," he began. Cassandra realized he was trying to take off her coat. She let him, easing out of it as he stepped around her. "But today my daughter has been chased by a man who had no reason to chase her and I've been run off of the road only hours later."

Cassandra had completely forgotten about what had happened at school while she'd been dealing with the sinking truck. Now her acute worry at seeing him get close to drowning evened out into a blanket of anxiety that weighed her down.

"You think it's connected?" she asked.

Jones threw her jacket on top of the car and then took her hand again.

"All you all right?" he asked. "You shouldn't have been in that cold water. Neither one of you."

"I'm fine," she responded. "We're both fine."

He moved her gently to the passenger's seat. Cassandra silently took the directive and lowered herself into the warm interior. Heated air hit her face and stomach directly just as the sirens in the distance became flashing lights seen clearly in the rearview.

Jones glanced back at them but answered her before dealing with the newcomers.

"I might think that it was all some kind of coincidence had this morning been normal routine for me."

Cassandra gave him a questioning look.

"What happened this morning?"

Eyes as deep and serious as the creek they'd just struggled to get free of met Cassandra's and held them fast.

"I found out someone was lying in the Annie McHale investigation."

A LOT OF information came in all at once. Jones met the first wave in the hallway of the sheriff's department.

"Miles is in Oklahoma with his mother," Detective Foster Lovett said, voice low. "He's also ten and hasn't been to Kelby Creek since his mother and Bill ended things when he was four."

Jones crossed his arms over his chest. His shirt didn't like the movement too much. It was tight and a loaner from Sterling, the only Kelby Creek officer who came close to his size. Thankfully, Jones had his workout joggers and tennis shoes in his office so he didn't have to scrounge for pants or footwear. It felt odd to wear the mismatched outfit with his badge. He was, at least, glad he had the shining star. It was the only piece of his uniform he'd had on him as the water had overtaken the truck.

"So he's probably not out here building bombs and singing Bill Burrows's praises," he said, deadpan.

"Not unless he can magically transport himself across the country without his mom, his Boy Scout troop and his little brother catching on, no. I'm going to assume not."

"Then that means Jimmy was either very ill-informed or he told one heck of a lie."

Foster nodded.

"I figured you'd want to ask him yourself about that."

Foster eyed the sheriff's office behind Jones. His wife, Millie, and Cassandra were inside. Both women had been told they could go home and both women had wanted to stay for answers. Though, Jones had a sneaking suspicion that Cassandra was still worried about him. When the EMT had checked out the cut on his head, she'd been hovering nearby, insisting he go to the emergency room. The last he had heard they were in deep conversation about Millie's job as a social worker for the county.

When Foster made another quick glance that way, Jones decided to give the man a bone. His wife had already brought something for Cassandra to change into and he himself had left family dinner to scour the town for Miles and Bill's possible bomb.

"What's on your mind, Lovett?"

Foster put on a smile that was partially apologetic. His voice went even lower than it had before.

"I just didn't know you were dating, is all."

Jones had known Foster before The Flood and had been happy to see him as the lead detective when Jones had become sheriff. He trusted him. Jones knew that he was a good man. He also knew he was a better detective.

Jones wasn't about to waste both of their time by trying to fib out an excuse.

"We weren't on a date, just trying to catch up," he answered. "We had a few moments a while back before parting ways. We didn't even know each other lived in Kelby Creek until what happened at the school today."

That was a very vague way to say something big because their "few moments" had, apparently, become a child.

A baby boy.

Jones had already suspected, based on the timing alone, but hearing Cassandra tell him that he was the father had been a sucker punch.

To the stomach?

The heart?

Both?

He didn't know.

The only feeling he could grasp was that guilt, and it ran deep and spanned years. He'd had to deal with it when Helen was pregnant with Bonnie, and when he'd picked out pink paint for the nursery and hummed some song he never figured out the name of.

Happy, healthy, unable to hold in her excitement at the vision of watching their child grow and be happy and healthy and have their own excitement.

But that wasn't how Helen's story ended.

All because of The Flood, all because of Annie McHale's kidnapping, all because Jones hadn't seen the bad right in front of him.

So when Cassandra was there, risking herself to save *him* while carrying their son?

Jones had done the only thing he knew to be right in that moment.

He'd taken a cold woman to find some warmth and become the sheriff at the scene.

That's what he needed to be now, too.

The sheriff of the department.

Foster, knowing he wasn't going to get more than that answer, nodded. He had the great good sense to set aside his curiosity and cleared his throat. He thumbed back down the hall toward the interrogation room.

"Well, I suggest you get going on Jimmy before he spooks and lawyers up. I don't think he realizes that we've found Miles and also not any kind of bomb, never mind in connection with Bill."

Foster didn't have to tell him twice.

The Dawn County Sheriff's Department had two interrogation rooms. Both were always thoroughly cleaned after use, but one always had a slight dingy feeling to it. Fluctuating temperature, a chair that wobbled just a little and a smell that ran between a hint of mold mixed with staleness all created an uncomfortable feeling for those sitting inside.

That was the room they had Jimmy sitting in. The door was open and maybe that gave him the idea to look a little cocky. But, bad day for him, Jones shut the door tight when he walked in.

"Hey there, Jimmy."

Jones took the chair that didn't wobble and dropped down into it with a sigh. Jimmy's eyes widened a bit but

Jones wasn't sure if that was because of his current outfit, or if it was because he wasn't currently on the bottom of the creek. Jones decided to address both in the moment.

"I hope you don't mind my clothes. I know they're not up to snuff for the sheriff, but, well, the damnedest thing happened after I left you in the parking lot earlier." Jones leaned forward, placing his elbows on the table between them. "A car actually ran me off the road, just like in the movies. I went off of a bridge, even. Straight into the water until it ate up my dad's old truck." Jones swooped his hand through the air to pantomime the car going over the edge of the bridge. Jimmy watched the movement. "Thank goodness for one of those emergency hammer things, or else I might not be sitting here across from you right now."

Jones clasped his hands together. He dropped his fake politeness as fast as his truck had dropped into the water.

"But, look at that, I am here now. Sitting with you."

Jimmy, a man who never minded talking, was awfully quiet. If he hadn't had a clue what the mood was, now Jones suspected he was catching on.

"That's rough." That was all he managed to say after it was clear Jones wasn't going to keep on talking. "Some people really need to go back to school to learn about driving. All ages, not just the young'uns."

Jones didn't respond. He didn't nod, and he didn't move an inch. He kept his gaze planted on the smaller man.

The silent treatment was effective when Bonnie used it on Jones; he'd learned that effectiveness still rang true when used in questioning.

People weren't innately fans of the quiet.

That was true for Jimmy after a few more moments of it. He readjusted his posture, jumped a little when the chair wobbled at the movement and went to talking quick.

"I was going to follow you, like I…like I said, you know,

earlier but then I got this call in the parking lot and had to take it," he began. "My nephew, you know the one that was married to Mari—Marigold, I mean—well, he called all upset about some date he was on not going the way he wanted. I couldn't leave him all upset like that, you know, so I was trying to figure out what was what. That's—that's why I didn't follow you or else I woulda seen whoever did that and, well, you know, help you."

Jones unlaced his fingers and rubbed at his chin.

"Your nephew was on a bad date and upset about it," Jones repeated.

Jimmy nodded. He was starting to sweat.

"Must've been really bad considering we were on the way to try and find a teenager with a bomb. One who, according to you, was going to use it to hurt me and mine."

Jimmy went still.

So still it was almost impressive. Like he was a robot who'd just been turned off. Jones marveled at it a moment before Jimmy appeared to restart.

His movements this time were more rigid.

"I love my family," he said. "Nothing more important."

Jimmy was no longer babbling. His tone had gone flat.

Jones didn't understand why. So he took a leap to find out.

"It probably helped matters that you knew Miles wasn't in town—hasn't been in town for years—and held no soft spot for Bill. That's not even mentioning that he's only ten. Also probably helped your conscience to know that there was never any mention of a bomb by Bill."

Jimmy's eyes widened. He didn't confirm, he didn't deny. Which, in itself, was loud.

Jones leaned forward again but not into a casual position. He was getting mad.

"See, the thing is, Jimmy, I'm pretty sure you told me

that wild story to get me moving. To get me out on the road. And I think you knew that I'd take Wayne's Road so I could speed my tail off because, well, a bomb's a pretty damn urgent situation. Then, I'm guessing, you found a reason to stay back because, even though you needed to get me out and going, you didn't need to be the person who was supposed to meet me out on the road. But, what I don't get, is the why of it all. Is it because of me arresting Bill?"

Jones had lived through many a surprise in his career in law enforcement. Runners, fighters, people who had nothing in their hands one moment and then holding a weapon the next. He'd used those experiences and his career to become better at spotting the subtle changes, the barely hidden emotions. The spark that was about to ignite a fire that he didn't need to get burned by.

Yet, for all of his experiences, Jones never suspected what the man said next.

Jimmy, a man who'd had a clean record for upward of twenty years with no real issues, sat to his full height. His words were ice.

"You're going to destroy this town and we're not going to let that happen."

Jimmy leaped across the table.

It was only when Jones reacted and pushed back that he saw the knife in the man's hand.

Chapter Eight

Everyone was running, most were yelling.

Cassandra was standing behind Millie while her husband told her to lock the door behind him. She listened but with extreme hesitance.

Cassandra had her hand on her stomach when the yelling stopped. Millie shared a look with her, but neither one of them spoke until a few minutes passed and Millie's phone vibrated. It was a text.

"Foster said everything's okay," she informed Cassandra as she read. "He said to give them a minute and he'll be back."

The words were reassuring, but the locked door between them and the rest of the department was not. Cassandra was tired of all of the adrenaline that had been pumped into her system that day, and all of the worry, too.

However, the day she was having didn't seem to compare to the day that Jones was.

It was part of the reason she had insisted on coming back to the department with him in the first place. He had been through the stress of a parent seeing his child in jeopardy and a head trauma within hours of each other. The man should have been at home.

Then again, she probably should have been, too.

Cassandra was looking at the clock over Jones's desk

when footsteps echoed outside of the door. It was ten o'clock at night and Chief Deputy Park told Millie it was finally okay to come out.

"Where's Foster?" she immediately asked, voice pitching up into a higher octave. Park put his hands up in quick defense.

"He's fine," he said. "He's dealing with a suspect right now and wanted to make sure he got in a few questions before he was sent to the hospital. The suspect, not Foster."

Park shifted his gaze to Cassandra.

"The sheriff asked me to escort you home, if that's all right. He would do it himself but he's…busy right now."

The man probably hadn't meant to, but the way he said the word *busy* came out all wrong.

Cassandra knew she had no real claim to Jones—she wasn't his girlfriend or his wife, just a onetime lover recently reunited—and the fact that she was pregnant with his child really didn't change anything about that. Yet, she gave Park a look she reserved for stubborn kindergartners.

"You tell him I'm fine waiting until I can talk to him myself."

Just like Park had said *busy* all wrong, Cassandra knew how she'd spoken had resonated as something that the man was better off not fighting.

He nodded.

"You did save his life earlier, so he at least owes you a good-night."

Park led both women down one hall, across a large room and down another hall. The first two spaces were devoid of people, but the room they entered was filled with chattering men and women in uniform.

Their sheriff stood off to the side, shirtless and bleeding.

"Oh, my God."

The sudden appearance of Cassandra and Millie barely registered with anyone inside of the room. Whatever happened was way more interesting than a pregnant elementary-school teacher suddenly in their break room.

Jones, however, looked up in an instant.

Then he rolled his eyes at Park.

"You had one job," he said. "One stinking job."

Cassandra ignored both men and moved to Jones. She stopped right in front of him, eyes going straight to the cut on his side.

"What happened?" she asked. "This isn't from the crash, is it?"

Jones sighed, the sound heavy and true.

"No. This is from a conversation that took an unexpected turn."

Cassandra knew that Jimmy had been brought in to get more answers about his accusations about some teenager and a bomb, but she didn't understand how that had gone to Jones being shirtless and bloody less than five minutes after she'd seen him.

"Wait. Jimmy did this?"

This time the sheriff wasn't as forthcoming with his answer. Instead, he grabbed for the first-aid kit open next to him on the counter. It gave him time to construct a vague statement.

"There's a lot of questions still up in the air right now. Don't worry, though, I'm also itching for answers."

Cassandra watched as he took a sanitation wipe and moved it across the cut. The wound didn't look deep and the man didn't wince at the pressure.

"Let Park escort you home," he added. "He's a good man and I trust him. He also said he didn't mind."

A deputy close to them glanced over at Cassandra. It

prompted her to take a small step forward. She lowered her voice so only Jones could hear.

"I think you should be the one to go home," she said. "I mean, haven't you been through enough today? Surely somebody else can do a little work while you take at least a little rest?"

Jones gave her a calculating look.

It caught her off guard.

So did his demeanor as it shifted to something more stony.

"I have to go over some things here before I can go home," he said. "And that's probably going to take a while. I can get rest later. *You* should probably think about getting rest now."

He eyed her stomach with quick purpose.

And it put straight anger into her veins.

"Just because I'm pregnant doesn't mean I'm glass," she countered. "And if I can't get you to take a much-needed break, then you don't have any say so about when I should and shouldn't rest, either."

Cassandra understood enough about trauma, herself and pregnancy to know that her anger was coming from a lot of places.

First of all, he was right. She did need to rest. Plain and simple. She was pregnant and she'd been through two significant situations that had been terrifying in their own right.

Secondly, she knew that not getting that rest had made her truly exhausted and, even before pregnancy, a tired Cassandra was never a good Cassandra to be reasonable with.

Lastly, there was a good chance that she was still afraid that something was going to happen to the father of her child. And that held weight. Weight that had her a little panicked.

Plus, there was also the bonus detail that being pregnant often meant being a little hormonal. The week before, she'd all-out sobbed at a grocery-store commercial about buying the right kind of bread from the bakery. It only made sense that seeing Jones again after all of these months on top of seeing Jones hurt was stirring up a lot of those more pronounced reactions.

Still, just because she knew why she was feeling the way she was, didn't stop the feelings from happening.

Before Jones could try and convince her to go, Cassandra decided to listen to him. But, of course, she wanted to make it feel like it was her decision.

She spun around on her heel, hoped that she wasn't making a scene and found Deputy Park next to the door.

"I don't need you to escort me to my house, but if you're offering to walk me to my car, I'll take it."

JIMMY WASN'T TALKING to anyone the next day and no one knew exactly why. His warning, attack and lie about a bomb made no sense. Not to his friends, his coworkers and certainly not to his sister, Nan.

Most concerning was Bill Burrows's lack of connection with Jimmy. As far as any of them could tell they weren't even friends.

"I have never seen Bill around Jimmy," Nan had said, sounding like someone who prided herself on knowing everything and yet was surprised by something unknown so close to home. Jones had questioned her late last night, and she hadn't been happy to be called to the station. "I can count on my hand how many times Bill's been to the restaurant and of those times he hasn't been sitting there talking to Jimmy about nothing. Don't you go saying those two are the same kind of man. Bill went after kids, Jimmy went after the law. And, if you don't remember, that was something the whole town did pretty hard a few years back."

She hadn't wanted to talk to Jones after that. She wanted a lawyer for her brother, though Jimmy had done one smart thing and had already called one in.

"It truly could not be connected," Carlos offered as the end of the shift came near, the long previous night and new day now over.

But Jones wasn't so sure.

"It's the 'we' part of what Jimmy said that has me thinking that something else is going on," Jones said. "And even if the two incidents aren't connected there are still two different problems." Jones held up his index finger before holding up his middle. He ticked off each as he made his points. "What was Bill trying to do at the school and why did Jimmy come after me?"

"Don't forget about who was the one who tried to get you after Jimmy sent you off on that wild-goose chase about the bomb?"

"There is that."

No questions got answered by the time Carlos convinced him to leave.

"You went home for an hour and then you came back here raring to go," he said. "Miss West was right. You need rest. The department can handle it from here."

Jones was surprised he didn't bring up their friend, and the former sheriff, Brutus Chamblin. During his last stint as interim sheriff, he'd suffered a heart attack on the job. It was during a singularly intense event, but the stress and long hours he'd been swimming in had put him on the road to it. Sure, he had a few years on Jones, but that didn't mean Jones was going to go nose-to-the-gravel, not stopping until he saw blood. He spotted the picture of Bonnie on his desk instead and sighed deeply.

"Call my cell if anything happens."

Carlos seemed surprised, though he didn't say anything out loud.

"Isn't it at the bottom of the creek?" he asked. "Don't tell me that waterproof phones these days are *that* good."

"Definitely not," Jones said. "No amount of rice could save it. Dad gave me one of his old ones. I had all of my numbers transferred at lunch."

Carlos whistled low. Then sobered.

"I still can't believe that happened. Every year I hope to say this job has been boring, but every year here I am shaking my head and wondering if it's something in the drinking water."

Carlos wasn't alone in wishing for a boring year.

What Jones didn't tell his chief deputy was that he'd already known things were going to get interesting before they settled.

And that had everything to do with the folder that had been destroyed by the water while riding shotgun beneath the passenger seat in Jones's truck.

It felt like a lifetime ago but had only been yesterday morning, when Jones had met someone to talk about the Annie McHale kidnapping.

Then *it* had happened.

I found out someone was lying in the Annie McHale investigation.

Jones shouldn't have told Cassandra that, but it was as true as the need for answers.

He'd caught someone in a lie and, as far as he could tell, it was the first time the lie had been said.

Jones hadn't had the time to process it yet given his

father's call to get him to the elementary school and the downward spiral after that.

And maybe that was the point?

Jones growled into the cab of his rental after leaving the department when his talk with Carlos was through.

This was what Kelby Creek had felt like after The Flood. All the uncertainty, the questions. How everything felt like it was coming at you from every direction.

It was infuriating.

It was frustrating.

It…

Jones cut off his own mental downward spiral. The sign for Holly Oaks went past his window. His father's. house wasn't in Holly Oaks.

But he realized he knew someone's house that was.

Jones went to the second street and the third house on the left. A car was parked in the drive. He parked behind it and took a moment to look the two-story up and down.

It was nice. The landscaping, too. There was a wreath on the front door that looked like only succulents. A Home Sweet Home sign stood propped up against one wall of the front porch. Jones spotted the Welcome doormat. He could see the rainbow printed beneath the word.

Jones took a deep breath and followed it out into the cold.

He kept steady and true as he walked up the drive and across the sidewalk, and when he pressed the doorbell.

He was resolute in his decision to come here, unannounced, and at dusk.

He was sure as sure could be that it needed to be done.

He needed to be *here*.

Yet, the moment the door opened, the man once called "the towering sheriff" by a reporter felt two inches tall.

Cassandra might have been wearing an outfit that reminded Jones of a Christmas tree covered in glitter, but her face held nothing but anger.

"I should have called," he said quickly. "And a lot earlier than now, but—"

Cassandra shook her head as she cut him off.

"I know why Bill came after us yesterday." There was no waver or uncertainty in her voice. "And I need you to take me somewhere to prove it."

Chapter Nine

It was five in the afternoon and Cassandra grabbed her third bag of fruit snacks since coming home from school. Or, actually, Jones did, after she waved him into her home.

"So you think that Lila Shaw, Keith's foster mom, was having an affair with Bill," he mused after her hurried follow-up. She didn't ask, but Jones grabbed another bag of fruit snacks from the back of the pantry and moved it down to a lower shelf as he spoke.

Cassandra nodded emphatically.

"Keith ended up taking lunch with just me in the classroom so he could have some space to talk. I could tell something had him quiet, but I just assumed it was what happened. But *then* he said that he didn't know why Bill chased us since the last time he saw him he was so nice."

Cassandra was doing her version of a grid search of the first floor, looking for her purse. Pregnancy brain was certainly real for her, especially when it came to misplacing her things. The week before she'd had to get June to pick her up because she couldn't for the life of her find her keys.

They'd been in the fridge next to a box of cereal. The milk had been in the pantry.

Cassandra had already looked in both places for her bag. Jones dutifully followed her around.

"After that comment I asked a few strategic questions,

and according to Keith, who, by the way, I trust, Bill frequented their house…but only when Lila's husband, Joel, was away."

"Bill and Lila were having an affair," Jones said, finishing her theory.

"That's what I'm thinking." They'd made it to the laundry room. Her purse was on top of the dryer, along with a jacket half covered in glitter. The casualty of the day.

"What if Bill thought Keith was about to spill the beans to Joel? What if Keith already had and Bill was coming for, I don't know, revenge?"

"What if Keith isn't the reason at all why Bill was there?"

Cassandra slung her purse across her shoulder. It put the bag on her belly. She readjusted as she gave the sheriff an incredulous look.

"I checked Joel's social media. He checked his marital status to 'separated' *three* days ago. Then *yesterday* his wife's lover chases down his kid? And after Lila told us yesterday that she didn't know Bill that well?"

Jones considered that for a moment. She could tell the line of thought intrigued him.

"Okay, say you're right," he said, changing his stance to arms over his chest. It made an already intimidating man seem all the more giantlike. "What exactly is your plan now?"

Cassandra had seen the man naked, *felt* him naked; there was no reason to be shy about a possibly ridiculous plan now.

"Keith has a T-ball game in thirty minutes that he said he and Lila will be at. I want to go over there and catch her in a conversation and, now that you're here, you can do your sneaky conversation bit to try and get to the bottom of her original deceit. A smooth operation consider-

ing the T-ball games are open to the public and you can
say you were thinking about signing Bonnie up and that's
why you're there."

Jones surprised her with a laugh.

She narrowed her eyes at him.

"What?"

"A 'smooth operation'? You sound very James Bond,
is all."

Cassandra wasn't having it.

"I'm sure you could go through more official channels
to talk to Lila—something you should do, James Bond–
style or not, because she definitely lied—but I think a
more casual approach might do everyone some good." Her
gaze dropped to the cut that Jimmy had dealt Jones the
night before. His button-up might be hiding it, but they
both knew it was there. Maybe an unofficial questioning
might work better on Lila.

When Cassandra looked back up, Jones was watching
her with no more humor.

Instead the man appeared right tired.

"I wouldn't mind checking on Keith myself, anyway,"
he decided. "If we can get some answers while we're at it,
then that works, too."

Cassandra clapped her hands together. Excitement
flushed her cheeks with warmth. She wanted to get to the
bottom of what had happened to stop it from ever happening again.

"Great! You're driving, right?" She opened her bag of
fruit snacks and led him to the front door as he nodded.
Cassandra stopped, house key raised in midair. "Wait. Did
you need something? I mean, is that why you're here? Are
you in the middle of work?"

A look she couldn't decipher crossed his face.

He shook his head.

"I came here to talk, but talking can happen anywhere so we're good."

Cassandra would have turned them right back around and sat down on the couch, ready to have any kind of conversation about their child and what that child would mean for the future. But she had already set herself in motion and wanted to see it through.

Plus, he was right. They could talk in the car about their situation just as easily as on a couch.

"So let's get this spy mission going before it gets too late," Jones added. "I promised Bonnie a nighttime story if I missed supper tonight."

Cassandra followed him out to what must have been his rental. She smiled as he opened the door for her and then waited until she was inside before closing it carefully behind her.

Jones Murphy was a gentleman. He had been one at the hotel months ago and that hadn't seemed to change now.

"The game is at the Woodland Complex near the entrance trail to Kintucket Woods," Cassandra began when Jones was seated beside her. "It's free admission and apparently something of a rivalry. Another boy from my class, Donavon, is on the team. The Winter Tigers."

"Now, *that* sounds like some kind of spy talk."

He pulled out of the neighborhood and had them driving a little bit before Cassandra's curiosity just couldn't hold anymore.

"You know, I spent a lot of today driving myself crazy about everything going on. Honestly, I even contemplated using my classroom's whiteboard to try to get my thoughts straight in my head. I didn't, of course, but I have to admit I don't know how any of you do it."

"Do it? You mean solve cases?"

"I mean any of it," she answered with genuine feeling.

"It's not like all the bad keeps to a normal schedule or has a nighttime routine or curfew. I've felt constantly on edge and I was only wrapped up in this mess for less than a day."

Jones seemed to be considering his response.

"This job, any law-enforcement job, can be a lot. But sometimes that *a lot* can be a lot of good, too. That helps when the bad stacks up."

"I guess I can see that," she said. Cassandra decided to creep up to the point of conversation she'd been hoping to hit. She smoothed out the fabric of her dress over her thighs and tried to be gentle.

"It probably doesn't help the bad stack when The Flood keeps getting brought up at almost every turn, even years later."

Jones stiffened.

He actually *stiffened*.

"I was wondering if you knew about that," he said. "I suppose it's hard not to here."

Some towns had endearing or odd stories that were detailed out by the locals.

Kelby Creek had corruption.

"June told me the local version of the story after I moved here. The man who hired me gave me an impassioned speech about how little ol' Kelby Creek was out of the past and looking to a brighter future. A few bad apples couldn't poison the orchard seemed to be his sticking point."

Jones snorted. It was a particularly nasty sound.

"It was more like the orchard was the poisoned part and the few apples were the only good."

He zipped up as soon as the last word left his mouth. Cassandra was outright staring at him. She turned her head and kept her gaze out the windshield.

But she didn't stop.

"Annie McHale," she said, reserving a good dose of awe for the name. "Kelby Creek's beginning of the end."

That got a look from the sheriff.

She tried to explain.

"It's what June told me once," she said. "That had Annie McHale not been kidnapped, the investigation into her wouldn't have uncovered all of the corruption. Her disappearance became the beginning of the end for the town. The downward slope."

"Well, jeez, that June sure is poetic."

"Don't worry, Sheriff." She reached out to pat his leg. It was an automatic move. Cassandra took her hand back as quickly as she'd touched him. She smiled at his glance over at her. "June was just as poetic about how, despite the inevitable end, there's been a growing light, too. Seems a lot of locals have lessened their stance against the sheriff's department in the last few years."

He took a turn and flipped on the headlights. The time change was plunging them deeper into darkness earlier every night. It's why the teeball games that had been added to the schedule for this time of year were played under floodlights. For now, it fit the mood in the car.

"Sheriff Chamblin, the one who hired most of the staff and is the reason why the department is still standing, told me that every bad moment in life will find a balance. All the betrayal, anger and pain… It'd be met later with some kind of cosmic reckoning." He snorted again. "Chamblin's a good man—smart, too—but I think it's too clean a thought to think every bad spot in your life is going to always find a good spot to make it better. Always waiting for the second shoe to drop is a tiring thing, and placing all of your hopes that it's going to be a good second shoe is downright cruel."

Cassandra had been after one question since she'd sat

down, but now, she got caught in his double talk. Jones was saying something without saying it and she didn't know why.

"I only came back here to help my dad and now look at where we are," he continued, a good amount of loathing in his words. "Driving to a children's game in the hopes of finding out why a grown man attacked two kids and a pregnant woman, right before trying to figure out why after twenty years of good standing, a man decides to attack the law for some unknown and probably ridiculous reason."

She placed her hand on his leg and kept it there. This time Cassandra meant the contact.

The pressure seemed to still him.

She finally got around to her question, though she phrased it so he wouldn't have room not to answer.

"And, on top of all of that, you're reinvestigating Annie McHale's case."

The silence was profound.

And short.

Jones nodded.

"Something, I'm guessing by how sensitive the topic is, that's not public information," she added.

The man let out a long, low breath.

"No. It's not. Actually, only a few in the department even know I'm doing it." He shared a look with her. "And you."

She didn't smile but felt a warmth spread in her.

She shook it away quickly.

"That's why you think you're the connection to Bill at the school and being run off the road. And, well, Jimmy. Because you found out someone was lying about the original case."

He didn't look like he wanted to talk about work, yet he continued with no hesitation.

"You said June caught you up on the story of Kelby Creek, but how in-depth did she go about Annie?"

"Not too deep, I suppose. Annie was kidnapped by the sheriff at the time and the mayor. The FBI came in to help and one of their agents went missing, too, before her partner found the evidence that linked everyone together and then to years of corruption. Annie and the FBI agent were never found. The FBI came back and tried to weed out all of the corrupted in what everyone around here calls The Flood."

The sign for the Woodland Complex was lit up as they drove past it. The street that they followed in had several other cars making the trek to the different lots and fields inside. Despite her excitement to talk to Lila, though, Cassandra's attention was all on the sheriff.

"That's true but leaves out a lot of the gut punches. See, the timeline goes—Annie goes missing and the entire town bands together to look for her. Then the ransom call comes in asking for money in exchange for her. Sheriff Barkley, friend to the McHales and godfather to Annie, takes over. He decides to give backup to Annie's father at the exchange meeting at the park and, when the time comes, it turns out to be an ambush." His voice went flat. Cassandra searched his face for an emotion, but it was nothing but blank. He continued. "Several people were killed or hurt but the kidnappers didn't get the money, Annie's parents didn't get her. After that, the town's official website was hacked and a video recording of Annie tied up to a chair and bloody, crying for help, was uploaded to it. That's what went viral, that video. It's also what got the FBI's attention and brought Agent James Delamere and Agent Jacqueline Ortega to our humble little town. They got to looking and then Agent Ortega went missing, too.

But not before she left her partner a message saying she found a lead."

Jones was deep in his story but he still had the focus to pull them into a parking lot next to one of the fields. They were early, which was good.

Because Cassandra couldn't look away.

"Then, it started raining," he continued, putting the car in Park. "Then that rain turned into a flash flood and made the mayor hydroplane himself right into a ditch. By pure luck, the first person to come along the road was Agent Delamere. He went to help the unconscious mayor and, in doing so, accidentally found a necklace had come loose in the crash. The same necklace Annie had been wearing when she went missing. After that? Well, Agent Delamere started turning over those rocks and it led to a whole lot of other people in positions of power, until finally he needed backup to deal with all the snakes he'd found hidden beneath those rocks."

"That's why locals call the investigation into the corruption The Flood," she realized.

He nodded.

"It's the reason why the department has had to work so hard for redemption in the eyes of this town. It's why a lot of us couldn't stomach being around here right after the investigation ended."

Cassandra didn't know what to say to that, but she did come back to the original question.

"But something has happened since then to get you to go back over Annie's specific case?"

Jones let out another deep sigh.

"Annie doesn't just come from what was once the wealthiest family in Kelby Creek, she comes from the most beloved family in Kelby Creek," he said. "The entire town, for some unknown reason, just... loved them. When

Annie went missing, we all looked for her. When we realized she was taken, we rallied alongside them. When they finally moved away after no leads or clues, we grieved with them. So when Annie's uncle was found to be involved in a human trafficking operation recently and his son testified against all of his father's bad without anyone being the wiser…it changed everything."

"If Annie's uncle had gone under the radar with his bad, then maybe the rest of the family had, too?"

It was a solid jump to make, easier for Cassandra, too, considering she hadn't been around to know the McHales. Definitely not to love them.

"That was the thought," he confirmed. "I started officially yesterday by going through the last day Annie was seen alive. Including all of the notes taken by everyone investigating the first time around. I wanted to step through Annie's every minute in the public if possible."

"That's where you found the lie."

Jones nodded.

"Annie spent the night before at Melinda Deacon's house, her neighbor and friend. The next morning she was seen walking across the acreage between the two houses to get home. Two people claimed to have spoken to her then—the Deacon gardener, Jeff King, and the Deacon maid, Vera Lohan. I spoke to Jeff yesterday to just confirm his earlier statement and, wouldn't you know it, he lost his top. Said there was no reason in the world to question him again. So I said I'd just move on to Vera. She's living in Huntsville now with her own business number so it's not hard."

He shook his head.

"Let me guess—Jeff the gardener didn't like that," Cassandra said.

"Nope. Yelled me out of the garden completely."

"So, naturally, you called Vera."

Jones chuckled.

"Yep. She also didn't want to talk but when I told her that the gardener had said the same thing, do you know what she said?"

Cassandra shook her head with bated breath.

"She said, 'What gardener?'"

Cassandra's bated breath turned into a surprised gasp.

"He lied, the gardener," she exclaimed. "Or, maybe she did."

"If she hadn't hung up on me, and then skirted my calls after, I would have kept pressing. Now I'm waiting for a call back from her daughter, who's still in town with her grandson. Maybe I can get her to open up a little to figure out what's going on."

Cassandra had pictured Vera as a younger woman, but if she had a daughter still in town and a grandson…

"Wait. Lohan. Her daughter's name isn't Jasmine, is it?"

Jones's eyes went wide. He nodded.

"Yeah, Jasmine Lohan."

A new wave of excitement went through Cassandra. She cut eye contact with Jones and surveyed the growing crowd of kids and adults on the brightly lit field and stands in front of them.

"I know this sounds wrong to say after everything, but, Sheriff Murphy, today might be your lucky day."

Cassandra saw the young boy with dark hair cropped close that she was looking for. Next to him was a woman holding a baby. Cassandra pointed.

"Because I have a Christopher Lohan in my class and he just so happens to be very good at T-ball."

Jones followed her gaze.

"Well, I'll be damned, that's Jasmine Lohan."

Christopher was waving frantically to another boy, who came walking up.

It was Keith.

"And I'll be damned by two," Cassandra said. "Because there's Lila Shaw."

Jones cracked a smirk.

His voice went a little deep when he met Cassandra's gaze.

It did something to her that was wholly inappropriate in the moment, but she was more than game for what he said next.

"Well, Miss West, looks like our night is about to get interesting."

Chapter Ten

The kids went to the field after the coaches. The rest went to either the stands on the other side of the fence, or the lawn behind them. Everyone could still see and it was that everyone whom Jones tried to avoid as they walked up to Jasmine Lohan, the maid's daughter.

"She might not be happy to see me if her mom got to her after my call," Jones warned Cassandra with a whisper near her ear as they were walking. "If she gets to fussing, you might need to give us space."

Cassandra, who was all energy now, shrugged.

"She might not be happy to see you because you're the sheriff, but I'm the one teaching her son how to read. She might fuss at you, but she's not fussing at me."

Jones couldn't help himself. He chuckled.

"Miss West, if I didn't know any better I'd think you're having fun."

Cassandra laughed.

"On a normal night I'm looking at craft supplies, lesson plans and a bedtime of eight, where I just lie around and try to get comfortable. So, yes, I might be a *little* enthused for a livelier existence right now."

Jones didn't want to, but he imagined Cassandra in bed, pregnant and alone. It was the first image that popped into his head and he abruptly made it leave.

He needed to focus.

Cassandra was already there.

She quickened her pace and met Jasmine before he could. She was all smiles and warmth when the other woman took them in.

"Hi there, Jasmine," she said in greeting. She went to the baby in the sling next. "And this must be little Oliver. Boy, aren't you growing!"

Jasmine took the bombardment in stride. Her lips stretched into a smile when she realized who Cassandra was.

"Miss West! Hey! How are you doing? You come out to watch the game?"

Cassandra had told him in the car that she tried to have a relationship with all of her kids' parents, but Jasmine had never been too chatty at school functions or meetings. That was okay, she'd reasoned, since some parents didn't even show up, but she still wasn't sure how far her presence would go when he started asking questions.

"I'm actually here to check up on Keith," Cassandra admitted, which was partly true.

Jasmine immediately was sympathetic. She nodded knowingly.

"I still can't believe what happened. You know, Bill used to be one of my mom's clients and she said nothing but nice things about him. Kristine said as much, too, when we were talking at lunch today."

Cassandra's eyes widened. Not enough to be terribly noticeable, but when she looked at Jones he understood the meaning of what she was trying to convey.

They didn't have to force a segue to talking about Vera. Jasmine had just done it naturally seconds into their conversation.

"I truly hate that the kids had to go through that, but I'm

sure glad this one here was able to come in and save us before things got any worse." Cassandra did an almost talk-
show-host type of hand sweep toward him. "I don't know if
you two have met, but this is Bonnie's dad, Jones Murphy."

Jasmine had all the markings of a nice, pleasant woman
who was schooled in the ways of Southern politeness. She
was going through the motions of someone about to ac-
commodate a stranger—her smile stretched, her hand
started to rise—but then, like Jimmy had flipped at the
interrogation table, she changed the instant she registered
his name.

Her smile was gone when Jasmine met Jones's eyes.

"You mean, *Sheriff* Jones Murphy."

Cassandra must have caught on to the change.

And she didn't like it.

"Now, Jasmine, I need you to take that tone and flush
it," she said sharply. "Flush it right on down. There's no
need for it here."

Jasmine was as surprised as Jones at the admonishment.
Jones readied himself for a prickly response, but Cassandra had been right. Jasmine wasn't going to fuss at her.

"Mama already told me this one here was bothering her
today," she told Cassandra with a notably more respectful tone. Jasmine kept eye contact with Jones, however.
"I'm not going to help him drag her back into the black
hole that is this town's awful past. Just because some of us
won't move on, doesn't mean all of us have to be stuck.".

Her eyes narrowed.

She'd meant that comment specifically for him.

Too bad he'd heard worse.

"I'm just trying to figure out some things that need figuring out," he defended. "That's all. I'm not trying to drag
anyone into any kind of black hole."

Jasmine crossed her arms over her baby. The movement didn't wake him, but it did show Jones that he wasn't going to get anywhere with her. She was physically closing him off without saying the words.

"If the FBI and a slew of other law enforcement didn't figure it out, I'm not betting on your horse there, *Sheriff.*"

Frustration came up like bad heartburn. Jones understood the distrust in Kelby Creek law just as much as he loathed it. He couldn't do his job if he couldn't even get people to answer one question without pushback.

He was about to say as much when a soft hand took his.

Just like that the frustration ebbed.

Jones looked down at Cassandra's smile. Out of focus beneath it was her pregnant belly.

"Hey, Jones? I see Keith's mama over there. Maybe it would be a good time to go see how she's doing, too." Cassandra squeezed his hand. "I'll stay here and keep Jasmine and this adorable kiddo company in the meantime."

Jones lost his words.

For a lot of reasons.

He didn't want her to be alone with Jasmine because he knew, deep down, that she'd get the woman to talk. It's what he wanted, what he was trying for, but involving Cassandra? He didn't like that.

But then he felt the warmth of her hand. *Really* felt it.

Jones was amazed that it calmed him without any effort.

He was also amazed that he stepped back and took her subtle directive.

He nodded to both women.

"I think that's a mighty fine idea."

Cassandra let go of him.

Jones flexed his hand.

It felt as wrong as walking away from her.

CASSANDRA WATCHED HIM until it was clear that Lila was more welcoming than Jasmine had been to the man. She also gave some time to the woman at her side, so when Jasmine spoke again, there was a calmer tenor to her voice.

"I didn't realize you were friendly with the sheriff," she said. "I actually didn't realize the sheriff was friendly with anyone anymore."

Cassandra was only a little bit uncomfortable. The sheriff had been plenty friendly with her at every turn, but it wasn't her place to correct her.

"He's a good man," Cassandra said. "And he means what he says. He's just trying to help."

Jasmine huffed.

Baby Oliver moved at the sound but didn't wake.

"Everyone always says that, you know? 'He's a good man.' Like that's some kind of magic phrase that makes strangers trustworthy all of a sudden. 'He's a good man.' We thought Bill was a good man. We thought a lot of people were good men and women before him. I'm sure someone even told you the same thing about the sheriff. 'He's a good man, Cassandra West.' Now look at you, coming to my child's T-ball game with some attempt to what? Get me to convince my mother to talk to him about something she doesn't want to talk about? I know you're not a local, but those of us who are don't look at the badge the same way you do. 'He's a good man' just isn't going to cut it."

Cassandra hadn't expected the amount of passion that Jasmine had forced out of every word. But maybe she should have. Jones had the same intensity to his words when he spoke of Annie McHale.

Cassandra was also sure of something else.

There was something Jasmine wasn't saying that she could have been.

"Do you know why I teach kindergarten?"

The words came out before Cassandra realized where she wanted to go with them.

How could she expect Jasmine to ever possibly open up if she didn't?

"My mom left my family when I was six," Cassandra continued, not that Jasmine had tried to answer. "I used to think one of the worst things she could have done was leave without saying goodbye. That waking up one day and her just not being there was a pain that my little mind couldn't handle. But, then I got older."

Cassandra smiled. She felt it and she knew exactly what it looked like. Quiet, barely there. Sad but with some peace to it. Sorry that she was sharing something painful, even if it didn't necessarily hurt the person she was sharing it with.

"See, it took me a while to realize that the worst thing my mother ever did for me was announce that she was leaving before she did," she continued. "I was six and *that* announcement became a core memory very quickly. It was like she was reading a grocery list that she'd already read several times. There were a lot of reasons she was going, but there was only one that really stuck with me."

It was like it was yesterday, hearing her mother speak in the living room next to the front door. Her father, so shocked he was quiet as he stood next to her.

"She said I was too much to handle," Cassandra explained simply. "Said she wasn't built for small children. That I would be better without her even trying. That way, I didn't feel her failure later."

"That's cruel." Jasmine's voice was quiet, but she was correct.

Cassandra agreed with a nod.

"It also followed me, in every choice I ever made. I was terrified of biting off more than I could chew and I was just so sure that having children was too much to chew. I mean, if it was for her, it had to be for me."

Jasmine not so subtly looked at Cassandra's pregnant belly.

"But then, that part of me that was resentful and angry at her for years started to show up. I still didn't want children, but then I started to wonder if I could teach them instead. And not just kids, but the same age my mother couldn't handle. It was a dare to myself, and a way to prove that I could do what she couldn't. So I became a kindergarten teacher and, well, it changed everything. Now, look at me—I'm pregnant and I'm not watching how much I chew."

Cassandra was surprised at herself. She'd only ever told that story to one other person and he had died in a car accident before she even had the chance to tell him that she was considering having children with him.

"That's a nice story," Jasmine said, also clearly taken aback by the share. "But why are you telling me this now?"

Cassandra pointed to Jones.

"Because seven months ago, I listened to that man anguish over whether or not he should run for sheriff. No part of him wanted to come back to Kelby Creek, but when his father got hurt he did. He left a life he never thought he'd leave behind and came back to the one place in all the world he didn't want to come back to. He sacrificed because he was asked to, because he said he was needed, because a good great part of that man wanted to undo years of anger, resentment and pain. Because he *is* a good man, Jasmine, even if the phrase is overused. He came back to help. But he can't do it alone."

That was as good as she was going to be able to give in the way of trying to convince Jasmine to talk. A vulnerable story and the truth about the man behind the badge.

Sure, she didn't know him that well objectively, but, as sappy as it sounded, Cassandra really felt like she *knew* him.

That she had for a while.

She placed her hand on her belly and thought about their son.

Jasmine was quiet. The game started after the sound of the whistle being blown. Parents and spectators cheered. Cassandra suddenly felt tired. Jones was still talking to Lila, but she couldn't read either one's body language.

Baby Oliver made a soft coo in his sleep.

It served as a way to break the silence.

"I'm only going to say this once and after that you, the sheriff and anyone with a badge will leave me and my family alone about this. Understood?"

Cassandra nodded. She was relieved that her speech had resonated.

"Your goodhearted sheriff there was asking about the morning before Annie went missing, about my mother's original statement. And about some gardener who had given one, too." Jasmine shook her head. "The gardener was never scheduled the same day as my mother. If he was there, he wasn't on schedule."

"He lied, then."

"He wasn't the only one." Jasmine chewed on her lip, and she seemed to really consider her next words carefully. "I thought I'd take this to the grave. Mom would have, too, but her memory…well, it isn't what it used to be." Jasmine did a quick look around them. Cassandra leaned in. "Annie didn't leave the Deacon house alone that morning. Someone was with her."

Jasmine's entire demeanor changed. Like she was closing in on herself. Like she was lost.

Cassandra had to egg her on.

"Who?"

Jasmine's answer was so quiet, Cassandra barely heard her.

"Me." She turned to look Cassandra right in the eye. "And we didn't go to her house when we left."

Her words came out in a rush after that. She told Cassandra something she herself claimed she had never told another soul other than her mother. Cassandra made sure to burn every sentence into her memory. She wanted her recap to be perfect for Jones, because she knew there was no way Jasmine was ever going to repeat herself again.

When Jasmine was finished, Cassandra thanked her from the bottom of her heart. Yet, the woman looked far from happy.

"My mother was protecting me when she chose to keep all of that a secret and I've kept that secret, just like you will about my involvement, to protect my family," she said. "I know why I did what I did and I stand by it. But I can't claim to know why everyone does what they do. Neither can you, great teacher or not. So let me be maybe the first person to tell you about that man." She nodded toward Jones and Lila. "He might've come back for his father, but he didn't take the mantle of sheriff to do good in Kelby Creek."

Jasmine's voice hardened. They were past whatever amicable connection they'd had. There was nothing but warning in what she said next.

"Believe you me, Jones Murphy only came back to town for revenge."

Chapter Eleven

Jones glanced over his shoulder. Cassandra and Jasmine seemed to be okay. They were talking and Cassandra didn't look to be upset. Not that he knew what exactly it was that she did when something had her going. Well, other than at the department, when he refused to go rest. She'd gone from polite to pulsing pretty fast. Then she'd just gone all together.

Now, though, she looked to be okay. Open and a small smile across her lips.

Jones wanted to keep his gaze on her for a little longer, but Lila Shaw had finally decided to drop the heys, hellos and how-do-you-dos and address his presence head on.

"Keith told that teacher of his about Bill," she said outright. "Didn't he?"

Jones wasn't going to betray the little man's involvement, but he was going to stick to the whole admitting-it thing.

"It's a small town, Lila, you know how news travels," he said, sidestepping. "And how when you don't want it moving, it only travels all the faster."

Lila dropped her chin a little, defeated. Or, really, it looked more like she was tired.

"Having a relationship with someone isn't a crime," she said.

"No, but lying to law enforcement is."

She sighed. Everyone had been sighing a lot lately it seemed. Everyone was tired. Everyone wanted things like this in Kelby Creek to end. Everyone wanted some kind of peace they weren't getting.

But Lila had lied about an attack against children and a pregnant woman, and if she didn't tell him the truth now, he definitely was going to be the opposite of her peace.

Jones was about to start in, thinking she'd already caved, but Lila surprised him. She spoke bluntly.

"I started seeing Bill after running into him at the bar one night. He was nice and funny and, I don't know, it worked. That was back in February. Joel was gone on his trucking route for weeks at a time then. I wasn't a fan of that, but, well, communication has never been our strong suit, so instead I guess I turned to Bill." She paused, looking lost for a moment. Jones wasn't going to press just yet. Not if she was willing to keep right on talking.

Lila ran a hand through her hair. Her words were drenched in regret.

"It was a casual thing at first, me and Bill, but a few weeks ago he started talking about being with me. Full time, no hiding. Said we could leave town together and start over, happy." She snorted. "I told him the truth that happy doesn't fit everyone, and plus, I couldn't leave Keith. Not when he's in the middle of looking for a forever family. It's not his fault that I'm broken, you know?"

Jones's ears had already perked up.

"When did you tell Bill that you wouldn't leave without Keith?"

That's where the regret was.

She'd unknowingly given Bill an obstacle to his happiness.

Now, though, Jones could tell she realized it.

"Last week."

They let that sit for a second.

"I didn't know what he was planning—I guess I still don't—but I never should have used Keith as an excuse. It wasn't fair to the boy…and it wasn't fair to your kid, who had to go through that, too. I'm sorry, Sheriff. I really am."

"You aren't Bill, Lila. I'm not going to blame you for what he decided to do or try to do. You should have told me, though. Would have saved us some head scratching."

She nodded.

Someone on the field hit the ball and sent it flying. Parents and visitors alike stood tall, whooping and hollering.

Jones didn't need more from Lila, but he didn't want to leave her yet, either. He looked back over his shoulder again. Cassandra was still talking to Jasmine. She was rubbing her belly.

Jones felt a whole lot at the sight.

He cleared his throat and tried to put some of that feeling to good.

"You know, Lila, broken people can be happy again. It might not be the way we thought it would happen, but maybe that's what makes it work. We don't see it coming so we can't worry about it, just enjoy it when it happens."

Lila blew out another breath. This time it wobbled.

Jones softened even more.

"I'm sure you and Joel can work this out. Find a way to maybe start again."

The woman was crying now. Not hard, but he saw a tear streak down her cheek. It alarmed him.

However, not as much as when she turned to face him full on.

Lila Shaw was angry.

"Joel and I can't start again," she growled. "We never started because *he* wasn't who I was supposed to be with."

Jones liked to think he did a fairly good job of keeping up with the details, but that one had him pause.

"I don't understand," he admitted.

Lila laughed. It was harsh and pointed.

"Of all of the people to forget about them, I didn't think it would be you."

Lila… Breckinridge.

Jones remembered her maiden name a split second before he made the connection he should have already made.

"Max," he said.

Jones hadn't forgotten about Max, Detective Juliet's brother. A young man who'd left town after The Flood only to die in a car crash a few months later.

What he *hadn't* connected together was Max's girlfriend at the time was one Lila Breckinridge. Now Lila Shaw.

"Max," Lila repeated, but with a world more of a feeling. "The love of my life, the man I wanted to spend forever with. Did you know that he asked me to leave town with him, too? He did. He said he'd pack me up himself if I wanted." Lila's shoulders drooped. More tears followed down her cheeks. A woman near them turned around to look, but was quick to avert her gaze.

Lila continued, uncaring of a potential audience.

"But, what did I say? Not yet. Not yet because my mother was so *heartbroken* about what happened in this damn town that she quit her job at the hospital in protest. That she conveniently forgot about bills and health insurance and future employers all over a principled stand against the big, bad corruption. And do you know what that got her in the end, Sheriff? Nothing. Nothing but debt and a daughter who had to stay around to try and get the finances fixed before she could go be with the man she loved and *start a new life*. And what did that get me? A funeral, a loveless marriage and absolute rage at the fact that I'm still stuck in this awful town."

She was all-out crying now.

The woman who had turned earlier was now clearly listening. Jones tried to readjust his stance to give Lila more privacy.

Which didn't matter much when the woman took a deep breath. Followed by another one. The crying lessened, and her words were clear.

Though, they would have hurt regardless, if they were in between sobs or not.

Lila met his eye.

"Why couldn't you see they were bad?"

Silence.

It flooded between them.

Lila didn't have to explain her question. She didn't have to say anything anymore.

Jones knew what she meant.

He'd asked himself the same thing.

Why hadn't he known the sheriff was an evil man? Why hadn't he picked up on the backroom dealings? The cover-ups? The cold cases growing faster than they ever should have? The plot to ransom Annie McHale?

Why hadn't he seen the bad?

If he had, their world would have been much different.

He could have protected everyone.

Annie. Max.

Helen.

But he hadn't.

Jones wrapped his arm around Lila's shoulders.

He said the only thing he could.

"I'm sorry."

He wasn't sure if she could forgive him, but Lila let him hold her steady while she went back to crying.

They stood there for a few minutes like that.

This time around Jones didn't turn around and look for Cassandra.

He looked ahead instead, but all he saw was the past.

THE CAR RIDE out of the Woodland Complex was, the best Cassandra could describe it, strained.

Jones had slid into the driver's seat with a quietness that had been loud in its own way. He'd sat straighter, yet seemed to be dragging downward.

Exhausted wasn't the right word.

Cassandra wondered if the same could be said about her.

After her mission was a success, Jasmine had continued to talk about the past until Jones had ended his conversation with Lila.

It hadn't been about Kelby Creek.

It *had* been about Jones Murphy.

And his late wife, Helen.

Cassandra had never asked about Bonnie's mother, about his romantic life in general. There had never been the place or the right time. He hadn't asked her, either. It wasn't like they'd been living distraction-free, after all. The last two days' problems could have filled two years' worth of stress, as far as Cassandra was concerned.

Still, she'd known logically that the sheriff might have been a widower, just as he might have been divorced.

Cassandra had never once thought that his wife had been killed.

Caught in the cross fire at the ambush during Annie McHale's ransom exchange.

Cassandra could have cried on the spot for how awful her heart hurt for the man. No wonder he'd left Kelby Creek to start a new life with Bonnie.

How had he had the strength to come back?

And not only come back, but also reinvestigate the case that had led to his wife's death?

"Sometimes singing praise for finding justice is just noise to hide the fact that you're really looking for revenge," Jasmine had said before Cassandra had said goodbye. "Don't get caught in the cross fire, too."

Cassandra hadn't liked the phrasing, and she also didn't like how the warning had made her feel. She tried to push away those thoughts as she and Jones shared what they had learned.

"Jasmine and Annie had become friends after Vera took Jasmine to work with her a few times while Annie was visiting," she explained after recapping the two lies told in the original investigation. "They spent the night at the Deacon house, but the next morning they were woken up by Vera instead of her watching Annie walk to her house. She wanted to make sure they didn't miss their study slot at the library."

Jones, who in silhouette still seemed impossibly big behind the car's wheel, cocked his head to the side in question.

"Their study slot?"

"It's for one of the two rooms in the back of Redman Library, you know, the public one near downtown. You can reserve them for studying or meetings or just to read without any interruptions."

"And Annie and Jasmine signed up to study that morning?"

His eyes stayed ahead on the road so Cassandra made sure to say no instead of just shaking her head.

"No. Jasmine said that Annie had been going once a week to the library to read this one book series she'd become obsessed with, but knew her parents would flip out if they found out she'd checked them out. That morning Jasmine said Annie reserved the room as soon as it opened at eight, which was a little weird since she typically did it in the afternoons. Jasmine didn't think anything of it, though, but admitted books weren't her thing and Jasmine left her there to go to her boyfriend's place, where she went back to sleep for a few hours. She didn't have any plans to meet Annie later. They only really hung out after bumping into each other or at the library when Jasmine had the time."

Jones shook his head and growled.

"According to her parents, Annie was in her room from seven twenty in the morning until nine ten in the morning. Not the library."

Cassandra shrugged.

"Maybe she lied to them and they didn't know? According to Jasmine, she wasn't even sure they knew she was friends with Annie. No one came to question her after Annie went missing. Her mother was only questioned because she was on schedule with the Deacons. Oh, and speaking of the schedule, according to it the gardener shouldn't have been there. Jasmine couldn't explain that, said her mother couldn't, either."

Jones was back to shaking his head.

"Why didn't any of this come up the first time around?"

It was a rhetorical question. The corruption in the department was the answer.

Cassandra tried to answer it, anyway.

"Vera thought she was protecting herself and her daughter by taking them out of the picture. It sounds like she only dropped the facade on the phone with you because she's having issues with her memory due to old age. Or else I'm pretty sure all of that would still be locked up tight based on how much Jasmine didn't want to talk about it now."

"But she did," Jones pointed out. "She told you."

Cassandra waved off his comment.

"Honestly, I think she needed to get it off of her chest."

Cassandra expected some follow-up questions.

She didn't get any.

"Lila confirmed she had an affair with Bill," he said after a moment. "We talked a little more and I think Bill was trying to take Keith so they could all leave town together. At least, that's my hope. I'll get Foster to follow up with Bill, but my guess is that, for once, a coincidence in Kelby Creek was actually a coincidence. I don't think Bill at the school was connected to my look into Annie's case."

"Do you think Jimmy used Bill's name to try and throw you off?"

Jones nodded.

"I think he did it to make me waste some time. I just don't know why."

The drive to the Woodland Complex had felt like a good stretch of time. The drive back to Cassandra's house felt like a blink.

Suddenly she was staring at her front door, standing on the welcome mat and the sheriff towering behind her. She unlocked the door and stepped inside with a little heat in her cheeks.

They hadn't had a lot of time to be alone together, at least not with a mystery to solve pressing down on them.

Now?

Now it could be the two of them, finally talking.

Cassandra dropped her keys in her catchall and waited for the door to shut behind them.

It didn't.

She turned to find Jones still on the welcome mat.

He looked more exhausted than before.

Cassandra knew then that he wasn't going to come inside.

"We've been going a mile a minute and I know part

of that is on me and me alone," he began the second she found his dark eyes on her. "I want to talk, I really want to talk, about everything. About you, about me and about our son, but right now I need to go back to the department and I can't take you there with me."

Jones took a startlingly quick step forward. Before she could take him all in, he was a breath away. He bent down enough that his words were closer and not lost in their height difference.

"But I want to tell you right now that, in no uncertain terms, I want to be a part of this child's life. I want to and will be a father to him, and do whatever I can and whatever you want me to, to see that happen. You don't have to worry about that or question me ever about that. I will love him like I love Bonnie. With everything I have."

Cassandra might have melted at that admission.

She might have cried or kissed him, whichever struck her fancy first.

Yet, as much as she heard the sincerity in his words, she also heard the *but* coming next.

"But, as much as I may want to say otherwise, I can't be with you. Not like we were before we both came back to town. I don't even know if that's something you'd want, but I wanted to go ahead and let you know that it's something that I can't have. I'm sorry."

He took a step back, left no room for her to respond and was back out on the porch in another blink.

"Thank you for tonight, Cassandra. I really mean it."

Jones gave her a small smile, a quick nod and then was gone.

Cassandra watched his taillights disappear down the street, Jasmine's words of warning blaring in her mind.

Chapter Twelve

He saw her there.

In the crowd.

She was wearing a thick jacket and her hair was shorter. A different color, too. But he knew it was her.

What he didn't know was why she was there.

Why she was watching the sheriff so closely.

He half expected her to go to the man, to try and warn him. Or scare him away. Given her moods, she could go either way.

But she didn't approach the sheriff. She just watched him and then watched him and the teacher as they walked back to their car.

It wasn't until they were off and gone that she went, too.

She was casual but she was careful.

She'd have to be by now.

He blew out a breath after her car was a pair of taillights in the distance. He couldn't see his breath in the air, but the forecast called for much colder weather in the coming days. He liked fall in Kelby Creek. The storms were much less frequent.

"It's done."

Dark hair and a sweet voice took up the space to his left. Jasmine Lohan wasn't smiling. The man on his right stayed quiet. They were all standing at the edge of the field, the sound of children yelling and playing ever present.

"I told them the truth," she added. There was bite to her words. She didn't like helping him.

She didn't have a choice, though.

Her mother's jumbling thoughts had become a problem. If she hadn't helped him, well, then there would be another victim of Kelby Creek's past.

And she didn't want that.

Hell, neither did he.

But that didn't mean he wouldn't continue to be proactive.

"That's good," he said. "Now your part is done."

Jasmine might not have been happy to have been tangled together with him, but she'd stopped herself when given the chance to leave. He could tell she was looking out at the field. Looking at her young son, while wearing her second.

He'd never thought Jasmine the type to be a mother. She'd never liked commitment. She'd proclaimed that loudly and often. Then again, she hadn't married her partner. So maybe she'd compromised with herself.

One commitment instead of another.

"I only came to you so the sheriff could find out about Annie's *other* life in a more organic way," he reminded her. "You told the truth, which is what I wanted. Everything else—" he found her son on the field, running between two bases "—is fine now."

Jasmine was noticeably relieved.

But she still stuck to her spot.

"How did you know they'd come here tonight?"

"When no one talks at the department, it's because they're out gossiping." He shrugged. "I knew once he talked to your mother, you'd be next in line. Since he doesn't want everything he's doing out in the public, coming here to see you was a possibility I thought might pan out. If it hadn't, well, there were other ways to get the information to him. Though, I'm glad we didn't have to resort to them."

That did it.

Jasmine was done with him.

She nodded and walked away. Jasmine was a loyal friend but a more loyal daughter. However, he suspected being a mother trumped those two for the woman.

Using her sons would have done the trick if needed.

The man at his side made a noise.

He was grumpy.

He always was.

"You guessed the sheriff might show up," he said, voice low and the epitome of being annoyed. "But you had no idea he'd bring the teacher."

It wasn't a question.

"No, I had no idea he'd bring the teacher," he admitted. "I also had no idea he'd rely on her to question someone about Annie."

He stretched tall and wide.

He was bored now.

"Let's keep an eye on them, see what they do next."

"They're going to go to the library. That's what they'll do next if Jasmine told them right."

He didn't like the man's know-it-all tone.

He rolled his eyes.

"They can go to that library every day for a year and it won't do them any good if they can't find out what Annie was up to."

"What if they don't? Or, what if they do?" The other man followed him as he walked around the crowd and headed toward their car. "I know you're all 'big picture' with plans, but the rest of us would feel a lot better if you at least gave us an idea of what to expect next."

He let another breath out, becoming more bored by the second.

"If they don't then we'll have to find a way to get them where we want them," he said simply. "If they do, well, that's when I make a phone call."

He had to turn to see the other man's eyes widen in realization.

"This is too complicated," he objected. "It's too much. Can't we just leave? Can't we disappear and just live out the rest of our days happy, healthy and not behind bars or dead?"

He shook his head.

He wasn't leaving.

Not now, not ever.

"This is my town." He had his car door open. He paused before settling inside. "No one is making me leave. Not the sheriff, not his teacher friend, not you and certainly not *her*."

The man went quiet.

Which was good because there wasn't a thing he could say to make him change his mind.

Kelby Creek was his.

And he was about to make sure everyone within its town limits knew that.

A WEEK WENT BY.

One full week of no word from Jones, no mention in the news of his attacker being caught or even identified and not even a whisper of Annie McHale's second investigation.

It was driving Cassandra batty.

Not to mention, playing havoc on her emotions.

One day she cried, a lot. Another day she was angry

and fussed at almost every inanimate object in her house, including an Amazon package from her father. It had a baby-naming book inside along with a blanket covered in sailboats.

She said some curses at it after wondering if Jones had a boy name he was fond of.

That anger came with some self-reflection, but only a day later.

It was *great* that Jones wanted to be in his son's life.

It was *fine* that Jones didn't want to be anything other than a co-parent with her.

She was *good* with both of these things and hadn't expected to rekindle any kind of relationship with him after their surprise reunion.

Sure, had she fantasized about being wrapped in his arms or listening to his deep monotone as he talked to her in the last seven months?

Absolutely.

Did that mean that she wanted to be his—his, what?—girlfriend?

His wife?

Cassandra decided to bury any and all questions about her feelings deep down until a later date.

She spent the next few days instead focusing all of her energy on Annie McHale.

And the Redman Library.

It was on Saturday morning Cassandra put on her maternity jeans and her least conspicuous blouse, and went to the library by herself. She wasn't sure if Jones had done the same already, but it was such an odd clue that she couldn't stand wondering about it any longer.

Redman Library was one of the few public spaces in Kelby Creek that hadn't received some kind of funding, donation or gift from the McHale family's fortune through the years. That made Annie's dedication to its study rooms all the more interesting. Doubling that interest was the fact that Annie had already graduated high school and hadn't yet enrolled in college. If she had been going to a study room merely to read, the material wasn't for school.

Why go to a public space for privacy when you're the wealthiest heir in Kelby Creek, Cassandra thought as she mounted the four steps up to the front doors. It wasn't the first time she'd wondered. Even if the material she was reading was scandalous, at least scandalous enough to want to keep it from her parents, then surely she could find somewhere else to read it?

"Hi there!"

A chirp of greeting came from a young man behind the front desk. Cassandra recognized him. He'd substituted at the school before, usually in music class.

Cassandra sidled up to the desk, polite smile coming alive.

The main reading room opened up to their right. Tables and chairs were placed at random throughout the space, making way for themed book stands and endcaps. Cassandra hadn't been there in a long while but remembered the layout well enough. The children's room was located in the back left corner. The study rooms were located along the back wall. Neither door could be seen from the main room unless you walked through the nonfiction stacks toward the back.

If Annie had wanted privacy to read whatever she was reading, reserving one of the rooms was definitely the ticket.

"Hey, there, Lloyd," she said. "I didn't realize you were working at Redman."

Lloyd was wonderful with children but terrible at confrontation. Cassandra had once seen him bullied by a fourth grader so she could see why he'd be more comfortable out of the classroom.

He was also too young to have been at Redman during Annie's original visits.

Lloyd started to laugh but then caught himself. He looked over at two men sitting at the computer bay near the middle of the room. They didn't appear to be offended by his burst of noise.

"Lady, I've been here for over a year now." He leaned over the counter, all dramatic. "And apparently you've missed my career news and I've missed your expecting news?"

Cassandra felt her cheeks heat.

It was amazing how, even in such a small town, she was still managing to run in to people who were so shocked to find her pregnant.

"I guess we both did." Cassandra rubbed a hand over her stomach. "Six and a half months along, baby boy, cravings include Doritos, but only the Cool Ranch flavor."

Lloyd laughed in good humor.

"So, basically, Baby Boy has good taste."

Cassandra shared in the mirth.

"I suppose so."

Lloyd settled back into his chair.

"Does this mean you got married, too, and I wasn't invited?" He looked to her hand. No ring. His smile fell a little. "Or, am I being too nosy into something that has nothing to do with my body or life?"

If Lloyd had been someone else, say Coach Rich, who had asked almost every time he saw her who the father was despite her open desire to keep that to herself for the time being, Cassandra might have gone the defensive route. But she liked Lloyd. He was one of the few people she'd known who truly enjoyed helping children.

Cassandra also was, admittedly, more in her emotions than normal lately.

Either way she responded without worrying about spending the next few minutes dodging more and more questions.

"His father is a wonderful man but we're just friends," she said. "Baby Boy was a bit of a surprise."

Cassandra made sure to show that she wasn't at all put out by the situation. Lloyd picked up on her mood.

"Well, can I just say you're absolutely glowing," he said. "And I'm not just saying that because that's what most people say in lieu of an actual compliment."

Cassandra laughed.

"Thank you, I'll take it."

Lloyd seemed pleased with himself. He opened the door to the real reason she was there.

"So what can I help you with this fine Saturday morning?"

Cassandra had already rehearsed this part in the car. She tried to keep her request casual.

"I'm actually thinking about renting the study rooms for a few tutoring sessions I'll be doing next year after school. I wanted to go ahead and get the logistics down before baby here comes and I get lost in bottles and diapers on top of lesson plans and my planner. Do you think I could check them out now? Are they in use?"

It wasn't a total lie but it wasn't the total truth. Cassandra was often asked if she was open for extra tutoring during the school year, but she usually took those at the coffee shop or at school, given the time of need. She also had already decided to leave tutoring off her docket for the current school year since she had to believe she'd still be getting used to the balance of teaching kids and finally having one live with her.

Lloyd was unsuspecting of her half-truth. It made her feel even more guilty when he nodded profusely.

"You know those rooms have been pretty popular this week. I had to chase a couple of teens making out away from one, and then a few other people wanted to see if we were like Hogwarts or something and had the forbidden books hidden in them. Then there was the actual sheriff who came in on Tuesday, asking about using one of the rooms for a party for his kid." He laughed. "I had to remind every single person that this is a *library* and all the study rooms are for studying, hence the name."

He shook his head. She made sure to control her expression.

So Jones had already been there to check out the rooms. He'd also apparently done the same as her and kept his real curiosity out of the request.

Had he found something there?

Was it pointless for her to go look now?

Cassandra didn't know what her eyes could do that Jones's couldn't, but she decided she had to try or it would drive her anxiousness through the proverbial roof.

"Before I take a look, how do you reserve the space, anyway? Do I need to fill out a form or something?" she asked.

"I wish," Lloyd said with a sigh. "We're not that organized. We just enter the request in a log. Paper records. Can you imagine? I'm trying to convince them to digitalize that system. There are tons of scheduling apps for free, you know? We'll get there."

Paper records. That meant there was a written log somewhere of who signed out the study rooms, and Cassandra thought she might know who had the older ones.

She let Lloyd give her the short directions to the first study room and thanked him twice.

When she made her way to the door, passing by four stacks of old and severely used books, Cassandra couldn't shake a new, creeping feeling.

Despite no one being around, she felt the rising sensation that someone was watching her.

But why would anyone do that?

It wasn't like she knew anything important. It wasn't like *she* was important.

She shook her head at the silly thought and opened the first study-room door.

Had she known just how wrong she was, she would have never gone into that room.

But she had no idea what was going to happen.

So she shut the door behind her and tried her best to think like Annie McHale.

Chapter Thirteen

Jones grunted.

He readjusted, trying to get comfortable.

He grunted again.

He couldn't move from his seat and that was starting to really grate against his nerves.

"Watch it," he told his captor.

She did nothing with the warning. The cold hit his foot like a slap to the face.

"Bonnie," Jones yelled out. "I told you that you could paint my toenails only if you didn't touch my toes with those freezing little-kid hands of yours."

Bonnie, sitting beneath his desk, let out a devious cackle.

"It's not my fault your feet are so big! It's hard *not* to touch them."

Jones rolled his eyes as his father let out a burst of laughter from the hallway.

"She's got a point there," he said, appearing in the doorway. "And may I just say that when she did my nails? No issues whatsoever with the size of my feet."

Jones couldn't see Bonnie, but he felt her nod.

"Yep, yep!"

Jones lifted his eyes from the notes on his desk. They were in his father's office, which was filled with spillover from the hardware store he owned. Ever since Jones had convinced his father to become partners with his long-time employee, some of his dad's free time had become dedicated to trying to figure out which hobbies he truly liked. That pursuit somehow had turned into a lot of random things finding their way into both the hardware store and their home.

Plus a storage room, which Jones visited more than he liked.

Right now the three of them were in close proximity to a desk covered in sheriff-department files, a cabinet filled with the miniature planes, most half-painted, and a bookcase that held more how-to manuals for various hobbies than probably most stores had in stock.

Then there was what Bonnie added to the mix, which, at the moment, included a manicure-and-pedicure set she was using on Jones's feet.

"Better my big feet than that thing you call a nose," he told his father with a grin. "We're almost at funding for the K-9 unit at the department. Maybe you should apply?"

It was a joke and it landed.

His father laughed.

"Remind me in a few years when you realize your nose finally matches mine."

Jones waved his father to the lone seat across from them. The chair was upholstered in a floral print that was dark and busy. It had been his mother's favorite and one of the few things that had followed him through every move he'd made after she passed away when he was twenty-five.

His father settled against its fabric with a brief smile. Then he looked at his son with concern.

"You told me you were taking the weekend off, but it looks like you just took the work home for the weekend."

Jones leaned back in his chair, officially giving up for the moment.

"I can't help it because it's here," he said, jabbing his finger down on top of one of the loose pieces of paper that had his notes on it. "The answer, the next lead, *something* is here. I know it—I can feel it. I just can't see it. Not yet, at least."

"And you still haven't told anyone at the department what you found out about Annie."

Jones made a half-and-half gesture with his hand.

"Carlos knows I found something new but is giving me some space to pursue it solo. He's taken charge of trying to make sense of Jimmy and all of that that came with him."

His father shook his head.

"I can't imagine why Jimmy said and did what he said and did to you. Do you think he knew you were looking into Annie?"

Carlos had already asked a similar question.

Jones could only shrug.

"I'm not sure how he would've known, but I also don't know why else Jimmy would do that."

His father glanced under the desk at Bonnie. They could only talk about it so much in front of her. Jones didn't want to worry her with their adult problems, after all. His father included.

"Maybe you could use a break then, once your pedicure is finished, of course," he added. "Maybe even invite your new friend over for some lunch?"

Jones knew his father was talking about Cassandra. He also had been told in no uncertain terms that he would love to be the grandfather of their son. Just as he'd shown immediate distaste that Jones wasn't sure what any of their futures looked like yet.

This woman was, after all, someone he'd been thinking about since they'd met seven months ago.

Now that she was within the town limits?

Surely that was the end of that problem, right?

It'd been more than a week since Jones had seen Cassandra and even though he'd spoken his mind to her about their unborn son, he didn't at all feel settled. He wasn't avoiding her, but he also wasn't rushing to try and be at her side.

He just kept thinking about Annie McHale, Lila Shaw and Helen.

Their lives had been taken in one way or another and he'd hadn't done a thing about it.

Not yet, at least.

Lila's tears had been a startling reminder that he could want the world, but wanting wasn't the same as deserving.

Then there was the simple fact that he couldn't protect everyone.

Not when his guard was down.

Not when he was vulnerable.

Not when he was thinking about a future that he'd never once planned on having.

"You talk about someone needing a break? I'd point you right at Cassandra." Jones forced a grin and pushed back in his chair. Bonnie laughed and swatted at his leg.

"Hey! I have the pinky toe to go!"

Jones pointed down at his daughter.

"Cassandra has to deal with little terrors like this every day?" He was all dramatic with his scoff. "I can barely function with this little terror."

Bonnie, having heard the beginning war cry of a play session, scrambled out from under the desk.

"Terror," she yelled. "Terror!"

Jones was up in a flash. He ran around Bonnie until he

was out in the hallway. He heard her laugh in delight. She was a girl made for running around.

She was also fast.

They streaked across the one-story house before spilling out into the backyard. Jones might have had much longer legs than his daughter, but Bonnie was lightning-fast. Their chase turned into tag and Bonnie legitimately earned a few of her tags against him.

"When did you get so fast?" he asked after her little hands slapped against his thigh.

Bonnie's cheeks were rosy—her nose, too.

"From the playground," she exclaimed. "I practice there. Practice is how you get good at everything. So I practice and I run and now I'm *super speed*!"

He could tell she was gearing up to run around him again, but she stopped herself and looked down, deeply concerned.

For a brief moment Jones thought something was truly wrong.

But then Bonnie pointed to his foot.

"*Dad.* You smeared your polish!"

Jones laughed as they together surveyed the damage. Running barefoot from the office to outside had upset his glitter-blue toenail polish, leaving some of it on his skin.

"I guess I should've waited for it to dry," he said matter-of-factly. "Then again…"

He hunched over and stuck his hands out to make claws.

"Sometimes you just can't wait to *run fast*!"

Bonnie devolved into giggles as Jones led the charge this time, trying to tag her. He was thankful for his father's large backyard and its lack of prickly weeds, holes and random dog droppings. It made for a more peaceful playtime.

They looped the perimeter without any issues before the back door slid open.

Jones scooped up Bonnie as his latest catch. Her laughter reverberated through him. It hugged into his chest, making all of the uncertainty in life feel less than in an instant.

When he turned to see that his father wasn't watching them alone, he wondered if that warm feeling showed on his face.

"Cassandra," he stated, seeing the woman on the back porch, too. She was smiling.

She was beautiful.

"Miss West!"

Bonnie squirmed out of his hold. She ran full-tilt toward the porch. Her arms were wide open as she collided with Cassandra, who, Jones saw, turned just at the last second to keep her belly from being Bonnie smashed.

"Hey there, Miss Bonnie, how are you doing this lovely Saturday?"

Bonnie, being six, was always one of two things. Talkative and precise with what she said, or talkative and completely random.

She went for random here.

"I had popcorn at school yesterday and Miss Forehand gave us paint for our fingers so we could do some leaves. Mine were really good."

"That's wonderful," Cassandra commented. Jones made his way to their small group.

As soon as he was close enough, Bonnie pointed to his bare feet.

"I painted Dad, too. His toenails. They weren't great before but now they're really pretty. He won't let me do his fingernails because he said it might make everyone else at his work feel left out. I told him that I could come there one day and do everyone's nails, though."

Cassandra nodded and shared the humor in a glance with Jones.

"That would be something I would love to see," she said.

Bonnie was starting to build up to that chaotic energy that small children often got after playing. Jones could sense it and so could his father.

"Hey, Bonbon, I think Ms. West is here to talk to your dad, so why don't we give them some space and go ahead and make some popcorn here?"

Just like he could sense the chaotic energy, Jones could see that his daughter was conflicted between staying with the new company or eating one of her favorite snacks.

Popcorn won out.

"I can save you some" was all she managed to say to Cassandra as she bounded inside after his father. The little girl could already be heard asking if she could press the buttons on the microwave before the door shut behind them.

Cassandra was still smiling in their direction.

Jones didn't have time to comment before that smile disappeared.

"Did you figure out why Annie McHale kept visiting the study rooms at the library?" Cassandra asked, cutting straight to the point before he could say a word. "Because I think I know how to find out."

CASSANDRA ASKED IF they could continue their conversation on the front porch. She was ready to go, even before she'd stopped by.

She said as much as they backtracked to the porch.

"I'm sorry I showed up, but I was going to call, then realized that we haven't actually exchanged numbers. At least, I don't have yours." She gave him the piece of paper she'd scribbled her number on in the car. "I only know where you live because Millie mentioned your dad's house when we were talking a week or so ago. She's a fan of his flower beds."

Cassandra was vibrating with energy. It was a stark contrast to the exhaustion pregnancy that had been pressing down on her in the last trimester.

So she wanted to go with the flow until that flow stopped.

"I would have just asked for your number from the department, but I didn't want to raise any suspicion."

"Suspicion?" Jones's question had a lot of confusion in it. He'd had his brow scrunched up good since she'd said Annie's name.

"About you doing a second investigation." She dropped her voice a little low despite them being the only people outside that he could see. "I wasn't sure who all knew and if you wanted anyone else to. We end up talking a lot but don't actually answer the important questions around that talking. Like, if I need to ask someone about something that happened on Annie's last day, is it okay for me to come up with a little fib so *they* don't get suspicious?"

Cassandra had been driving herself crazy about this conundrum in the car. It was the only reason she'd come by Jones's house.

At least that's what she was telling herself.

Seeing Jones had been a shock to her system that she hadn't realized she'd needed.

Seeing him playing with his daughter while sporting toenail polish?

Every hormone in her had felt that.

She'd all but needed the walk from the backyard to the front porch to cool herself down and get back on track.

"You shouldn't be doing any investigating." Jones's voice was stern. Authoritative.

Cassandra waved him off.

"It's just me talking with an old friend and then trying to slyly work a question into the conversation. You probably know her. Megan Hamilton. Used to work at the library. Harmless as a container full of Tums. I just don't want to get into any kind of trouble for digging a little if I have to stretch the truth a little."

Jones was shaking his head but not at her concern.

"You aren't in law enforcement, Cassandra. You're not investigating anything. This doesn't concern you."

Cassandra's cheer waned.

Her excitement paused.

She knew she was drawing into herself based solely on the way he was searching her face at the change.

"You didn't see you, Jones. Unconscious behind the wheel of a sinking truck. I did. And I may not have a badge and we might not be a couple, but *you* concern me now." She placed her hand on her stomach. "So I'm going to go ask an old friend a question and if it's worth more than salt, I'm going to call you. It's probably nothing and won't amount to a thing, so don't worry yourself about it, okay? I probably shouldn't have even come by."

She turned on her heel, trying to put a lid on the tangling emotions that were starting to come up more and more frequently around the man.

"Cassandra—" he began.

She didn't turn around but yelled out loud enough so he could hear her.

"Just make sure to keep your phone on, Sheriff."

Chapter Fourteen

Regret.

Fear.

A woman with golden curls and a cot with a plaid blanket.

Cassandra blinked in confusion.

The woman sitting on the bed opposite her was kind enough to explain.

"He didn't hit you, he said, but you have some blood in your hair." Her voice was honey thick with an accent. She touched a spot on her own head. "You were also out like a light when he brought you in. I'm guessing you gave him some trouble and he fought back."

Cassandra was beyond confused, but her first instinct was to touch her stomach. The woman noticed.

"My mama once broke her leg while she was pregnant with my brother. Lost consciousness from the pain for a while. But the doctor said the baby was fine and so was she. It was probably just like you went to sleep. Baby probably doesn't even know otherwise."

Deep and pure fear ran through her, but she finally took in her surroundings.

Which didn't help matters.

"Are we in a motel?"

They were in a room with beige walls, beige carpet, a

beige door and beige curtains. The only spots of coloring were on her and the other woman, the flannel blanket and the TV to her left. It was a small flat-screen and had dust covering the screen.

"Looks like it, right? I thought the same." The woman pointed to the nearest window. "I can't tell if we're somewhere high or low. There's no window behind the drapes. That door over there's a bathroom with green tile and that door there—" she pointed to the door across and to the left of Cassandra "—is locked and, I'm thinking, has something mighty heavy against it."

Cassandra didn't know where to go from there.

"I— Why am I here? Who are you?"

"It's the shock. Denial, too, most likely. I had a hard time remembering what happened, too, when I first woke up." The woman sighed. "I know he hit me. I fought him good until it happened."

Cassandra realized she'd been propped up, two pillows behind her. Her memories were fuzzy but starting to come in.

"I was kidnapped by a man." She shook her head, clutching her stomach. "Oh, my God. I was kidnapped."

The woman put her legs over the side of her cot and her back against the wall. She slid up one leg and looped her arms around it.

Resigned—she looked resigned.

"I'm Lottie, Lottie Henderson, and we're in Kelby Creek as far as I know," she said. "He said you're Cassandra?"

Cassandra nodded. A knot was forming in her throat.

"I knew a Cassie once. Pretty name." The woman let out a breath. "So where did he get you from?"

Cassandra struggled to stand.

She let out a laugh that was close to tears.

"What an awful question," she said.

Lottie wasn't unsympathetic, but she didn't try to apologize for the bluntness. Instead she leaned her head back against the wall.

Cassandra wobbled her way to the door. The lock was on the wrong side. The doorknob didn't budge. She went to the curtains nearest her next.

Lottie was right. There was nothing but smooth wall behind it.

Cassandra's heart plummeted at the sight.

"He said you were a teacher, too," the woman prattled on. "I bet you're good at a lot of things."

"Who has us? How long have you been here?" Cassandra didn't understand why she was getting casual conversation in an absolutely terrifying surrounding.

The woman went on like she hadn't heard her. Cassandra hurried to the other door while she continued. Sure enough it was a small, green-tiled bathroom.

"I've only ever really been good at one thing. Faces. I'm real good at faces. Like, now that I've seen you, I won't forget you. My one dang gift."

Cassandra felt close to tears. She didn't know what to do. Her purse was gone, her phone with it.

She thought of Jones.

She'd called him before she'd seen the man.

He hadn't answered, but surely he'd come for her?

Surely, he'd find her?

Cassandra found Lottie's eyes. She was young and beautiful and tired. Her clothes were clean, but she had bruising along the side of her face and a scab over her lip. She had no shoes. Her toenails were painted pink. It was too cheery in contrast.

Cassandra felt her own life fade a little just looking at the woman. She sat back on the cot she'd regained consciousness on and did the only thing she could think of at the moment.

She answered her earlier question.

"New Beginnings Mental Health Facility," Cassandra said. "Well, the old building. The one across the street from the Redman Library."

Lottie snorted, shaking her head as she did so.

"I guess grabbing you wasn't some kind of mistake then."

"What do you mean?"

"My daddy used to work there, at New Beginnings—a name I've found funny since it shut down so quick, by the way—when I was in middle and high school. He did a lot of group therapy there. I used to go there, too, sometimes, since Mama had my brother by accident and I never liked hanging around the house with a toddler." She shrugged. "It wasn't a bad place. Boring since I wasn't let into any of the group meetings and half of that place was closed off to visitors for the more intense cases."

Lottie paused.

Cassandra's adrenaline spiked.

Had she heard something?

Lottie continued after a moment. Cassandra stayed on edge.

"But one day I went to exploring and met a boy in the part of New Beginnings you're not supposed to go. He was nice enough. I thought he was funny. Kept me entertained and feeling all rebellious since no one knew I was hanging around with someone who wasn't even allowed to have shoelaces." She paused again. Cassandra saw now that it was to keep herself collected. "But then one day I went in to see him and he was gone. His things were there but he wasn't. I finally asked my daddy about it and he got so mad. Said he didn't deal with that side of the place. I didn't think anything of it until the Rosewater Inn murder."

Cassandra raised an eyebrow at that. Lottie saw it.

"You're not local, are you?" she asked.

Cassandra shook her head.

"Rosewater Bar used to be the Rosewater Motel, kind of looks like this place if you ask me. Rosewater's had a bunch of owners but the current one finally got some good use out of the building. Split it into three parts. The offices on the left, the bar on the right and the old bed-and-breakfast attempt in the middle. The original owners, though, never wanted all that. They just wanted a motel to make money. Instead they were killed in the lobby one night by some passing guest. At least, that was what everyone thought before they became another cold case in Kelby Creek."

Lottie sighed.

"I didn't think much on it because I was young and self-absorbed, but then on my daddy's last week of work I went back to see if the boy was there," she continued. "He was and he had a look about him that was different. Then he asked me about the killings and I just couldn't get over how he looked when he did that. I swear, every part of me stood on end. It was like he was bragging about something he didn't do. But then, I realized he'd been missing the same time as the owners were killed."

She shook her head.

"I told my daddy about it, he told his boss and I didn't go back. Which worked out since Daddy started working at the hospital after that. But nothing happened and I got older and forgot about it. Met a man who drives me crazy and decided it was time I tried to show him how much I did love him."

Lottie had tears in her eyes now.

"There's a clearing in the Kintucket Woods that looks just about heaven on a clear night. Stars as far as you can dream 'em. I wanted to surprise him with a little camping trip, so I went on out to the hardware store in town to get a tent. That's where I saw a man and, even though he'd aged, I hadn't forgotten his face."

"The boy at New Beginnings." Cassandra wanted to be clear.

Lottie nodded.

"I guess he hadn't forgotten mine," she said. "He surprised me at the woods when I was setting up. Must've followed me. I've been here ever since."

"Who is he?" Cassandra asked. "What's his name? And *why* are we here?"

Lottie pulled up her other leg and turned her body until she was lying down across her cot. She answered but she kept her eyes up at the ceiling.

"Killian Carmichael," she said. "He's tall, slender. Has light brown hair. Pale, too. He's given me food, clean clothes and hasn't touched me since he brought me here. I think he's really smart, too. I think he has some kind of plan, but I don't know what it is. If he got you because you were poking around New Beginnings, then I'm thinking you ruffled his feathers somehow. Maybe he likes his privacy."

"I wasn't there for him." Cassandra had been there for Annie McHale. For what she'd found out at Megan Hamilton's house.

Lottie shrugged. The movement made her cot squeak.

"Whatever you did, you got in his way."

Cassandra had no idea.

She'd never heard of the name Killian Carmichael.

She didn't know what he could possibly want with her.

A pop of pressure went against the palm she had over her stomach.

Cassandra could have cried.

It was a kick.

Relief washed over her.

Just as fast as despair.

She should have listened to Jones. She should have never tried to play detective.

Now she only hoped he could follow her misguided path to save her and their child before it was too late.

JONES HAD EVERY intention of following Cassandra after she left, but like when they first met, their timing was off.

Jones had gone back inside for his rental car keys and run smack-dab into a problem. His dad had his phone out to him.

"Carlos called, then Foster, then Brutus. Followed by Carlos again."

"I've only been outside a minute," Jones said. "What has everyone calling?"

His dad didn't know but they both found out soon enough.

Carlos was nearly breathless when he answered Jones's return call. He got straight to the point.

"Jimmy and Nan just told the press that you're reinvestigating the Annie McHale kidnapping case. And, Jones, everyone is losing their minds over it."

Jones had started looking for his shoes.

"We knew this would happen eventually," he told his chief deputy. "I'm not ashamed of what I'm doing. It's no secret."

"I agree with all of that," Carlos said. "But, Sheriff, the news is running through town like wildfire and a lot of people are having some feelings about it. We might need you at the department sooner rather than later."

Jones had meant what he said—he wasn't trying to keep the investigation a secret. He *was* trying to keep it on the down-low until he knew more.

"I'm on my way," he said, finding his socks and slipping them over his glitter-covered toenails. "Don't say a word to anyone until I'm in."

After that Jones became the sheriff he didn't like. The PR sheriff. The one who talked to the press and said vague things and sidestepped any information that would hurt an ongoing investigation. He talked to the local news anchor only and said he was looking into a lot of older cases. Annie's was among them.

That was it.

That was enough.

The next two hours were a swamp mess of phone calls, drop-bys and social-media-comment wars.

It wasn't until he found the space to breathe by himself that he realized his dad's old phone had a piss-poor ringer.

He'd missed a call.

From Cassandra.

Guilt struck him like lightning.

He should have called her after the news broke.

He hoped Megan Hamilton hadn't given her too hard of a time if they'd found out together she might be looking into Annie, too.

The phone call had been left an hour before.

There was a voice mail.

"Hey, Jones, it's Cassandra. I just finished with Megan and I think Annie wasn't actually interested in the library at all." Jones could hear a car door shut. *"I think she was sneaking out across the street. I'm—I'm there now and going to give a quick peek around. It's—it's okay. Wow*

I'm out of breath. Ha, ha. It's this pregnancy stuff. I used to be in shape. Anyway, I'm here and just going to look around. It's not like anyone is going to stop me. This place has been closed a while. All right, long rambling message over. I'll call you after just so you know my super sleuthing hasn't gotten me into trouble."

The recording ended.

Jones looked at the time stamp again.

There were no new calls.

He pressed the call-back option.

It rang and rang and rang.

Cassandra didn't answer.

Jones hung up.

Then he tried again.

No Cassandra.

Jones stood. He replayed her message as he pulled his coat off the back of his office chair.

"You don't say where you are, Cassandra," he said, griping at the phone.

No, she had told him. Across the street from the library. That's what she said.

Jones took a second, but he figured it out.

New Beginnings, the mental health and rehabilitation center.

But it was closed, like she said.

Why was she there?

And why wasn't she answering her phone?

Jones had his keys and was out of the department in a flash.

He decided right then and there he wasn't letting Cassandra out of his sight from now on.

Not until they figured out what was going on in Kelby Creek.

Chapter Fifteen

New Beginnings had once been housed in an expansive building. Some parts had two stories, the back half had a still-impressive fence despite being abandoned, and even with some of the doors and windows boarded up, it was in relatively good shape.

Jones got out of his car and experienced an awful sense of déjà vu.

Cassandra's car was in the side parking lot, but she wasn't in it.

Jones tried to call her again.

No luck.

He took a second to look toward the library. A lead he'd been obsessing about meant nothing to him now.

"Do you think she went inside?"

Carlos was with him. Jones hadn't wanted to take any chances. If Cassandra had found trouble, he wasn't going to lone-wolf it if he didn't have to.

"She said she was going to poke around." Jones tapped his service weapon in its holster twice and headed for the sidewalk. "Since she's not answering her phone, I'm really hoping she *is* in there sleuthing around."

Carlos fell into step behind him, the chief deputy also on high alert.

On the car ride over, Jones had caught him up on everything Cassandra and he had found out in the last two weeks. He'd been impressed by Cassandra's go-get-'em attitude. Jones had shaken his head, angry with himself that he'd let her go out alone.

The side door was locked tight. Carlos spread out across the windows trying to see if they had a line of sight inside.

They didn't.

Jones led them to the front doors to the same setup— locked.

Carlos knocked.

There was no movement inside as far as they could tell.

The back of the building had more potential access points, but all were boarded or locked up.

"Let me call again," Jones said, feeling as tense as could be.

Where was she?

Why was her car in the lot?

Carlos walked to the back door that fed directly into the staff parking lot.

"I never understood why this place didn't sell," he said, more to himself than to Jones. "It's not like anyone is using—"

Carlos stopped talking.

Jones moved the phone down to his side.

A ringtone was going off inside.

It timed perfectly with the ringing phone in his hand.

Carlos shared a look with Jones, but he was already moving.

With a kick that had no forethought, just anxious power, Jones broke the wooden door like it was nothing more than a toothpick.

"Cassandra?"

His voice echoed out.

Nothing but a ringing phone came back.

Lottie was quiet for a while.

Cassandra couldn't handle it.

"Listen, there's a man out there I have to apologize to, a kid in here that I have to watch grow up, and I can't do either one if this Killian guy decides to really hurt me." Cassandra was up on her feet, pacing. "I get not being able to escape earlier when it was just you, Lottie, but now you're not alone. I'm here and I'm going to need us to be somewhere other than here real quick."

Lottie, who'd been weepy on and off after her story before going stone-cold quiet, stirred a little.

"No offense, but he's a big guy and you're pregnant. What if he has a gun? A knife? Any kind of weapon?"

Cassandra had already thought about that.

When she'd first seen him outside of New Beginnings, his hands had been free. When he approached her, she didn't remember seeing anything that was a weapon, either.

"When he comes in for you, does he ever have a gun or knife or anything?"

Lottie sat up.

"He had a Taser once, a baseball bat another time. Once he said if I got past him I'd regret it quick. The last time he came in, before you, I got a hit in and he got…well, this."

She motioned to her bruising along her face.

Cassandra winced.

Then she tried to rally.

"Me and my kids got trapped in a storage room at my school last week and how I got us out was by bum-rushing the man as soon as he opened the door. Just literally running at him. Maybe we could do something like that? Catch him by surprise?"

Lottie clearly didn't like the plan.

It wasn't like Cassandra did, either.

"We could be killed in this room for trying and no one would ever know."

"Who's to say that isn't already the plan?"

Cassandra felt sick for saying it.

She knew Lottie knew it was true, though.

She nodded.

"Okay, then but let's try to be smart about this."

There wasn't much smarts to be had about rushing at a kidnapper, but they tried their best. Cassandra went to the bathroom and managed to get the towel rack free from the wall. It was old, cheap plastic, but it could do something. She looked wistfully at where the mirror should have been. Shards of glass wrapped in the linens.

It was a movie-magic move that she'd seen a few times.

It would have been nice to have the option now.

"Maybe we can do something with the cots," Lottie mused out loud when Cassandra deemed the rest of the bathroom's contents unusable. "Maybe flip one up and use it like a battering ram? I think it would fit through the door okay. Push him down at least."

"That could work! We can ram him and then hit him with everything we have. Literally everything we have." She pointed to the standing lamp between the cots. Then the TV.

It was a wild plan, one built on absolute desperation, but Cassandra felt a flair of hope at it.

A flair that fizzled when the sound of a door unlocking filled the room.

"He doesn't come until night," Lottie whispered, panicked. "He's early."

Cassandra didn't have time to rally again. She moved to her cot and was glad Lottie went with her. They had it hoisted up between them and were turning toward the door, not at all ready to take on Killian when he came through.

But the door didn't open.

They took a few steps closer, listening.

Footsteps, clear as day.

Yet, they were retreating.

Cassandra shared a look with Lottie.

"Is this a trick?" the woman whispered.

Cassandra didn't know but she wasn't going to let an unlocked door go unopened for long.

"Come on."

They put down the cot and collected their individual makeshift weapons. Cassandra had the plastic towel rack, Lottie picked up the lamp. Unplugging it caused the room to be dotted in darkness. Cassandra hadn't been there long, but she knew she would have nightmares about it and its beige awfulness.

She motioned for Lottie to stand to the side and tried the doorknob.

It was smooth as it turned.

Adrenaline rushed through her. Cassandra took a breath and nodded at Lottie.

She opened the door slowly, then stopped, waiting for resistance from their kidnapper.

There was none.

There was no one and nothing on the other side of the door.

Cassandra tapped Lottie's shoulder.

She waved her to follow.

The room opened up into a small hallway that led to a landing that made no sense to Cassandra. To the left and right there was only enough space to walk a few steps to each side. The walls matched the floor—both were concrete. An electrical box was on the left wall, a metal box sat on the floor to the right.

Straight ahead were steep, metal stairs.

Cassandra only cared about them.

Lottie stopped her before she could step on the first one. She pointed to Cassandra's belly and pushed in front of her, taking the lead.

Cassandra let her but she tightened her hold on the towel rod as she followed up.

The stairs squealed under their weight. Cassandra winced at each step. The door at the top of the stairs matched the metal. It, however, didn't make a sound when Lottie opened it.

Cold air pushed into them the second it was open.

If Cassandra hadn't equated moving forward to survival, she might have stopped to question what it was she was seeing with more attention.

They'd gone from a motel-looking room with carpet and a bathroom, to concrete and metal, to...a dirt floor and wood walls and a ceiling that had seen better days.

Lottie must have been on the same wavelength. She looked around but never slowed down.

Not until they got to another door.

It was wooden, too, but looked new.

She waited until Cassandra gave her the nod to go ahead before opening it.

The cold that pressed against them was several degrees lower. Lottie put her hands over her eyes in what must have been reflex. She hadn't seen the sun in a week.

"Where are we?" Cassandra breathed out, as she peered out at a stand of trees.

Trees stretched all through Kelby Creek and beyond, the heaviest area at the Kintucket Woods near the town limits. At least that's what June had told her when a field-trip idea to go on a nature hike through them had been suggested.

Cassandra wasn't local, though.

To her she was looking at a foreboding forest, one cutting her off from safety.

She turned around to where they'd come from.

It looked like a utility shed or small barn from their new vantage point.

That made the imagery and its placement all the more menacing.

"Let's go," Cassandra said. She took Lottie's free hand and pulled her along into the closest tree line. There was a small path, but she wasn't going to walk right into Killian returning.

Or whoever had unlocked the door and then promptly left.

Lottie didn't argue with the plan of fleeing into the woods, even as her feet started to bleed the more they went.

Cassandra wanted to mull over their situation, trying to put two and two together, from her looking into Annie McHale at New Beginnings, but the longer they went, the more her mind only settled on one thing.

Jones.

He had to find them.

He was local.

He was the sheriff.

Surely, he could figure out what happened?

And if he didn't?

Cassandra stopped her train of thought there before looping back and replaying it again.

It wasn't until Lottie slowed that Cassandra realized she wasn't just thinking of Jones in desperation.

Thinking of him was bringing her comfort.

She trusted him without knowing him all that well.

She just *did*.

And that wasn't some small thing.

"There's something—something up ahead." Lottie's voice came out, panting.

Cassandra wasn't far behind. She'd been winded for the last mile or so, she guessed.

If they didn't find something soon, she was going to have to stop and rest,

Lottie pointed out in front of them and a little to the right.

"I see it!"

The woods ended a few feet from them and Lottie was right. There was something in the distance beyond that.

A house.

A big house.

Cassandra started forward, thankful all the way to the tips of her toes that they would be getting out of the woods, but Lottie stopped her dead in her tracks.

Her face had contorted into a mixture of what seemed to be confusion and fear.

"What is it?"

Lottie shook her head.

"I know where we are and—and we don't need to go there." She pointed to their left. "There's a—there's a road we can walk along for a little bit. More houses."

Cassandra didn't understand.

"Where are we?"

Lottie started to walk along the tree line, giving the house in the distance a wide berth that was worrisome.

"That's the McHale Manor."

Cassandra didn't move to follow.

"The McHale Manor? Annie McHale's home?"

Lottie didn't break stride.

"Yep. Right before she disappeared forever. I don't know about you but I don't want to disappear forever too. Let's—"

"Cassandra!"

Lottie stopped dead in her tracks. Cassandra froze too.

"Cassandra!"

The call came again. It was far off.

It was near the house.

Lottie's eyes were wide, terrified.

Cassandra was thawing.

"I know that voice," she whispered, as if saying it any louder would somehow make it less true.

She waited for one more call.

It came.

"Cassandra!"

She didn't need any more confirmation.

Cassandra took a step forward and yelled out for all she was worth.

"Jones!"

It was like her voice had a line tethered to the man. She and Lottie watched as the towering sheriff came running around the house in the distance. It was too far away to see his exact expression, but Cassandra knew he was searching for her.

Cassandra ran out of the tree line but stopped before she was in the open clearing between the woods and the house.

"Jones," she yelled again.

The sheriff's head turned. He saw her and he was running.

Cassandra wanted to say a lot of things—warn him of Killian, whoever freed them, explain Lottie and say how she knew he'd come—but the second Jones was close enough to touch, she crumpled.

"I'm sorry," she cried out before he could touch her. "I'm so sorry."

Jones had never slowed on approach. He collided into her with warmth and care of her stomach.

She accepted the strength of his arms as they wrapped around her.

"You're safe now," he said into her hair. "I got you."

Cassandra didn't think their troubles were over yet, but in that moment, she found she didn't care.

Chapter Sixteen

Ray Cooke came into the hospital lobby like a bat outta hell. His eyes were red. He was upset.

And Jones knew half of it was at himself.

"Ray," Jones called, waving him over. Jones knew he was coming and had been waiting by the first set of elevators.

Ray ran to him, not wasting a second.

Jones figured he'd do the same so he hit the button to call the elevator down before the man had made it to him.

"She's okay, right? You said she was okay?" Any animosity Ray had been harboring almost two weeks ago, when Jones had found him drunk on the bridge, was long gone. He was a man worried and sick with guilt at the same time.

"Lottie's good," Jones confirmed. "She's got some bruises and her feet are a bit scraped up but she's still as good as she was when I called."

The elevator doors opened. Ray only seemed partially relieved. He stepped inside after Jones shook his head.

"I—I was sure she'd left me again. You know? She was gone, the car was gone. I—I didn't know she'd been—"

The doors shut in time for Ray to make a noise somewhere between a yell and a groan.

Jones felt for the man.

After he'd found out that Lottie had been held captive for a week with no one knowing, he'd gone through a volley of emotions as sheriff. As someone meant to stop this sort of thing from happening.

He couldn't imagine how Ray felt knowing he'd not been looking for Lottie the whole time she was gone.

Cassandra had been missing for almost two hours and it had been eating Jones alive every second.

"The important thing is that she's okay. She's safe now. And the first person she asked after was you. She's not upset, Ray. She's just tired, scared and wants nothing and no one but you to be by her side."

Jones wasn't exaggerating or fibbing to make the man feel better. The first thing Lottie had said in the car on the ride to the hospital was that she wanted Ray.

Cassandra had held her hand in the back seat and promised her they'd get him.

Jones would never forget how calm her voice was then, how reassuring.

How tired and drained it was at the same time.

Tears streaked down her face, and there was blood in her hair.

Even now Jones wanted to punch something to get his anger out.

Instead he took a breath.

The doors to the third floor opened. A deputy from the department nodded to Jones.

"Now, Ray, you're one of three visitors allowed on this floor at the moment," Jones told him, turning the man in the right direction. "I don't know Lottie's family-and-friend situation, but we'd like to keep it to you for now."

Ray nodded. His anger and guilt had turned to an anxiousness that was rubbing off on Jones. He didn't even ask any follow-up questions.

Jones didn't blame him.

He showed him to the door of Lottie's hospital room.

Ray knocked once then disappeared in a rush inside.

Before the door closed behind him, Jones heard Lottie cry out. Ray was blubbering in an instant.

It made Jones soften.

The door across the hall was already cracked open. Jones went inside and walked into a conversation with Cassandra and Carlos.

Seeing her sitting in a hospital bed made his blood boil. She shouldn't have been there at all.

"Ask her already," she said to Carlos. When she saw Jones, she went from smiling to concerned. "Did you get Ray to Lottie?"

Jones nodded.

"I think that's the first time I've spent with Ray without threatening jail time." He took a seat on the chair next to the bed. It had become his designated spot since they'd brought the women in. "I gotta say, it was nice."

"I just hope that will give Lottie some good to go on." Cassandra shook her head. "I was in that bunker for way less than a day and I don't think I can ever go into a windowless room again. I can't imagine being down there for over a week."

The three of them were quiet a moment at that admission.

Whatever Carlos and she had been discussing beforehand fell by the wayside. Carlos cleared his throat.

"I'm headed back to the McHale house to talk with Foster and Kenneth," he told Jones. "Then I'm back at the department. Cole is taking night shift."

Jones nodded. In between trying to figure out what was going on, they'd had to deal with their schedules.

Especially since Jones had changed his around, something that he hadn't yet had the chance to tell Cassandra about.

Then again, they hadn't been alone together since he'd embraced her out behind the McHale house.

Carlos dipped his head to Cassandra, said he was glad she was feeling good and then headed out.

Jones caught himself looking at Cassandra's belly before *she* caught him looking, too.

"The doctor gave us the all clear," she reminded him. "Baby boy and me. Strong heartbeat for him, no concussion for me. We're good."

Jones growled a little.

"You shouldn't be in this place at all."

It was a comment he'd doled out several times already. This time, though, Cassandra smiled.

"Well, I'm going to count it as an impromptu practice run for when I most definitely *have* to be here in a few months. At least now I'm not in any pain."

Jones did his best job at giving a smile to her attempt to lighten the mood. She must have realized it hadn't budged him much.

"I shouldn't have played detective, I'm sorry," she said. "I just wanted to help and I thought I could do that without getting in anyone's way. Honestly, had I known what would happen I never would have risked it. Risked us."

Her hand smoothed over her belly.

It did something to him. Jones tried to let go of some of his tension.

"You don't have to keep apologizing, Cassandra. I'm the one who didn't go with you. This is on me."

She reached out and took his hand in one fluid movement. He was glad there were no IVs in it. The sight would have brought out his rage at whoever had done this to her again.

"Unless you managed to attack and kidnap me during a press conference, I'm not blaming you at all. Especially since you're the one who found us after the fact."

Jones could have taken the comment with grace. Then simmered down because his heightened stress wasn't helping anyone.

But they hadn't been alone yet. He hadn't had the chance to tell her what had really happened.

Why he had been at the McHale house in the first place.

Cassandra let go of his hand, an eyebrow raising in the process.

"What?" she asked.

Jones used to think he was a closed book. That wasn't the case with her.

He had a few more specific questions for her before he dove into his answer.

"You said you went to the library study room and found nothing, just like I did when I went, but noticed the window in one showed New Beginnings across the road. What made you go to Megan Hamilton about it?"

"I noticed Lloyd was still using paper logs for reservations and, since Megan used to work there before him, I wanted to know where older logs might be. I taught Megan's granddaughter two years ago and became friends with Megan so she had no problem when I asked about it. Or, at least she didn't pick apart my lame explanation for looking for a former student's older sister. I phrased it to kind of sound like the student had been adopted and I was trying to find her family on the down-low." Cassandra squirmed a little. "I'm not proud of being dishonest, but, well, it worked out alright."

She motioned to her phone on the table next to him.

"Megan had some of the old logs stashed in her attic.

She was told she could take them when she retired and use them to make her flowers."

Jones gave her a look.

"She makes and sells paper flowers on Etsy," she explained. "Her house is filled with them."

Jones lifted her phone and handed it over.

"*But* she hadn't gotten to using them yet since her neighbor gave her crates of old newspapers, so I was able to look at the logs myself." She clicked through her phone until she got to a picture. She handed it back to him. "Annie's name wasn't on any of the old ones, the ones before she was kidnapped, but Jasmine Lohan's name appears on the reservation log every Saturday, Monday and Thursday morning for at least two months and only for the room with the window. I asked Megan if she remembered Jasmine, noting that the name appeared a lot, and she actually laughed. *She said* that half of the time Jasmine would slip in and out without her even noticing. That it happened so much the staff started calling her the Ghost in the Stacks." Cassandra was clearly amused by the name, but that feeling went away at the next part.

"Then Megan said Annie McHale went missing and the whole town kind of stopped. Jasmine stopped reserving the room and, at least while Megan was on schedule, didn't come back to the library again."

Jones looked down at the picture on Cassandra's phone.

"This is one of the old logs?"

She nodded.

"So it sounds like Annie wasn't the one reserving the study room, it was Jasmine."

"Or Annie reserving under Jasmine's name. Ghost in the Stacks sounds like someone who doesn't really want to be seen."

Jones conceded that.

"That got me wondering about the why of it all and I started thinking about that window and New Beginnings and looked it up." Cassandra started talking with her hands, excited as she continued. "Did you know that New Beginnings was partially funded by the Delphi Group? And, did you know that the Delphi Group is an offshoot of the McHale Foundation?"

Jones did know about the Delphi Group but he hadn't known that it was a part of the McHale charity organization.

Jones cracked a quick grin.

"Remind me after the baby is born to see if you want to switch jobs to detective."

"I don't think it's some big, dark secret or anything, but I don't think a lot of people know that," she said. "It got me a lot more curious about New Beginnings, though. If Annie was reserving the room with the window that faced New Beginnings, a place her parents helped create, then maybe she was going across the street during her reservation times."

"Why go through the trouble of going to the library at all if you're just going to use someone else's name and not stay?" Jones added.

At that, Cassandra shrugged.

"Maybe in case she got caught she wanted an alibi? One where she could get Jasmine to admit that it was Annie reserving the room so Annie could get some privacy? I don't know but that's a good question. I would be more inclined to think the whole idea of her going to New Beginnings was ridiculous had I not gone there myself and, well—"

"—been taken," he said, finishing the thought.

Cassandra nodded.

"Then there's the whole secret room thing I woke up in that just so happened to be on the McHale property. I thought I was somewhere in that New Beginnings place. If that's all unrelated then you can slap my butt and call me Sally."

Jones chuckled at the phrase.

Then he sighed.

"It's definitely related." It was his turn to pull out his phone. He went to the gallery app. "I didn't just guess that you were at the McHale house. *This* was left next to your phone inside of New Beginnings."

He clicked the picture he was looking for and handed it over. The picture on the screen was burned into his mind.

A single piece of paper with one line perfectly written on it.

"'She's at the house—Annie.'"

Cassandra read the message, twice.

It gave him chills both times.

"Wait. Annie? Annie McHale?"

Jones shrugged.

"We don't know who Killian is yet, or why he's doing what he's doing, but this could be his way of being dramatic," he offered. "Or trying to distract us. I wouldn't read too much in to it yet. Not until we know more."

Cassandra didn't respond right away. Her eyes were scanning the message again.

Jones watched her.

He marveled at how much she'd grown to care about Annie's case, his case, since finding out about it.

Then again, Jones had a sneaking suspicion that that's just what Cassandra did.

She cared.

But even those who cared got frustrated enough from time to time.

"Ugh. This is all giving me a headache." She handed

him his phone back. "Every time I talk to you I feel like I have more questions than there can possibly be answers to."

"I can say ditto to that."

Cassandra let out a breath that sunk her low.

She was tired.

He didn't blame her.

"The doc said we can leave when you're ready. Then we can run by your place and grab your things. Carlos already had someone get your car from New Beginnings."

"Why are we grabbing my things?"

Her confusion was genuine.

It made Jones smirk, despite how serious he was when he answered.

"Because, Miss West, you're staying with me tonight."

Chapter Seventeen

Bonnie was over the moon about the company. She yelled Cassandra's name like she was some kind of movie star and Bonnie was her biggest fan.

"You've made quite the impression on our girl," Jones's father, Ted, said when Bonnie ran off to get her favorite toys to show her.

Cassandra had felt a blush rise at that comment. There was just something special about being accepted by kids. Even more so by being accepted by Jones's daughter.

"I'd have to say likewise to that," she told him. Ted smiled. He'd been doing it off and on between the several times he'd asked how she was feeling since she and Jones had arrived at the house earlier.

She'd told him, at every turn, that she was fine.

She was, after all.

Her baby had gotten the all clear and she would sleep better knowing that Lottie was safe at the hospital under guard. Not to mention half of the Dawn County Sheriff's Department now were looking into the bunker, New Beginnings and the man named Killian Carmichael.

As far as Jones said, after the update he received when dinner was wrapping up, Killian was still their biggest mystery. There were no records of him at New Beginnings or in their system, and no one recognized the name. Ted had even pulled security-camera footage from the hardware store after Lottie's statement that she'd seen Killian outside of it before he'd followed her to the clearing.

All customers seen on the camera were regulars and well-known. Still, Lottie looked at pictures of each when they'd been brought to her in the hospital. She recognized none.

"A sketch artist should be here in the morning. Hopefully with the description Lottie gives we can find this Killian guy."

Jones concluded his conversation with Carlos and dropped down onto the couch. Cassandra and Ted had been talking about the upcoming school schedule and field trips. She'd caught him looking at her belly several times.

Once again, she realized that with all the talking that she and Jones had done at the hospital, they hadn't broached the subject of who knew the identity of her child's father.

It didn't feel right to potentially be the first to tell Ted. That was Jones's decision to make, she decided.

"So what happens now?" Cassandra asked when Jones closed his eyes to rest for a moment. "Surely you're not going back to the department. You're clearly exhausted, too."

Jones shook his head.

"I'm not going back to the department until we've gotten some more answers."

Cassandra hadn't expected that response.

"He took himself off schedule for the next few days," Ted said. "He wanted to make sure we were all safe. We also have a cruiser outside. I think it's Sterling, if I'm not mistaken."

"It is. He insisted. Marigold, too." Jones opened his eyes. They were red.

When was the last time he'd gotten good sleep?

Cassandra focused on the significant part a second later.

Jones had stepped aside to keep them safe. Keep all of them safe.

It warmed her.

Him demanding she stay by his side?

That had done a bit more.

She hadn't known she could get butterflies while carrying a baby.

But she had.

She got them again now.

"Both are good eggs," Ted continued. "I'll get them some food in the morning. I know Sterling's a fan of my coffee."

He rocked up out of his chair. He was wearing cargo shorts and the two scars around his knee were shining and wide.

He noticed her stare and smiled.

"Us Murphys are a strong breed. Every single one of us."

Ted winked and then said good-night. His room was on the far side of the house. Jones didn't speak until they heard the door close.

"He knows about the baby." Jones gave a soft chuckle. "Heck, he even knew about us meeting all those months ago. I'm actually impressed he didn't outright blurt it at you when you first came in."

That blush came back quickly.

"I thought he might. The whole Murphy-strong-breed comment and all."

Jones snorted this time. He didn't follow it up with a comment on his father, though. He nodded to the hallway across from them.

"Dad gave me the master bedroom when I moved in since it's got this weird step-down situation and the bathroom isn't as crutch-and-wheelchair friendly. I got him to set it up for you when we were at your place earlier."

Jones stood up and reached a hand down to her. She was thankful for the assist. Her belly wasn't exactly beach-ball-size, but she was finding it harder and harder to stand up from anything with comfortable cushions.

"Bonnie is on the other side of the house and a hard sleeper, so if you need to get up and go to the kitchen or just move around, don't worry about waking her," he continued. They'd made it to the door. He opened it and waved her in. "There's new sheets on the bed and clean towels and whatnot in the bathroom. I also made some space in the dresser for you, top drawer."

"You didn't have to do all of this," she said honestly.

Jones waved her off.

"Least I could do. You did, after all, jump into a creek to save me."

His smile was teasing.

Cassandra couldn't help her third blush of the night.

She went to her bags on the bed to create distance from him and those dang butterflies that started flapping.

Jones had already made his position on them together clear and she respected that.

In fact, she agreed with it.

Being co-parents might be difficult, but it wouldn't be heartbreaking.

Not like what they had both already experienced.

If she could avoid that again?

Then she could handle swatting away butterflies every now and then.

"All right, well, I think you're just about right on the dot with the whole rest thing." He grabbed a pillow and blanket that was sitting on top of the dresser. "I'll be out on the couch if you need me."

"The couch?" Cassandra hadn't thought about his sleeping arrangements yet. "Oh, that isn't fair, Jones. Take the bed and I'll take the couch."

The man shook his head.

"Good night, Cassandra."

"Jones, really I don't mind if you—"

"Good night," he repeated. The door shut between them. Cassandra stared at it a moment.

"Good night, Jones."

THE HOUSE WAS QUIET.

Though, since Bonnie had come into his life, quiet didn't really mean the same thing.

Jones stood in the doorway of her bedroom. Her sound machine's white noise was whirling by the window. Her stars of blue and green light swam across the ceiling. Bonnie was breathing deep and steady.

Jones took his pillow and blanket and laid on the carpet next to her bed.

The Almost Pink paint still seemed bright in the dark.

Jones wished Helen was here, wished she could see the paint. Wished she could see Bonnie sleeping, and laughing, and living wild.

He wished he could tell her that Bonnie, despite all of his failures as a father so far, was kind and smart and filled with more courage than he thought was possible for her small size. That she was loved deeply by his father and, although they hadn't been close, Helen's parents came to visit them always for Christmas.

He wished he could tell her he was afraid that one day Bonnie would blame him for everything that had happened to Kelby Creek. To her. To their family.

That one day she'd be old enough to understand that a

lot of people in this world were broken by one thing or another. That life could be mean for no good reason.

That some things just couldn't be fixed.

Jones also wished he could tell Helen about Cassandra, as odd as it might have sounded.

About his fear of being a father again, to a boy, at that.

And, even though he spent his time behind a badge, his courage about the future had been crippled by her death.

When the sun goes away, you just don't look at light the same way anymore.

Jones listened to Bonnie breathing, unaware of him on her floor, wishing he could talk to her mama.

Unaware that his heart was stretching across the house to a woman who had shown nothing but kindness and patience to her.

Jones tried to sleep, he really did, but the usual quietness of the house had him tossing and turning.

He didn't know why until he was standing in front of his bedroom door.

The soft light of the bedside lamp reached out beneath it. Jones almost turned around. Then he heard the sound of a phone being laid down on the nightstand. The same sound he heard overnight when he plugged his phone into the charger.

He knocked lightly.

Cassandra called out, just as quietly.

Jones let himself in and shut the door back behind him.

Cassandra was propped up with two pillows, her body covered by his sheets. She gave him a look of such acute concern, he hesitated.

"Is everything okay?" she asked, trying to sit up straighter.

Jones had every intention of saying he just had come in to check on her. That he was anxious given the last two weeks, especially that day.

But he didn't come close to his intention.

Jones went to the side of the bed. He placed one hand on the headboard over her and the other under her chin. She watched him, bright eyes wide, as he bent low.

Jones pressed his lips to hers.

It was a slow kiss. It was a soft kiss.

It was his way of opening up.

Of saying he was sorry.

Of saying he was glad she was okay.

That she was there with him, with his family, all okay.

That he was sorry he couldn't say all of that out loud.

That the kiss was all he could give her now.

So he made it last.

Cassandra returned it, her hands coming up to either side of his face.

For the first time in a long while, Jones felt content.

He knew it couldn't last.

He ended the kiss and met her gaze, still cradled in her hands.

He didn't know what to say.

She did.

"Stay with me tonight. I don't want to be alone."

Her voice was soft.

Jones nodded.

Cassandra let him go. He went to the other side of the bed and took off his shirt. The sheets were cool against his skin as he slid between them.

Cassandra kept quiet while he molded around her body, arm around her, leg between hers. She reached over to turn off the light.

Darkness filled the room.

Jones let Cassandra adjust beneath him. When she settled he put his chin on top of her shoulder.

He remembered the first night they'd lain together.

The lead-up to it had been a quiet kind of chaos.

They'd eaten at a restaurant but hadn't wanted to part ways yet. So they'd gone to a coffee shop. It had closed right as they'd hit the door. They'd then found themselves walking around the hotel before taking a stroll by the pool. There, their conversation had turned into something more.

When she'd invited him in after her, when he'd walked her to her room, Jones knew what saying yes would become.

He'd kissed her deep and true two steps inside. His hands had caressed her cheek before he'd used them to take her to the bed. She was nothing to his size, like moving air.

She had laughed at the quick move.

He had kissed that laughter.

Then he'd kissed all of her.

After that they'd been a tangle of skin, warmth and the best kind of movement.

The morning after, she'd smiled up at him. Quiet, bright. The sunlight that had managed to find the only crack between the curtains, lying across her shoulder—the same shoulder he was pressed against now—and Jones had suspected something then, right then.

Despite not really knowing her, he was never going to forget her.

Jones moved his hand over her stomach in the dark. She covered it with her own.

A few minutes later and Jones was fast asleep.

Chapter Eighteen

There were three doughnuts in a bag sitting next to the bed when Cassandra awoke the next morning.

One was chocolate, one was powdered sugar and one had a bite taken out of it. A little perfect Bonnie-size bite, if she had to guess.

Cassandra ran her hand over the empty spot next to her in bed after making the discovery.

Last night had been…different.

That kiss?

Every butterfly Cassandra had been swatting away had come back in full force. They'd brought their friends and families and even coworkers to the party.

It had been all Cassandra could do to not completely melt into it.

Into him.

But then she'd seen it in his eyes.

Jones Murphy had been feeling something and that something wasn't up to her to define. So she'd let him take the lead.

That had led to a giant of a man wrapping around her in the darkness.

Cassandra had felt him relax against her and then, sure enough, his breathing had evened out.

She'd fallen asleep a little later.

She was a little let down that she hadn't felt him leave when he'd woken.

Cassandra stretched wide and tried to stay in her happy bubble for the moment. She found her phone and unlocked it. It was nine on Sunday. Which meant, for once, she'd slept through the night without having to readjust or use the bathroom. It was a small blessing.

Now that blessing had run its course. She went to the bathroom, decided to go ahead and shower and found herself back in the bedroom getting dressed while eating a doughnut.

She dipped into her purse for her prenatal vitamins and looked at the bed.

Then she was thinking about the cot in the bunker on the McHale property. They'd been told the day before that it was a storm shelter for tornadoes. One that had been installed by Annie's grandparents and then shuttered and locked down after Annie was taken and her parents moved.

They'd had no idea that someone was using it.

Why would they?

They were living in Montana now.

Cassandra ran a hand over her stomach. Her heart hurt just thinking about the possibility of her son being taken.

Gone for years with no answers.

So depressed and heartbroken that she'd have to escape the town they'd spent their life in.

But Cassandra wouldn't leave, no matter how much it hurt.

She'd have to stay, go through every tree in the woods and turn over every pebble by the creek.

Jones would do the same, she was sure of it. He might have left Kelby Creek behind after his wife was killed—hadn't Cassandra left her previous life after Ryan had passed?—but she had no doubt that he'd stay if Bonnie was gone without a trace. That thought led Cassandra down a rabbit hole of what-ifs and more questions.

She knew she could get lost there, but now wasn't the time.

They didn't need her help to solve their mysteries. She'd already overstepped once and look where that had landed her.

Cassandra thought about that cot again, and pictured Lottie's bruises along her face. She thought about the man who'd taken her, but she'd barely seen him before she was attacked.

Then she left.

Ted was the first to greet her once she made it to the kitchen. He had coffee and the paper in front of him. His attention was focused on an ad for a sale at the hobby store in the city.

"You should make those into flowers," she said, motioning to the newspaper. Cassandra had picked up on the fact that Ted Murphy was a man who enjoyed trying new things to do. "Megan Hamilton makes different flowers out of the paper. I've seen them. They're pretty cool. She said they're complicated enough to keep you focused but not troubling enough to make you swear." She winked. "Most times."

Ted eyed his paper again.

"I've never tried making anything with paper."

"Could be something there, Pops."

Jones came in through the doorway behind them. Carlos brought up the rear. There was a file under Jones's arm. He extended his smile to her.

Cassandra got all warm again.

"Morning," he said to her. "Do you want me to make you anything for breakfast? I'm a mean egg scrambler."

The man was definitely well-rested. Or, at least, not

as dragged down as he had been. She was glad he'd gotten the rest.

"The doughnuts did the trick. But thank you."

"You can thank Bonnie for that. Her doughnut vice pays well for the rest of us." He turned to Carlos. "Want some coffee?"

"Are you kidding me? I'm now thinking about those mean scrambled eggs and doughnuts."

Both men laughed.

"The lady gets the good eggs, the kid gets dibs on the last doughnut and the man gets the coffee because I saw him woof down a sausage biscuit in his car."

Carlos pretended to take offense.

"Look at the 'towering sheriff' out here humbling me."

That got everyone laughing. Jones went to the coffeepot and, for a few minutes, Cassandra forgot about the rest of the world.

It didn't last long.

Ted went into the backyard to play with Bonnie while the rest of them hung around the dining-room table. The file beneath Jones's arm landed on the top.

"All right, we have our hands in a bunch of pies right now." Jones was addressing her, but Carlos was listening with rapt attention. "The department is looking after the Taurus that ran me off the road, also trying to figure out the Jimmy angle of it all. New Beginnings has eyes on it, same with the bunker and the McHales. Killian has Foster on him and, last I checked, the sketch artist should be coming into the department this morning to meet with Lottie to get a sketch on him since she's left the hospital already. Then there's the note."

Jones opened up the folder and spun a piece of paper around and out of it.

Cassandra recognized it as the paper that had been next to her phone in New Beginnings. The one signed by Annie.

"This is what we're going to focus on here." Jones tapped the signature twice.

"You want us to focus on Annie," she offered.

Jones nodded.

"The gardener who said he saw Annie on her last morning lied. I'm sure of it now, even without confirmation from the Deacon household and the schedule that Vera Lohan talked about. I'm not convinced, though, that this lie is relevant. He could have genuinely been mistaken and here we are chasing it as a lead for no reason. Though, it did lead us to the library and New Beginnings. Either way, it stands that Annie's parents saw her last, before the ransom demand."

"That's if no one else lied." Cassandra said it as an under-her-breath thought, but Jones agreed with it.

"Exactly," he said. "Before now no one even knew about Annie's friendship with Jasmine Lohan, definitely not their library scheme. I think we only got what we did by accident since Vera's memory has been coming and going. It might also have been why Vera left town."

"To keep the chances of her slipping up down," Carlos added.

"It's possible. Then again, people do move for reasons unrelated to Annie," Jones said, playing devil's advocate. "Regardless."

He tapped the paper again.

"Jasmine gave us the info on the library. Maybe she knows more."

Carlos nodded. "I can have her brought in."

"No," Jones said, the single word coming out sharp and fast. "I don't want to spook her. I'll find a way to get to her."

He paused.

"This whole thing has blown a weird hole into what we thought of Annie. Whoever wrote this might have known what was really going on or know enough to use Annie's name to make us jump when they say go and that's what we need to figure out. Who might do this, what was Killian's plan, who let the girls out of the bunker, and what might be their next steps."

Carlos nodded and put down his writing pad, pen already out. Jones settled at the head of the table, pulling his file closer to him.

Cassandra finally said a thought that had been floating around in her head since she'd woken in the bunker. It was quiet but impactful.

"Or it *is* Annie."

Jones and Carlos's heads snapped at attention.

"If she went to the library only to use the room for cover to go to New Beginnings, and if Killian was a patient there at the same time, then maybe they were seeing each other. And if they were seeing each other then, maybe they're seeing each other now."

Carlos's brow furrowed.

"We checked the timeline of his stay, the murders at the Rosewater Inn and Annie's kidnapping," he said. "Other than Lottie and her father, we can't find anyone else to even confirm Killian *was* a patient. It's possible Annie was sneaking in to see him or knew someone who let her in, just like Lottie. We have no evidence to back it up, though."

"If she was seeing Killian, then this goes back to who the hell is this guy?" Jones had his hands fisted on the table. "And, if he's tied to Annie somehow and Annie is working with him, or against him, or doing anything at all in the shadows, this town is going to burn at the knowledge."

Carlos nodded. Cassandra didn't understand.

"Wouldn't it be a good thing to know that Annie is alive after all of these years?"

"No."

The one syllable was hard, unmoving.

Jones took a second to explain.

"Annie's kidnapping might have opened our eyes to all of the bad in this town, but it also created a lot of bad, too." His jaw clenched.

He was talking about the ambush at the park.

Helen's death.

"If Annie's kidnapping was a lie? If it was some kind of game or setup?"

"The Annie McHale this town has been praising for years will go from the angel of this town to its villain." Jones's frown was deep, severe. He snapped. "Just like that."

THE CONVERSATION COOLED as the three of them put their heads together for theories. An hour in and none were panning out. Carlos left for the department soon after and Cassandra went to the backyard to stretch her legs by walking around with Bonnie.

Jones watched them in deep conversation, trying to still piece together the mystery. It's why his father surprised him when he spoke at his side.

"I got up last night for some water and noticed you weren't on the couch or in Bonnie's room."

Jones sighed.

"I'm not talking about this right now, Dad."

His father shrugged.

"I didn't ask you to, now did I? I was just making an observation, is all. But, since I'm here, I'll make another one." He nodded out the window. "She's got the heart for this, you know?"

Jones lifted an eyebrow.

"This? You mean talking to Bonnie about the show *Bluey* or her fascination about how turtles breathe through their butts?"

Jones was joking. His dad wasn't.

"All of this. Bonnie, you, sheriff, Kelby Creek. Being a mom. She has the heart for it and I wanted to make sure you realized it. Though, I think you already do."

Jones had woken up that morning and hadn't been able to wrap his head around the kiss the night before.

Why had he done it now?

Why hadn't he done it earlier?

But what had been a more pressing question was, why had she accepted him?

And was that what she'd done?

Or had she just been tired and gone along with it?

Jones sighed.

"It's that heart I'm worried about."

His father surprised him with a laugh.

"We've both had the privilege of sharing our lives with two wonderful women. To find someone else to love? That's an absolute gift, son. Don't waste it because you can't get out of your own head. I think your mother and Helen would tell you the same if they could."

Jones felt his father's hand on his back.

He often missed his mother, but he never once was ungrateful for his father's presence.

He let his dad give him a good, reassuring pat, until the moment ended by Jones's phone ringing.

"I'm going to make some snacks now so Bonbon doesn't become a sea monster. Try not to stress too much, if you can."

He went back to the kitchen while Jones took his call in the living room.

"Murphy here."

He didn't recognize the number but he did the voice.

"You're not going to believe this hot garbage, Sheriff."

It was Detective Howard.

Lily had never called his cell before.

"Hot garbage? Be more specific."

Lily went to talking fast.

"Jimmy just got out on bail with the fanciest lawyer I've ever seen. Some man from Birmingham with a suit Marco and my husband, Ant, agreed cost more than our cars combined. So, Juliet goes and asks Nan the million-dollar question—how in the devil's name could they afford this guy—and *Nan* tells her that it's none of her dang business and I've been digging deep and I can't figure out why this guy took the case and how he's being paid for it. I mean, this guy stabbed the sheriff. It's hot garbage that he's apparently out and has been since this morning. I mean, it's also Sunday, for gosh sakes."

Jones had tensed on the first part, and at the end he joined in on her confusion.

"Text me the name of the lawyer and the judge who signed off on this," he said. "Do we know where Jimmy is now?"

Lily seemed a might happier with the next news.

"Ant saw him first over near the restaurant and is sitting out there waiting. Don't worry, he's good at being sneaky, but I'd like to head out there myself since I'm not doing anything here that needs me tied to a desk."

Jones was nodding hard.

"Go on out and keep an eye on him for now. I still don't know what his deal is, but maybe you can catch him meeting with someone or doing something that gives us some insight."

"Will do, Sheriff."

They ended the call and Jones felt all the hotter for it.

Jimmy's attack and threat had been weighing on everyone. Now, given the last two weeks, Jones wasn't sure if he was a target, Cassandra was a target, some combination of the two, or if Jimmy had had one hell of a day when he'd brought a knife out at the department.

Either way, as Jones walked back into the kitchen he reaffirmed his stance that he wasn't leaving his family unattended.

He certainly wasn't leaving Cassandra alone.

Not while Killian was out there.

It was a stance that was immediately put to the test.

Bonnie came in, but Cassandra was still outside on her phone.

Her brow was creased. She was upset.

"It's Keith," Bonnie exclaimed before he could ask what was going on. "He called Miss West. He's crying!"

His dad appeared with a plate of chopped fruit. He gave Jones worried eyes.

"Then let's give her some space, Bonbon," he said. "This sounds like an adult problem to solve."

Bonnie agreed but looked out the window before she followed him.

"You don't leave your friends behind," she told Jones. "It's the pirate code."

"We're not leaving anyone behind," he assured her. Jones's gut was on high alert. He swooped down to give Bonnie a kiss on the head before going out to Cassandra.

She was ending her call.

"That was Keith." Worry was vibrating through her. "He said that Lila is crying in the kitchen. He asked if I'd come over and see them."

"Is *he* okay?"

She shrugged.

"I asked and he said he is, but his little voice was wobbling." She looked at the house behind him for a second. "Jones, I know you have a lot going on, but I'd really like to go see them. Poor Keith's been through a lot, never mind Lila."

Jones nodded.

"Let's go."

"I can't ask you to leave Bonnie and your father."

Jones pulled out his phone.

"I'm not leaving them alone."

He scrolled to Sterling's number.

"Still, I can't ask—"

Jones cut her off.

"You aren't asking me to do anything. I'm telling you that I already had a plan in place if I needed to leave the house."

He hit the call button but kept his eyes on her.

"Plus, we don't leave our friends behind."

Cassandra nodded.

"Pirate's code."

"Pirate's code," he repeated.

Chapter Nineteen

Lila and Joel lived in a one-road neighborhood five minutes from downtown. It was a quiet few houses, helped in part by the good amount of yard space between them, and Lila's was smack-dab in the middle. It was a nice two-story home with a cute Welcome sign and a stack of ceramic pumpkins on the porch.

The festive decorations didn't strike a festive mood.

It was cold outside and the clouds reflected it in their varying shades of gray.

That feeling had found its way into Cassandra's stomach.

She wrung her hands together as they parked at the curb.

"I'm sure they're fine. Nothing we can't help."

Jones's one hand enveloped both of hers.

He squeezed.

The worry abated. But only a little.

"And Bonnie and Ted have someone with them?" she asked. Again.

Jones didn't seem to mind the repeat. He helped her out of the car.

"Sterling, Marigold *and* Juliet."

"Won't that mess up the investigation?"

"Not at all. Juliet's a pro at phone duty. She can find

out more using a cell than most people can sitting in front of a big screen. Dad's going to set her up in the house and Sterling and Marigold are going to stand guard outside. Don't worry about them."

She *was* worried about them, but at his confidence, Cassandra allowed herself to switch tracks.

Jones knocked on the door, but made sure to step aside when it opened to reveal Keith.

His little eyes instantly went to her, just as Cassandra instantly crouched to get to his level.

"Oh, Keith, what's wrong?"

The little boy's eyes were red and rimmed with tears. His cheeks had stains across them. Otherwise, he seemed in good physical health.

He didn't seem at all happy to see them, though.

He looked up at Jones.

"I didn't call you." Cassandra was taken aback at the tone in his voice. It was hard. She'd never heard it from the boy.

"This is Jones, remember him? He's my friend. I asked him to come to help. He knows Mrs. Lila, too. He can help."

Keith looked absolutely lost for a moment. Like he'd escaped into his own head and almost didn't come back out.

Cassandra shared a look with Jones.

He'd already picked up on what she was thinking.

"Hey there, Keith. I'm Bonnie's dad, too. She couldn't come to check on you so she sent me. Why don't you let me go inside and talk to Mrs. Lila now, okay?"

He didn't wait for Keith to agree or not. Cassandra moved in tandem with him. She reached out to take Keith's hand. It was clammy with sweat but he held her fast. Cassandra stood and gently pulled him out and onto the porch.

Jones gave her a quick nod and disappeared into the house.

Cassandra shut the door softly behind him before focusing on the boy. She lowered herself again and squeezed his hand.

Keith took one look at the gesture and burst into tears.

"Oh, Keith, what's going on?"

The boy shook his head. Cassandra used her other hand to steady it.

"Keith, you can talk to me," she said softly.

But Keith wasn't having it.

He took his hand out of hers so quickly that Cassandra had to rock back on her heels so as not to fall over. She stood to keep the momentum from sending her down again.

Seeing her almost fall did something to the boy.

He slowed his breathing and seemed to be actively trying to stop crying.

It wasn't working but he did manage to talk through his tears.

"He—he made me do it," he stuttered out. "He said he'd hurt her if I didn't—didn't do it."

Cassandra's stomach, already cold, became a frozen wasteland in an instant.

"Who's he? Joel?"

Keith shook his head hard.

"I don't—I don't know him. He just told me to do it and I had to."

Cassandra heard the change in her own voice.

It pitched low, quiet.

"What did he make you do, Keith?"

Images of Lila crying filled her head.

Cassandra never imagined his answer.

"He—he told me to—to get you here."

The timing couldn't have been more perfect.

And maybe that was the point.

Footsteps thundered up behind Cassandra. Keith shrunk back and uttered one last thing through his tears.

"I'm—I'm sorry."

The house was warm, the lights were nice and it smelled like cinnamon.

It was a complete contrast to the awful scene he found in the downstairs bedroom.

"Lila!"

Keith's foster mom was tied to a recliner, facing the door. Her head was drooping down, but Jones could see the blood and bruises. Just as he could see the same around her wrists, where she was tied to the chair arms.

"Lila," Jones said again. He crouched down and gingerly lifted her chin. Her eyes remained closed. Jones felt for a pulse next.

It was there.

Barely.

"Hang in there, Lila," he told the unconscious woman.

He took his phone out again and immediately backtracked through the house toward the front door. There was no way Keith had done that. Something else was going on.

Dispatch answered when he was next to the stairs.

Jones barked out for an ambulance and assistance, but didn't get to finish explaining what he'd found.

The front door burst open and Cassandra ran in.

She was dragging Keith and yelling.

"Jones!"

It was the only thing she could get out before Jones focused on her reason for running.

Jimmy was behind her, gun out.

Jones reacted on instinct.

He dropped his phone and ran at Jimmy, and in the

space between put himself in front of Cassandra and Keith's backs.

Jimmy's eyes widened at the sight of Jones coming to meet him. Still, he looked as though he was about to pull the trigger.

There were cons to being well over six feet tall, but there were definite pros, too. In this case it meant a large wingspan and strides that got him to where he needed to be faster than the average man.

Jones made it to the gun before Jimmy could squeeze a bullet off. He managed to push the man's arm up just enough that the bullet went into the entryway ceiling and not Jones or the two he was protecting behind him.

Jimmy tried to correct his misfire but Jones wasn't having it.

He threw a left hook so hard it knocked the man off balance. He released his hold on the gun. It clattered against the hardwood.

Jimmy staggered back as Jones went for it.

This time he could see the knife coming.

Jimmy let out a war cry much like he had in the interrogation room at the department and struck out. Jones jumped back to avoid the hit, but ran into a wall.

Jimmy ran the knife deep into his shoulder.

Jones yelled out in pain and Jimmy had the audacity to gloat.

"Killing you will be as nice as killing her," he sneered, pushing the knife with all that he had.

Too bad for him he'd chosen very poor last words.

Jones wrapped his hand around Jimmy's holding the knife. Instead of trying to push off the man, Jones kept him there.

Once again, that wingspan was saving the day.

Jones used his other hand to grab Jimmy's head. His thumb pressed into the man's eyeball.

Jimmy yelled out in pain and tried to pull away, but Jones held him fast. He clawed at Jones's hand on his face.

"Nothing but small men hurt women," Jones growled.

He let go of Jimmy's hand and face, and the man staggered back, still yelling.

Jones knew his wingspan well, his stride, and his resolve to see that bad men like Jimmy never got a second chance.

But what he knew most of all, had spent his entire life learning?

It was how powerful he could be when he wanted.

Jones stood to his full height and brought up his fist.

"But big men like me have no problem returning the favor."

Jones wanted a knockout and that's exactly what he got.

His fist collided with Jimmy in a spectacular crack.

The other man crumpled to the ground in an instant.

Jones didn't waste time. He got the discarded gun and took it apart just as quickly.

"Cassandra?" he called out. "Are you okay?"

Movement from the room across from him caught his eye. Cassandra nodded; Keith's hands could be seen around her.

Her eyes widened. She clutched at her shoulder.

"Are you okay?" she asked, voice wobbling.

Jones turned and pulled the knife from him. He sucked in a breath.

"Yeah, I'm okay, just a little—"

Footsteps hit the porch.

Jones kept the knife in his hand and raised it, turning once again to block Cassandra and Keith from view.

This time, the man holding the gun held it with distance in mind.

Ray's face turned as pale as a ghost as he stopped outside of the opened front door.

He didn't even look down at Jimmy's prone body between him and Jones when he spoke.

"They got Lottie, Sheriff. Took her from my hands like it was nothing." Ray's voice shook, but not enough to suggest he was about to break. He was steady, deliberate.

Jones didn't understand.

"Who took her? And how?"

Ray moved his head from side to side, but kept his aim true.

"I don't know. She got discharged from the hospital and we were at her house and one second she was there, the next she wasn't. Then I got a call and a man told me only one way to get her back." Ray continued to calmly hold the gun. But now, he moved it to the side and aimed it right at Cassandra and Keith. "I take her with me now and give you a chance to get her back later, or he takes your daughter and you'll never see her again."

Jones's heart dropped.

Ray didn't look pleased with his words.

He said as much.

"If it isn't me holding this gun, it'll be someone else, and there's nothing the two of us can do about it."

"You can put the gun down," Jones yelled out. He realized he'd never hung up his phone.

Where was it?

Was Dispatch hearing this?

Ray shook his head. He changed his gaze to Cassandra. He also changed his aim back to Jones.

"He can get you back later. If you don't come with me

now, then he'll never leave this house." To put a deadly emphasis on his words, he cocked the gun.

"Wait! No, stop!"

Cassandra's footsteps were fast. Jones reached out to her. Blood from his hand skimmed along her jacket in the process. It was a horrible contrast.

"No, Cassandra," Jones growled, but she was looking at Ray.

"How does he get me back?"

Ray opened his mouth, but someone else spoke over him. Someone from behind them.

A woman.

Jones wanted to turn his head to look at the new voice, but Ray still had his gun on him. If he decided to use it, Jones had to be ready to react.

"Ray Cooke, you put your gun down right now or it'll be you who doesn't leave this house," she said. "You and I both know that Lottie would rip you into two if you used a pregnant woman and a child as a bargaining chip for her."

"He'll kill her," Ray said, visibly breaking. "He said he would if I didn't do what he wanted."

The voice got closer.

It was strong and as steady as steel.

"It might be in his name, but Killian won't touch a hair on that woman's head. He's been in love with her since he first set eyes on her when they were kids. The only people he's planning on killing are you, me and these two love-birds and their kids. If you help him now, then you're only hurting the same people who are going to help get Lottie back. So put that gun down so I don't have to shoot you in front of this kid. He's already going to have nightmares because of this idiot Jimmy."

Whether for effect or not, Cassandra put her hand on her stomach, cradling their unborn son.

Ray eyed the move.

Then he dropped his arm and let the gun go loose.

"Now, give that to Sheriff Murphy here. And, Keith? Could you take these to the sheriff to use on Ray there?"

Keith made a noise that must have been a yes. Soon after Jones felt his hand and something cold in his.

They were handcuffs.

"I'm sure you have some in your car, but I don't want you getting a chance to run off or fight me yet. So go ahead and make sure Ray doesn't make any other foolish decisions in the name of love. And, Ray, I'm going to need you to slide that gun off the porch before he gets to you, okay?"

Jones didn't like the orders, but he followed them. He wasn't the only one. The gun was already sliding away from Jones as he took Ray's arms and put them behind his back. He cuffed the man's wrists. When he turned back around the woman had positioned herself directly behind Cassandra, obscuring her face.

But not her voice.

"Now, Sheriff, I want you to bring Ray inside here and shut the door because I already have some bad news for you and we need to talk it out."

Jones stood still. He'd had enough. His shoulder ached, his head filled with angry resolve.

"I'm not moving until you tell me who you are. Plain and simple."

Cassandra nodded to him, agreeing with the directive.

The woman, who he expected to fight it, let out a low sigh. She took a step to the side so Jones could finally see her face.

In that moment he felt a lot of things.

But, all he could say was a name.

"Annie McHale."

The woman smiled.

"In the flesh."

Chapter Twenty

Seeing a ghost would have been less jarring; seeing Annie McHale, alive, after six years, had the room so shocked that only the sheriff could break the silence.

And even then, Cassandra heard the great effort behind his words.

"This is Annie McHale," Jones said to the group that had formed in the room around them. Although she needed no introduction. They were all locals. They had known Annie for most of their lives. "Along with me and Cassandra, you now are the only people who know she's alive."

Jones didn't take his eyes off Annie. He hadn't since she'd shown herself. He wasn't the only one. Cassandra looked around Jones's father's living room and the people who had been contacted by Jones over the last fifteen minutes. All were law enforcement. Specifically from his department.

Lily Howard had an open face, but her brow was drawn—she was ready to take in whatever was said with great detail. Kenneth Gray was right there with her, standing with his arms crossed over his chest, jaw tight. Foster Lovett was in his street clothes with an impassive face, his wife, Millie, at his side, though she had originally come for Keith, who was with Bonnie in her room, and he was all worry. Kathryn Juliet was at their side, standing.

And angry.

It radiated off her so clearly that Jones had given her a quick word as everyone filed in.

Carlos, a man she'd only ever seen as even-tempered, looked stuck between being professional and joining Juliet.

Sterling Costner rounded out the group. His cowboy hat softened his severe expression, but only a little.

Then there was Jones Murphy, Sheriff.

Cassandra already knew what it meant to see Annie, alive.

He didn't know if the town's golden star was the bad guy or not.

And it was eating him up while he was having to force himself to listen and let that someone take control for a little bit.

Annie knew she held that power, too.

Cassandra could see it in her demeanor.

How had she gone from the girl who triggered The Flood to the young woman sitting in front of them like they were at a normal social event?

Annie, to her credit, addressed Jones with a more respectful tone than she'd given Ray.

Ray had been squirreled away to the department by Deputy Rossi, even though he still wanted to search for Lottie, while Lila and Jimmy had gone to the hospital with Deputy Marigold. As per Annie's request, and Jones's great hesitance, they were keeping the incident quiet.

For now.

All he'd managed was the barest of medical treatment for his shoulder from one of the EMTs who had shown up at Lila's. It was a quick bandaging job followed by a promise to Cassandra that he'd get it checked out more thoroughly as soon as possible.

"There's a few other people who actually know I'm

alive," Annie began. "Of those, Killian Carmichael is our real problem."

"Who is he?" Jones's voice was even. He'd found calmness.

Annie didn't hesitate.

"He's my brother."

Everyone stayed quiet, but there were a lot of heads turning this way and that.

"I've never heard anything about the McHales having another child," Jones responded.

"I missed the news, too. Killian isn't just the skeleton in my family's closet. He's the graveyard." Annie didn't have her gun anymore, but she didn't need it to have their rapt attention.

"I found out about Killian by accident," she continued. "My parents were arguing. This, despite public opinion, was a common thing in our house, but when I realized it was them arguing about moving out of Kelby Creek, I listened. My mom didn't want to go but my father kept on, saying that we could all just leave it behind. I was young and dumb and self-absorbed, so I thought they were talking about leaving silly things behind. Pageants, town fairs, ribbon cuttings, that kind of thing. But then, my mom said that they couldn't just leave 'him' behind."

Annie laughed. It wasn't in humor.

"It drove me crazy. That one little word. Like a song you can't get out of your head or an actor's name you just can't place. So I tried to figure it out. I asked them directly, at first, which only really sold me on digging deeper. My dad blew up. My mom got so nervous she knocked over a new glass of sweet tea. After that I noticed they also started keeping a better eye on me. I couldn't go two steps without needing a handful of excuses."

She shook her head.

"They kept acting so weird that I started looking into them. A hard thing to do to the most *beloved* couple in all of town." Her words were angry. She almost spit them before returning to her normal tenor. "But, being who I was and having money definitely helped. I found my way into not one secret but tons of them. My 'flood' happened months before yours, I just didn't realize how bad it was until I found him. Killian Carmichael, a teenager locked away in a mental health facility partially owned by his parents."

She snorted.

"Once you've pulled the curtain back on the lovely McHales, you realize that one of the problems of their *generosity* is that they somehow now own almost everything. Every gift, every good deed, was them trying to tip the scales of karma in their favor for when the world finally found out about their long-hidden son."

"Why keep him hidden?" Jones's voice was deep. It shook the room out of the trancelike state they'd fallen into.

Annie didn't seem to mind.

"He was the product of an affair by my mother," she answered. "Not the most original soap-opera-y thing to happen in this town, but it was enough to send my father into deep resentment. It only helped matters that as Killian got older he showed some sociopathic tendencies. As far as I could find, he lived at the house when I was little until he was moved to New Beginnings."

"The bunker."

Cassandra said it without question.

Annie nodded.

"If the McHales say they're building a storm shelter, who's going to question them? The town who loves them?" She snorted again. "But I didn't know any of this until after I'd already found Killian. He knew who I was instantly.

Told me that our parents were the crazy ones and that I wasn't safe as long as I stayed with them. I believed him. After all, they'd been lying to me my whole life. I went to visit Killian every week and he spent those moments telling me about all the bad he'd learned about them. About how we were going to come up with a plan to help him escape or convict them so we could be free together."

For the first time, Annie looked wistful.

Sad.

Wishing for a different outcome to a story that was about to get bad.

"Then, one day, he said he'd been out. That escaping for him was possible. I didn't believe him until Lottie showed up. She didn't know I was there. I listened as he talked to her about the Rosewater Motel murders. I could hear her tone change, saw her face. Just like I saw Killian, and I knew. I knew that while my parents lied, they hadn't lied about everything."

"He killed them." Kenneth was the one who spoke this time.

Annie nodded.

"And then, I made another mistake." She looked at Jones directly. "I told my godfather."

"Sheriff Barkley." Jones had ground out the name.

The man who had betrayed the entire department, the entire town.

She nodded.

"He said he'd handle it and I went back the next morning to see if Killian was still there," she said. "He wasn't, but the sheriff was."

Annie paused and seemed to consider her next words.

"I know my being here, alive, might make a lot of you here angry," she said after a moment. "That if I'm walking around like nothing ever happened, then who did the kidnapping? If I wasn't really taken, then that means some of you lost a lot." Her eyes trailed back to Jones. They were shining. "But I'm here to tell you, he really did take me and I really did try to escape. I just couldn't until they grabbed Jackie."

No one spoke for a moment.

Cassandra knew that being the only one who wasn't a local gave her an emotional advantage. She spoke up and no one seemed against it.

"The FBI agent who went missing, you mean."

Annie nodded.

"She figured out the sheriff was behind it and then she was drugged. They put her in a chair next to me and she fought them off with everything she had. She told me to run and—and I did. I never saw her after that. But I tell you, I've spent all these years looking."

Cassandra stood, her hand on her belly. She wanted answers for the people around her. The one that could change everyone's minds about the woman.

"And what else were you doing all these years, Annie? Why not come forward and tell your story?"

Annie opened and closed her mouth, twice. She dropped her chin a little. For a moment, she truly looked like a girl, lost and alone.

"I didn't know who to trust after The Flood, especially with Killian out there. So I left for a while. I waited to see what the investigations would bring up…but then nothing happened. I realized that everyone here was working with half of the board, they couldn't see the whole picture because this town put one family on a pedestal so high up they never thought to do anything but praise them." Annie was crying now. Tears ran down her cheeks, but her voice was strong. "So when my parents left town—no doubt knowing exactly what happened to me and worried that it would come back on them—I came back to help the only way I thought I could. In the background, as a ghost."

"You've been in Kelby Creek, trying to help us, for six years?" Foster asked.

Annie nodded.

"Then what made you come out now?" Carlos asked next.

Annie's whole demeanor changed. It hardened. She wiped at her tears with her hand.

"Two sheriffs came to this house and I knew that they were going to ask Jones to be the next one." She adjusted her gaze to Jones. "And I knew you'd accept. Just like I knew you'd look into my kidnapping again. It seemed like a full-circle kind of sign and time to come forward. I guess Killian got wind of it and decided the same. I've been trying to figure out what he's planning while also being a step or two behind."

"You wrote the note at New Beginnings."

Annie shook her head.

"No. He did. But when he let me let you and Lottie out, I finally realized what he wants."

"He wants us to know you're alive." It wasn't a question. Jones's words were definite.

"I think he wants to come out of the shadows, condemn our family and use me as the catalyst. I think that's why he's using other people for his dirty work. Trying to keep his hands as clean as possible. I'd bet he already has someone framed up for it."

"And he can't come out of the shadows if we know what he looks like," Jones added.

"And me and Lottie are the only people who have seen him," Cassandra realized. "That's why he took her. Why he wants me."

Jones growled.

Annie spoke before he could follow that with words.

"This is where the bad news I was talking about comes in."

"You mean none of this has been bad news?" Carlos asked.

Annie ignored the comment.

She was back to Jones.

"Killian is smart. He's going to see this through. The only way we can stop him and make every McHale pay for what they've done—what they've covered up—through the years… Ray already told you where he was supposed to take Cassandra. Why not see it through?"

Jones shook his head in one aggressive no.

He went taut with tension.

"No way am I taking her there."

Cassandra knew his immediate dismissal was more than warranted. Ray had admitted he was supposed to exchange Cassandra for Lottie at the park.

The same one where the ransom exchange and ambush happened all those years ago.

The same place where his wife had been killed.

It was a hard ask and maybe that was why Killian had chosen it.

The park was a sore spot for most of the town.

"If we just go in guns blazing, he might run. He might not even be there."

"He might also shoot her on sight."

Annie stood up. She pointed to Cassandra.

"He needs her first. He needs her to draw me out, just like he did when he left that note at New Beginnings. He knew I wasn't going to stay hidden when I saw he'd taken her and Lottie. He'll only get her after I'm out in the open and we're all going to make sure that doesn't happen."

"Then go reveal yourself to him," Jones growled. "If

he wants to draw you out, just step up and let him see you! No need to put anyone else at risk." His frustration was palpable.

Annie shook her head.

"That's not how he works. He's not some rational man. It's his way or no way. We either play his game or it's game over for Lottie. I wish it wasn't the case but, it is. We need Cassandra if we want Lottie. If we want him."

Jones was violent with the no this time. His voice was concrete.

Yet that's not what made his words so startling.

"I am *not* losing another woman I love to that place, especially not when she's carrying our son."

The room, minus Annie, quieted.

Those from the sheriff's department weren't coy with their looks of surprise.

Cassandra wasn't coy with hers, either.

Annie, though, didn't care.

She wanted justice.

She wanted six years of her life alone to matter.

She wanted the town that broke because of her family to find some kind of peace.

And, by God, if Cassandra didn't want that for her.

For all of them.

For the man she'd fallen for the second he'd agreed to play the question game in that hotel.

For their future, their son, Bonnie, Ted, Keith…

Cassandra took a step forward. She placed her hand on Jones's arm.

Her words were as strong and definite as his.

"I'm going." Jones turned, mouth already opening, but she shook her head. "But only if you can answer this question honestly."

Cassandra nodded to the room behind them.

The men and women with badges who'd spent the last six years trying to redeem the department once riddled with corruption and betrayal.

"Do you trust *them*?"

Jones didn't like the question.

But, perhaps, he disliked the answer more.

"Yes."

Cassandra turned to Annie.

"Then let's do this."

Chapter Twenty-One

The park was beautiful. Always had been.

Good for walking, great for playing, the best for picnics.

That's why Helen had been waiting for him that day, on the grass, straightening out a picnic blanket next to the lunch she'd made for them. She didn't know about the ransom exchange and he hadn't known she was there.

Until it was too late.

Now, he had no excuse.

He knew what was happening and yet there Cassandra was, walking over the grass with Ray Cooke at her side.

"You can't control everything that happens," she had told him before they left. "No one person can. I want to do this. I want this all to end so we can be safe. So our kids can be safe. If me showing up does that, you need to let me."

"She'll be okay." Carlos was down to a whisper. That was the rule. If this plan was going to work, they needed to be like Annie.

They needed to be ghosts.

Jones kept watching Cassandra.

She was walking toward him.

Because everyone in the sheriff's department was currently hiding in the woods, the surrounding businesses and the park itself. Killian didn't realize it, but there was about to be a second ambush at the park, this time with the good guys in the lead.

At least, Jones hoped.

He believed Annie and her story. He just did. Right down in his gut.

To his surprise, though, it was a mutual feeling among his friends.

They'd gone to working on the plan faster than he'd ever seen them work.

Ray was released and told to play his part, saying that he and Cassandra had to hide from deputies until the coast was clear to come to the park, as if he'd lured Cassandra. They used an all-points bulletin for her along with one for him. Meanwhile, deputies were scouring the town everywhere but the park to look for them.

On the outside, it looked like Ray's plan had worked.

Jones just hoped it stayed that way until Annie could trap him.

Carlos tapped his elbow.

Cassandra and Ray were almost to the set of benches closest to the tree line.

Jones took out his gun and waited.

Carlos started looking around them while Jones watched Cassandra and Ray sit down on one of the benches.

Five minutes went by.

Then a few more.

Carlos tapped his elbow again, but this time with force.

Someone was walking through the woods next to them.

It was Lottie.

And a man Jones was guessing was Killian Carmichael.

He looked just like Annie but a bit taller and with long dark hair.

Snake in the grass was what came to Jones's mind at the sight of him. That and several other derogatory terms.

Killian was too confident. He was smirking as he pushed poor Lottie along.

He kept that smirk tight as Annie walked up, cutting him off from Cassandra and Ray.

"Well, well, I was wondering when the golden child would show." Killian's voice carried. "For a second I thought you were going to let me take the poor pregnant teacher without any fuss. Not very like you."

Annie's anger was real.

Her calm was, too.

She was ready for this.

So were they.

A text came in and lit up Carlos's phone.

Carlos repeated the message so low Jones barely heard it.

"Sterling found a silver Taurus across the street. A man is inside. They're surrounding it, but won't move until we say."

Jones nodded.

Good.

Annie had said there were two men working directly with Killian as far as she could tell. Jimmy and the man with the Taurus.

If they had them handled, then all that was left was Annie and Killian.

The siblings had finally stopped across from one another, but left enough space to show that they weren't about to trust that the other didn't have a weapon ready. Jones was surprised that Killian, for all of his planning, didn't have a gun out.

Then again, he thought he had the upper hand with Ray holding Cassandra.

"What do you want from me?" Annie asked. "What could I possibly give you that you don't already have?

Mom and Dad already give you money to keep you away from them. You haven't been caught for the murders you've committed, the crimes you've helped orchestrate and fund. I mean, no one even knows who *you* are, Killian. You could leave now, let Lottie and Cassandra go, and never look back at Kelby Creek again. What could you possibly want?"

Killian wasted no time.

His answer was boiling.

"I want them to know *me*."

Jones almost stood as Killian pulled a gun.

Annie didn't flinch as her brother pointed it at her.

"I want them to see what I see, what I've seen," he continued. "I want this whole town to realize they've been worshiping the wrong McHales. That it's time they get to know me. The son who's spent his entire life trying to build a legacy that will crush Mom and Dad's. A legacy that shows I triumphed in the face of absolute adversity."

From his hiding spot, Jones could see the man's smirk rise again.

Killian's gun was on Annie.

"One that truly begins when I finally show the world just how wrong they've been about little Annie McHale. The girl who could have shown herself for years but instead let everyone suffer." He laughed. "But I suppose you already guessed how this little meeting was going to go. Which means you must already know how they'll treat you."

His smirk dropped.

"So are you here to join me, Annie, and beg for forgiveness? Or are you here to try and save the day?"

Jones stood to his full height. He nodded to Carlos.

Killian aimed his gun.

Annie took a second.

Then she smiled.

"I think the sheriff can save the day just fine."

A lot of things happened all at once.

Carlos told Sterling to get the man in the Taurus.

Cassandra, who was connected to Jones by Bluetooth earbuds and an open phone line, yelled to Ray to run.

Lottie, of her own instincts, ducked down.

And Jones, the Dawn County Sheriff, took one precise shot.

The sound ricocheted through the forest around them.

Killian Carmichael dropped to the ground, screaming.

Annie picked up his gun and Carlos rushed over with his.

Jones followed.

"Are you okay?" Cassandra's voice was in his ear, and it was the most beautiful sound he'd ever heard.

Before Jones could answer, the woods had men and women running inside to meet them, all guns pointed toward Killian.

"Are you okay?" Jones asked her instead.

"I'm okay."

Jones smiled at the men and women around him, then to Annie.

His trust had paid off.

He let out a sigh of relief.

"Then I'm okay, too."

A YEAR WENT BY.

Then three more.

Joshua was born, Keith was adopted and Bonnie finally got her a sister when Adriene came into the world one late night in November. Their family grew when his father married Megan Hamilton and, finally, it was time for Jones to fulfill an old dream and build a house big enough for all of the family and friends they had collected over the last four years.

It was that house that they were standing in now, party food out, music playing softly, that had them all laughing together.

Foster came in with Millie and their three kids, Carlos and Dr. Amanda Alvarez helped carry the baby. Amanda was pregnant with twins and Carlos had the sonogram framed on his desk next to their wedding picture. Marco Rossi, now captain at the department, came in with his wife, Bella, and their kids ran straight to Keith and Bonnie's rooms the second their feet were in the door. With Millie's help they'd adopted a brood of their own, two of their kids the same age as Bonnie and Keith.

Marigold and her boyfriend puttered in next, all tangled up in laughter with Sterling and his wife, Mel. Their daughters went to Bonnie's room faster than the earlier kids had. Kenneth and Willa's son at least said hi before he jetted off. Willa rubbed her pregnant belly and laughed at them.

"The only reason he stops and says hello is because of Lily and Ant's kids," she said. "Honest to goodness, they try to make everyone they meet smile."

Sure enough, when Lily and Anthony showed, their six kids sounded almost rehearsed as they yelled off hellos and how-do-you-dos.

Ant let out a loud boom of a laugh as Marigold explained why the rest of them were laughing.

Ray and Lottie came out of the kitchen, wondering what the fuss was all about. June and her wife yelled loudly over it all to say they were crazy for the sheer amount of children in the house, but Jones heard the smiles in it. Lila had once joined in with the mock jeering at so many kids but now she and her new husband, Charlie, were working on their second.

His dad, someone who thrived in a kid-filled house apparently, showed up with Megan and the party went on for a while as the best kind of chaos and noise.

Then the doorbell rang and most of the adults quieted when Jones answered the door.

"Sorry, I'm late."

Annie McHale sported a smile. It was one that Jones had come to recognize as sincere.

"Before I come inside, I was wondering if I could talk to you first?"

Jones, who'd had Adriene hanging on his leg, nodded to Cassandra. She swooped in with Joshua already on her and told Annie hello.

Annie returned the greeting and then waited for Jones to lead them to the corner of the wraparound porch.

In the last four years, she'd been through a lot.

Not as much as the six years before that, of course.

But enough.

After the recording of Killian admitting to what he'd done had come out, Annie had, too. What followed was an investigation into her, Killian and the rest of the McHale family that garnered no nickname, as The Flood had done.

Annie had been telling the truth.

So had Killian.

It took until his trial but he finally found a place he couldn't escape. He cooperated to reduce his sentence and, in the process, implicated his mother and father in several cover-ups and financial schemes that benefited them and them alone.

They'd also admitted, when their time came, that they had thought Killian had killed Annie and had been paying him for years to keep him away from them.

Jasmine Lohan had been brought in too for her involvement with Killian but had been given a deal for any information she'd had on him. He'd used her to try and get Annie through Cassandra but he'd also threatened her children in the process. No one, not even Jones and Cassandra, had ever blamed her for her part in the ruse.

She'd also implicated the man in the Taurus, Brandon Ross. He'd gone to school with her as a teenager and had struck up a friendship with Killian through the years. He hadn't cooperated and neither had Jimmy when it was his time to talk. It was only when Nan came forward that she admitted her brother had spent the last few years after The Flood growing more and more angry. He'd often said that he'd played by the rules that had been forced on him by the law for decades and The Flood had shown him his innocence had been pointless. So, he'd tried to move on but every few months it seemed like the town was dragged back to the investigation into Annie McHale. Nan had admitted they'd both hated when that had happened. They'd agreed that it had sometimes felt like the sheriff's department was dragging the whole town back into the bad, making them suffer old wounds on repeat.

"I think all Jimmy had wanted to do was make y'all stop forcing us to relive it all," Nan had said. "He was trying to save the town."

Her testimony hadn't helped her brother. He'd tried to kill people, including a pregnant woman. There was no amount of good intention in that.

The trials had gone on for two years regardless. They were made all the more complicated when the body of Agent Ortega had been found buried on the McHale property.

The investigation into Annie herself had ended that morning.

"I'm going to leave," she said now to Jones. "I've decided it's time to find my place in this world and it's not in Kelby Creek. Not anymore. I just wanted to be the first to tell you since you've done so much for me. You and Cassie. Thank you."

Jones had been expecting this. He didn't blame her for trying for a new start. Still, he was sad to see her go. He said as much.

"It'll be a lot less interesting without you around. I know we're all going to miss you."

Annie was still having trouble when it came to being vulnerable, but he saw her cheeks redden at the affection. Jones wanted to make sure she knew how much she really meant to the group.

He nodded back to the house.

"You hear all that in there?" he asked. "The yelling and general wildness of kids and their grown-ups?"

Annie laughed and nodded.

"That is, in a way, because of you. Because of what you did through the years. You helped all of us, at some point. Now, we're loud and outnumbered and, well, this town doesn't deserve you anymore, Annie, and I think there's some beauty in that."

Jones put a hand on her shoulder.

"I can't wait to see where you go next."

Annie was all blush.

She looked back at the house.

Cassandra had come outside.

"Sorry, I didn't want to interrupt, Jones, but Marco said he needs your help. Keith and Jordan might have gotten their heads stuck in the banister again."

Annie laughed.

"That I have to see." Annie walked back to the house, but Jones caught Cassandra's hand.

She was close enough to kiss, so he did.

It was perfect.

"So you want me to go rescue some kids from our banister again, huh? I guess I have to. We do have a code, after all."

Cassandra nodded.

She kissed him one more time.

"Pirate's code," she said.

He laughed.

"Pirate's code."

* * * * *

COLTON COUNTDOWN

TARA TAYLOR QUINN

This book is for Holli Anne. I've been waiting for a heroine that I thought you'd be proud of, and I think Suzy is it! She's an awesome mom, an amazing person and is stronger than even she knows. Basically a rock-star human, like you! Thank you for being my beautiful, rule-breaking moth and also the best Anne out there. Love you to the moon and back, Perkins/Knope!

Chapter One

Ezra Colton's chin hit his chest and he jerked awake. Every muscle tensed, he quickly assessed his immediate danger level to be zero and relaxed back into the quite comfy-for-his-big-shoulders chair, in his great-aunt's lovely, homey room. Glancing across at the woman who'd been mostly dozing in a matching chair during the entirety of his afternoon visit, he noticed she was also awake and staring at him.

His smile was immediate, and he tried to shrug off her lack of response. His siblings, his mom, had all warned him that his aunt's memory loss had drastically worsened since he'd last been home. Still, fingers tapping on bare knees beneath the army-green shorts he'd pulled out of his duffel that morning, he couldn't accept that she didn't know him. At least a little bit.

"It's pretty hot outside," he offered, looking her right in the eye. "People are grumbling a bit, but after being in Afghanistan, I'm fine with the heat. You remember that time I went tubing in the river without Mom and Dad's permission and ripped my swim trunks on that tree limb? I came straight to you. You had me change into some of Uncle's old shorts, and you fixed those trunks for me. And then told me to go home and tell my parents what I'd done."

Not a snippet of response. Of any kind of recognition, even.

But she was still looking straight at him. So he kept chatting until she dozed off again. Figured he needed to get his lumbering butt up and active. A month of leave could make a guy soft, and no way he was letting his men down. His sergeant stripes were way more than uniform decoration, and he'd die before dishonoring them.

Still…a few more minutes to relax… That was what leave was for, right?

What did it say about him that he was more relaxed hanging out in a room at the Sunshine Senior Home than with most of the siblings who'd all, for once, gathered in the same town at the same time for his big brother Caleb's wedding?

The home—at least, the wing where Aunt Alice's room was located—might be filled with memory-care patients, but there was order to the day, to the rooms and the patients who wandered in them. You knew what to expect and how to deal with it.

Unlike the chaos and drama that attached to his huge, well-known family like bees on honey. And sometimes stung like bees, too.

But…did sitting there make him a coward? He ran a hand across the top of his close-cropped hair. Stood, stretching muscles that, while difficult to fit into some shirts, served him well, and glanced again at his greataunt. When she was sleeping, she looked…as he remembered her. Like herself. The vacant stare when she was awake…

His mom had been right. He hadn't been prepared.

He should just go. It wasn't like she'd know—or remember that he'd been there. Still, she was Aunt Alice. He couldn't just walk out on her.

With a hand on the back of her chair, he bent to kiss her cheek like he'd done every time he'd left her since he was a little kid, moving slowly so he didn't startle her. And then, with a hard bump in the butt from behind, nearly fell over.

"What the…?" Swinging around, his first instinct to defend and protect, he had an arm half raised in front of him as he shielded his aunt with his body and had to drop his gaze to meet that of his attacker.

Big brown eyes gazed soulfully up at him from a mutt's tilted, light brown head. Before he could even drop his arm, a very young voice, in a place filled with old voices, called out, "Charlie!"

And two dark-haired urchins appeared in the doorway. "Charlie!" The girls, in identical sundresses and sandals, didn't even seem to notice him as they hurried straight to the errant dog. "We're really sorry, sir." The child with braids and holding a book spoke up. The other one, wearing her long straight hair down, patted Charlie on the head.

"He doesn't like it when someone claps at him, and he ran off," the bookless one of the two of them—and, he noted, the one without freckles as well—added to the first's apology.

With virtually zip experience around children—his little niece, Iris, didn't count because she was only a few months old, still just sleeping, eating and being held, and because with his career mostly out of the country, he'd only seen her, sleeping both times, in the few days he'd been home—Ezra was mesmerized by the pair, clearly sisters and most likely twins, until a slight movement caught the corner of his eye—and his attention.

Charlie had a paw on the edge of Aunt Alice's chair, and her hand moved to cover it. His gaze rose slowly from that gesture to his aunt's face, and he could hardly believe the small smile he saw there. He'd been there a couple of hours with no sign of life from the woman other than a blank stare, but Charlie had a response out of her in less than two minutes.

Bookless was reaching for the dog's collar.

"I'm a triplet," he blurted, grabbing her attention before she pulled the animal away. Even if the girls weren't twins, they were dressed alike as though someone wanted them to be. "And I have three sets of twins for brothers and sisters," he added, as though someone was adding up multiple birth values.

"We're twins," Bookless told him, her little fingers resting on her dog's neck. And not holding the collar. "We were born at the same time," she added.

"I'm Claire and she's Neve," the girl with braids told him. Her adorable freckles made him want to smile at her. And he might have if she hadn't worn such a serious expression. "We aren't supposed to be in here."

"We can't help it, Claire," Neve said, shrugging. "We had to get Charlie. Claire was reading to Mrs. Sally and Mr. Bo, and I've heard the story a gazillion times—" she rolled her eyes "—but I like the part where Flow—that's the smaller horse who everyone thinks can't win—gets ahead of everyone else because she's trying harder—and I guess I forgot to hold Charlie's collar tight enough right when Mrs. Sally clapped for Flow and, well, what's a triplet?"

"It's three instead of two, Neve," Claire said. "We're two. Triplets is three. But—" she peered up at him, nose scrunched "—what's three twins?"

"Three sets of twins, right, mister?" Neve said. "And that's…" Letting go of Charlie, she held up the fingers on one hand, pointing with her other to individual fingers as she tried to count to two, three times.

"One, two, one, two, one, two," Claire butted in then, holding up a finger each time she named a one or a two, and then looking at the total of held-up fingers when she was done. "You have six twin brothers and sisters?"

"That's right." He nodded, noticing that Aunt Alice's hand was moving atop the paw still resting on her chair, as though Charlie knew that the lost old woman needed him.

"Six kids being born at once?" Neve burst out, her voice rising markedly by the end of the question.

"Just two at once," he said. "Remember, that's twins. Two born at once. They were born three different times, years apart."

"Is triplets years apart, too?" Claire asked.

"Nope," he told her, suddenly enjoying the moment of diversion more than he had anything else since getting off the plane in Denver. "It's three born at the same time."

"You have two more of you born at once?" Neve asked, giggling.

Thinking of Dom and Oliver, he couldn't in any way see his brothers as two more of him. He and his fellow triplets were very different guys. But he ended with, "Yep," because the girls seemed so delighted by the thought.

"Two against one," Claire said. "That's what sometimes happens if someone wants to play with Neve but not me. Is that what happened to you?"

"I always say you can play, Claire. You just sometimes want to read."

Not sure if he was still required to answer the question Claire had posed, but certain that he didn't want to do so, he asked her, "Are you the younger or older twin?"

"I'm younger," Claire said, her gaze serious.

"I'm her big sister by two minutes!" Neve chimed in, standing next to her sister to gaze up at him. "But I'm a little person. You sure are big," she said. "Almost like a giant."

"Are your other triplets as big as you?" Claire, full of questions, apparently, asked.

"My older triplet—" he used her word for him and his brothers "—is named Dom, and he's taller than me by one inch. And the younger one, his name's Oliver, is my same height, but he's a little skinnier than I am." Lean, Oliver was lean.

"Oliver?" Neve asked, her nose scrunching up as the lilt in her voice rose. And then she giggled. "He's a cat! And him and Jenny are together forever, just like Claire and me."

When Ezra stood there, his brain racing trying to figure out the reference, Claire said, "Did you ever watch *Oliver & Company*, mister?"

The Disney movie. Right. Had he ever seen it?

"You're like a sandwich." Neve popped back into the conversation, once again sparing him from Claire's question. "Smooshed in the middle of two more!" she pronounced, clearly pleased with herself. "A giant sandwich."

He followed the conversation, and also noticed something pretty cool going on apart from the girls. Aunt Alice's hand rose to Charlie's head, her fingers moving slightly. Wanting to prolong her enjoyment, and unable to come up with any interesting reply to a giant sandwich, he motioned toward the book that Claire had been hugging to her chest since they'd come in. "So your book's about a horse named Flow?"

She held it up, showing him the cover. *Flow Goes to the Races.* The title was in bold purple-and-pink lettering.

"I have a brother and sister, one of the pairs of the twins I told you about, who run a ranch, the Gemini, and they have horseback riding. Have you been there?"

The question gained him identical shakes of two little heads, in tandem. And while Neve stepped back beside Charlie's head again, Claire pointed to Aunt Alice. "You want me to read it to her?"

"Sure, if you want to," he said, as another movement caught his eye. This one from the doorway—a woman hovered there, just off to the side, mostly out of sight.

For the first time since the kids had appeared in his great-aunt's room, he wondered why two young girls were roaming freely through the halls of the memory-care unit.

And had a feeling he was about to find out.

And perhaps get chewed out as well, for engaging with them.

Figuring he'd much rather have it be him than them, he invited Claire to start reading and backed slowly toward the door.

SHE'D BEEN MADE. Dealing with all the feels, Theresa Fitzgerald stepped farther back from the door, but not so far she couldn't still hear her daughter's sweet, so serious voice as she read her beloved story to the memory-care patient. She'd never have believed it was possible to love anyone as much as she loved her twins.

And she most certainly hadn't expected to be caught eavesdropping—by one of the gorgeous Coltons, no less. Embarrassment joined the flood, but there was so much more. Her girls...the ease in their tones, the innocent, unfiltered chattiness...

As she came down the hallway, the sounds had stopped her in her tracks.

She hadn't heard them talking like this since their father died...

Mark.

A year later, and she still lived with the gaping hole his death had left in their lives.

But the girls... She'd had to see who'd managed to elicit natural engagement with them...who'd had the ability to draw them out of whatever darkness had held them captive. Even if just for a moment...

"Are you...?" The man broke off, his gaze going to the badge she wore pinned just above her left breast. "Oh...you manage this place? I sincerely apologize here," he continued on, his blue eyes meeting hers with none of the complexity or veils she'd have assumed a Colton man would wear naturally. "I know I should have sent these girls out immediately, the second they came into the room to retrieve their runaway dog, but…" He glanced at her badge again. "Senior Care Manager?" he asked.

To which she nodded, intending to say more, but he said, "Then you know Alice," nodding at the scene playing out in the room. "Maybe you see this all the time, you know, if the dog is a regular or something, and Alice always responds this way. But from what my mom told me, my aunt is almost always little more than a breathing statue, showing no reaction or awareness at all, and she's smiling. Kind of petting him. I'm afraid I purposely kept the girls chatting so that the dog could stay a moment and…" He glanced down at his feet, showing her the top of his head, covered with shortly cropped light brown hair, before looking up at her once again.

The quick look shot a flame through her…one she hadn't felt since Mark got sick…shocking her so much she barely heard his next sentence: "Please apologize to whoever is in charge of them. I swear they weren't harmed…"

"I know they weren't. I've been standing here listening." She had to fess up. It was just her way. "Enjoying the conversation."

Claire's voice carried over to them, the words filled with the emotion of the story and yet a very distinct pause at the end of each sentence, too, as the little girl read, rather than recited, the book Theresa knew she had completely memorized. Neve, bless her energetic little heart, stood right there, listening, her little fingers on Charlie's collar, as though she hadn't done exactly the same, hearing exactly the same, far too many times to count over the past months.

"They bring Charlie to visit specific residents every Tuesday afternoon," she said, when there was so much more important information to glean in the minute or two she had. What had he done to draw them out?

Why him? What quality did he possess that had performed this small miracle for her daughters?

"And I'm sorry for eavesdropping, Mr. Colton."

"You know me?" the man asked, frowning. "I'm sorry, but I don't remember us ever meeting. Did we know each other in school?"

She shook her head. "No. Your mom talks about all of you, has shown me, and others, pictures of all of you…" But nothing had prepared her for this Colton in the flesh. If her girls hadn't been on the other side of that door, she'd have turned tail and run.

Or walked away as quickly as proper protocol and manners would allow.

"And… I know you're Ezra because you told the girls your triplet brothers are Dom and Oliver." There, could that be enough baring of her soul, please?

He was sorry. She was sorry.

And there they stood, with Claire pronouncing every single word, slowly and distinctly.

"I've not had much experience with kids, but they're a delight." Ezra Colton warmed her mother's heart that time. The woman heart, the mother's heart—what was the man trying to do to her?

"Thank you."

He looked at her. Back into the room. "They're yours?"

She'd taken for granted he'd known that. When he'd had no way of knowing. "They are," she told him. And then, with her heart so discombobulated, more came pouring out. "And I don't know what kind of magic you came bearing, but what you're seeing, well, not the reading, that's how it is every week, every visit. But the way the girls were talking to you, so open and friendly... It's just kind of sent me into a state of flux here."

He shook his head. Probably thinking her a blubbering person incapable of maintaining responsibility for an entire care home.

Not wanting to hear what he was thinking, she hurried forward with, "They've been... They haven't been comfortable around strangers since their dad died."

And you want to know my slightly-larger-since-I-gave-birth pant size, too?

"Their dad...your husband?"

Looking at the girls, not him, she nodded, embarrassed. "I can't believe I just laid that on you... I'm just..." Her chin trembled. That meant tears were imminent. Stiffening her shoulders, she continued, "I'm just glad to see them happy."

They were talking softly, standing so that Ezra Colton was the only one immediately visible to those in the room. She blamed her wayward tongue—and emotions—on the false intimacy their little tête-à-tête created.

"I'm...sorry. I had no idea." Ezra's soft tones seemed to carry a rare brand of tenderness, coming from such a muscled, imposing figure. "I've lost comrades, who were family to me. And—" he glanced toward the girls, who were nearing the end of their story "—like them, I lost my father at a young age."

She knew the story, of course. She'd been too young to remember much more than hearing Ben Colton's name in the news, but pretty much everyone who'd been in Blue Larkspur for any length of time knew the story. And eventually heard how the revered justice had been taking bribes and sending wrongfully convicted individuals to prison. She'd even heard it said by an old-timer at the home that the car accident that took Ben's life had been a blessing…

She'd never figured a wife and children would find the loss of their loved one a good thing, though. No matter the wrong choices he'd made, Ben Colton had loved his wife and kids. Or so she'd heard.

"How old were you when he died?" she asked.

"Just turning sixteen."

Which made him, what, thirty-six? "You were ten years older than my girls are," she said aloud. "They were five when Mark died, but he'd been sick for a while before that."

They'd been through a lot, her twins, strong, sweet, and compassionate beyond their age.

Too much. She would not have any more of their childhood robbed from them—no matter what Mark's parents said or tried to do to her.

Claire's voice faded away. Neve slid her fingers under Charlie's collar. Ezra's great-aunt was dozing off, and he straightened, moving back into the room.

As always, Flow, against all odds, had won the race.

Stepping away from the wall, Theresa rounded the corner into the room, showing herself to her recalcitrant daughters with a smile, not a frown, and silently promised them that they were going to be winners, too.

Just like Flow.

Chapter Two

As soon as the twins saw their mother, they immediately made a beeline in her direction, Charlie and Flow book in tow. They were leaving. Shocked at the sudden onset of disappointment the realization begot within him, most particularly since he much preferred order to the chaos of kids, Ezra blurted out without forethought, "There's a big Colton summer barbecue coming up this weekend, on Saturday, at the Gemini Ranch. You all could come as my guests, and the girls could see the horses."

After one look at the shock on Theresa's face, followed by a frown, he saw his misstep. The twins jumped up and down and said, "Yay! Can we, Mom?" First Neve and then Claire, followed by a chorus of "Can we?" He'd never been a man to speak without thought. What had the visit to Sunshine Senior Home done to him?

"I'm sorry," he quickly backtracked. He'd never meant to put her in a precarious position, period, and most particularly not with her daughters. Possibly forcing her to disappoint them. "I should have checked with you first, asked whether or not you were working," he stumbled, words over thoughts, hoping he'd given her an easy out. She could say she had to work.

Who could argue with that?

Glancing from her daughters' expectant faces back to him, she smiled. And Ezra had to take a physical step back. The woman…the way her gaze, her grief, and probably recovery from grief, too, seemed to resonate with him… It was like he'd known her his whole life but just hadn't met her until now.

"If you're serious, then thank you. We'd very much like to be your guests. Can we bring anything?"

Had he just asked her out on a date?

Had she just accepted an invitation to go out with him?

Or were they just treating two young kids, who'd already lost a lot, to an outing that would bring great joy to them?

He had no answer to any of the three questions.

But as he arranged to pick her up Saturday afternoon, and actually thought about showing up to a Colton family function with a gorgeous widow and her two fatherless daughters in tow, he knew his family would assume he was on a date.

He didn't hate the idea as much as he'd assumed he would have, either.

THERESA LISTENED TO her girls chatter on about Ezra Colton as they walked back to her office, holding on to Charlie while she shut down for the day. They walked with her and the leashed dog out to the parking lot and climbed into their booster seats and belts in the back seat, while she got Charlie settled in the passenger seat beside her. The twins were calling him Mr. Giant, though Theresa told them he was Mr. Colton, and they wanted to know if someone as big as him could ride a horse without hurting it.

She wondered if the man had some kind of potency potion. As much as the girls were talking about him, she'd been in her own thoughts thinking about the man. She'd never met any of the Coltons other than their mom, Isa, face-to-face—

Never met any men of the family, period.

The experience had her way hotter—in that way a woman got when she was near a guy who did it for her—than she had any business being. Hotter than she'd been since Mark had gotten sick.

She'd loved her husband. And even when he'd made her promise that she'd love again, she'd half wondered if she'd ever be able to feel sexual feelings for any other man.

Well, there were no more doubts on that score.

And now she had a date with him.

Of sorts.

Maybe.

She was less than a block from the senior home when she had a feeling that she was being followed. Not wanting to alarm the girls, she tried her best to act natural, while constantly checking both side and rearview mirrors for sign of a twenty-year-old, over-large, four-door blue pickup truck. In mint condition.

Just because she couldn't see it towering behind her didn't mean it wasn't there, though. Lurking at corners, waiting to see her pass, moving on to another intersection where her progress could be tracked.

Mark's parents, who'd never even met the children before his death, were determined to have rights to their grandchildren, to indoctrinate them, by any means necessary. Mark had been estranged from the doomsday preppers—children during the Cold War who still, decades later, felt that a nuclear blast was imminent—since before he'd met Theresa. He'd told her about the guns they'd been stockpiling since he was young, about the apocalyptic bunker they'd built out in the middle of nowhere in preparation for the nuclear attack they were sure was coming from somewhere. But after he'd died, they'd contacted her for visitation, talking about their grandparental rights to know their flesh and blood.

About Claire and Neve's right to know their father's family.

So many years had passed since Mark had first told her about their tendencies.

And they'd been shocked by their son's death, even though Mark had kept them at a distance while he was alive. Grieving as only parents could.

She'd insisted on mediation first. To make sure outside sources found them suitable to visit with the girls. And had eventually allowed a couple of playdates. Their first visit had been like a dream come true. Eric and Jennifer Fitzgerald had been overwhelmed with emotion—and devotion—for Mark's children. Had mourned their son's death. And been so utterly grateful to her.

To think she'd let them take the girls for even one afternoon playdate… She shuddered.

The night after that one and only unsupervised visit, little Claire had come to her, asking about their plans if the blast came that night, wondering if she'd be safe to sleep in her bed through the night or could the end happen before morning. Neve had come home talking about the gases that were going to kill people and Claire had asked, the next time they'd filled up their car with gasoline, if they were all going to die…

No truck in sight at the next intersection, but having to keep her gaze on the road meant that she couldn't peruse every parking lot of every strip mall and store they passed. The truck could be lurking in any of them.

The Fitzgeralds had told her point-blank that they weren't going away.

Would they wait for just the right moment and T-bone her front end with just enough force to disable her, maybe denting her door shut, but leaving the girls unharmed behind her so that they could snatch them and run?

They'd been…upset…when she told them they couldn't see the twins again. She hadn't expected the threats that had followed. Nor had she ever in a million years thought that that old blue pickup would show up outside the elementary school. But the week before, it had been there. Had she not beat them to the pickup lane, would they have taken Claire and Neve and run with them?

Theresa shook her head.

She'd actually tried to talk to the Fitzgeralds, to get them to see that they were scaring the girls, but when they'd grown belligerent with her, calling her a horrible mother who wasn't preparing her children properly…

She'd had to cut them off. There'd been no other choice.

And they weren't respecting her wishes. Seeing them parked outside the girls' school…

Still, maybe she was being a bit paranoid, she acknowledged silently as she pulled onto their street and into the driveway of their little three-bedroom house that needed some work—including a new coat of paint. There was no sign of a big blue pickup anywhere around. The couple had said they'd been at the school, at a completely safe distance, just to get a glimpse of the twins. They loved them and missed them so much.

She'd had no concrete reason to call the police, in spite of her threat to get a restraining order taken out on them. Keeping weapons in a private bunker for personal safety in the event of a doomsday event was perfectly legal.

Their threats, to that point, had all been veiled enough that they could just seem like the result of grief and lonely desperation. And the mediator who'd interviewed the Fitzgeralds separately and together had found them to be sane and rational. They were both retired, but had held regular jobs, paid their bills on time.

Maybe she wasn't being followed at all.

Maybe she was feeling guilty—having the hots for a man who wasn't Mark. Feeling like she was being unfaithful to Mark's memory, and to any regard his parents held for her because their son had loved and married her—the fact that they'd never met her before his death had been his choice, not theirs.

Maybe she was overreacting to the entire day, she allowed. She watched the girls race each other to the door to see who could get inside first, never minding that neither of them could enter the premises until she was there with the key.

"Charlie, my boy, what did you get us into?" she asked the dog as, holding his leash, she waited for him to jump down from the car. "Of all the rooms to seek solace in, you had to choose the one bearing a gorgeous man?"

She'd just unlocked the door, hadn't even had a chance to follow the girls inside, when her phone rang.

Ezra Colton? Calling to cancel?

Or…just to further their acquaintance?

Heart pounding, she pulled the phone out of her pocket, checking the screen, wondering if she'd actually answer or not.

If she didn't, would he leave a message?

Did she want him to?

Her heart rate sped up even more when she read the number. Sped up and pounded harder, too.

She'd deleted the contact.

But knew the number.

It belonged to Eric Fitzgerald.

Theresa didn't pick up.

EZRA FOUND HIS mom in the kitchen Wednesday morning. He'd looked for her when he'd come in the night before, but she'd either been out or already in bed. Isa out at night, without telling her visiting son where she'd be, brought questions to mind.

She'd been looking more than just polite, dancing with chief of police Theodore Lawson at his big brother Caleb's wedding. The eighty-one-year-old lawman might have some age on him, but Ezra had heard Naomi—his TV producer baby sister—call the chief a silver fox, and he couldn't deny the tall, charismatic man had the kind of aura that attracted attention from anyone around him.

Pouring himself a cup of coffee and landing his butt on one of the white square bar stools at the kitchen island, Ezra didn't ask any of the questions he wanted to ask his mother about her personal life. He didn't want to scare her off from having one.

Pushing aside the tablet she'd been focused on, her finger moving with precision and flair as she chose virtual tools and colors to design on-screen, she smiled at him. Told him there was leftover breakfast casserole in the refrigerator.

He'd had it a couple of times already, appreciative of her effort, if not as fond of the result, and went for it again, while she continued to watch him, her mature, beautiful face beaming.

He could crash with siblings, or even get a hotel room when he came to town—which wasn't often—but Isa wanted him there. And so there he was.

The wedding and all…

"I met Theresa Fitzgerald yesterday," he said. "She seems quite fond of you."

"She's a sweet woman," his mother responded with a long look at him that put him a bit on edge. But she continued with, "She's been through some rough times… and those two little ones of hers. We've talked a few times about raising twins."

"You'd be the supreme authority on that one," he said and smiled at her. "If anyone could give tips, you could."

Isa shrugged. "I just told her to honor their individuality," she said, as though her contribution had been nothing, but Ezra figured there'd been more than that.

"I met the girls, too," he said.

She frowned, briefly, and then nodded. "Right, it was Tuesday. They're always there with the dog on Tuesday."

"Have they come in to see Aunt Alice before, then?"

Just because it had been a first for him, one that was still holding center court in his head, didn't mean the unexpected encounter had been all that much out of the ordinary for Theresa or her daughters.

"No. Didn't seem much point, since Aunt Alice is so unresponsive. Better that the residents who get true joy out of the visits be given the time slots."

He glanced up, midchew, swallowed and blurted, "But she did enjoy it, Mom! She smiled. Put her hand on Charlie's head. I saw her fingers moving like she was trying to pet him. She continued that way for most of the time little Claire read her story…"

Maybe the occasion had been momentous after all. And he wasn't merely losing his perspective on reality.

"Seriously?" Isa sat forward, her gaze intent. "She smiled?"

He nodded, thinking he should have pulled out a phone and snagged a picture. Wishing he'd had the mental wherewithal to do so.

The girls, and then their mother…their instant effect on him…was bothersome.

"And she reached her hand to touch him," he told her. "It wasn't like Charlie headbutted her for attention. He just had a paw on her chair and she touched that first."

Isa's teary but clearly happy smile was worth the monthlong visit home to a town he'd been happy to escape.

KNOWING SHE WAS being overly cautious but bothered by Eric Fitzgerald's number showing up on her phone, Theresa took Wednesday as a work-from-home day.

Her employer allowed her two days a week at home, but she mostly preferred to be on campus.

The girls grumbled about missing day camp. They wanted to swim.

She didn't want them in any other public space where their grandparents could just be hanging out, hoping for a glimpse of them.

Because she didn't believe that was all her in-laws had been doing. If they'd had the chance, they'd have taken her daughters. She'd bet money on it.

She just had no proof of anything criminal to report.

Nothing but hearsay—which wouldn't be enough for any kind of subpoena or warrant, and…

At five after twelve, normally the day-camp attendees' lunch break in the park, her phone rang.

Jennifer Fitzgerald.

She'd left a message.

Wanted to know if the girls were okay. Requested at least a text as reassurance that Claire and Neve weren't sick.

And Theresa knew…they'd been watching the park.

Looking for their chance.

Knew it and had no way to prove it. The only way she could get protection would be if they actually did more than talk and watch.

And then it would be too late.

Chapter Three

With only a few days shaved off his month of leave, Ezra went against better judgment and headed back to the Sunshine Senior Home. He'd been fond of Aunt Alice while growing up. Had found at her house solace from the cacophony in a home with eleven siblings, many close in age.

He liked order. Aunt Alice had been orderly.

She'd also been unimpressed by Ben Colton's stature in the community or his wealth. She'd liked her niece's husband for the love he gave to his family.

And after the scandal, that hadn't changed. Ben had done very wrong things. The man had used his ill-gotten gains to pay for the best of the best for all of them.

Ezra had never needed the best things, though. He'd needed his father to be the hero he'd once thought him. Aunt Alice had helped him see, in part, that Ben hadn't been all bad. After Ben's arrest, the shame he'd brought to his wife and dozen kids, Ben had still cared for his family. On some level, that mattered.

In Alice's current state—even if she hadn't been sleeping soundly in bed that afternoon—she wasn't able to remember who Ezra was, let alone the lessons she'd taught him.

Or the familial love she'd bestowed upon him at a critical age.

Which was why Aunt Alice hadn't been his sole reason for visiting the home today. When he didn't see Theresa around, he found her office.

The door was locked. And an aide, seeing him standing there, offered the information that Mrs. Fitzgerald was working from home that day.

Since he'd been spotted lurking, he figured the only decent thing to do would be to stop by Theresa's place, to let her know he'd been looking. Just so she didn't hear about it through the grapevine and figure she had to seek him out to see what he'd wanted.

A stretch…but with just enough logic to have his rental Jeep pulling into her drive a few minutes after three. He had a legitimate reason to talk to her.

A phone call would have worked.

If he'd had her number.

He'd been so bowled over by his encounter with her and her girls that he'd failed to ask for basic information. Her address had been a matter of public record.

She hadn't invited him to call her.

She hadn't invited him to knock on her front door, either. The place needed paint. Though Ben's crimes hadn't left the family penniless, Ezra had painted a house or two to earn money the summer before his senior year in high school. If wealth had been the cause for his father's walk to the dark side, Ezra had figured he wanted no part of it.

He had a month to kill at home. Maybe, just like the work had helped him deal with being around family so much that summer, he could do a little painting over the next month, too. And help out a widowed mother in the process.

Lord knew, not a lot of people had helped out his widowed mother back in the day.

There was no hesitation in his knock on the door of the modest home. He had information, an activity invitation of sorts, and was eager to share it. He'd asked his younger brother for a favor—and the smirk Jasper had sent him, the slightly snarky comment about Ezra asking favors on a woman's behalf, had been well worth the chance to be the bearer of good news.

"Ezra?" The surprise in Theresa's voice as she pulled open the door was obvious. He didn't know her well enough to be able to tell if there was pleasure mixed in there as well. "I just had a call from Bonnie that you'd been by to see me."

The aide. He'd made the right choice, following up with her at home. Better that than have her wonder why he'd stopped to see her.

"I guess, in light of the fact that we have a barbecue to get to on Saturday, we should have exchanged phone numbers."

She came outside, pulling the door mostly closed behind her. Her hair was up in the same messy kind of bun she'd worn the day before. He noticed right away that he hadn't imagined the auburn glints in the dark strands.

"I apologize for the shorts and T-shirt," she told him. "Since I'm working from home, and the girls wanted to go down to the river for lunch…" She shrugged.

Did she think he was on a business visit? He'd thought mention of the barbecue had made his intentions clear…

"Should I apologize for my shorts and sandals, then?" he shot back at her. Same basic attire he'd had on the day before. Different-color shorts and shirt.

And he'd changed his skivvies, too. Not that she'd have any cause for the information.

"I'm just not used to…a Colton, here? I…"

"I'm an enlisted army man," he told her. "Straight out of high school. You've got your master's degree in health management. I saw from the letters behind your name on your office door. I'm guessing that if anyone should feel lesser here, it would be me."

He had no idea who her parents had been or what kind of family she'd grown up in, but he'd bet everything he had that her father hadn't been headed for spending the rest of his life in prison before dying in a car crash.

"You're driving a luxury Jeep that could easily buy my old van four times over."

"It's a rental. And I don't vacation much."

They could go on. He grew up in a big house—was staying there with his mom.

"Just to be clear," he said, "I've already told my mother that I don't want any Colton money, which is really just whatever she's made in her graphic design business and from her investments. I'm never going to be a rich man. Wealth doesn't equal health and happiness, in my book."

The compassion that filled her expression about sent him to his knees.

What the hell…?

Before she could speak, and split him wide-open, he said, "I came by to tell you—and the girls—that I've made arrangements for them to have horseback rides on Saturday. It'll probably be best that they wear jeans, to protect their legs from saddle burn and horse-hair, and boots."

Somehow, he came off sounding all lord of the manor. Not him at all.

To defend against any pity she might have been about to bestow upon him.

He wasn't that guy, either. But… "My brother Jasper stopped by Mom's this morning, and I cleared it with him," he allowed. It wasn't his manor he was lording over.

"I don't want to impose," she said then, her eyes squinting somewhat in the afternoon sun. The bright-ness also gave them a glow he was pretty sure he was never going to forget.

The kindness that seemed to emanate naturally from the woman…

To a man who spent his life fighting enemies—al-ways expecting bad guys to be lurking around every corner—she was…nice.

For a brief moment.

"You aren't imposing. The horses are going to need exercise. Jasper was actually glad for the chance to get new bodies up on them. I guess several of the build-ings at the ranch experienced storm damage a while ago, and they have to close for repairs."

A fact that could have been financially difficult for Jasper and Aubrey, except that Naomi was going to be renting the ranch out for filming, so it had all worked out.

Sometimes, being from a big, dynamic family had its benefits.

"Well, then, the girls will be thrilled!" Theresa said. "And I'll let you tell them about it yourself, if you'd like."

He'd like to. And was suddenly loath to walk inside that home, too. To get in too deep. "It's hot out. Why don't we all go for ice cream? Unless it's too close to dinner?" There'd been strict rules in the Colton household—at least, according to his memory—about snacking too close to mealtime. Maybe because he'd always been the one trying to snag cookies before he had to contend with vegetables and other such things.

Her hesitation that time was unmistakable. She actually stepped back, and there was no sign of a smile, or even any welcome on her face.

She was a widow whose husband had been gone only a year. He totally got it.

"Just as friends," he quickly assured her. "I'm in town for a month, and then it's off to another assignment God knows where. I'm not making moves here. I just…felt good around you and your daughters yesterday and would like to ease your way for a second or two, if I can." He'd get to the painting offer later. A military man knew how to pick his battles. "Seriously, you'd be taking pity on me," he added, thinking about how he'd just eschewed the idea that she'd do so. And then he told her in all truthfulness, "You and Claire and Neve are much easier to be around than the pack of Coltons waiting to take their turns at grilling me and then giving their opinions as to my life choices…"

He loved them all. Would give his life for any of them.

And hated that they always tried to get up in his business. Like they knew better than him what was best.

The fact that their concern very likely stemmed from worry did ease the burden a bit.

But Coltons versus ice cream? The choice was a no-brainer.

Luckily, Theresa seemed to see the value in the choice as well. With one last glance at Ezra, she called the girls, and within minutes they were all bundled into his rented Jeep, car seats installed and seat belts fastened, and heading out to a little family-owned place he knew of not far from town that had been serving homemade ice cream since before he was born.

To anyone on the outside looking in, they probably looked like a real family.

A happy one.

Shaking his head at the thought, Ezra turned his mind to more important matters.

With a quick glance in the rearview mirror, he asked, "What flavor of ice cream is your favorite?"

And tried not to notice the sexy bare knees within hand's reach on the passenger seat beside him.

THE GIRLS JUST wanted chocolate; she could have told Ezra that. Didn't matter what kind of fancy, one-of-a-kind flavors the place made; they'd just want chocolate.

It was all she really wanted, too, but at his suggestion, she ordered a chocolate brownie concoction that he'd said was to die for, and…he was right. Ambrosia in the mouth. So much so that she hated to swallow a single bite.

Or maybe his smile was part of the reason she wanted that ice cream cone to last forever.

That and the easy way he had of talking to the twins.

Like they were equals, not little girls, and yet seeming to stay on topic for a six-year-old.

Mostly, she noticed, he didn't look at them or speak to them as if he felt sorry for them. Or was in any way trying to compensate for their loss.

A change from everyone else who'd been around the girls over the past year.

Out of town, in a vehicle no one would recognize, at a place no one would ever expect her to be, she actually started to relax, to let herself believe, just for a moment, that she was on a real date and she could one day have the happy family they must appear to be to all those around them at the outside picnic tables and going in and out of the shop.

Right up until Claire said, "Grandpa said that we should wear our breathing helmets all the time when we're sitting outside around other people. 'Cause the explosion will happen when lots of people are gathered together. Is this lots of people, do you think?"

Neve shook her head. "No, Claire, this isn't that kind of lots of people. Is it, Mom? That kind is bunches and bunches like you could build a really, really tall people tower, one that could almost reach the sky, huh?"

"Remember, I told you, there isn't going to be an explosion," Theresa said with a twist in her gut, careful to look only at her girls—so they'd have her full attention and be better able to trust her words. But also because she suddenly wanted to look anyplace but at Ezra Colton.

So much for the real date.

Or ice cream lasting forever.

"But Grandpa said you're wrong about that," Claire

told her, solemn as ever as she licked her ice cream, a chocolate ring surrounding the edges of her lips.

Theresa didn't want any more ice cream. She wanted to snatch her girls and run. Far. Fast. Forever.

"When did Grandpa tell you that?" she had to ask—airing family problems in front of Ezra be damned. She'd explained about the explosion being a figment of their grandparents' imagination after she'd banned the Fitzgeralds from seeing her girls.

"You know," Neve said. "The other day ago when we were on our swing set."

In their gated backyard? The couple had been on her property?

"You were swishing the toilet," Claire piped up. "They said not to bother you and they'd come back another day."

The only time she'd had the twins out of sight had been when she'd been cleaning the bathroom. Otherwise, she'd had them in view from one window to the next as she'd cleaned the house. That had been Saturday.

Her in-laws could have taken the pair from their own backyard.

The fact that they hadn't didn't mean as much as she'd like to hope. They were planners. Investigating their options. Collecting information that they'd process well, allowing for every eventuality, before making their move.

Horror-struck, she could hardly pretend to enjoy the rest of the outing. She had to get home. The couple had been on her premises. Could that rank as rating a call to the police?

Would anyone listen to her fears?

Or merely find her as irrationally out of touch as she considered the older Fitzgeralds?

They'd merely say they'd been by to visit her, that the girls had been outside, they'd asked for her, the girls had said she was busy, they'd said they'd come back...

She heard the mental play-by-play with a sinking feeling of helplessness and dread.

Tried to keep up with the chatter going on between Ezra and her daughters.

And had never felt more alone in her life.

Chapter Four

The girls wanted to show Ezra their swing set. There was nowhere else he had to be.

Nowhere else he wanted to be, either. He'd never hung out with a woman with kids before and was finding the experience enlightening.

Children, their innocence, their lack of conversation filters, brought life to a different level.

He wasn't opposed to hanging out on the level for a second or two.

His sister Rachel had recently become a mother. Isa's first grandchild. Ezra had just met little Iris for the first time recently. Maybe that was why he was suddenly noticing a part of life he'd heretofore ignored.

With one hand on each of the two little backs, he pushed both girls in tandem on their swings. Then he watched them take turns sliding down the slide in all kinds of contortions, meant, he was sure, to impress him.

Truth was, the two feisty little beings did impress him. As did their mother, who was a lot quieter than she'd been at the beginning of their outing.

He was pretty sure he knew why, and wasn't leaving until he had a chance to make sure she and the girls were okay.

Whether she sensed his intention or not, Ezra didn't know, but when the twins tired of outdoor play and asked if they could go watch *Frozen*, she didn't even pretend that she might follow right behind them. Unlocking the door for them, she stayed outside on the stoop with Ezra.

Leaning a hand against the small porch support, he said, "I have to ask."

"I don't have to answer."

"No. But I spend my life fighting bad guys to protect my country and all of her citizens," he said, deadly serious. "That includes you and your daughters. What explosion? What helmets?"

She said nothing.

And she didn't leave, either, when she could so easily have escaped into her home.

"I thought, at first, that it was just some kind of game the girls played with their grandparents, but your reaction... When you heard they'd been in your backyard, you went white. And haven't been the same since."

That time she nodded.

"Are they your parents or their father's?"

"I never knew my parents."

Filled with a ton of new questions, all about her, Ezra waited. And knew that that conversation wasn't any of his business.

Obviously Theresa felt the same as she continued, "Mark was estranged from his folks." A small peek into what he knew was going to be something bad.

He needed to know how bad.

And even with that, the way she said the man's name… Mark…the familiarity and warmth, stung him. With jealousy. He was jealous of a dead man.

But welcomed the needed reminder that Theresa was a grieving widow.

"They're extremists," she said. "Irrationally obsessed with the belief that there's going to be a nuclear attack that's going to wipe out anyone who isn't prepared. Mark walked away, refusing to have anything more to do with them when they started talking about giving some guy tens of thousands of dollars to build them a bunker somewhere. He said they hoarded everything from medical supplies and food, to guns and ammunition. But that was nearly fifteen years ago."

He straightened, every hackle he owned standing on end, as she continued. "After Mark died, they contacted me, expressing deep grief at their loss of him before they could make amends. Asking to see the girls."

Appealing to her compassionate, motherly heart. He gritted his teeth. Remained silent.

"At first I refused, but then they started talking about grandparents' rights. In Colorado—and elsewhere, I've discovered—grandparents have the right to visitation if their son or daughter who parented the child has died."

"No way the courts would give irrational theorists visitation rights." The words tore through him, and out. He wished he could have been a sounding board back then, even though he had been on the other side of the world and hadn't known her.

To offer advice, or use his connections to get her help, if need be.

There was no room in either of their lives, or time,

for him to be getting emotionally involved, he reminded himself. Not with her, her children, or her situation.

"They seemed to be over all of that. They were so rational on the phone, and in letters…"

It took all Ezra had not to grab her and the girls up and take them to his mom's house.

"I didn't want to take a chance on the court ruling in their favor, so I suggested that instead of forcing them to file for rights, I'd agree to visitation willingly, as long as we all went through professional mediation first. Which we did." She glanced behind her, and then back up at him. "They appeared to the mediator and social services specialist to be caring, rational people. So I introduced them to the girls. We met for lunch, that kind of thing. Eventually I let them take the girls for a playdate, following the guidelines we'd all established. They couldn't take the girls for more than two hours, they had to have cell phone access at all times, and they couldn't leave the Blue Larkspur city limits."

That sounded reasonable to him.

"So they had a right to be here on Saturday? Looking for you?"

Had he so grossly overreacted?

He wanted to believe he had, but his gut—and Theresa's reaction to her daughters' news—told him different.

She shook her head, and he asked, "When did things start going wrong?"

"After the first playdate. Claire was afraid to go to bed in case the blast came while she was asleep." She hugged herself with both arms, her brow creased beneath the few loose strands of long dark hair that had escaped from her off-center bun.

"I tried to talk to them, to explain they were hurting the girls, but they got belligerent, told me I was going to send the twins to their death, too, along with Mark. I ended up telling them they couldn't see the twins anymore. They said they'd sue for rights, and I threatened to get a restraining order against them, testifying about their bunker filled with guns and ammunition. I was so upset I just blurted that out, going only from what Mark had said, but it seemed to work." Her brown eyes wide and imploring, she seemed to be asking him for something.

He wasn't sure what, but knew he wanted to give it to her, whatever it was. Knew, too, that he was in no position to allow this woman to rely on him for more than a few fun outings.

Not only was he army all the way, and leaving as soon as he got his next assignment, but he most definitely wasn't a family man. Any of his siblings could vouch for that one. While most of them had stayed local after their father's duplicity was exposed, devoting their lives to making up to the community for their father's sins, Ezra had split.

Along with Dom and Oliver.

"And then on Friday, I saw them parked down from the girls' school. And now I hear they were here, at my house, on Saturday?" She shook her head. "They're making me as paranoid as they are…building up this whole conspiracy theory that they're watching everything we do, investigating the best place and time to take the girls and hide them away in their bunker for the rest of their lives, indoctrinating them until they won't be able to think straight, either."

Maybe she was a little bit right about being paranoid. Her theory, while understandable, was a bit farfetched. And yet he understood it, too, which meant he couldn't completely discount it.

"Have they tried to get in touch with you directly?"

She nodded. "They called yesterday and then again earlier today. They left a message."

He asked to hear the message.

She played it for him.

The expression of concern seemed completely appropriate, given that their son had died and they were clinging to what was left of him. He told her so.

She nodded again. "I know. I was telling myself to calm down, but now I hear that Eric told the girls I was wrong about there being no imminent nuclear blast?"

Yeah, he didn't like that, either. But the Fitzgeralds had left the kids alone as soon as they knew Theresa was busy. Maybe they'd come to the front door, to try to work something out with her, and, after their knock went unanswered, they heard the twins in the back and hoped to find Theresa there?

"Have they threatened to take your daughters?" he asked. Families, as much as a pain in the butt as they could be sometimes, were also sacred. Grandparents wanting to be a part of their grandkids' lives was understandable.

"No. Just to go to court for visitation rights until I threatened to counter the motion with the request for a restraining order. That's how Mark got rid of them in the past. They never bothered him again after that.

He said that they'd feared losing their bunker and their stash more than they'd loved him."

"That's somewhat comforting," Ezra said slowly. "Did you get the feeling, when you made the threat, that it still carried the same weight?"

"I did until recently." She shook her head, and he waited for the bun to topple. It didn't. And neither would she, he realized. "I'm probably just overreacting."

He mostly agreed with her. "Probably," he offered. "But just to be safe, do you mind if I put a word in with the chief of police?"

"You know the chief of police?" she asked, then shook her head one more time. "Of course you do."

Ezra let the comment go. "Do I have your permission to speak to him?"

"Of course. Yes!" And then, after a glance that seemed almost shy, she said, "Thank you."

And suddenly there he was, standing there wanting to kiss her.

Backing away, he confirmed the time he'd pick her up on Saturday and told her he'd see her later.

No kissing. As far as anything intimately personal went, Theresa was off-limits.

As soon as he'd switched back the car seats and was headed down the street, he put in a call to Chief Lawson, the man who'd been dancing so closely with his mother at his brother's wedding. He didn't mention Isa, though. And was grateful when the top lawman said he'd see what he could find out about Eric and Jennifer Fitzgerald.

TALKING WITH EZRA had helped. Theresa stretched out in the tub in the bathroom attached to her bedroom, letting the bubbles soothe her as she listened to a popular New Age album and watched the candlelight flicker against the walls.

She and the girls had had a fun night—baking cookies and using the new markers she'd bought them to draw on the whiteboard she'd mounted in the playroom the previous weekend, with one of their favorite animated films playing in the background. It had been the most just plain fun she'd had with them since Mark had died.

It wasn't because of spending time with Ezra earlier in the day personally. He hadn't done anything anyone else couldn't have done—just talking to another adult about her concerns regarding the Fitzgeralds had helped her step outside the situation and see how large it had loomed in her imagination.

Consuming her.

Instead of being a victim, she was drinking a glass of white wine and remembering how to relax. Pampering herself in the attempt. She hadn't done that since Mark's death, either.

She wasn't going to think about that. Or the past year's worth of struggle. She was there to grab a few minutes of good feels and…

Her phone rang.

And her stomach sank.

Grabbing the cell off the counter, wet hand and all, she wouldn't let the dread seep through her veins. Wouldn't…

It wasn't the Fitzgeralds.

It was Ezra Colton.

She answered before she could stop herself. And except for her head and the hand holding her phone, she promptly slid down to hide her nakedness beneath the bubbles.

"Is it too late to call?" he asked, leaving her wondering if she'd sounded sleepy.

As long as she hadn't come across as aroused, she didn't care. "No. The girls go to bed at eight, and I was just settling down for a few minutes to myself..."

"I won't keep you, then," he said. "I just wanted to let you know that Chief Lawson is going to check into the Fitzgeralds for you. If nothing else, this will put them on police radar."

Okay, now the relief was because of him personally. Him and his Colton contacts. "Thank you."

"I also talked to an old buddy of mine and was wondering how you'd feel about having your house painted."

Jolting up so fast water sluiced around her, over the sides of the tub, splashing onto the floor, Theresa sat there barely holding the phone. Mouth gaping.

The house needed several repairs, but the paint... It was the most crucial. If she didn't get it done, there were going to be structural issues. And it was the most expensive thing, so the farthest down on her budget, too.

How did you tell a man that you couldn't afford to keep up your modest little home?

Like a strong woman, that was how. "I can't afford to have my house painted."

She worked hard, but with Mark's lingering illness, there'd been so many medical bills. Things insurance didn't cover. And his modest life insurance policy hadn't done so, either. Another year and she'd be out of debt. Just one more year...

"I'm offering to do it for free," he told her. "I painted houses when I was in high school—it was my way of working my way out of the mess of crap my father had landed us in—and I just ran into this buddy I painted with. I mentioned to him that I might have a job he could help with, and he said he'd like to get back up on a ladder, too. Give us a chance to catch up."

"I cannot let you paint my house for free."

"You just said you can't afford to pay for it."

"I can't."

"So I'm hoping you'll reconsider and let us do it for free. I've got three weeks left in town, and I'm going friggin' bonkers just hanging around Mom's place, a sitting duck for whichever Colton wants to stop in and save me from myself."

"I'd think your family would be proud of you—the job you do."

A dangerous job. One she didn't want to think about.

"Maybe. They'd be happier, though, if I came home and painted houses."

After holding her breath for a second, Theresa slowly let it out. Reminded herself of her recent foray into letting her imagination run away with her. But then she asked, "Is there a chance you'd consider that?"

"Not one in hell," he said. "But since I've committed to being here, and I'm already buzzing with claustrophobia, I'd appreciate it if you'd let me help you out. It's what the Coltons do, helping others, so no one will give me a hard time about being busy."

"And your friend? He has nothing better to do, either? Or does he have a family he needs to escape, too?"

"Nope. He's a cop with a wife, two kids and a full

schedule, but he wanted us to get together on Friday, and I told him painting was the only way."

"I don't…"

"He was actually kind of happy about the idea," he said. "For some of the same reasons. No grief, and an excuse to hang out…"

"Well…then…" She couldn't believe she was actually considering it. The thought of having the huge worry off her mind was so tempting, and…

"I'm taking that as a yes," Ezra said. "I'll come by tomorrow to get started. Don't call if you change your mind," he added, and while there was no laughter in his tone, she could tell he was teasing her.

"You're a good man, Ezra Colton," she said softly, suddenly more aware of her nudity than she'd been in years.

"Nah, I'm just not a vacationing type of guy, so hovering on the desperate spectrum."

She believed that, too, but his words didn't negate her opinion of him at all. To the contrary, every time he opened his mouth, she was moved more.

He talked about paint finishes, and then brands, asked about colors, and hung up as though he was no more than her hired help.

Who was working for free.

As she sat there in the cooling water, staring at her phone, she had to strictly remind herself that no matter how wonderful Ezra might seem in the moment—how wonderful he might be, period—he wasn't wonderful for *her*. Not only was he only in town—a town he clearly didn't want to be in—for just a month, but his job was super dangerous. She'd already lost her heart to one man who'd died.

She couldn't go through it again.

Nor could she risk her girls getting too fond of him and having their hearts broken.

Period.

He was going to be around. The kids would be outside playing at least some of the time. She and Ezra were bound to run into each other—more than just an afternoon at a barbecue as she'd originally thought.

She'd have a talk with them in the morning. Make certain that they understood Ezra was only a visitor in their lives; he was not even going to be around long enough to be a friend. They had to get that Ezra needed and wanted it that way.

And Theresa had to accept that while her body had chosen that particular inopportune time to come back to life, Ezra was not the man to engage with in that way. She'd promised Mark that she'd seek out happiness again.

Giving any part of herself to a career soldier who lived for dangerous assignments was not an option.

Chapter Five

Up at the crack of dawn on Thursday, Ezra did some cardio and was at the paint store when it opened. As small as Theresa's house was, and with help, he'd have it done before the barbecue. He'd hoped to get to her place before she left—for no real good reason—but no one was home when he arrived.

Considering their conversation the day before, and the fact that he hadn't yet heard back from Lawson, he called her cell just to make certain everything was okay. He heard that the twins were at day camp—an indoor pool and gymnastics day—with strict instructions to counselors that Claire and Neve were not to go outside for any reason. Just a precaution. Probably unnecessary, but one of which he wholly approved.

And then he told her, "I'll be at your place all day, up on a ladder for most of it, and will keep an eye out in the area." Enemy surveillance was what he did. He hoped there was no threat.

But when it came to irrational theorists, trust was just plain stupid. Unrequited love, even in grandparental form, was an aggravator.

He was probably just a soldier with too much time

on his hands and looking for trouble where it didn't exist—but looking didn't hurt anyone.

As it turned out, the day passed uneventfully, if you didn't consider the peacefulness, the completely un-expected relaxation that slowly settled upon Ezra as he first scraped where necessary, and then rolled and brushed, rolled and brushed. How weird was it that he actually had fun moving his rented ladder around the outside of Theresa's house?

The physical exertion helped, too. He'd learned long ago that the best way to keep himself mentally alert and healthy was to exercise his body, expending energy before it built like nerve bombs inside him.

And though he might have hoped to see Theresa and the girls at the end of the day, he had to take off before they showed up.

After a quick shower, pulling on jeans and a gray T-shirt, he called her again, on his way to meet his fellow triplets for a bit of letting loose at The Corner Pocket, before Oliver left the next day. And he ended up sitting in his car for a couple of minutes after he'd pulled in, looking at the riverfront and listening to Neve tell him about hanging on rings that day and having bumps in her arms just like him—muscles, he realized. The-resa apologized for her six-year-old's insistence that she had to tell him something and took the phone back the second Neve was done, leaving him no chance to respond to the remark.

Rescuing him was more like it. What did you say to something like that?

But he was smiling as he walked into the English-feeling pub, turning right to head straight for the bil-liards, finding his brothers—Dom with somewhat shaggy blond hair, and Oliver with his slicked-back blond hair and lean runner's look. Both wore jeans and stood at their favorite pool table in the back, balls racked, three beers already on a small high-top close by.

"Uh-oh." Dom was wearing a knowing grin as he nodded.

Seriously? "What?" Ezra's tone had a bit of an edge. He was going to take Colton crap from his own triplet sibling now?

"Nothing, just know that look."

"What look?"

"The 'a woman I know is making me smile' look." He glanced at Oliver, who gave a bit of a cynical shrug.

"Whatever, dude, you break." Ezra took a long cool swallow of beer and decided to whip Dom's butt at the table. Winning was always a toss-up between the three of them, but Dom had just given Ezra a reason to want it more.

After an hour of daring each other, taking foolish, behind-the-back shots, acting like they thought they were pros, Ezra had met his goal, thrice over.

Clearly, Dom had his head still too filled with thoughts of Sami, his newfound life love, to fully concentrate and had come in last all three times.

Ezra, who was starving by that point, told him he had to buy food. Dom obliged, bringing a huge tray of unhealthy and delicious bar munchies back to the table. Cue sticks resting up against their small high-top, with balls already racked and ready on the table, they leaned butts to stools and dug in. Except that Oliver was keeping up appearances with a wing in his hand, rather than gorging himself as usual.

"What's up?" Ezra asked, as Dom looked at the wing and raised an eyebrow.

With a shrug, and an odd look of…feeling… Oliver took a bite, and then another, put the wing down and said, "I had dinner before I came."

"Let me guess—at the Atria," Dom said.

To which Ezra frowned, looking between the two of them. "What gives?" he asked.

"A certain waitress is working in her family's restaurant," Dom said, then ate half a potato skin in one bite.

Ezra's gaze shot to his clearly-cynical-about-women financial wizard brother. "Seriously?"

"It's nothing," Oliver said, swigging from his beer like he did it all day, every day. And that was the end of that.

"You notice Mom dancing with Chief Lawson at the wedding?" Dom asked then, obviously reading, as Ezra had, their brother's lack of amusement regarding the waitress.

"I noticed."

"I actually called the chief yesterday," Ezra told them, though he maintained Theresa's privacy on the issue. "Had him check into something private, unrelated to any of us, that I kind of walked into at the Sunshine Senior Home the other day."

"I don't want him pressuring Mom," Dom said. "I'm keeping my eye on things."

"She didn't look unhappy," Ezra admitted, but he was glad to know that Dom, who lived in Denver, would be around.

"She needs to sell that house," Oliver piped up, helping himself to a jalapeño popper. "It's too big."

Ezra nodded. "I just talked to her about it this morning. She's hanging on to it because it's where we all grew up, but there's no way we're all twelve going to be staying with her at the same time, not with some of us having places here in town. It just doesn't make sense for her to be rambling alone in all that space so much of the time."

"Agreed." Dom said the word. All three of them were nodding in unison. "I hear you kind of walked into something else at the Sunshine Senior Home," Dom continued then. "Or should I say some*one*?"

Ezra shook his head. He wasn't getting into that.

"Who?" Oliver, looking between the two of them, appeared completely interested all of a sudden, until Dom filled him in on Ezra inviting a widow and her twin daughters to the Colton barbecue on Saturday. "Taking up with a widow with kids? That's not like you, man," Oliver said then, holding his beer in both hands, his expression concerned. "You can't just have a quick fling with a family. What happens to them when you leave in a few weeks?"

Dom was clearly waiting for an answer as well— which was probably why his brother had brought up Theresa to begin with.

"Cool it, guys." He gave them each a stern, I'm-not-fooling-around look. "Theresa's still grieving her ex-husband and isn't interested in dating. She made that very clear. The barbecue is a chance for the girls to be at the ranch and ride horses, that's all. Just something nice."

And when they heard, as they surely would from some family member or another, that he was painting the widow's house? "Anyway, did you hear about

Naomi filming some reality TV thing at the Gemini this summer?" he asked to change the subject. "Can you believe the baby is really a TV producer?"

"Here's to the Coltons making good," Oliver said, raising his beer mug.

Dom and Ezra clinked heartily, ate a bit more and got back to the real feature of the evening. Finding out which one of them most had his eye on the ball that evening.

Ezra needed it to be him.

He had to know that Theresa Fitzgerald, her daughters and their problems were only ships passing in the night. They were not personally meaningful to him and absorbing his focus.

THERESA WAITED UNTIL the kids' bedtime to have a "talk." She'd been thinking about it on and off all day, wondering if, like with the Fitzgeralds, she was overreacting to Ezra Colton's effect on the girls. Seeing more than was there about the potential for heartache that an association with Ezra Colton would bring her girls. He was only in town for another three weeks or so. How attached could they really get in that time?

But when Neve had started to cry earlier that evening when Theresa had been ready to hang up without giving the six-year-old a chance to tell Ezra about her newly discovered arm bumps, and Claire had corrected her that they were *muscles*, with a bit of an attitude, after looking sad that she hadn't had a chance to talk to Ezra, either, Theresa knew an Ezra conversation had to happen.

The only way she could allow any further interaction with the man at all—including Saturday's scheduled barbecue and horseback riding—was if the twins understood, clearly, that they were not making a new friend for life.

"Remember when we went on vacation right before Daddy got sick?" she asked them as, snuggled in their double bed in the room they shared, they both lay, heads on their pillows, looking up at her.

"Yeah, we went to Disney World, and I peed my pants," Neve said, giggling. They'd had to wait in line for a couple of hours, and though Theresa and Mark had continually questioned the girls regarding their bathroom needs, they'd both shaken their heads every time they were asked. That was, until right before they boarded the boat that would take them on a ride through a tunnel into a world of fantasy, song and color. Neve said she had to go. But when told that they'd have to get out of line, she'd insisted she could hold it.

And, of course, the excitement of seeing the magnificent, larger-than-life moving figures, and hearing the music, the boat ride, had been too much for her...

The memory of the girls enjoying the ride, even with the peeing, was sweet. But not where she could hang out at that moment.

"You remember the princess you had lunch with?"

"She was so pretty!" Neve said.

"I liked her hair," Claire added, nodding, her young eyes bearing a bit of her sister's sparkle.

"Remember how she was ours just for a little while and then we had to go away and we'd never see her again?"

"Yeah, and remember her lips? They were so red, even when she drinked," Neve continued.

Okay, this probably wasn't the best analogy.

"Our time with the princess is like our time with Mr. Colton," she pressed on.

"Mr. Giant's not a princess!" Neve giggled.

"Shhh, Neve, you should call him Mr. Colton 'less you make a mistake and say that in front of him, right, Mom?" Claire, her hair still in braids and brown eyes big, was looking at Theresa for support.

"Right, but it's not going to matter what we call him for long, because he can't be our friend forever. He's just like the princess having lunch with us, and then he will be gone."

"You said he was the one who made the front part of the house so pretty, Mom," Claire replied. "And he's taking us horseback riding. That's way more than lunch with the princess was."

"Yeah, horseback riding," Neve repeated, nodding. Her loose, long dark strands lay like a halo around her on the pillow, and Theresa had to hold back tears.

God, she loved them so much.

"You're right," she acknowledged, refusing to give up. "It's more than just eating one lunch with someone, but the going-away-forever part is exactly the same as what happened with the princess. Mr. Colton is only in Blue Larkspur for a vacation, like the time we were in Disney World, and then he has a home and a job that he will go back to."

She didn't actually know about the home part. Isa had said Ezra traveled all the time. From one assignment to the next. She'd never mentioned Ezra having a home base. But surely he at least had permanent barracks someplace where he kept whatever personal stuff he had. Or an apartment.

For all she knew, he could have a girlfriend tucked away there, too.

"He's going away like Daddy did?" Neve asked, frowning.

Life shouldn't be so complicated—not at six.

"Sort of," she told them. "He will still be living, like the princess is, but he'll be too far away for us to likely ever see him."

"Why?" Neve asked.

"Because his job is far away, and he's very good at it."

"People have to work their jobs to earn money," Claire announced to the room in general.

"That's right."

"Why can't his job be here?" Neve asked then, no hint of levity in her tone this time.

"Because he works for our country, Neve, and has to go where the president sends him. He keeps the whole United States safe, like our policemen here keep us safe." She was winging it, and not doing a very good job. Had no idea if the girls would get the concept of a much bigger world, of which Blue Larkspur was a part.

Not sure she wanted them to, at this age.

"Is the president nice to him?" Claire wanted to know.

"Very," she said, but then had to be clearer because she and Mark had determined, when he'd gotten sick, that they'd always be honest with their girls. "The president doesn't actually know Mr. Colton to talk to him, but he sends the thousands of people who do jobs like Mr. Colton all over the world."

Neve yawned, and Theresa took that as her cue to

kiss the girls' cheeks one more time, tell them she loved them, wish them sweet dreams and head for the door.

"Mom?"

Claire's voice called her back.

"Yeah?"

"Can we talk to Mr. Colton the whole time he's here on vacation?"

"We'll see. Now, go to sleep. We have to be up early in the morning." Disappointed in her total cop-out response, she flipped the switch in the hall, plunging herself into near darkness, heading toward her room.

A flash of light caught her eye through the door of the playroom, from the street outside the window. Heart pounding, she moved along the wall to get a better look, and she relaxed when she noticed the police car passing through the neighborhood.

If she wasn't careful, she was going to be jumping at her own shadow like some kind of helpless woman.

And helpless she was not.

She couldn't afford to be.

On her way to a full-out pull-on-your-big-girl-panties talk, her mental tirade was interrupted by the sound of a text coming through on her phone. She bet it was from Eric and Jennifer; she hadn't thanked them for the box of the twins' favorite cookies that had been waiting for them when they got home. Sent via a respected and well-known shipping courier, not delivered in person.

Jennifer trying to be a grandma without disrespecting Theresa's wishes.

The text was from Ezra, wanting to know if she'd be up in an hour or so. He was with his brothers but would like to speak with her that night if he could.

No way she'd be going to sleep after that—not that

she'd intended to go to bed anytime soon, at any rate. She'd brought work home with her—accounts to go over—and was too het up to sleep.

She texted back a simple Yes and then pretended that she wasn't feeling a new burst of energy coursing through her as she watched the clock, waiting for the hour to pass.

He probably just had a question about the house, the paint job he'd be working on again the following day. Maybe he'd found some dry rot and she'd have a bigger problem on her hands than getting through a couple of weeks without throwing herself at a visiting soldier.

Maybe he had another function he wanted her to attend. With just her. Like a date.

Her stomach flipped at the thought. And then flopped.

She prepared herself.

If Ezra asked her out again, she had no choice but to tell him no.

Chapter Six

"I'm sorry to be calling so late," Ezra said as soon as Theresa picked up the phone. Sitting in his car in the parking lot of The Corner Pocket, he'd dialed her as soon as he'd seen the taillights of both of his brothers' cars turn out of sight. "Oliver's leaving tomorrow to head back to Malaysia…" he started in, then stopped, Oliver's words ringing in his mind. *What happens to them when you leave in a few weeks?*

A question followed by his own… Even if he wasn't leaving for good, or she was willing to be hooked up with a career soldier, he worked a dangerous job. How could he ever ask a woman who'd already buried one love prematurely, or those precious little ones who'd suffered far too much in their young lives, to chance their hearts with a man who faced the possibility of death as a regular part of his job?

His personal business was no concern of hers…

"No, no, it's fine." Theresa's tone sounded stilted—because it was coming over the car's audio system? Or because she wasn't "fine" with him calling so late?

Which brought him back to business.

"I heard from Chief Lawson," he jumped right in. "He didn't find any immediate cause for worry. There are no police reports on the Fitzgeralds, period, anywhere in the state. Not even a speeding ticket for either one of them. If they own a bunker, that's not something that would show up, but a surprising number of government officials have them, too. He found nothing at all that could lead to any sign of criminal behavior. But he didn't like what I told him you'd said, and so, just to be safe, he's putting extra patrol around your home, the day camp and the nursing home."

It was overkill, and he knew it. He also knew that he was probably getting special treatment because he was Isa's son. He didn't care why. He'd use whatever influence he had if it meant keeping a widow and her two daughters safe. Any widow.

"I had a package at the house today."

He started his Jeep and put it in Reverse with one hand, ready to back up and get to her house. "You didn't open it yet, did you? Why didn't you call sooner? That's the kind of thing that warrants…" He'd made it out of the parking spot, and with the Jeep in Drive, foot on the gas, he shot forward.

"I opened it," she interrupted. "It was just Jennifer's homemade chocolate chip cookies. Mark used to talk about them. And every time they saw the girls, both with me and that one time alone, she sent some home."

He still didn't like it. He turned toward her part of town—the opposite direction of home.

"Have they already consumed some?" Maybe he spent too much time living on guard, ready to go up against the worst of the worst…

"No."

"I'd like to pick them up, if you don't mind. Take

them to have them analyzed. Just to be sure. We can do it on the down-low. No one needs to know…"

"I can leave them for you in the morning," she said. "I don't want them here, anyway."

Right. The morning. It wasn't like forensics would be called in that night, or even that the job would be top priority, if he collected them that night. They'd sit until early the next day, no matter what.

Slowing, he turned his vehicle toward his mother's house. "I'll get them to the chief first thing," he assured her.

"I don't know how to thank you…"

"For what? Making a few-minute phone call and taking a ten-minute drive out of my way to deliver a box?" She might make more of it. He knew better. He couldn't have either of them making more of his interest than was there. "Look, for what it's worth…the one thing my siblings and I have in common, other than our name and growing up in the same household, is a need to make up for what our father did to people in this county and beyond. Before my dad got greedy, to keep his huge family with all of the creature comforts and monetary security he'd wanted to provide, he was a good guy. I was in the second batch of births and remember him back then. He ruined his own legacy, but we're determined to right as many wrongs as we can. To help where he hurt. We started The Truth Foundation ten years ago, to exonerate everyone he wrongfully imprisoned and to help others in similar straits. We're the new Colton legacy…"

What the hell? Him, part of the legacy? Where had that come from him? Ezra had skipped town at eighteen by joining the army and had never looked back. Oliver and Dom…pretty much the same.

"The painting…and the riding… I'm not one who takes charity," she said, her voice soft. "We're doing nothing in return."

Slowing, he took a detour down by the river. Parked and looked out over the moonlit water. "Aunt Alice is my great-aunt, but I was closer to her than most of my other relatives. She was on Mom's side, not a Colton, and she was where I went to escape being a Colton. You're doing things for me in return every single day that you're at work, making sure that my aunt has loving care, offered with patience and respect, at a time when she can't possibly look out for or speak up for herself. If anyone's in debt, it's me, not you."

All true. And maybe too personal, which he sought quickly to correct. "I wasn't kidding about the painting being something I enjoy, which also gets me out of sitting at my mom's, the unwilling recipient of nosy drop-in visits all day long. Most people have to pay for their vacation entertainment."

And if painting as entertainment made him a dull guy, all the better.

The activity was actually serving a much more important purpose for him. Up on a ladder at her house all day, he'd be able to guard the place easily. No subterfuge necessary.

He'd already decided to slow his pace. And to find other jobs he could do, if necessary, to keep him at Theresa's all day until the Fitzgerald situation calmed down.

And if it didn't calm down before he left?

Ezra shook his head. He'd learned long ago to take his battles one at a time. He didn't borrow trouble.

"And, actually, there is one thing you can do," he said then, already congratulating himself on his flash of insight. "You can put Aunt Alice on Charlie's list, for as many visits as he can make. Did you see the way she was petting him?"

"I noticed the slight smile on her face most," Theresa said. "I haven't seen that expression out of her since she came to us."

"Family took care of her as long as they could."

"Rest assured, she's on Charlie's list from now on."

Which left them nothing else to discuss. "So, I'll see you in the morning." He didn't want to hang up.

"We'll probably be gone by the time you get here," she told him. "I'll leave the cookies on the bench in the garage."

Unless she was leaving before dawn, he'd be there before she left. Figuring the Fitzgeralds for nighttime sleepers, since their known activities had all happened during the day, he'd assigned himself daily painting shifts, dawn until dusk. He was hoping that, since the grandparents apparently wanted to get the girls without alarming them—their motivation being to save the twins from whatever blast they thought was imminent—they wouldn't break into Theresa's home to kidnap them.

"By the way," she said, when he'd braced for the goodbye that had to come next, "I saw a patrol car passing by outside when I put the girls to bed. So... thank you. What you're doing might be small to you, but it's making a huge difference to me. I just want you to know your efforts are appreciated."

His male part went to immediate attention, misunderstanding her appreciation for something much more personal. At first, he felt like a skunk, until he realized that her tone of voice had changed.

"I'm glad," he told her, equally soft. And personal.

And then hung up before he ruined everything.

EZRA, IN PAINTER'S pants and a T-shirt that left the remarkable muscles in his upper arms in plain view, was already up on a ladder at the garage side of her house when Theresa pulled out the next morning. She hadn't even known he was there but noticed him at the same time as the girls did.

"It's Mr. Giant!" Neve yelled, drowning out Claire's more restrained, but equally enthusiastic, "Mr. Colton's here!"

The eagerness in their tones was sufficient to keep Theresa from stopping the old vehicle for a quick good morning.

She waved instead, as did the kids, and tried not to make anything of the man's smile and lifting of his paintbrush as she drove away. She walked the twins into day camp—another mandatory indoor day for them—and arrived at work. Same thing in reverse that night, except that he was in his truck, just getting ready to drive away, as they got home.

He waved, she waved, the girls excitedly gesturing, and off he went. The timing of that one was almost meant to be—as though she was supposed to see him there—and she sent up a silent prayer to whatever angels were watching over them. Thinking of him that way, as a gift sent from above to help her and her daughters out of a tight spot, felt…wiser.

Safer.

And so, on Saturday afternoon, when Ezra's Jeep pulled into the drive to collect them not five minutes after they'd returned home from a morning spent at gymnastics and then shopping, she scurried the excited girls along with the thought that the angels watching over them had arranged an afternoon of horseback riding, too.

The butterflies in her stomach were a little harder to explain.

Reminding her daughters that Ezra wasn't a permanent friend, but rather a fleeting companion, she checked their jeans and matching princess T-shirts. She'd handed out the new tops that morning as a reminder of their only lunch with the princess. She'd spared a quick glance down to ensure that her tie-dyed cotton sundress and matching red sandals bore no morning stains, and led her small family out of their home, locking the door behind her, and supervising as Ezra quickly loaded the car seats.

The friend reminder might or might not have worked on her daughters. But the second she climbed into the passenger seat next to Ezra, smelled his musky scent and saw those arms only partially contained in a short-sleeved polo shirt above faded jeans, she started to quiver from the inside out. More so when he leaned in to quietly let her know he'd dropped off the cookies, but that it could take a while to get results from the analysis. The man was too good to be true.

So angels, fate, whatever, had an ironic sense of humor, she mused. And ended up with the thought as a mantra as they arrived at the Gemini after ten minutes of nonstop six-year-old chatter on the ride over.

Nine of the twelve Colton siblings—Gavin wasn't in town, Oliver was in Malaysia and Caleb was on his honeymoon—had gathered for the barbecue. From the adult conversation that flowed with almost as much abandon and cacophony as Claire and Neve's, she was able to ascertain that Ezra's presence at the event was a near miracle.

"You haven't attended this function since you were eighteen?" She leaned over to whisper to him as they walked through too many adults for her to remember all at once, toward the tables and grills set up behind the massive lodge.

Cheers went up as someone threw a ringer at a game of horseshoes, and she heard a large splash right before Neve cried out, "Look, Mom, a pool!"

"Crap, I didn't think to tell you to bring their suits," Ezra said, a frown on his face. Wondering how he handled being disappointed in himself, she almost didn't have the wherewithal to comment.

But that same look drew words from within her. "Are you kidding?" she said, wanting only to let the man know that rather than being a disappointment of any kind, he was a miracle worker. "The girls swim all the time at day camp. You're giving them a chance to be close to horses. To actually sit on one, which neither of them have ever done, by the way. Their outfits are perfect for what their little hearts desire today."

It was all the chance they had for any kind of private conversation before they were swarmed by another gaggle of Colton siblings and some significant others, too. Some in bathing attire with cover-ups. Others in shorts.

And then she saw Isa Colton, who had been a great support during Mark's passing.

"You finally get to meet my crew," Isa said with a smile as Theresa and Ezra approached the table behind which Isa was standing, arranging covered dishes. The woman came around the table, dressed elegantly in white close-fitting pants and a colorful, formfitting top that showed how lovely her hourglass figure remained, even at seventy-two. The lovely blonde didn't try to hide her age. She just looked fantastic in it. "Though I have to say," Isa continued before Theresa could respond, "Ezra is the last person I'd have expected to bring you to us…" She was grinning, gazing so adoringly up at her son that Theresa almost felt envious.

To be loved to that extent, that someone didn't care you'd missed eighteen years of parties, because they were so happy you'd come to one…

Isa took over the girls then, taking them first to see baby Iris, who was sleeping, and then showing them a kids' hut on the other side of the large grassy area where the picnic tables had been set up.

An hour later, Theresa still hadn't had her girls back at her side or had a chance to speak with either one of them. Nor had she had a chance for any private conversation with Ezra. The first made her a tad bit uncomfortable. The latter she knew was for the best.

"You think we should take Claire and Neve to ride before or after we eat?" The man in her thoughts spoke into her ear, leaning from just behind her. They'd just finished listening to Naomi talking about her plans for the show she'd be filming at the ranch soon, and Theresa figured they had about five seconds or so before someone else came up to join them.

"That's entirely your call," she said, and then took the rare private chance to tell him, "You can go play horseshoes or cornhole or whatever with your family. You don't have to stand here and babysit me."

She needed him to go. Give her a breather. She loved having him there, too much. Loved listening to him banter with his siblings almost as much as she loved the serious answers he gave to a couple of sincere questions Dom had asked about Ezra's last assignment in Afghanistan.

A very strongly needed reminder to her that Ezra Colton had a real life.

And how very far away it was from anything she could live with.

"Are you kidding?" he asked, leaning toward her again, as though anyone else could hear him in the chaos going on around them. "You're my excuse not to have to whup their butts or pretend that I'm not letting them win."

The bravado was only more of what she'd been hearing from the brothers and sisters for the past hour, but in Ezra's case, she had a feeling he was speaking the truth. At least somewhat.

Mostly, she had a feeling the man really did prefer standing with her rather than hanging out with his siblings en masse. He'd seemed to relax when Dom had joined them for a few minutes, but the man had been so clearly besotted with Sami—a landscaper who Theresa had thoroughly enjoyed speaking with—and had been eager to show her around.

Get her alone was more like it, though Theresa kept that thought to herself.

"I had no idea the girls would be the only kids here

besides the baby," she said, as they had another minute with no one approaching. "Everyone is spoiling them so much I'll never be able to get them to sleep tonight. I was expecting a slew of kids running around."

"Nope, Iris is it," he said with a shrug. "Who'd have thought—twelve kids, the oldest two being thirty-nine, and only one grandchild." Who was still sleeping. Or maybe sleeping again. It wasn't like she'd been privy to the baby's activities all afternoon. The girls had come out of the kids' hut with a couple of horses painted with watercolors, running to show them to her, and then had been called over to play cornhole. One on each team. They were laughing, hollering encouragements and having the time of their lives.

And they hadn't even been on the horses yet...

"It looks like Dom could be providing a grandchild in the not-so-distant future," she said, happy for her daughters, and worried, too. Disney World was half-way across the country. Gemini Ranch was right there in town.

"I'd never have thought Dom would ever settle down or want a family, but it does appear like he's on his way there," Ezra allowed, frowning as he looked over the grounds at clusters of siblings and others they'd invited. "Caleb's married now, too. And Aubrey, Rachel and Gideon have all found happiness..."

"You don't like the people they're with?" she asked.

"Yeah!" He glanced at her then. "I do, actually."

And she felt stupid for thinking she knew him well enough to read his expressions. "Sorry... I just thought you sounded...not happy about it..."

His shrug brought her attention to those massive

shoulders, but only until she saw the troubled look in the blue eyes trained completely on her.

A woman could happily melt right there...

"I don't like the change," he said then. "Or maybe, better put, I don't like that things can change so drastically in such a short time." The words seemed to make him more uneasy.

And Theresa went into immediate nurturing mode. It was what she did best. What she was born to do. "And yet you know that they can," she said softly. "Your experience with your dad taught you that."

A tragic course of events that, at sixteen, could mar a man for life. Ezra clearly liked order. His military haircut might be mandatory, but everything else about the man was in place as well.

Even the way he seemed to need a solid explainable reason for every single thing that he did.

Something that drew her to him in a very dangerous way.

"Just as it taught you that it doesn't take away your own ability to make choices for yourself," she added. "If Dom didn't want to give up undercover work, I'm guessing he wouldn't be doing it."

"True, that..."

Whatever else Ezra had been about to say was interrupted as another attractive, dark-haired woman joined them. Ezra introduced her as Morgan. Twin to the Caleb who just got married. An attorney like her twin, in partnership with him at their own firm. They were the firstborn Colton heirs.

And had made the news a number of times as they ran The Truth Foundation, an organization they initially spearheaded to help free the innocents their father had wrongfully put away. Last she'd heard, they'd taken care of almost all of them.

Morgan's welcome of Theresa sounded sincere. She praised Claire and Neve. Was polite, kind, and seemed to be heading somewhere, a purpose for coming over to them with no one else around. But when the pleasantries were done, she just turned to Ezra and said, "So, how were things at The Corner Pocket the other night?"

His night out with Dom and Oliver. The night he'd texted Theresa, and then called late...

"Same as usual. I beat the crap out of them. They said I cheated."

"They let you win. You know that, right?"

"Ha! That's what they want you to think." Ezra didn't seem the least bit concerned one way or the other.

"I'm guessing Roman comped your beers," she said then. Roman DiMera, owner of The Corner Pocket. Theresa knew who he was, of course. The man owned the entire waterfront building that housed the pub, but lived in a little apartment above his eatery and bar. But she'd never met him personally, let alone had him offer to comp as much as a French fry.

"No clue," Ezra told her. "I wasn't buying." She asked a big-sister question confirming that they'd had two apiece, to stay within legal driving limits, and walked off when Isa called out to her, leaving Theresa to wonder why on earth she'd brought up the bar at all.

Figured it was probably just Morgan's way of engaging her recalcitrant soldier brother in conversation, but she took the whole episode as a needed reminder that she was way outside her league at a Colton barbecue.

But so it went for most of the afternoon. Introductions. Kindness. Great food. Conversations that gave her insights into Ezra.

The Colton siblings enthusiastically taking turns entertaining the six-year-old twins their brother had invited into their midst.

And she and Ezra, side by side.

It took all of Theresa's great well of strength to keep herself from falling for the moment.

Chapter Seven

Who'd have thought that seeing the glow on the faces of two little kids could bring such pleasure? Glancing up at Claire and Neve as Jasper and Aubrey helped the girls into their saddles and then asked if they were ready, Ezra felt the jolt like lightning shooting through him.

As though he had some ownership in the joy and happiness of anyone's kid.

He was so not a family man. All it took was an outing with all of the Coltons, a reminder of a lifetime of cacophony, and he knew that, unlike Dom, he wasn't open to a major life change.

He was a normal guy who noticed an incredible woman when he met her, though. From the way Theresa held court with his siblings, engaging with them so naturally, keeping track of who was who, to the way her long dark hair—free from the bun for once—flowed around her upper body…she'd snagged his attention.

In a huge way.

And the beauty was, he could enjoy the moment, without having to fret about any of the rest of it. Theresa wasn't at all interested in, or probably even capable of, falling for any guy. Not while she was still a young widow grieving for the husband she'd lost.

Having her at his side for the entire afternoon, someone whose conversation was an immediate draw, not a potential threat, with a body that tantalized in a hands-off kind of way… The combination distracted him from his constant need to put up walls where his family was concerned. Not once, in all the hours they were at the Gemini, did he think about lands far away.

Or long for escape.

In the Jeep on the way home, while the girls took turns reading from a new horse book Aubrey had given them from the kids' hut, Ezra couldn't remember ever being so relaxed—and so alive at the same time.

As he glanced at Theresa, a curious desire to unburden himself came over him. He fought it. Made it most of the way home. But when he turned a couple of blocks from Theresa's place, he glanced at her again and said, "You thought you didn't have any way to pay me back for what you perceive to be huge favors on my part, and I just have to tell you, the favors you do might not seem like much to you, but back there, the afternoon we just spent… I owe you."

She frowned. But wasn't looking at him. He was turning the corner onto her street and she was staring down the road.

Following her gaze, he understood immediately. The mint-condition old blue truck would have stood out on any street. In front of her house…

Slowing, with a quick glance in the rearview mirror to ensure that the girls were still engrossed in their story, with Claire correcting Neve on a sentence she was sounding out, he asked, "You want me to turn around?"

His instincts insisted that was what he should do. Immediately.

Theresa shook her head. "They have an end goal that I can't allow, but they aren't violent people," she said softly. Always the nurturer.

He admired the hell out of her. And wanted to shake her, too.

Years of training had taught him how best to save innocent lives. When danger was posed, you went into defensive mode first, made a plan, then attacked.

And the call wasn't his. She'd made her wishes clear. If he did anything but deliver her and her daughters to their home, he technically became a kidnapper.

And law aside, Theresa's life and the lives of her children were hers to run. Not his.

Besides, she knew the enemy. He did not. Making her intel better than his.

Driving around the offending vehicle to pull in the driveway, he took a quick but detailed glance at the older man and woman sitting inside. Noting…nothing but a couple of grandparent-age people waiting outside a house.

They definitely weren't hiding their presence. In that truck, they'd be noticed pretty much anywhere they went.

Had Lawson's extra patrol already checked them out?

Or had the couple just arrived a minute or two ahead of them?

Before Ezra had even turned off the engine, Mark's parents had exited their vehicle and were walking up toward the back passenger-side door of Ezra's rented vehicle. If they so much as touched...

"Grandma's here!" Neve said, bursting out of her door before Ezra could figure out how to stop her.

A feat he'd have failed at, no matter what, because Theresa was already exiting his vehicle as well, heading immediately toward the Fitzgeralds.

Hearing the click of a seat belt behind him, Ezra turned around to look at Claire, who'd been seated behind him.

"Grandpa says scary things," she told him.

"I heard."

"Do you know about the blast, Mr. Colton? Grandma and Grandpa say it's coming, and Mom says it's not."

Keeping an eye on the two females who'd already exited his vehicle, while also giving Claire his attention, Ezra noted Neve hugging her grandmother, and Theresa standing right there, with a hand on her daughter's shoulder the entire time, while he tried to figure out how to answer the frightened and confused, hurting child relying on him for...promises he couldn't keep?

"I can promise you that I believe that the blast is not coming," he told her. He gave his life up every single day to ensure that threats of the kind Claire now feared did not hit American soil. "You know what's worse than the blast?" he asked her then.

Wide-eyed, she shook her head. "Being afraid to have fun because something bad might happen." He heard the words, and then had to quickly qualify, "Not to be confused with doing something you know is wrong, but doing it anyway just to have fun. That kind of fun you should be afraid of. You should always make good, safe choices, but if you're afraid of things that could happen that you can't stop, then you won't ever be happy or have fun."

"Like when Daddy got sick." The serious little voice broke his heart in one sentence. And climbed inside it, too.

"Yes. Just like that."

"Is the blast like Daddy's sickness? It happens to some people only and they didn't do anything to make it there?"

Theresa! Panicking at his lack of response, he glanced her way. Saw her arm around Neve while they stood there in what appeared to be serious but non-threatened conversation.

And knew, for better or worse, he was on his own.

"No. Because sickness does come from time to time. The blast doesn't." And the rest of the answer occurred to him. "It never has, Claire. Not even once in all the thousands of years since the world has been here, there's never been anything like the huge blast that can ruin the whole world your grandparents talk about."

Wide-eyed, she stared at him. "You sure?"

"Positive."

Claire nodded. Gathered her new book to her chest and, without looking his way again, climbed down out of his vehicle and walked around the Jeep to stand on the other side of her mother.

Feeling as though he'd just come out of battle, and not sure he'd won, Ezra followed right on Claire's heels.

"Who is this man who's carting my son's kids around?" Eric Fitzgerald didn't present as a nonviolent kind of guy as he glared from Ezra to Theresa. Landing on her with obvious accusation.

"He's Mr. Giant!" Neve popped in, before either adult had time to respond. "You know, like the princess at Disney World, only he's not a princess, but a soldier man who goes far away to keep everyone safe."

"Soldier!" Jennifer said, shooting a mistrusting look at Ezra before turning to her husband, as though he had to do something about Ezra's profession immediately.

"What are you doing exposing our granddaughters to a man who kills for a living?" Eric practically spit the words. "One whose job will take him to God knows where, and, if you two hook up, could take them, too, into God knows what. No way Mark would want them palling around with such a dangerous man!"

The guy was clearly unstable in his thinking, but hadn't made any moves toward Theresa or Ezra, in any physical sense. When she sent him a pleading look, directing his attention with a nod toward Claire's distressed expression and holding out her house key, he stepped forward, noting the irony in the older couple being so singly focused on their own conversation that they didn't seem to notice him ushering the twins away.

Taking one of each of the girls' hands, reminding them that they'd told him they'd show him the wall of horse drawings in their playroom before he did his best to make the exit seem natural.

He'd been going to help them choose where on that horse wall to put their watercolor paintings from that afternoon, so though Ezra wanted the kids away from their grandparents immediately, he took them around the Jeep, putting the vehicle between them and the Fitzgeralds, but made himself stop at the truck to retrieve the paintings first, then spoke loudly enough to at least distract from the tirade emitting from the other side of the truck.

"I had a lot of fun today," he told the girls, leaning down as he walked to be more easily heard. "What part did you like best?"

Neve, as usual, was the first to answer. Horseback riding was first, of course. And cornhole came in second. For third she wanted to know if she could go back and try the swimming pool sometime. She didn't give her twin a chance to answer, but Ezra was fairly certain Claire's attention wasn't on the question anyway. The little girl had reached up her free hand to hold on to Ezra's arm above their clasped hands.

He said hello to Charlie, who greeted him at the door as though he'd known him forever, and put the dog out back for his business as Claire instructed. Then he followed the two dark-haired urchins down the hall to their playroom.

And while he tended to the girls, thumbtacking their paintings to spots on the wall too high for them to reach, not seeing much at all of the house for the glances he kept sending out the window, keeping Theresa in sight, he knew that he was never going to forget this little family.

Or his brief time being a part of them.

SHE COULDN'T REASON with them. Theresa tried again. Failed again. And warned the Fitzgeralds that if they came anywhere near her home, her place of business, the girls' school, day camp or anywhere else any of the three of them might be, or called or texted her again, she was going to file for a restraining order against them.

Let them try to take her to court for visitation rights. She'd have a child psychologist interview Claire if need be, to prove that Eric and Jennifer Fitzgerald were not a healthy influence on her children.

And if they didn't leave her property immediately, she was going to call the police.

The last threat was a new one. And one she wouldn't have made if not for Ezra's intervention. He'd alerted the chief of police regarding her family struggles, and the chief had found the situation worthy of extra patrol. Her worry was understandable, actionable, even if in the end it turned out not to be warranted.

As her former in-laws turned and silently walked away, Theresa swallowed back tears. She'd wanted to love them. For her girls to have a loving relationship with them. Shaking, she wished so hard that life had been different. That Mark had been able to grow up with emotionally and mentally healthy parents. And that he hadn't been struck down with a terminal illness.

She'd had her time to say goodbye to Mark. And as she turned to go into her house, stopping first to retrieve the car seats from Ezra's Jeep, she thought of the promise she'd made Mark that she'd find happiness again. She was ready to be happy.

To give her girls back as much of their carefree childhood as she could.

And she felt helpless. It wasn't like you could just order up a pound of happiness on the internet, pay for same-day shipping and have it simply show up.

Just as no amount of hoping had helped Mark get well, she couldn't positive-think his parents into people they were not.

Feeling defeated, worried, like she had to find some

way to scale an impossibly high mountain in order to give her two precious angels the emotional and physical security that had been robbed from them, she entered her house to hear Claire say, "Thank you, Mr. Colton. The paintings look beautiful up there. Are you for sure you have to go far away and be a soldier?"

Fear struck through her. Her talk with the girls… She should have known there wouldn't be anything she could say that would be strong enough to prevent them from falling for the man.

How could she have expected two innocent six-year-olds to guard their hearts when she hadn't been completely successful in doing so herself?

Ezra Colton was a sergeant in the army. He'd be on active duty again in less than a month. And might be killed at any time.

She could not take on that possibility of loss for herself. She most definitely couldn't subject her girls to it.

With the resolve a viable source inside her, she headed back to the girls' playroom, only to hear Ezra say, "Why don't you two draw pictures of the horses you each rode today, while I go talk to your mom for a minute?"

He knew she was there.

She quickly backed into the kitchen.

She'd been quiet entering the house. Had greeted Charlie with the scratch on his chest that he liked best to keep him calm.

Knowing what she did of Ezra Colton, she figured he'd probably been watching her the whole time she'd been outside. Had seen the Fitzgeralds' truck drive away. The man didn't seem to miss anything.

At least, not with her or her twins.

Much like Mark had been with them…

Ezra had his phone in hand as he came into the kitchen—the only place in her small home where they could speak without being heard in the playroom. "I'll call Chief Lawson," he said.

"No!" The word came out far more sharply than she'd intended, and she softened her tone. "At least… Just…no." The girls, the problems, were hers. "I'll call the police myself," she told him. "To make an official report of the unannounced visit." And to make sure she knew exactly what to do, straight from law enforcement, if she saw or heard from the Fitzgeralds again. "I don't think they're going to bother us anymore." She told him what she actually believed.

There'd been resignation about their withdrawal from the fight that afternoon. A sense of knowing that they'd gone too far and had lost their chance.

Probably because they'd been through it all before with their son.

And they'd never contacted or been near him again.

"They didn't seem ready to just walk away," he told her, and the way his words immediately ramped up her anxiety had her walls shooting up higher than they'd ever been around him. "You don't have to go through this alone, Theresa. Let me help. We can explain to the girls enough about conspiracy theories to help them understand that people just sometimes get caught up in stuff, like thinking cartoon characters are real and…"

She'd thought of comparing Ezra's time with them to eating lunch with a princess, but she hadn't thought about easing her daughters' fears by likening their grandparents' beliefs to cartoon characters. He was good.

And as soon as her heart started to reach out toward

him in gratitude, she knew it had to stop. Him in her home. Interacting with her girls.

Touching her heart…

"Stop." She hadn't actually meant to say the word aloud, but knew when she did that it was the right thing. "Just stop, Ezra. You aren't their father. You aren't even going to be in town much longer…"

He didn't so much stiffen as just stand up straighter, but she knew her words had done what she'd set out to do.

"I apologize," he told her. "You're right. And it's probably just better if we don't see each other again."

Her nod was the right thing to do, too.

"I'll be back to finish the painting and, to that end, would like to work tomorrow as well. Carlos, my friend, was here yesterday, but I'll be alone tomorrow. Can you make sure the girls don't see me?"

He was even good, decent, about ending things. In that moment, the truth pissed her off. "You don't need to finish painting."

Even if they weren't there, she couldn't handle knowing he was at her house. Still taking care of them.

He didn't need to be spending his vacation working free of charge for a virtual stranger.

"I already bought the paint. And would appreciate the activity."

"Fine." She quickly added, "And…thank you. I'll take the girls to the river for the day. We'll leave early, and I'll keep them out until you text to let me know you're leaving. And if you need Monday to finish, we can do the same. Communicate with each other so the girls aren't here to see you. Same for Tuesday, if it takes that long."

She had no idea how she was going to tell them that Ezra had left without saying goodbye, but she knew it had to happen.

The long look they shared then might have said things that she couldn't afford to acknowledge. And maybe she'd only imagined that it had.

"You've got this," he said as he pulled his keys from his pocket. "Just, please, call the police."

She nodded.

He gave her a smile filled with warmth. Friendship.

Then turned around and walked away.

Out of her house.

Out of her life.

Theresa quickly brushed away the tears that fell.

Chapter Eight

Thank God for rotting eaves and fascia board. The need to replace them—with paid help from another high school friend—in order to paint them kept Ezra busy Sunday and Monday. With all signs of wood and sawing removed before he left the premises.

Theresa had enough to worry about without thinking she owed anyone anything else.

And he could leave town knowing that he'd done all he could to help her and her kids.

As long as the Fitzgerald situation was resolved. Though how he'd measure that result, he wasn't sure. There'd been no sign of the older couple at Theresa's house. His surveillance skills were top-notch. And he'd had a few calls from Chief Lawson as well.

He knew Theresa had called the police to report Saturday's incident. And he knew that there'd been no sign of, or reported trouble about, the Fitzgeralds since that time.

Did that mean the situation was resolved? As Theresa expected?

Or was the couple just lying in wait? Formulating a plan, as Theresa had once intimated?

Finishing up at her house on Tuesday, he wasn't

ready to just pack it in and call the job done. Doing so on a personal basis—he'd handled that one just fine.

But leaving a woman in potential danger?

Not his style.

He pondered the matter as, still in his new white painter's pants and a white T-shirt and tennis shoes, he turned into Sunshine Senior Home on Tuesday afternoon, his gaze automatically searching for, and not finding, the mint-condition old blue pickup truck. He saw Theresa's old vehicle, though. Parked right where it had been the last time he'd been there.

He was at the home to see his aunt—having promised himself he'd see her at least once a week, and it had been a week—and if he saw Theresa, he would let her know that the work at her home was done.

He could text her the message. Their brief communications to arrange their departures and arrivals at her home so that they didn't coincide over the past couple of days had worked fine.

He just couldn't bring himself to admit to her that his work was complete.

The painting was done.

His job, self-appointed as it was, protecting her from the bad guys, didn't feel done.

And the twins... He knew Claire and Neve would be on the premises. It was Tuesday. They were there with Charlie every Tuesday. He shouldn't go in.

His phone rang while he sat there. His oldest brother, Caleb, back from his honeymoon, and all business. He was calling all of the siblings to let them know that Ronald Spence, the last man to be let out of jail due to their father's illegal dealmaking, had been seen multiple times at his old haunts, and Dominic's suspicion that the man was back to his old smuggling business was looking likely.

"It appears that he's working right here in Blue Larkspur," Caleb said, "or pretty close to it. I'm hoping you, in particular, with your skills and time on your hands, can keep a watch out for anything suspicious."

"Of course," Ezra told his sibling. He was always on the lookout for suspicious activity. No matter where he was or for what reason. His belief that evil lurked in the world around him was just part of who he was.

The reminder had him out of the Jeep and heading toward the senior-home entrance as soon as Caleb hung up. Either he needed another job to do at Theresa's house, and he had one or two to suggest, or he had to be straight with her and let her know that he had a bad feeling about her in-laws and would be obliged if she'd let him continue his surveillance for a little bit longer.

He'd learned to trust his gut, and it was upheaving on this one.

He'd avoid all contact with the girls. Neve could always be heard from halfway down the hall, at least, and if they got close to Alice's room, he'd slip into the bathroom before they saw him.

Plan in place, he was barely in the door of the spacious, warm and somewhat elegant reception area before he saw Theresa. He'd known her office was there, but hadn't expected to get lucky and have her sitting at her massive desk with the door open.

She stood, giving him a full view of the black jacket and short skirt covering her delicious-looking curves. Professional dress had never been a particular turn-on for him before. Nor had auburn highlights in messy buns, but his body was sending a new memo.

At thirty-six.

He didn't have time to reject the message, but with his shirt hanging over his fly, he could ignore it. Refuse to listen.

Discipline himself so the body didn't have a say.

"Ezra, can I see you for a moment?" she asked, politely, all business. The warm gaze peering at him from those expressive dark eyes seemed to carry a much more personal note.

Since he was there to speak with her as much as see his aunt, he took the invitation as an omen that his gut had been correct in terms of needing more time to watch over her safety from the Fitzgeralds.

Which honed his nerve endings to the edge, and gave him need for a plan, too.

In her office, with the door open, but with no one else in the lobby, she stood just inches from him, her face turned up toward his, and said, "I owe you an apology for my waspishness on Saturday." Eyes wide, filled with concern, and that constant hint of reaching out with her heart, she didn't blink as she continued, "Seeing Mark's parents again unnerved me. And with you there, and them attacking my right to have you there... I overreacted, and I'm sorry."

"I'm sorry, too." The words came. He didn't approve of having uttered them.

"What could you possibly have to be sorry for?"

The conversation wasn't supposed to be on the course it seemed to be following. It was supposed to be serious, but only in terms of the threat she might be facing, and his ability to help alleviate it to some extent.

"For letting you ditch me so easily," he told her. Theresa compelled his honesty. "I took the route of least resistance, and while I'm here to see my aunt, I also came to see you. To talk about…"

Frantic dog barking erupted, cutting him off.

"Charlie!" Theresa cried out as, together, they hurried in the direction of the memory-care unit from which the barking was emitting.

Swiping a card rather than having to type a code on the keypad as Ezra would have had to do, she was on the unit and heading toward Charlie's anxious-sounding alerts coming from behind a closed resident door. Moving past Theresa, Ezra ran the length of the hall, skirting a couple of people in wheelchairs set along the wall, heading straight for the back exit.

Charlie locked in a room…

The back door was set to an alarm—he'd noted all details the week before, when he'd been taking stock of security measures for his aunt's safety. An alarm hadn't gone off.

The door was closed. But a quick glance at the sensor had his blood raging. A kitchen magnet covered the sensor, triggering the alarm to think the door was closed even if it wasn't. The door was set to prevent confused residents from wandering out alone, unattended, not to keep people from leaving the building in case of emergency. With the slide of a security bar and a hard shove, he had the door open.

And saw a flash of metal through the trees along the road behind the home. The Fitzgeralds' truck? He hoped to God he was wrong.

Pulling out his phone, he was connecting to the police by the time his gaze fell to a bush just outside the door.

Claire's new horse book.

The so-serious little six-year-old had let them know she'd been outside that door.

SHE SAW CHARLIE. Mrs. Wright, the room's occupant. Not her daughters. Gaze darting frantically around the room, Theresa didn't see Claire or Neve anywhere!

Her heart practically clogged her throat as she tried to speak to the elderly resident who was hard of hearing, and she couldn't get Charlie to stop barking, so she ran for the private bath attached to the room, hoping the girls had disobeyed orders not to use the patient facilities.

The small room, including shower, was empty. Blood pounded through her so rapidly she couldn't feel. Could hardly think. Ran out of the room, desperately searching, and saw Ezra coming toward her, his phone in his hand.

And a look of deep sorrow...

"*Noooo!* No." She toned her wail down to a command. "No," she said, shaking her head. Charlie, quiet all of a sudden, stood beside her. Ezra strode to the room where the dog had been shut in.

"Did you see anyone come in here?" Ezra asked the woman sitting in a chair by the window, but Theresa shook her head.

"She can't hear, and doesn't comprehend enough to..." She broke off, panic rising so high within her she started to see stars.

"You need to put the building on lockdown." Ezra's voice called her back from an abyss. Commanded her action. "When I was here last week, I read that there are protocols for that, in case a memory-care patient goes missing..."

"Yes," she cut him off. "Yes." Pulling a phone from her pocket, she pushed speed dial to tap into the building's rarely used intercom system, ordering all personnel to instigate an immediate lockdown. No one was to leave the building. She barely had the wherewithal to remember to assure everyone that there was no immediate danger.

That told staff that they were dealing with a possible resident escape, one or two people in a troubled situation, as opposed to a multiple life-threatening situation.

Except...multiple lives... Oh, God. The Fitzgeralds might not be violent, but if they'd actually kidnapped her girls...

"The police are on their way," he said next, striding purposefully toward the window. As though troops would be coming through it at any moment. But what about her girls?

She ran for the door. Intending to search every room, every closet, under every bed until she found Claire and Neve...

"I've already searched the rooms on this unit," Ezra said. "Can you check security tapes? I know cameras aren't in individual rooms, but they'd show us hallway activity, right? And outside?"

Yes. Absolutely. "Of course," she said, tearing out of the room, down the hall, past employees—who, under lockdown protocol, were standing at their assigned doorways—off the unit and over to her office, not sure if Ezra was even behind her.

It didn't surprise her when she pulled up the live feed on her computer and his face lowered right next to hers in front of the screen. For a brief second, it comforted her.

Until the blue truck flashed up on her screen from the top right camera image. Then all she knew was stone-cold fear.

"THEY'VE TAKEN THEM to prepare them for the nuclear blast." The wealth of terror, and of certainty, in Theresa's tone grabbed at Ezra's gut. "Oh my God, what are they going to do with them?"

He didn't have that answer. And couldn't think as emotion poured through him. Her emotion. His.

Until another glance at the blue truck galvanized the man he was into action. "They aren't going to do anything to them," he told her with a bit of his own certainty. "Their goal is to save them, right?"

The fact that some unstable family members had been known to take the lives of their loved ones with the thought that they were saving them hit him hard.

He didn't share it.

"Their goal is to hide them away in their bunker that's underground God knows where and train them to live like animals, with survival the only thing on their minds…" Panic filled her words, raising her tone as she spoke, and he could see her falling in on herself, literally bending her head, her back.

"Hey." With a hand at her chin, and another at her back, her lifted her head until she was looking him in the eye. "They need you right now. They need you to not give up believing that they'll be okay. They need you to find them. Because I can guarantee you, they're believing you will." The words flowed naturally, a sergeant talking to the troops that became family to him.

And when she nodded, he felt more like the sergeant

he knew himself to be. Capable of remaining calm. Aware. And outthinking the enemy.

The front door opened and Chief Lawson walked into the lobby outside Theresa's office door, followed by suited and then uniformed men. A glance out the window showed Ezra the entire road up to the home filled with police cars. Theresa saw the number of law enforcement filling her lobby and turned to Ezra, her gaze begging him for something.

Without another thought, he stepped forward, spoke to the man who'd danced with his mother at his brother's wedding. Spoke as though he and Chief Lawson actually really knew each other. As though he had a right to demand help. To speak and be heard in a professional sense.

And within minutes, a BOLO was out on the Fitzgeralds' blue truck, and an Amber Alert was being issued for Claire and Neve. Theresa looked shell-shocked by the speed with which everything was happening. Ezra wanted it all to happen faster.

Officers, detectives, janitors and other personnel who weren't preventing residents from leaving their rooms went over every inch of the place, making certain the girls weren't there, and then while some law enforcement started taking personnel and resident statements, others checked out means of entry and exit.

Ezra stayed with Theresa. He wasn't going to slow things down by getting in the way, but he did tell the chief, who relayed the message over his radio, that the point of exit was at the rear of the memory-care unit and the point of entry, Ezra believed, was the window in Mrs. Wright's room.

"She likes fresh air," Theresa said slowly, as though in a daze, standing in the middle of a circle of officers. Ezra, from right behind her, felt her shudder. "I never thought an open window in a senior home would be cause for a security breach. None of the residents on that particular wing are capable of getting the screens out, let alone climbing out of a window. We keep the more agile memory-care patients on a different hall because they need different stimulation and different types of caregiving..."

She was rambling. He was grateful no one interrupted. Those who had immediate jobs to do were doing them. And she was distracting herself, whether she knew it or not.

He'd seen the jimmied screen the second he'd entered the resident's room.

He'd seen Aunt Alice, too, sleeping in her chair as he'd stridden past her partially opened door. Resident families would be notified of the breach. His family.

He had to get to work. To figure out where the Fitzgeralds were going and stop them from getting there without endangering the girls.

And he couldn't walk away from their mother, couldn't leave her there trying to be a rock and floundering. She'd already lost one man who gave her strength. Had already lost too much. And not that he was a man in her life, but she'd turned to *him* in her time of greatest need.

His immediate response, the emotional one that drove his actions, shocked the hell out of him. As did the livid anger burning through him every time he thought of Claire leaving her book outside that door—a very smart and desperate cry for help—an action generated by fear for her life.

And also a sign that she held hope that she'd be rescued.

He cared—in a way he didn't understand and with a force he didn't recognize. Something he could ponder some other day when he was out in a desert hole spending hours waiting for the enemy to fall into a trap. Or working out in the gym during mandatory downtime.

He had two weeks until then. And if the girls weren't found before then…if they were in captivity for fourteen days… He shook his head. Fourteen days of being held in a bunker for what their grandparents perceived to be their own good…

No. He'd die before he'd let that happen.

Die to save his own from suffering. That was what he'd signed up for at eighteen, and he'd never looked back.

The girls weren't his to call his own. Their mother wasn't really even something as official as a friend.

Didn't matter how he felt.

He wasn't on the job. Didn't have an assignment. But he was going to move hell if need be to use his skills and bring those little girls home.

The powerful emotions prompting the actions would have to come under scrutiny at a later time. Every minute those girls were out there was another moment they might remember in the future. Another moment they could be emotionally or mentally scarred.

Lord knew Claire was already carrying heavy burdens of fear regarding the damned blast actually happening that was more a figment of someone's imagination than any real and valid threat. Because

the threat was guarded against. Things were in place.
Had been for many years. Things he hadn't been able
to explain to a six-year-old.

As he waited for Theodore Lawson to get off a call,
Ezra put a hand on Theresa's back, at the base of her
neck. More like a heating pad for relaxation than anything else.

An attempt to help her hold on.

While his mind spun.

Lawson was taking too long.

"The police have everything handled here," he told
her, not wanting to leave her, but not being able to just
stand there any longer. "And there are things I can be
doing, things my family can be doing…"

"Do them." She looked him straight in the eye. No
questions asked.

He nodded and headed out to his Jeep.

Chapter Nine

The second Ezra left the lobby of the senior home, Theresa started to shake. Her mind jumbled, bringing her images of Claire crying, Neve yelling, the girls hugging each other on the back seat of a truck. Without car seats.

Did they have seat belts on?

She saw them in an underground cave of mud with such pitch-blackness at night that Claire would wet the bed. Would there be beds there?

Oh, God, would the girls feel sun on their skin? Be warm enough?

Would they sleep with guns beside them?

Stop it! She stomped her foot and noticed several of the officers moving to and fro throughout the lobby stopping to glance at her.

Just when she thought one might lead her away, Ezra was back in her line of vision. "I'm assuming I can use your office to set up in?"

"What?" *Set up in.* She replayed the words. Or they replayed themselves. He was…staying?

"Yes!" she said then, too quickly, adding, "Of course."

Where was her calm? Her coping abilities? She'd nursed the father of her children through a debilitating end. Had worked, too, so they'd have money to pay his bills and still provide for the girls. She'd seen things she'd never expected to see. Had buried the man she'd expected to spend the rest of her life with.

She was not going to fall apart when their daughters needed her.

And…she didn't have to do it alone, either.

As she stood in the lobby, the only unmoving being, it seemed, just existing there like a statue surrounded by urgency, she saw Ezra in her office. Behind her desk. Typing on her keyboard.

And then he came out again. "I need your password."

Something she never gave anyone. "Cleave1!" she said without hesitation. "Capital *C*." Giving him access to a part of her she never gave to anyone. Ever. Not even Mark had known her passwords.

Weird, probably. But…

Was she really going to stand there and think about password habits? While everyone else moved with greatest energy to find her children?

"Claire and Neve combined in a word of promise. I will cleave to them forever. Exclamation because they are the most magical part of my life. And 1 because they both are my firstborn," she said, following Ezra into her office.

Giving no indication as to whether he'd heard or not, Ezra sat at her desk, his fingers flying on the keyboard, his gaze intent on the screen. He picked up his phone, pushed one button, waited a brief second and said, "Okay, now what?"

He typed, his eyes narrowing on the screen. And then, "Got it," and hung up.

"There are things my siblings and I can do faster," he said as he typed and moved the cursor with her mouse. "Dom's an FBI agent," he said. "I've got clips from surveillance cameras, and Dom's tracking phones for GPS coordinates," he said as he continued to move the mouse on the pad.

And suddenly, Theresa was behind him. Focused. With a resurgence of the toughness that had seen her through bad days, she studied images as they appeared. And when Ezra turned the seat so she could sit with him, she did so without hesitation, right there on one of his thighs.

There was nothing sexy about the move.

But it affected her more than she'd ever thought possible for a simple physical contact. It was like he wasn't just at her back, he was a part of it. In that moment, he was a part of her. Warmth to warmth. The panic, the fear…he shared it.

And in the sharing, there was strength.

The second he pulled Theresa onto his knee, Ezra knew he'd made a mistake. He'd pulled Naomi down to his knee tons of times when they'd been younger and he'd been teaching her things on the computer.

Theresa was most definitely not his little sister.

And he had no business treating her as though they were…something together. But he didn't have time to worry about any of it, either.

She stayed seated. He kept working. Aware of her. Of wanting her there. For more than just that moment. But not focused on any of that. More desert-hole stuff. The times in foreign deserts when he contemplated life.

At that moment all he was contemplating were

the images he was scrolling through on the screen as they downloaded through his brother's equipment. He wasn't getting the actual footage, but still shots from them. Some program Dom had access to that put the video in still frames.

And...there it was.

"It's the truck!" Theresa called out, and then lowered her voice to say, "Can you make it bigger? See if the girls are there?"

He tried, but neither of them could see the back seat of the truck from the view they had. They couldn't even make out occupants of the front seat.

But it was something. He made note of the photo designation—camera location and time. And continued scrolling.

Theresa sat still as could be, her gaze glued on the screen. She didn't chat. Didn't ask the questions that had to be racing through her mind. He didn't have any answers to them.

And then...he felt the muscles of her butt clench against his thigh. There it was again. The same distinctive blue truck. Ezra took one look at the camera's location—and the time the Fitzgeralds had been there.

"I gotta go," he said then, practically pushing Theresa off his lap as he stood up. Except that he didn't have to push. She was right there with him. Grabbing her purse.

"Where are we going?"

He didn't take ride-alongs. In the desert, on the battlefield, no one ever wanted to ride along.

"I'll be in touch soon," he told her. "I just have to go check something out."

"No way, Colton," she said, sounding as fierce as

his mother ever had. And having raised twelve kids, seven of whom were boys, Isa had a lot of practice at putting her foot down. "I won't be left behind."

He had a lot of practice at standing his ground, too. And didn't budge. He had no idea where his hunch would lead him. How dangerous it could be if he got lucky and there was a showdown with the Fitzgeralds to get the girls home in time for dinner.

Or how disappointing if it didn't pan out. He also didn't have time to fight her.

Unable to look at her, he grabbed his keys and headed for the door.

"Please, Ezra. They're my children. All I have. I can't just sit here..."

He paused, but didn't turn around. That last line... hit him where it counted. He'd had the same thought not half an hour before, and Claire and Neve weren't even remotely his.

With a glance back over his shoulder, he motioned for her to come with him and continued his determined stride out to the Jeep.

He was racing against time and couldn't afford to lose the race.

Most particularly not with the twins' mother sitting in the vehicle beside him.

SHE DIDN'T KNOW where they going. Didn't ask. Didn't even question her unwavering faith in putting her life in the hands of a man she'd known only a week.

Or stop to consider that perhaps she'd be of better service to the trained police force working to find her daughters. Ezra called Chief Lawson once they were on the road. Let him know that he'd had to get Theresa out of there for a few minutes. Told him to call if they needed her for anything.

And then it was just the two of them.

She didn't make the mistake of asking a second question. The first one had nearly gotten her sidelined.

"I'm not a magician." Ezra's comment was so odd, she stared at him. Trying to figure out what had prompted the words so she could reassure him. Got nowhere.

"I know."

"This could be a wild-goose chase."

And she got it. He was afraid he was setting her up for disappointment.

"If I was in on the details, I'd be more apt to realize that, and not build up unreasonable expectations," she told him. But in truth, she was just glad to be doing something to try to help save her babies rather than sitting around, letting worrisome scenarios take over her brain.

And doing it with him. Ezra made her feel more alive, more capable, than she could ever remember feeling. Even before Mark got sick.

"The area between the one camera and the second... I know it. There's a road that heads across state, away from any towns, and that road is not far from that second camera..."

"You think that's where they're headed."

His shrug drew her attention to his massive shoulders, to his strength, and yet she sensed a vulnerability about him. He wasn't sure.

How could he be?

She drew a deep breath.

"I know a shortcut to that road. Dom and Oliver and

I used to drag race out there. There's a gas station about an hour from where we saw that last camera image."

It had been time-stamped half an hour before they'd been in the Jeep.

"Do we have time to make it before they do?"

"Probably not."

"But we're going to try."

"Yes."

"Good."

For the moment, it was enough.

THEY DIDN'T MAKE IT. Ezra was actually hopeful—an occurrence that wasn't normal for him—as he pulled into the vacant lot at the little country station, that they'd arrived in time. Most people driving the long road into nowhere knew that the little family-owned place was the last stop until past the state line. Most stopped.

Pulling the Jeep around back, so that there was no chance either the girls or the Fitzgeralds would see it and recognize it, he suggested that he and Theresa head in to talk to the guy behind the counter. A younger guy Ezra didn't think he'd seen before. If the blue truck pulled onto the lot, he could be out the back door and in the Jeep to head them off before they knew they'd been made.

"Sorry, man, you just missed them," the guy said as Ezra described the truck. He'd explained that he was trying to catch up with in-laws. He hadn't said whose. "They was here maybe twenty minutes ago."

"You're sure it was the same truck?" he asked, certain that there weren't two of them in the state in the condition Eric Fitzgerald kept his vehicle. "They

had our daughters with them. You wouldn't be able
to miss them…"

"Twins," the man cut him off, nodding. "Yep. They
bought 'em each an ice cream sandwich," he said, as
though that solved all the world's problems.

"And they were headed toward the state line?" He
pointed into no-man's-land, refusing to let dread, or
fear for Theresa and her girls, sink in. Slow his thinking processes or inhibit problem-solving skills.

"Noooo." Frowning, the young man shook his head
as he drew out the word. "They headed back the way
they'd come."

"They were going back to town?" Theresa asked.

The guy shrugged. "Maybe. Unless they took that
turnoff that leads to McClintock and Benson and them
other small towns up that way. One of them girls had
to pee is why they came down here, I think. No places
to stop on that other road."

Which made it not likely to be on police radar. Or
have surveillance cameras.

A good choice of travel for someone wanting to
stay off the grid.

"Thank you." Ezra dropped a twenty on the counter and, taking Theresa's hand in his, hurried from
the store.

"THE GIRLS DON'T like ice cream sandwiches." They'd
been in the car a minute—just long enough for Ezra
to report in to his brother Dominic, the FBI agent, that
they were headed on a road to small towns upstate.

"Mark liked them," she continued. Made sense,
then, that Jennifer would think to buy for her grandchildren the same treat she'd bought for their father.

"He bought a box of them once, had the girls try them. They ate the ice cream and gave him the chocolate-cake part. After that it was tradition. He never seemed to mind eating the sandwich without the filling."

"You miss him." The quiet response came from the muscled, powerful man at her side. Filled with an understanding, a gentleness, that while in direct contrast to the look of the man, and to his job, still felt...right.

She thought about his statement. About the past year on her own. "I do," she said. There would always be a part of her that would be tied to the gentle man she'd known and married. "And yet if he were here now... I feel horrible for saying it, but I'm not even sure we'd work anymore. I've changed."

The thought slipped out, sounding blasphemous. It was also the truth. And if she hoped to get her daughters back safely, she had to make no mistakes.

Lying to herself, or anyone else, was definitely a mistake.

The ringing of his phone prevented any response he might have made. She cared little about their conversation when Ezra answered his phone with a push of a button on the steering wheel and said, "Yeah, Dom, what's going on?"

"I got myself officially on the case—kidnapping being within FBI jurisdiction—and should only be reporting to family or their designated spokesperson." The voice came over the Jeep's audio system.

Ezra looked at Theresa. "That choice is yours to make," he said, and then added, "You need to know I won't stop looking. I'll just stop talking to my brother."

"No." Dominic's voice came firmly over the line. "You don't stop talking to me. You tell me everything you know when you know it. I just stop giving you official updates on what I know."

"You aren't giving them to him. You're giving them to me." Theresa spoke up. "And, for the record, Ezra Colton is my official spokesperson." Her entire being warmed at the pronouncement. It was nothing. Getting around red tape was all.

But felt like so much more.

He glanced her way, a brow raised, as though asking her to be sure.

She nodded.

"There you have it, bro. Now, what do you know, for God's sake?"

"Authorities have been notified in every burg along the road you mentioned, cars have been dispatched, but so far, nothing."

"I'm heading that way anyway."

"I expected as much. I'll keep you posted. And… Theresa, I'm sorry about your girls. They were a hoot on Saturday. We'll get them back."

Her eyes filled with tears, and, chin trembling, she nodded but couldn't get words out.

Ezra, with a quick glance her way, said, "Later," and clicked off the call.

"I can't believe you all are doing this for me," she said when she could, feeling awkward, yet as though she was where she was meant to be in that moment. "I'm just a woman your mom knows because of her senile aunt. And you… You've only got a couple of weeks left on your vacation." She blurted the words more as a reminder to herself than because she thought he needed to hear them.

"All true, but you left out the part where you and

your kids have snagged my attention in a way no woman with children ever has, and you took pity on a restless military sergeant being emotionally blackmailed by his family to spend time in a town he bolted from years ago. For good reason."

His gaze never left the road. She wasn't even sure he was fully cognizant of what he was saying. The tone of voice was a bit...distracted.

"Seriously, Ezra, thank you," she said and pulled out her own phone, making a couple of calls to arrange for a health-care manager to take over for her, starting immediately, at the Sunshine Senior Home until further notice. The first woman she contacted from the pool of traveling health-care workers, a woman who'd filled in for Theresa during the week Mark died, accepted on the spot and said she'd be in Blue Larkspur by nightfall. She also agreed to look after Charlie.

Hanging up, Theresa stared out the windshield, reminding herself that Claire and Neve needed her to stay focused.

They'd be counting on her to find them before dark.

"We have to find them before dark," she announced.

"We're going to do our best," Ezra said, and she heard what was in his silence, too. They might not succeed by then. Or ever.

The man wasn't going to lie to her.

But he reached out a hand over the console, and when she took it, she believed they'd get through whatever lay ahead.

And that Claire and Neve would, too.

Chapter Ten

He couldn't give her false hope. Unstable people were also unpredictable—even to themselves. But Ezra believed that they wouldn't hurt the twins intentionally.

He had to believe it.

Never in his life had a battle meant so much to him. It had never been personal before. As he drove, keeping focus on his surroundings, the ditches, the trees, the road ahead and behind, looking for any signs of vehicles having pulled off the road recently, he kept his less understandable thoughts at bay, sending them to storage for a time when he could get them into order, label them and put them away.

And…there. He slowed.

"What's going on?" Theresa's question carried alarm.

He wasn't used to being questioned when he was working. He gave the orders.

Turning around, he drove back a few yards, got out of the Jeep, studied the fresh tire tracks in a pile of dirt and jumped behind the wheel again.

"A truck just turned right here," he said, heading down a one-lane side road. The vehicle's GPS system caught up quickly, showing him that the road was long, continuing on as far as he could see on the map. A likely road into open territory where one could dig a hole and hide forever.

She didn't say any more after that, just sat next to him, a second pair of eyes watching the landscape.

And he was glad she was there.

ONCE SHE KNEW more of what to look for, fresh dirt showing new tire tracks, for one, Theresa couldn't take her gaze off the sides of the road, the nearby ditches, as they drove. It wasn't like she actually expected the twins to be sitting there waiting to be picked up, but if they'd stopped, had a chance to leave any other tell-tale sign...

Claire had left her book outside the home on purpose.

She was a resourceful little girl. And Neve, once clued in, got things done. It wasn't that Claire was any more intelligent than her sister; she was just a lot more focused.

Kind of like Ezra.

The man's ability to concentrate on the moment at hand was a bit intimidating.

And wonderful, comforting and reassuring to have around. Ezra's attention to detail calmed her panic. Helped her focus and do her part.

As she actively worked to find her girls, just by looking for a minute clue like a clod of dirt that didn't fit, she grew in strength.

The ability to hang on.

And to think clearly. To use her knowledge of the Fitzgeralds to try to figure out their next move. Without attaching immediate panic to the answers that came to her.

The idea wasn't to imagine what the girls were going through, but to stop the Fitzgeralds before they reached their endgame.

And then Dominic called again.

"Yeah," Ezra said after a quick push on the steering wheel. She listened intently. She didn't take her gaze off the land passing by them.

"Pick up."

As Ezra reached for his phone, she shot out a hand. Stopping him. Grabbed his phone. Had he not been driving, there was no way she'd have succeeded. "No," she said to both men at once. "Whatever you have to say, I need to hear."

"The Fitzgeralds' truck has been spotted twice in Benson."

Oh, dear God. They were on the wrong road. Looking for signs of the twins in a place they'd never been…

Her thoughts were interrupted as Ezra did a far-too-rapid-for-safety one-eighty, managed it with expert skill and had them racing at twice the speed limit back in the direction they'd come as Dom relayed specific coordinates of the blue truck. One on the outskirts of town. "The other was twenty minutes ago," he said, "at an intersection two miles west of Main. Can't make out any occupants, but authorities are all over the area now."

Heart pounding, she almost cried out with glee. Their capture and her daughters' rescue were imminent!

"If you're in the area…"

"We aren't," Ezra nearly barked. "But we will be

within the hour." In very succinct words, he told Dominic about their detour. "Good news is I was traveling slow enough to survey roadside. Backtrack will be quick."

As she listened to her vehicle mate relay what she already knew, it occurred to her that there was nothing in what Dominic Colton had said that would prompt him to tell Ezra to pick up. As in, prevent Theresa from hearing what he had to say.

There was no logical reason for the request.

"Keep me posted," Dominic said, as though ending the call.

"Wait!"

Ezra glanced her way, raised his brow, and she said, "What else is there? Why did you want Ezra to pick up?"

She imagined the brothers exchanging a glance in the silence that fell. And then Dominic said, "One of the cameras got a good shot of the interior of the truck," he said, his tone not good. And while for an instant she wanted to cover her ears, the instant passed as quickly as it came.

"And?"

"We were able to identify Eric and Jennifer Fitzgerald in the front seat, but the back seat was empty. I'm sorry, Theresa."

He was sorry. Meant something to be sorry for. Bad for her. For her girls.

"They could have dropped them somewhere in town," Ezra quickly asserted. His hand found hers again. Held on, though her fingers didn't clutch his back as they had before. She was too numb to move.

"That's the theory we're going with."

As opposed to?

Did someone think that the couple had…?

"They love the girls," she said emphatically. "They won't physically hurt them." Not knowingly. And you'd have to do it knowingly for it to have happened to both of them so quickly.

"They could also have been told to get down on the floor," Ezra said. "Could have been covered up by a dark tarp. Theresa has said these people are planners. They're unstable in their beliefs, but smart. Look at the way they pulled off the kidnapping. They'd obviously been watching the home. Had done their research on the security system…"

Which they could only have done if they'd been inside. On her phone instantly, she called the home, asked for the charge nurse on duty and had her get someone to start watching security cameras over the past week to see if Eric and Jennifer Fitzgerald had been inside. She texted a picture of the pair while she was still on the phone.

And when she was done, she glanced at Ezra. Saw the caring, and also the approval, on his face and knew that, whatever it took, she would get the job done.

Just as she knew he would.

They were a team.

For the moment only, she reminded herself.

But in that moment, there was no future.

There was only finding her girls.

WHAT DID YOU say to a woman whose children were missing and she'd just been told that they weren't in the vehicle they'd been reportedly seen in an hour or so before?

Way out of his league, Ezra didn't say anything for a bit. He drove like a bat out of hell, to get her to Benson with the hope that by the time they arrived, the Fitzgeralds would be in custody.

And he worked on a plan B as well. The plan where they got the older couple but the girls weren't with them.

Theresa had been scrolling on her phone since Dom had hung up. Knowing that keeping her brain occupied was the single most important thing she could do to fight off a feeling of powerlessness that led to loss of hope and panic, he didn't ask if she was okay.

How could she be?

He didn't tell her things would be all right. That the girls were fine. He had no way of knowing either.

"Oh my God!" Her exclamation sent shock sensations from his chest to his gut.

"What?" Had she received a ransom note? A text? An email?

"I've been researching bunker buildings," she said. "Just in case…you know… I mean, their goal is to get the girls to safety, and we know they have a bunker somewhere, or did…"

"What, Theresa?" he asked, in a sergeant-expecting-an-answer tone. Not mean, but firm enough to stop the stream of useless information. There was only so much emotional tension a guy could take.

"There's this guy. He builds bunkers for people. There are a few of them, actually, right here on the internet, but this one, for a pretty hefty sum, he'll build a bunker for you…" She glanced over at him, as if to see whether he was still with her or thought her misguided for her research.

He couldn't help but nod with encouragement before turning his attention right back to the road. Driving twenty over the speed limit wouldn't do well if he lost control of the vehicle.

"His address is Benson, Colorado," she said softly.

She'd found his backup plan.

He glanced at her again. He couldn't help it. She was smiling.

It was a teary smile, but there.

And he smiled back.

They made a good team.

Chapter Eleven

Not long after the smile that had to be forgotten, Theresa's phone rang. Millie, her second-in-command at the home, let her know that the Fitzgeralds had been at the home on Saturday. They'd signed in as Frank and Janie Frederick, to see Alice.

Her entire body froze. With stark cold horror. Somehow managing to thank Millie, she dropped her phone in her lap, as though it burned her skin, and saw it sitting there, on the black material of her skirt...

She'd had a meeting with state health people this morning, hoping to win a grant to provide electronics for the residents who could use them. Had donned the black skirt and jacket so she'd be taken seriously...

"Tell me what's going on." Once again, Ezra's voice pulled her back into focus. Which sent her right back to despair.

"The Fitzgeralds were at the home on Saturday. They signed in to visit your aunt. That's how they got on the ward. They're diabolical planners, Ezra. I knew it. I knew it," she said, and continued right on, "They knew about the Colton barbecue, knew I was going to be there. Probably watched you come pick me up, followed us there and saw their chance. They've been watching me, us, all along. They knew when they were waiting when we got home Saturday that we were with you. That's why they were there. They were sizing you up. Sizing us up. I knew it. I should have…"

"What?" His tone had softened. "What could you have done that you weren't already doing?"

"Run."

"Someplace where there was no one to help you when they found you? Because if they're as good, and determined, as you say, they would have found you, you know."

"They've been preparing for the blast since Mark was ten. That's more than twenty years. He said it was pretty much all they did, all they talked about. But it was so many years ago, and people come to their senses…"

Or they didn't. They just got in deeper and deeper until planning and protecting their own from what they perceived as very real dangers was all they knew. And something they did at any cost.

"They're prepared for a blast, Theresa." Ezra's tone strengthened. A sergeant talking to his men, maybe? "They aren't prepared to be hunted by the best this state has to offer. They aren't prepared for me."

There was no bravado in what he said.

Just stone-hard truth.

She listened while Ezra called Dom, reporting Millie's news, and wanted to lay her head down against Ezra's chest, feel the rumble of his voice, and rest. When the thought struck, she sat straight up instead. And spent the next half hour perusing the internet on her phone, searching for anything to do with conspiracy theories about nuclear blasts, preparations for them, where to buy supplies. She read articles. Clicked on links to various outlets. Read a short piece about guns and ammunition—bunker living required stockpiling illegal types of both—and forced herself to see the Fitzgeralds, to try, as Ezra was doing, to predict what they might do next in an effort to get that one step ahead of them that they had to reach in order to save the girls.

If, peripherally, she was getting a glimpse into the life her sweet babies might be forced to live if they weren't successful, she pushed the impressions away. Just as she prayed that they'd be strong, cling to each other and continue to be smart as Claire had been in leaving her book, she knew they needed the same from her.

She had to stay lucid and capable, no matter what it took. She'd learned the hard way that there'd always be time to grieve. Her job was to prevent the need.

She'd get her girls back. And she'd do it without falling for a sergeant who'd be leaving. One who'd dedicated his life to danger and fighting enemies. She'd prevent reasons to grieve. Protecting her daughters from any more cause to fear.

They were six. Life was supposed to be about unicorns and rainbows. Horses and happiness.

She jumped as Ezra's phone pealing interrupted the concentrated silence in the Jeep. Every muscle and her fingers clenched, she waited to hear that the Fitzgeralds had been caught and her daughters were safe.

Stared at Ezra as he pushed the button on the steering wheel and said, "Yeah."

"Nothing." Dom's tone was equally stoic. "Not another sign of the truck, of the couple or the girls. More

than fifty law enforcement personnel from various ju-
risdictions, and they manage to get by all of them."

"How does that happen?" she cried out, uncaring
for the moment that she was supposed to be strong and
focused. Unable to hold back her terror. "Where are
they? How do they just disappear?"

But the answer came to her even as she asked it.

They went underground, that was how.

They were informed, prepared.

She'd known in her gut that they were making a
plan. They'd had everything in place, down to every
last detail, like using the magnet to fool the alarm system.

"We suspect that there's a network," Dominic said.
"From what intel we've gathered, there is a whole group
of these people, like a cult, spread all over the country.
They meet on social networks, mostly on the dark web.
We're on there and listening, but so far, there's been
no chatter regarding grandparents with young girls. Or
any special movement today…"

Dark web. Intel. Chatter. It was like she'd woken up
that morning a normal woman and had somehow face-
planted in the middle of a TV show.

"We've checked property records from all over the
state, and neither Eric nor Jennifer Fitzgerald comes
up. Either they're renting, squatting, living on inherited
property without legal deed change, or they've been
living under an assumed identity for a hell of a lot of
years. The address on both of their driver's licenses
is to a rented mailbox in a postal center they used to
own. Same for credit cards and cell phones. Phones
are turned off, but we've got someone monitoring in

case they come back on, even for a few seconds. We'll know as soon as it happens."

And she'd let these people drive off with her little girls? Even once? Nauseated, Theresa turned the Jeep's vent straight at her face.

Law enforcement had been alerted in all surrounding states. Dom let them know, as if that was cause to feel grateful. The pronouncement, the authorities' apparent belief that there was cause to make the call, scared her further. The Fitzgeralds were Coloradoans. Had always, as far as she knew, been in the state. The idea that they'd take her daughters farther than state lines...

Maybe it shouldn't surprise her. After Mark's diagnosis, she definitely knew that the worst did happen. But...

Dom said he'd stay in touch. Ezra told his brother they'd still head into Benson. Ezra wanted to do his own reconnaissance, and Dom agreed that he was the man for that job, like none other, and reminded Ezra to call him if he found anything. They hung up without saying goodbye.

She hadn't had a chance to say goodbye to the twins.

The last thing she'd said to them...she couldn't remember. Probably some reminder to keep a hand on Charlie's collar...and not to leave the memory ward for any reason.

Oh, God, did they think she'd be mad at them for disobeying?

Neve was better at discerning the difference between disobeying and situations being beyond their control. Hopefully she was reassuring serious little Claire.

"This is a setback, not a failure." Ezra sounded like a teacher in front of a class.

Looking over at him still in his painting clothes, she saw the way his jaw clenched and wondered if he had as many doubts as she did.

"You talking to yourself or to me?" she asked, hanging on to reason by a thread.

"Just stating fact. You don't stop until you fail. We haven't failed. Not by a long shot."

"You stop trying to do something the first time you fail?" The question had nothing to do with anything that mattered, but came out anyway. She wanted to know his answer.

"In battle, when you've failed to achieve your mission, you fall back," he said. "Doesn't mean you give up on the war, only the battle. It's not time for us to fall back."

It wasn't time to fall back. It was time to continue moving forward. He'd just given her hope.

Again.

"You're a good man, Ezra Colton." Emotion filled the words. The tone shocked her, revealing something she would not, could not, own.

If he heard it, received it, he didn't say.

And she didn't ask.

Or apologize.

Best just to leave it alone.

There was no place for personal emotion in their brief acquaintance.

He was just helping her find her daughters.

And then he'd be gone.

Like the girls' princess lunch, she was experiencing a prince investigation.

Nothing more.

EZRA THOUGHT ABOUT calling Dom back, letting his brother know that he was planning to visit the bunker maker—Tom Smith. Thought about the fact that the authorities, his triplet included, would demand that he let them know first, if they could.

He dismissed the thoughts almost at once. Then had another one. Theresa had a say.

As they neared Benson, he broke the silence that had fallen between them. "I have a plan."

Though he kept his gaze straight ahead—not wanting to deal with another jolt like their earlier shared smile had given him, or the tone in her voice when she'd proclaimed him a good man—he saw, peripherally, when she turned to look at him. "I'm not surprised, but I'm glad. What do you need me to do?"

No questioning what the plan even was?

Her trust in him hit him hard. Humbled him.

The woman was putting her daughters' lives in his hands. Was he up to the task?

He wasn't a good man. He was the guy who'd run out of town at the first possible opportunity. Run out on his family and their myriad problems and challenges.

He most definitely wasn't a good man. He was just good at what he did.

Still...with Theresa, those two endearing urchins, he was out of his league.

In the army he had lives at stake every time he went to work, but everyone understood, going in, that you couldn't save them all. There were going to be casualties. Your job was to minimize them as much as possible.

This wasn't that.

"Ezra? I'm not just going to stand back and wait."

"I know." Knuckles clenched on the wheel, he took a breath and plunged in.

"As soon as we get to town, we stop at a box store and get a couple of changes of clothes for each of us. Pants, button-up long-sleeved shirts, boots, in colors that match camo, but not actual camo pattern. Survival wear that also blends in. I'm going to buy a burner phone and call Tom Smith, tell him we're a married couple interested in a bunker, but need to see more. I'll tell him we're in town specifically to meet with him. From there, the plan is fluid. Our goal is to get inside his place—if we get lucky, even see a bunker—and collect as much information as we can. Anything could be a clue that might lead us to Eric and Jennifer."

He meant to give her time to speak, to question, disagree, but started talking again, justifying, before she could get a word in. "Law enforcement can question him. But as soon as he tells them he's never heard of Eric or Jennifer Fitzgerald, as soon as he looks at a picture of the couple and denies ever having seen them, and then asks them to leave his property, they'll be done. There's no known tie between him and them, and even if they could find one, that could take time, which we don't have. And if they do find a connection, it would have to be more than just that they've been in contact at some point in order to be enough to compel a warrant to search his place…"

The plan was solid. The best.

He needed her buy-in.

"I'm not going to lie to you about the danger. I don't foresee any, but when you're dealing with someone who builds bunkers for conspiracy theorists, you never know."

He would have insisted on going in alone, in spite of the fact that he believed the cover of a married couple would work in their favor, except that she'd refused to be left out of the search for her girls, and this part of the plan posed little danger. No matter what kind of business you were in, you wouldn't get far if you went around hurting potential clients.

He waited. And in the silence, found the flaw in his plan. Theresa was a nurturing, compassionate woman who spent her life taking care of others. She wasn't a soldier prepared to don the gear and go into battle. He'd misjudged…

"I'll have to get a wedding ring. Something cheap that can pass for real. They'll have a jewelry counter at the box store."

He glanced her way.

She was looking him right in the eye. "To support the cover," she said. "Guys always seem to look for wedding rings."

He glanced down. She wasn't wearing one. "When did you take yours off?"

"A month ago."

Before she'd met him.

A sign that she was ready to move on with her life? That she'd be looking for more than a barbecue with a guy who was only visiting town for a few weeks?

He'd told his brothers she was a grieving widow who wouldn't be looking to him for anything other than a momentary acquaintanceship.

He'd told himself the same thing.

So how did he explain the looks?

The smile?

The tone of voice?

He couldn't have her seeing more in him than was there.

And no way in hell could he abandon her, either. Not while her girls were missing.

He might be a runner, but he didn't leave jobs he'd taken on until they were complete.

So...what?

Did he let her know what was what...make sure she wasn't falling for him...or imagining something that wasn't there...tell her that she could only rely on him to find her girls and nothing more...before or after they posed as a married couple?

"I need to get something out there." She interrupted his thoughts, relieving him of the immediate need to make a decision that wasn't feeling in any way pleasant.

"What?" he asked, both hands on the wheel as the traffic picked up slightly on the way into Benson.

"I just...don't want to give you the wrong impression here. I could be speaking out of turn, and I hope I am, but...you asked me out, and here you are, risking your life for my girls, and...it kind of feels like we've had a personal moment or two, and now here I am, telling you I took off my wedding ring, something everyone knows is a sign someone is moving on and..."

His knuckles turned white as she paused, and he silently swore every word he'd ever heard. And then made up one or two.

She was really going to do it? Force him to hurt her in the middle of the race to find her daughters? To add insult to injury to a woman who was already at her brink?

Could he pretend that there was a chance for them? Just until she got her girls back, when she'd be overjoyed and better able to handle the rejection?

The idea took root, was the most logical, considering all aspects of the situation.

"I just… I'm so thankful for what you're doing, Ezra. And…having you by my side is about the only way I'm getting through this…"

Yes. Definitely. Go the pretend route.

She could find out later what a creep he was to lie to her. Women got over creeps all the time.

"But I need you to know that…once the girls are home…" She took a deep breath. And he just knew that she was saying a prayer that the girls made it home safely. "What I'm trying to say is that I can't get involved with a man whose career doesn't allow him to have a real home. And most importantly, not a man who faces danger every day of his life. I can't put my girls through it, either. We've already lost one man. We can't lose another…"

Talk about having the wind knocked out of you…

"No worries," Ezra told her. "I'm not a family guy, and most definitely will be leaving at the end of the month. I've never even dated a woman who'd ever had a kid." All true.

As was the huge wave of disappointment that hit him when she finally got out with what she'd been trying to say.

She didn't want him.

It was good. All good.

Right.

What he needed. What he'd need to tell her.

A huge relief.

And still...wow.

The light in his world had suddenly dimmed.

Chapter Twelve

Ezra gave her ten minutes in the store to get what she needed, change clothes and meet him by the exit. When he'd suggested that she grab clothes for a couple of days, just in case, her heart had dropped, but it didn't slow her down. Every minute they were in the store meant more minutes before she could see her daughters again.

In addition to clothes and toiletries, she managed to grab food supplies as she ran her basket past displays, and she snagged a big package of cleansing wipes as well. The mother in her couldn't pass them up.

In dark green jeans, a long-sleeved, lighter green cotton shirt and a pair of tie-up, waterproof, tan ankle boots, she met him, bags in hand, at exactly ten minutes.

Tried not to take a second look at the way the jeans and long-sleeved light brown tee hugged his muscles, failed, and then noticed the thirty-six-pack of bottled water in the cart behind him.

The fact that she hadn't thought of getting the life-sustaining liquid herself told her how far off her mark she really was. Shaking, she followed him out to the Jeep, promising herself she'd do better.

And kept her mind on that goal as Ezra handed her a new burner phone and then sent a text from a second burner phone. "We have no idea how connected the Fitzgeralds are," he told her. "For now, use that phone."

Of course, there were conspiracy theorists with friends in high places. Governors who had bunkers in case of a nuclear blast. She'd just read about them that afternoon.

And she'd grabbed candy, as though she and Ezra were on an adventure. A road trip.

She had to do better. Be better.

"We're Jack and Molly Wallace," he told her as he stood the phone in a cup holder beside him and handed her a cheap metal band, motioning toward the one on his left ring finger.

Feeling surreal, she slid her matching band in place.

She could think about being Molly Wallace.

She had to not think about what could be happening to her daughters. Not think about Claire's worries or Neve's need to make things seem okay when they weren't. Not think about them afraid and crying.

As anxiety rose up, ready to choke her, she turned to reach for one of her bags in the back seat of the Jeep, intending to get the bag of candy she'd snagged, to grab a piece of chocolate to give her immediate distraction, and instead, her gaze landed on Ezra's bag.

More particularly on the new package of underwear visible through the thin plastic.

A three-pack—red, blue and black—of cotton boxer briefs.

Ezra's...

Anxiety dissipated.

And she no longer needed the chocolate.

NOT LIKING GOING into battle with someone to protect beside him, Ezra drove toward Tom Smith's known residence with trepidation building within him. He only ever took armed and trained soldiers into battle with him.

A team of men who knew how to read each other and the situation, who knew how to preempt the unexpected and deal with it if it slapped them in the face.

Theresa was most definitely not armed or trained.

But if he hoped to get a good look inside Smith's premises, and around his property, he had to have an in, and Theresa was it.

With the Fitzgeralds seemingly off the grid, Ezra's chosen course of action could be the only way to get the girls back expediently.

Only if it worked perfectly, of course, and there was no guarantee of that.

As he thought over every aspect of the plan, he saw no reason to fear immediate physical harm. The man ran a viable business with a stellar rating with the Better Business Bureau. Smith was just an unknowing means to a possible quick and happy end to a kidnapping.

They were only a mile from Smith's place when he got an answering text, telling him that Smith could meet with him at his convenience that day. Not wanting to rush in like a fool, he texted back that he and his wife had stopped for a bite to eat, and asked if half an hour would be okay.

The confirmation came back within a minute.

And the thirty minutes he and Theresa waited were excruciating to him, as he ran the plan over and over in his mind, thinking about what to look for, where to look and what questions to ask.

"Dom's the undercover expert," he said aloud to Theresa at one point. She'd spent the majority of their time scrolling on her phone. After their very clear understanding that there couldn't be anything personal between them, he'd given up being friendly with her.

If only he could quit being aware of her as easily. Her scent. Her almost frantic touching of thumb to screen, more like jabs than the light touches that seemed more natural to her. Every breath she took...

"If I call him, to get pointers, he could very likely order me not to visit Smith, and send law enforcement there instead..."

"No!" Her gaze wide and alarmed, she looked straight at him for the first time since they'd exited the store. "Then we have the whole warrant thing to deal with. Please, Ezra, no matter how this turns out, I have to try."

"And I have to make you aware of all aspects of this situation, as best I can," he said. "I've never freelanced before. Or been on any job without explicit orders and protocols to follow. But here I am, listening to a gut that has led men into many victories, and I feel as though I have to do all I can to get those little ones back as quickly as possible, but they're your girls to save, not mine."

"And this is my choice," she said, her tone almost calm, and most definitely filled with strength. "When Mark was sick, there were choices to make, different treatments with different risks and levels of success rates... I wanted to go one way, he wanted to go the other, but it was his life. He had to be the one to make them. And in the end, when the choices he made didn't pan out as he'd expected, he was at peace with having taken his life in the direction he'd thought best. That was one of the last things he told me. He'd lived on his terms. If we don't do this, and I find out that having done so could have helped my girls… I would never be able to live with myself."

He nodded, went back to his game planning while she went back to her phone, and they didn't speak again until he pulled through an opened chain-link gate. They drove across a dirt yard and up to what looked like a metal barn with a storefront sitting just feet away from an old, but well-kept, white-vinyl-sided house.

He turned to her. "Ready?"

"Ready." She didn't hesitate.

With a nod, he reached over to the glove box in front of her knees, opened it and pulled out his handgun. He slid it into the waistband of his jeans and covered it with the loosely fitting shirt. "I have a concealed carry permit in my wallet," he told her.

"I wasn't asking."

"I'm Jack and you're Molly," he reminded her.

"Wallace," she confirmed, exiting the Jeep and meeting him at the front, visibly calm when he knew she had to be shaking inside all the way to her core. God, he admired the woman.

He took her hand in his as they headed toward the front of the store. To get into character.

And because he wanted to connect with her.

When she linked her fingers with his, squeezing tight, he was glad.

TOM SMITH WAS nothing like she'd expected. A short, thin man, with dark-rimmed glasses, a clean shave and short hair, he welcomed them to his store as though they were friends. Showed them to a table toward the back of the partitioned-off front room, offered them water or coffee or a bottle of soda and gave them a couple of notebooks loaded with page protectors filled with photos.

Walking around to the back side of the table, against the wall, Ezra pulled out a chair for her, and then scooted his right up next to hers, so they could look at the same photos at the same time. Smith, returning almost immediately with the bottled water they'd both requested, and a pad and paper, took a seat opposite them.

As the men started their conversation, Theresa felt surreal. Enjoying the imaginary story of Ezra and her as Jack and Molly Wallace more than anything else she'd had to face that day. Wishing she could lose herself in the make-believe and rest awhile. She couldn't remember ever taking as much solace from the warmth and nearby presence of another human being as she did Ezra Colton. He was a man of few words during situations when she needed words, and yet he said enough. Said what she'd needed. She'd calmed more through his silence than she'd ever have thought possible.

Smith started by telling them basics, recommendations based on type of location—city, rural, size of lot—and then trenching specifics. He likened his process to what was done for subway systems, rather than digging, to prevent cave-ins. Finally he moved on to dimensions. He built his bunkers ten feet underground and recommended ten square feet of space per occupant.

Much of which, just like the photos in front of her, triggered every one of Theresa's panic buttons.

Were Claire and Neve already hidden away ten feet under? Experiencing for real what Theresa was only looking at in pictures? Would they both already be claustrophobic for life, being trapped down there? Were they scared out of their minds?

As her imagination started to run away with her, she felt Ezra's hand on her knee under the table. And remembered that she had a job to do. Covering his hand with hers, she forced her focus to the room in which they sat, taking in whatever she could, in case Ezra needed it later.

"Do you recommend all steel construction?" Ezra asked, perusing pages so thoroughly she almost believed he was in the market for a bunker for himself. He talked about things she hadn't even read about, and it quickly became clear to her that Ezra Colton was no stranger to bunker construction.

And, of course, he wouldn't be. He was a career soldier, on special operation assignments. Dangerous ones. Where they'd need bunkers to keep them safe.

"I mostly do metal sheets with cement, reinforced with rebar in between them," Smith was saying, "but we can do steel if you prefer and are willing to pay for it." The man went on to talk about ventilation, generator sizes, furniture built into the wall to make more use of a small space.

"What about plumbing?" she asked. She was there to convince the man she wanted to live in a bunker. It was time to take ownership of the home, or she'd fail the task, and possibly her daughters. "I read about toilets that grind and then pump and dump up to one hundred feet horizontally, where the compost becomes natural fertilizer, keeping any odor from collecting inside the dwelling." She pulled from what little she'd remembered from her afternoon reading.

"We do pump and dump, yes. I don't generally add the grind feature. It adds a lot to the cost, and as long as you don't throw sanitary napkins or condoms in the tank, you won't need to grind."

He spoke pragmatically.

She could feel her face turning red as embarrassed heat crept up her skin with condoms and Ezra sharing her space at the same time. And celebrated the fact that she was doing her job well enough to feel something besides panic and growing despair.

"I'd still like the grind feature," she said. "I'll borrow the money if I have to, but we have quite a bit saved already from my father's life insurance policy. We're…" She glanced at Ezra, allowing herself to show the deep regard she felt for the man she barely knew, and continued, "We're trying to start a family, and I want to be prepared for a stray something to get flushed…"

Ezra held her gaze. The warmth in his eyes made her want things she couldn't ever have with him.

"Yes, we'll definitely want the grind feature," he said, blinking and straightening his shoulders as he turned back to the bunker builder.

And she wondered…did he have the information he needed? Could they get out of there?

Had he seen something in her that he'd wanted?

"Do you have any clients who would be willing to give testimonials about your work?" her soldier man asked as Tom made a list of their dimensions, preferences and specifications.

"I do," the man said. "They're designated by type

of bunker, and type of location, too, so you can contact those who have interests and needs similar to yours. I'll get you the list when we're through here."

Her heart started to pump. So hard she could feel her pulse in her chest, thumping through her. Hear it in her ears. Was it really going to be that smooth? They'd get the Fitzgeralds' bunker information, and maybe even an approximate location, handed to them on a printed piece of paper?

Clamping her hand down on Ezra's knee, she took the sustenance she needed without apology. For that moment, he was as a husband to her.

Tom asked questions. Jotted on his list. Retrieved a laptop and moved notes onto a form that would give them an approximate cost for their personalized bunker, to be set out on an old hunting lot in the middle of the Colorado wilderness. Something Molly had also inherited from her father.

Whereas Theresa Fitzgerald had never even known who her father was. Her mother, either, for that matter.

Feeling rather fond of the imaginary deceased figurehead, she gave Ezra a glance as, figures done, Tom slid them across the table. Assuring Tom that they'd look everything over and get back with him before they left town the next day, she watched as the man left them to collect his list of references.

Tom's phone buzzed, obviously a text, as he pulled out the cell and looked at the screen rather than answering it, and Theresa couldn't help but touch Ezra's knee one more time. "Thank you," she said, her heart pretty much in her throat, making her voice soft and guttural.

When Ezra stiffened, his immediate tension noticeable to her hand still on his lower thigh, she tried to snatch her hand back, but it didn't leave its location.

His hand held her fingers where they were as he leaned over to kiss her cheek and said, "I think we've been made. Stay behind me and follow my lead."

Clinging to the hand holding hers, she stood as he did, not questioning his judgment for even a second, as he walked her behind the man bending beside a desk in front of a tall filing cabinet and out of the odd little store.

"Keep to the wall," he said, his free hand under his shirt where she knew he'd shoved his gun. And then, "See that wall of trees? Run behind it, and follow it back to the far side of the Jeep. Climb in the back seat and stay down. Now. Go!"

She went. She didn't think. Didn't question what she wanted to do. She just ran. Reached the trees, hugged the first one she came to with her arms up against her chest, not spread wide, and looked to the next trunk, getting there as quickly as she could. Two minutes was all it took for her to reach the Jeep and scramble onto the floor of the back seat.

Two minutes, and then gunshots rang out.

Chapter Thirteen

Ezra heard the bullet hit the tree just to the right of his shoulder. And then tossed the rock he'd grabbed on an upward trajectory, to arch down and hit the ground near a tree a few feet over from him. Waited for the bullet to hit. And repeated it twice more, throwing the rocks up on an angle to land a few feet farther each time. When the fourth shot rang out beyond his last throw, in anticipation of where the path would go next, he spun and made his way stealthily through the woods, behind the barn and out to the trees on the other side where he'd sent Theresa. The side with more covering.

Years of training for battle had taught him how to move undetected, but he couldn't be sure how long Smith would be distracted by his movement in the woods before advancing on the vacant Jeep. He went on the hunch that the man wanted his prey badly enough to follow the path Ezra had laid. Keeping down, he slid into the Jeep and started it. With only enough of his head above the dash for him to see, he spun them around to head toward the property exit before Smith had a chance to figure out what was happening.

"Stay down." He bit out the words through gritted teeth.

Bullets flew at them, but Ezra had expected that. A couple hit the Jeep, breaking glass, embedding in the back of his seat. The doomsday preparer was an excellent shot. He'd counted on that, too. The bullets would have hit him if he'd been sitting in the driver's seat, instead of half lying across the console, his legs in a split formation, with one foot on the gas and one bunched up by the radio. He had one hand on the steering wheel, the other holding his gun, as he sped down the road that led to Smith's place.

"Stay down," he said a second time, less forcefully. "He might follow us."

"I don't think so." Her tone was...fine. Considering she could have been killed. And he wondered if she'd lost it back there—thinking that just because they'd managed to evade the bad guy once, they were automatically safe.

"Mark talked about how his folks were always teaching him how to defend house and home," she continued, as if conversing from the back floor of a Jeep was part of a regular day in her life. "They were always really careful about not breaking laws—no way you could save yourself from the blast if you were locked in a cell. They knew when and where they could fight with force, shoot their guns, whatever. And chasing someone down on a public road, shooting at them, wouldn't qualify. Legally, if Smith had hit us while we were on his property, he could have claimed self-defense."

He couldn't believe it. The woman had just nearly lost her life and she was conversing as though they were on a picnic or something. Almost chuckling with relief as half a mile passed with no further bullets flying at them, he slowed the vehicle, chanced a quick glance behind them, saw the roadway completely empty and stopped in the middle of the road just long enough to get himself in the driver's seat.

"Wait. I'm coming up," Theresa told him as sirens sounded.

He did as she asked, keeping watch around them for any activity in the woods on the sides of the road as well as the road itself, and saw the row of vehicles with lights flashing coming from the opposite direction toward Smith's property.

"I called the police," she said.

Of course she had. And Tom Smith would tell them that everything was fine. That Jack and Molly Wallace had been potential clients who'd left unexpectedly. Lay any trouble on them. If he was questioned about shots fired, he'd say he shot in self-defense.

"Did you use the burner phone I gave you?"

"Yes."

He had to call Dom. But first, when she looked over and smiled at him, giving him the urge to pull her against him and thank God she was okay, he put his foot on the gas and got them the hell out of there.

THIRTY SECONDS AFTER she'd climbed in the front seat, Theresa started to shake. Adrenaline dissipated, survival mode faded, and she was left with vivid sensations that wouldn't let her go. She'd heard shots. She surveyed every visible inch of Ezra's body for signs of red. Found none. Not even on his shirt.

"I didn't know if you'd been hit." He hadn't wanted authorities involved in their hunt. Protocols would slow their process. And if they were ordered to stand down and didn't...

Freezing in her long-sleeved shirt, she rubbed her arms and tried to get herself back under control. "I had to call for help."

"You did the right thing. I'll call Dom just as soon as there's a little more distance between us and the Smith residence," he said, sounding not at all upset or disappointed with her. "He'll be pissed, read me the riot act, but he'll arrange for us to have another vehicle. And he'll get his people looking at what they can legally access of Smith's business dealings and associations."

The slow route he'd wanted to avoid.

"I'm sorry you're in hot water with your brother."

She most definitely didn't want to get him in trouble with the law.

And she didn't want him to give up on them, either. She needed him.

Just until the girls were home and safe.

Then she'd be able to wish him a blessed life and say goodbye.

She'd never forget him. That was a given.

"If Dom were in my position, he'd do the exact same thing. And he'd expect me to do so as well. He'll be more pissed that I'm out here getting stuff done while his hands are tied," Ezra told her, giving her another glimpse into the man who was so quickly growing to mean so much to her.

Feelings that would dim as soon as life got back to normal.

"The aftershock will wear off in a few."

"What?" Looking over at him, she saw the concerned glance he was sending her.

"What you're experiencing right now. The after-shock. Every sense is on high alert. Emotions temporarily shut down. Your mind is in full charge. And when the battle is over, when all of that starts to subside, it takes a bit for all parts of you to come back in sync with each other."

He sounded so…normal. Like someone who'd just watched what had happened on a screen, not in real life.

Almost like a teacher in class.

The once-in-a-lifetime potentially debilitating experience she'd just lived through was only a day's work to him.

The reminder was another shock to a system that she was pretty sure couldn't take much more. And yet she wasn't backing out.

Wasn't quitting. And if he thought she was…

They'd turned onto another country road, surrounded by more woods and very few homesteads. He parked on the side, kept the Jeep running and pulled out his personal cell.

"Where are you?" The bullet-tattered Jeep filled with Dom's voice.

In succinct phrases, Ezra filled his brother in on Tom Smith, the plan to get inside the man's shop. "Everything was coming down perfectly, almost had a list with a very good chance of including the Fitzgeralds. It would tell us if not specific addresses, at least details about the physical location of the bunker and type of bunker. Then he gets a text. Looks over at us, looks back at the text, at us again, and bends down to his file cabinet…"

That was how he'd known…

"Getting a gun…"

She'd thought he'd been going to a file for a copy of his reference list. And seconds later, if she'd been there on her own, she'd have been looking down the barrel of a gun, instead of fleeing one.

Ezra continued his half-sentence statements, telling Dominic about his game play with Smith outside the shop, his escape.

"Then we got the hell out of there," Ezra said, while Theresa kept her own counsel.

"And the anonymous 911 call that couldn't be traced?"

Wow, they knew that already?

"Theresa. From the burner phone I gave her."

"How bad's the rental?"

"I'll need something else."

"Smith knows what we look like," Theresa finally blurted. Which meant the police might soon know, and they'd be ordered to stand down.

And maybe authorities would believe that Dom had been involved with his brother's off-the-grid vigilante enforcement? Would he be told to stand down as well?

Panic filled her anew.

Her daughters, who could have already disappeared off the grid forever, needed more than protocol at the moment...

"He'd have to reveal more than he wants to, maybe even give access to the information you were after, if he admits he saw you. If he's going to report it officially," Dom said over the line. "More than likely he'll say he thought he saw movement and shot, thinking it was an animal."

She hadn't thought of that. But clearly Ezra had. He was nodding his head. And reached out a hand, tucking a lock of fallen hair back into her bun. Automatically reaching up to tighten the scrunchie holding her hair in place, she accidentally brushed her ascending hand against his descending one.

Ice against warmth.

Dom said he'd get back to Ezra shortly with details of where he could pick up a new vehicle and leave the damaged one to be retrieved by the rental company. "You're lucky you paid extra for their insurance, bro," the FBI agent said.

He was lucky he wasn't dead, Theresa thought to herself, recalling the cat-and-mouse game Ezra had told Dom he'd played with Smith while she'd been face-down on the floor of the Jeep, listening to gunshots.

Neither of the brothers seemed to get that the danger they were taking for granted, their escape from it, wasn't at all normal life.

Because to them it was.

To her, it would never be.

As it turned out, Dom used Smith's shooting at Ezra and Theresa as a means to tie the incident to the kidnapping of Claire and Neve Fitzgerald, and by the time Ezra and Theresa were in a new, slate gray Jeep, picked up at a rental place in Benson, the FBI was attempting to get a warrant to search Smith's place.

"So our plan worked after all!" Theresa said when she heard the news. "Not like we'd hoped, but, as you said, once we got inside, the plan was fluid..."

They'd just pulled off the rental lot, and he had more to tell her. "There's been no sign of the Fitzgeralds." They'd agreed to drive through for something quick to eat, and then he had to come up with his next move.

"No credit card use, no sightings of the truck, and their phones are still turned off." He knew his words had to be striking terror within her, but if they were going to get through however long it took to get her kids back, she would have to be able to deal with the hard stuff.

No way, as darkness fell soon, that it wouldn't be coming.

He couldn't let her slow him down.

Because to do so would let her down.

"That's with reports from multiple law enforcement agencies across the state and in bordering states, and a check of all Benson surveillance cameras." The truck was seen twice in Benson and then disappeared.

He pulled into the lot of an Italian place that offered a drive-through window. Pasta was filling and easy on the stomach. And then he asked, "Do you like Italian?"

He didn't look her way. Couldn't afford to be compassionate at the moment. Either she had what it might take, or she didn't. With the chance for a quick rescue gone, he was going off the grid.

"Look at my hips. What do you think?" The somewhat waspish comment drew his gaze to hips that, while maybe a little filled out due to childbirth, looked way too good to him.

"No, don't do that," he told her, shaking his head.

"Do what?"

"Distract me. Look, here's how it is. I'm given a goal, I figure out battle plans, and I only work with the best of the best. At the moment, that's me. Alone."

"We've already been through this."

The car in front of him pulled forward, making it his turn to order.

"I want baked ziti," she said. He asked for two. Saw

her reach for her credit card as he inched the Jeep toward the pickup window, and pulled out his own wallet.

She stuck her card in front of his chest. He handed his own card to the teenager leaning out the window.

"Why are you being this way?" she asked, her tone marked down several notches. "I was good today. I helped."

He nodded. He'd like to have her along. When he found the twins, there was no telling what emotional state they'd be in, and they'd need her.

She had a right to be with him since he wasn't working in any official capacity, but rather, at her request. If it were his kids who'd been hauled off, no way he'd sit out the search.

It wasn't like there was going to be some kind of ransom call. No reason for her to be home. Worse, there was nothing for her to do there but worry.

Not his concern.

She wasn't even a friend.

"I need to know that you aren't going to fall apart on me. I have no idea what I'll be doing, or what I might find along the way. If I have to tend to you, it could make the difference between completing the job successfully or not."

"The credit card, that was a test, right?" she said, her brows drawn together as she pinned him with a knowing look.

How did she do that? How was it possible that a woman he barely knew could read him when no one else, other than Dom and Oliver, had ever been able to do so?

What was taking the damned ziti so long? He glanced toward the window.

"I'm the boss," he said. When it came to split-second decisions and life and death, there had to be one.

"And I proved that I won't fight that. You won. You paid. I conceded gracefully. And earlier, when you told me to leave, to run, where to run and how to enter the Jeep, I followed every command without question."

Yeah. She'd done good. He had good points, too, but he was being a jerk. Because the woman turned him on, and he didn't want her to do so. Had given no permission for that to happen.

Had no good outcome for the malady.

And that pissed him off.

The fact that he hadn't found her daughters before nightfall was eating his insides out.

None of which was her fault. Nor should she be bearing the brunt of his frustration.

She'd suffered enough for a lifetime.

And was carrying a burden far, far worse than his would ever be. Nighttime fell on his failure, but it fell on her children.

He couldn't even imagine...

"You showed me what I needed to see in terms of your ability to do what's asked in the heat of battle this afternoon." He glanced her way again, really looked at her, into those overflowing brown eyes, and let himself soak for a moment.

He shouldn't have doubted her ability to hold up even for a second. "I'm sorry."

"You're risking your life for my daughters, Ezra," she said softly, the glow in her eyes growing, not diminishing. "You have nothing to apologize for."

He needed to kiss those lips. To hold her tight and make the bad things go away.

"Here you go, sir." A hand reached a bag out to him. He took it.

And drove off into the setting sun with a sinking feeling in his gut.

For the first time in his life, he was in over his head.

Chapter Fourteen

He hadn't quit on her. From the time they'd talked to Dominic, Ezra had been chewing on something, and Theresa had been prepared to hear that he was stepping back to let law enforcement do their jobs.

She'd been prepared to beg him to stay, even though he'd already done far too much for her.

Instead, she'd had to beg to be allowed to stay.

He drove out by a river they'd passed, pulled into a lay-by and parked. Wanting, first and foremost, not to hamper his process, she didn't attempt to converse with him while they ate. And forced herself to chew and swallow a good portion of the pasta crammed into a very full Styrofoam container.

She might not be skilled in battle, and sometimes her imagination ran away with her when it came to worrying about her kids. But she would not hinder the finding of her children.

Nor would she abandon them solely to the abilities of others.

"You're too quiet." Ezra's words washed over her like warm water.

"I didn't want to interrupt your thoughts."

"Might have been better if you'd pulled me away

from them." The statement was odd, most particularly from him, but she let it go.

And said aloud what she'd just started thinking about. "When I was two, I was abandoned at a church. Just left there, inside the vestibule, with no note, no identification. I'm told I wandered around for several hours, at best guess, and eventually crawled up onto a lone pew that was out there and fell asleep. I was found there early one morning."

She took a bite. Chewed. Appreciated his silence.

"Authorities spent a lot of time trying to find my parents. They couldn't put me up for adoption without knowing that I hadn't been kidnapped. Maybe one parent not wanting the other to have me or something. In any case, I grew up in a children's home associated with the church. I was well educated. Well loved. But until I married Mark, I'd never had a family of my own. Two things about this are pertinent," she continued. "First, the authorities, through all of their effort and access to information and databases, were never able to find who'd left me at that church. I cannot just leave my daughters' fates to authorities. I trust them to do everything they can. I appreciate all that they're doing. But whether you're with me or not, I will be on the hunt for Claire and Neve until I find them."

There was nothing he or anyone was going to do to stop her.

"And second?"

She glanced at him, noticed that he'd completely cleaned his container. "What?"

"You started with 'first,' and I wanted to know what second was."

"Second, I will not abandon my children as I was abandoned. I'm not prepared for battle, I get that..."

"I'll prepare you as best I can every step of the way." The old Ezra was back. The one who'd spent an entire afternoon at her side while his family hovered around them. Who'd made her daughters' horse-riding dreams come true.

"We're a team again, then?"

He nodded. Didn't really smile, but he was looking her in the eye again. Telling her things that she couldn't really translate into words, but things that mattered.

Things that gave her strength.

And hope.

"THE GOOD NEWS is that Eric and Jennifer Fitzgerald's end goal is to protect their son's children." Ezra started in before they'd even pulled away from the river. "Which means that this kidnapping is different from many where hope for the child's physical safety wanes as the hours pass."

"I'm counting on that fact." Theresa was putting their containers and plastic silverware back in the bag they'd come in.

"Until we can figure out where they're homesteading, where their bunker is, we need them to feel confident in their ability to pull this off." He was thinking aloud. But also doing what he'd just said he'd do—preparing her.

If the Fitzgeralds were cornered, feeling desperate, the twins could get hurt.

"So, we need to make sure that today's situation with Tom Smith doesn't happen again," she said. "We don't want them to know we're closing in on them."

She was good.

But he'd known that.

"We'll need to be more discreet, yes," he agreed. "I'm not a profiler, per se, but before we go into battle, we profile our enemy as a whole. We have to be able to predict what they might do given various situations. We need to know what kind of weapons they have, for instance, how many days' worth of supplies, or what kind of barricades, physical or otherwise, they'll be using to stop us. I need to know these kinds of things about the Fitzgeralds. So what I suggest is that we get a room someplace in town and sit down and talk. I need you to tell me everything you can remember Mark ever telling you about his parents. And any and all details you can recall about the time you've known them. Things the girls have said, but also your own impressions."

They had to get a room. No way they were heading two hours back to Blue Larkspur when they knew the girls had been driven as far as Benson. And it wasn't like they could scour wooded miles in the pitch-black for any telltale signs of recent occupation.

Realizing her little girls were going to be spending at least one night with the unstable couple had to be soul-destroying, but Theresa was sitting up straight. Engaging rationally with him.

She was there, as she'd sworn she'd be, and he admired the hell out of her.

"There was that place kind of in the middle of town," she reminded him. "It had rooms with windows that look out over Main Street. And parking outside each door." So much for thinking the room idea was going to be a problem for her.

If only he could be so sure it wouldn't pose serious issues for him.

He'd shared bunks and slept sleeping bag to sleeping bag in bunkers, too, with both male and female soldiers.

He'd never, ever spent a night in a motel room with a woman he was hot for without sex being an already-agreed-upon mutual desire.

And there were considerations so much more important at stake…

"I just thought of something," she blurted as he pulled back into town. The streetlights were coming on to brighten the falling dusk. "Tom Smith had a pamphlet sitting on that desk when we walked in. I remember wondering if it was part of a packet he gives to all prospective clients."

He'd been sizing up the man, looking for weapons and planning escape routes. Not glancing at brochures on the furniture.

"And?"

"It was for guns and ammunition, Ezra. That store right there." Sitting forward, she pointed an obviously shaking finger at a small corner place attached to a long string of storefronts all under one roof.

He drove slowly past, taking in the nearly all glass front and what looked like cases in a U shape around the long, narrow room. Several businesses down, outside an ice cream shop, he parked. "You up for a walk?" he asked, studying the street and the area around the ammunition shop on the corner intently.

"Of course." She'd opened her door and was out of the vehicle faster than he'd have liked. Remnants of having been shot at—of knowing she was a target as well—still tightened his nerve endings.

He didn't see any sign of unusual activity. The street was calm. Shoppers, but not so many that the sidewalks were crowded. A few cars. A family sitting on a bench eating ice cream.

If Claire and Neve had been there, they'd have ordered chocolate…

"Let's go inside," he said, heading up to the door of the soda fountain and sweets parlor. Pulling his phone out, he spoke with the manager who'd been working all day, spoke with anyone who'd been there for more than four hours, showed the picture he had of the twins without saying who they were or why he was asking about them.

No one had seen them. And it wasn't like six-year-old twins who, while not identical, looked alike would be forgettable.

"How about these two?" Theresa asked, showing a picture of the Fitzgeralds standing by their truck, smiling. "We were supposed to meet them here, but we're later than expected, and I'm afraid we missed them."

She was good. Damned good.

Better than he was.

Interrogation wasn't his business.

"Yeah, them I recognize." A young guy with dark hair tied back in a ponytail nodded as he wiped his hands on a long white apron over jeans. "Mostly because they bought like two cases of ice cream sandwiches and paid cash for 'em, too. They wanted all we had, and I emptied out the back of the walk-in to get them. They got dry ice, too, you know, like they were going on a road trip. But they didn't have any kids in here with them, if they were all supposed to be together or something."

"The kids were probably still out in the truck," Ezra said, to cover for Theresa's suddenly white face and tighter expression.

"Oh, well, maybe it's not the same people," the kid said. "They looked an awful lot like that, but these guys were driving a van."

"A van?" Theresa voiced the question.

"Yeah. I offered to help load it, but the guy was pretty definite about being able to do it himself. I figured he was one of those OCD types, you know. Everything has to be just right. The van was older, from the eighties, maybe, brown, and sweet, really. Not a scratch or dent that I could see. Tires were fairly new, too, great tread on them."

The kid asked if he could get them anything…on the house…but Ezra shook his head. Took Theresa's hand. Making an excuse about hoping to catch up with their family, he got them out the door, and as soon as they were far enough down the block for the observant ice cream scooper not to see, he was on the phone with Dom. Authorities were looking for the wrong vehicle.

"They got the warrant and are on their way to Smith's," Ezra told Theresa as, still holding her hand— for show, he told himself—they headed down to the ammunition shop.

She missed a step, clasping harder at his hand as she righted herself, and looked up at him. "Oh my God! We might still get them tonight!"

He didn't want to get her hopes up, but he couldn't deny that he, too, saw the plausibility of such a possibility. And needed it to come to be.

Every second he was with Theresa, every breath of her he inhaled, he was getting in further over his head.

ONE STEP IN front of the other. It was all she could do. Life had spiraled so far out of control, out of any comfort zone, out of all realms of anything she'd ever imagined herself doing, that Theresa couldn't find any sense of a self she knew. So, she took the self she had and determined that that person was going to do whatever it took to find her children.

"Act natural," Ezra said, his tone striking a new shot of fear through her. "We're a couple on a stroll…"

About to get shot at? She clutched his hand harder. Whatever happened, holding his hand made it easier to bear.

"The guy behind the counter in the gun shop is watching us. And texting."

He'd told Dominic that Tom Smith's doing the same was what had alerted him to their danger at the bunker store. Was the ammunition shopkeeper going to reach for a gun as well?

Ezra wasn't urging her to run. Or hide. He wasn't rushing her to face-plant on the floor of their new Jeep. She walked as casually as she could beside him. Looking toward the window of the antique shop next door to their destination. Moving close enough to Ezra that their hips were touching.

"You okay to go in?" Ezra asked as they approached the gun shop.

"Of course."

She saw the shopkeeper, a skinny guy with a mop of curly red hair falling down around his face, coming around the counter as they got close. Her heart pounded as her gaze flew to his hands, her entire system rushing into flight mode.

The man's hands were empty. He reached toward the door handle just before they did.

He was going to hold the door open for them?

She'd just started to adjust to the information when she heard a click. And saw a shade come down over the door. Followed by quickly pulled shades on the windows on either side of it.

"He just locked the door on us," she said, standing there nonplussed.

"Yep." Ezra moved them quickly toward the antique shop storefront. "Not smart to stand in front of shaded windows," he said. "Most particularly when the room behind them is filled with arms."

It was as he said that last word that the blood drained from her face, and what felt like her entire body as well.

His statement brought a picture to her mind's eye, the glance she'd been taking in of the shop in the seconds before she'd expected to enter it—just before she'd heard the click of the turned lock.

She made it back to the Jeep, hand in Ezra's, and dropped down to the front passenger seat, hands shaking as she fastened the seat belt. Sweating, she shivered.

"We've done what we can do for the night," Ezra was saying as he climbed in beside her and started the vehicle. "We need to find a room."

She heard him. Accepted his words. They weren't enough to bring her out of the horror she'd been catapulted into.

"What is it? Are you hurt?" Ezra's tone, sharp then, drew closer as he leaned across the console, his gaze running intently over her. Looking for blood, she figured. He didn't know it had all drained away.

"Theresa." The tone was compelling.

She blinked. "Mariette." She barely got the word out. Coughed. Then said, "I was wrong."

"About what?" With a finger on her chin, he turned her head until she was looking into his very intent gaze. "Wrong about what?"

His hand dropped away. She had to hold her own head straight. Felt driven to lay it on his shoulder, to turn her head in until she got lost within his strength.

But couldn't do that, either. She couldn't escape, no matter where she went.

Her girls… The danger was so much worse than she'd even imagined.

"Mariette. That antique gun in the case in the middle of the gun shop. I saw it just before he closed the blind. Mariette. Not marionette. Claire was right."

He didn't look away and his gaze didn't weaken, either. "I'm not following you."

Looking at him hurt. Everything hurt. Tears filled her eyes. She knew it. Couldn't stop them.

"The one solo visitation. Eric and Jennifer gave the girls presents. They each got a wooden box. Pretty wooden box, Neve said. Claire said they were heavy and wouldn't open. Neve thought that part was stupid, but insisted the box was pretty…"

Who cared about the way the damned box looked?

And yet her mind clung to Neve's impression. Couldn't let go of her baby girl's positive take on her world. Issued a prayer from the depths of her soul that Neve would hold on to that perspective.

"Still not following." Ezra's voice brought her attention back to the black moment sucking her in.

"Jennifer told the girls they couldn't open the boxes just yet. Not until they were someplace where they could get set up to use what was inside. Mariettes, Claire said. That was what was inside, Mariettes. *Marionettes*, I corrected her, thinking that the Fitzgeralds really were trying to be good grandparents, buying the girls real marionettes to play with, and keeping them for them until they had a stage set up to stand behind and put on a show. The girls said their grandparents were going to teach them how to use them. I pictured a puppet play. Was relieved..."

She saw the change come over Ezra, as though in slow motion. He stiffened. His eyes grew harder. His jaw tense.

"They gave those little kids Mariettes?"

She nodded, knocking tears over her lids and down her cheeks. "Oh my God, Ezra, they bought my babies their own guns!"

Chapter Fifteen

Mariettes were small guns, but precise and designed to kill. Ezra burned from the inside out as he drove to the motel Theresa had mentioned. The inn was well lit, beautifully manicured with gardens and fresh paint, and had a lit waterfall pond feature with benches out in the spacious, freshly mowed lawn. The type of place he was pretty sure she needed to be.

She was a natural nurturer, and beauty and peace had been horribly vacant from her day.

He asked for two rooms, adjoining if at all possible, and was told there was only one left, period. And that due to a cancellation.

He turned to Theresa, ready to offer to try one of the other two motels on the outskirts of town, when she said, "We'll take it," and slapped her credit card down on the counter.

Ezra had intended to pay. With no mortgage and very little upon which to spend money, he'd amassed far more wealth than he needed over the eighteen years since he'd left home for the army, while Theresa was a single mother who'd struggled with massive medical bills.

And he recognized that Theresa needed to be in control of something in a life spiraling out of control.

He recognized it because he'd been there since he was sixteen years old.

Five minutes after they'd registered, they were using a key card to enter a much more welcoming, homey place than he generally frequented. Bare-bones was good enough for him. He was glad that Theresa would have nicer than that.

It did feel a bit low-life to be entering the spacious accommodations carrying box-store plastic bags as their only luggage—a firm reminder that they weren't there on vacation.

Or even because they'd planned a trip.

They'd be in the room only until they had their next maneuver planned out and had gotten at least a little rest.

Or until Dom called and gave them a more immediate assignment.

Like picking up Claire and Neve.

"Obviously you've got the bed," he told Theresa, scouting out the room for safety and defense purposes. Only allowing himself to think about being on the job. Period. Might be a self-imposed, unofficial assignment, but he was there for only one purpose. Win the most important battle he'd ever fought. "I'll take the sofa thing."

"That doesn't make sense, Ezra," she said, moving over to the window alcove and dropping her bags on the iron-barred mattress filled with pillows and frills. "I'm fine with the daybed. You're a lot bigger than I am. And you're the one who is more apt to be called upon for physical exertion."

He'd just determined that he needed to let her win, to call the shots, wherever he could. This wasn't that. "I take the window," he told her unequivocally. "You take the wall." He nodded his head toward the bed with a wall at the head and another one right beside it.

She gave him one glance and moved her bags. He dropped his in one of the four chairs pushed up to a round table set in the twenty feet of space between the bed and the window. Opposite a two-cushion couch and two armchairs also sharing that space. They'd passed the door into the separate, private bath as they'd entered the room.

Feeling slightly as though he'd landed in a minefield like none other, Ezra grabbed the pad of paper and pen he'd purchased, along with his cell phone and a bottle of water, and sat down at the table. He made columns. Filled them in with what he knew. Heard movement in the room. The bathroom door closing. Silence. Water running. Door opening.

And stared at the page that he hadn't touched since the door had first closed.

It had been a while since he'd spent the night with a woman. Heard her moving. Couldn't look. Not for a minute or two, at least.

"What can I do to help?" Her phone landed softly on the table. The chair next to him moved. And...she'd taken the band out of her hair.

Long dark strands cascaded...everywhere. For a second there, they were all he could see. Thick dark strands, with those hints of fire in their depths.

And then he noticed the eyes in the middle of the array. They bore...agony.

His mind clicked into immediate gear. He asked

her to start with everything she could remember Mark
ever saying about his home, growing up. "I'm hoping
that Dom's going to find that referral list in his search
of Smith's place, and that we'll have good direction in
terms of finding the Fitzgerald bunker, but in case he
doesn't, we need to know where to head in the morning." He turned his phone around, showing her a topographic map of the state. Asked her to call up Smith's
website and get his list of suggested bunker locations,
to designate the most likely bunker sites. "Knowing
as much as we can about the Fitzgeralds' choices—do
they prefer woods or open fields, for instance—will
help us more accurately pinpoint where they might be."

"You think they've already taken my girls down
into their bunker."

Lying only added insult to injury. "I think we want
to assume the worst so that we're prepared to fight
under the worst-case scenario and win." He looked
her in the eye as he spoke, and then continued immediately. "What do you know about where Mark grew
up? Were they out in the country? In a neighborhood?
Anything about the surroundings might help."

She didn't know much at all. "Mark had to fight
hard not to be brainwashed, manipulated or influenced
by them. When he left, it's like he locked off that part
of his mind. I do know that he had a dog that got in a
fight with a bear once. The dog won. The bear ran off."

Her smile, though distant, was genuine. Like fresh
water to look at. A massive lake of it.

In Colorado, bears could come into neighborhoods,
but it wouldn't be as likely. And it made sense that they
were looking for someplace isolated, though from what

they'd been told by Smith that day, people had bunkers in the middle of big-city properties, too.

"And he learned to shoot a gun in his own backyard."

Very likely more remote than city or neighborhood living.

"Did he ever say how he got to school?"

"He was homeschooled."

Isolation.

Everything was leaning toward the Fitzgeralds living off the grid.

Which was going to make finding them a lot more difficult.

And also made him one of the best men for the job. He'd spent more time in foreign desert and mountainous land off the grid than in his home country in recent years.

What he didn't add was that Colorado had a load of state land—mountainous, nearly-impossible-to-access land—where someone could live an entire lifetime and never be seen.

No point in giving her more than one mountain to climb at a time.

"Tell me about Mark's skills. What was he good at? What were his hobbies? What did he enjoy doing?"

He had to ask the questions. And wanted to know the answers, too. Not just because he needed them. Who was this man who'd won Theresa's love and life partner commitment? Who'd fathered two very special little girls.

"He was a good swimmer. Insisted that the girls start taking lessons before they were even a year old. But he didn't particularly like swimming. He liked food trucks and festivals. He liked going to the zoo, and he loved amusement parks. I always kind of thought that he was a kid having the childhood he'd missed, but he never said so."

She caught Ezra's eye and didn't look away. He couldn't desert her, even as he knew he should. Eventually, she blinked. Looked down. Pulled at a string on a cloth thing set in the middle of the table with a bowl of fruit on it. And then said, "He was great around the house. Knew how to fix anything and everything."

Mark's parents had trained him to be self-sufficient. Something Ezra hadn't learned until after he'd accepted the fact that his father hadn't been the man he'd thought him to be.

"Oh, and he must have been pretty good at mountain climbing," she said. "We never went, but one time when we vacationed at a little resort in the Rockies, Neve asked if we could go to the very top and sit in the clouds, and he'd told her that he'd climbed that mountain to the very top once, and there were no clouds there. It just looked like they were the same from down below."

And…damn.

The man the Fitzgeralds had raised was proficient enough to climb a mountain. One that, considering his daughter thought it was high enough to be in the clouds, could likely take superior skills to scale.

Unless… Did Ezra dare hope that the guy had just been spinning a yarn for the sake of his little girl?

It was possible.

But he couldn't risk going with that more palatable theory.

He couldn't risk reaching out and touching the fingers that were unraveling a corner of the table's center decor one thread at a time, either.

But, God, how he wanted to.

SOME SECONDS, THERESA felt like she was holding on by a thread. And then she'd have some question to answer, some task to do, and she came back into her strength again. At some point, was that ability to persevere going to run out?

She couldn't let it. Whatever it took, whatever she had to do, she would acquire the capability by any means to find her girls and bring them safely home.

"I know this is hard, Theresa." Ezra's tone had softened again. She didn't need or want his pity. Sympathy weakened her.

But his personal attention... Life kindled inside her just a bit. Keeping her...present.

Giving her impetus to sit forward and tend to his next question. "Anything else you need to know?"

"I need anything you can think of."

"Jennifer and Eric risked discovery to stop and buy ice cream sandwiches. Probably because they thought the girls would be thrilled with them. Means they are trying to tend to the girls' happiness." It meant that they didn't even know their granddaughters well enough to know their food preferences. It also meant they were planning to keep the twins someplace where they wouldn't have access to purchasing ice cream sandwiches for a long time.

Ezra's hand covered hers on the table, stopping her fingers from moving. And she realized she'd been pulling at a string on a doily to the point of damaging the lacy work. "You can talk about it," he said, giving no definition to his vagueness. "I know I'm not the most sensitive guy in the world, but I get that this has to be killing you and you're stuck with me at the moment, and…if you need to talk… I can sit and listen. Not too many ways to screw that up." He grinned with the last line, probably trying to lighten the moment—and kind of screwing it up, too.

She wanted to smile back. Was tied too tightly to do so. She couldn't show any loose threads. The slightest tug and she'd unravel.

"I'm fine," she told him. "This isn't about me." And she didn't need him wasting any of his precious brain cells on worrying about her. She needed him coming up with a plan by morning that would get them closer to her children.

"So, you've been shot at before today?" he asked.

Of course not. And, yeah, she'd been shaken there for a bit. She was over it. "Technically, I wasn't shot at. Only trees were shot at." Thanks to his training and skills. "And the Jeep, of course," she added, remembering the terrifying moments when she heard breaking glass so close by and a horrifying thud as bullets pierced the back of the seat just above her head.

Her heart had cried out for Ezra as she'd braced for a wreck. And worse.

But she was over that, too, she told herself, pushing memories, emotions away from conscious thought by focusing on other things.

"It's okay, you know. The aftershock. I've gotten many of my men through it…"

His men were part of his team. She was…a blip in time. They could afford to lean on him. She couldn't.

"Believe me, I'm far more ripped up inside about my daughters than I am about a few flying bullets." Truth.

Ezra sat back, was studying her. "Those bullets could take your life." The words were calm. Matter-of-fact. Just like she was being.

And she answered without a second's hesitation. "I'll die if I have to to save my children…"

"Death is the end, Theresa. If you'd been shot today, how would you then go on to save your kids?"

Good point. She started to shake, as she had after they'd escaped from Smith. He leaned forward again, took her hand and held it on top of the table, sand-wiched between his much larger ones. Warming her.

"Your girls have already lost one parent," he said quietly, and yet the words hit her core. "They need you to be waiting, healthy and ready, when they return." He was right. And had understood something she had not. The girls didn't just need to be found. They needed her to be present and ready for them.

Ezra Colton might not be in her life for long, but his impact was huge. The man was one of those special beings who'd always hold a place of importance in her heart. He was leaving. She knew that. Just as she knew she needed him to go. But she would never forget him.

"One way you prepare to be capable of providing whatever emotional sustenance and understanding they're going to need once we find them is accessing the help offered you," he continued, unaware that he'd just been on the stage of her heart, being awarded top honors. "Finding your daughters, bringing them safely back to you… This isn't something you can do alone."

"So why do I feel like I have to?"

"Because it's easier than opening your emotions up

to the help that's being offered." His statement was like a confession. She had the thought, sat there studying him, and he said, "I adored my father when I was a kid. And as I grew, I idolized him. I wanted to be just like him. To help so many people...and to rid the world of the criminals that hurt people." He paused, pulled their hands down from the table to his knee, bringing them closer. Playing with her fingers, he continued, "When his duplicity first came to light, I didn't believe it. I fought anyone who tried to speak evil of him—and at that point, pretty much everyone was talking about him. On the news and everywhere else. I would have died defending him. Even after he called me into his office alone, and told me what he'd done and why, I still didn't believe him. I thought he was protecting someone..."

Her heart aching, Theresa swallowed back tears. She could feel the grief of the young boy he'd been. Wanted so badly to make the pain go away.

"Once I realized that he'd really done what every-one was saying he was doing..." He sat up, letting her hand drop. Leaned back in his chair. "I needed no one," he finished. "Let's just say it wasn't a pretty last two years of high school. Not until I joined the army, became a part of a unit of people again and found my purpose. I found my way to being the man I'd thought my father was."

If there'd been any minute hope that Ezra Colton would ever decide to hang around Blue Larkspur, or change to a less dangerous career, that hope had just been dashed.

If possible, her respect for him had grown. And her

trust in his ability to find her daughters had expanded so far there was no room for doubt.

"My whole point here is that I know what I'm talking about, Theresa, and I know how to minimize the fallout. This is what I do for a living—get soldiers prepared for battle and go into battle with them, yes—but a big part of my job is also teaching them how to cope with the aftershocks of shooting and being shot at or walking through a field that could explode under your foot at any given moment. If you don't deal with the residual emotions, you might survive or even win the battle, but you won't be good when the war is over."

He'd drawn the curtains across the window, mostly hiding the darkness that had fallen. A somewhat blinding light shone through a crack where the two sides of the drapes came together. The parking-lot security lights.

She appreciated that they were there. Knew she couldn't stare straight at the light or she'd be blinded.

Much like Ezra. She was thankful for his presence, but she couldn't get too close and be burned.

"I'm not saying you have to speak to me," he said then. "Obviously, the kind of coaching I know how to do is vastly different from a parent dealing with child abduction. I just… You haven't made a single phone call to anyone since we've been together. Other than to get your duties covered at work. If you need some privacy to talk to someone, I'm fine to provide it."

She'd texted a few people, a neighbor, the day-camp coordinator, and the mother of the twins' closest friend. Their horror and sympathy had only fed her own at a time when she couldn't afford to be weak.

"In a way, I've been going it on my own since I

was two," she told him then. "And with Mark's illness ongoing as it had been, I learned how to carry
the weight on my shoulders." She was going to leave
it there. Meant to. Looked over at him, held his gaze…
and couldn't keep it in. There was something he could
do for her. Right then. Right there. Something that
would instill some good feeling in the midst of all the
debilitating pain.

Something that would give her a few minutes of escape from the horror that had become her existence.

In the morning, for the rest of her life, she'd probably regret opening her mouth. The morning seemed
light-years away.

And uncertain. For over a minute, he'd sat there
maintaining their visual connection.

"You know what would help?" She was doing it.
That in itself was a relief.

"What?" And then, with a softening in his expression, "Tell me."

Leaning forward slowly, she opened her mouth…
and his phone rang.

Chapter Sixteen

Ezra and Theresa turned at once to look at his phone vibrating against the table, the screen fully visible.

Dominic.

Reining in the chest-weighting disappointment that hit him, he turned from his chance to receive Theresa's confidences and find out how to help her and picked up the cell.

"Yeah."

"Am I on speaker?" Code for *don't put me there*, which couldn't be good.

"No."

Something had happened and he sat unprepared. Seconds too late. Lacking in the knowledge he needed to help an incredible woman over the impossible hurdle in front of her.

"We got the client list. It's as thorough as you'd hoped, but the Fitzgeralds aren't on it."

Steeling his face to show nothing—another talent he'd honed to perfection—he didn't respond, either, waiting for his brother to lay it all out for him before giving Theresa any board from which to dive off.

"He didn't build their bunker. Doesn't even know where it is. Four years ago, they bought a plumbing system from him to pump water into the bunker from an underground well. And two years before that, a pump-and-dump toilet with one hundred feet of piping to shoot waste one hundred feet from the bunker on a diagonal to the surface, where it apparently composts and fertilizes. We've got the paperwork for both, and the measurements of the diagonal, which tell us that the bunker is ten feet down from the surface. They paid cash for both, picked both up at Smith's shop. He assumed by the questions they asked that they were doing the labor themselves."

Feeling Theresa's gaze on him, and because there were some good points in the conversation, he nodded. "Sounds like they trenched it in," he said, speaking of the bunker based on what Dom was describing about the plumbing designs he'd also seen.

"Trenching's good." Theresa's words drew his gaze to her. He left it there. Holding her up in whatever way he could. "Prevents cave-ins," she told him.

At the same time, Dom was saying, "He claimed self-defense on the shots fired. Said that you two acted odd by just getting up and leaving without a word, and he saw you go for your gun…"

"He did not. My hand was on it, but it was stuffed in my jeans, under my shirt."

"No cameras to prove that. And all he'd need to do is convince police that he had reason to believe he saw a gun."

"That's bull…" He finished a string of words Dom had heard from him before.

"You were on his private property," Dom continued. "Colorado law gives him the right to defend himself…"

Yeah, yeah, yeah. He got it.

"So what now?"

"We've got a specialist looking for underground wells starting around Benson and branching out three-sixty from there. And we've got the referral list. Doomsday preparers tend to be in close-knit groups. Hopefully one of them knows something…"

"You think they'd turn on one of their own?"

When the line went quiet, he knew Dom had hung up.

His brother had told him what he could. And hadn't hung around for Ezra to say something that Dom would have to warn him against.

Theresa sat watching him, her features the most beautiful thing in the world as they reflected the woman glowing inside her. She was waiting.

Not demanding.

"We don't have an address. Or bunker type." He laid it out clearly. "What we do have is some building specifications. We know that the plan is for long-term underground living…"

"And that it's trenched," she said, as though needing some encouragement to help her hold it together.

"Six years ago they bought a pump-and-dump flushing toilet system. And then two years later, a plumbing system that taps into an underground well for water."

"They bought the toilet system the year the twins were born. You think they somehow knew? And have been planning this since then? Even before Mark got sick? I mean, they don't have just a bunker. They've got an underground home," she said, her lips pursed as she nodded. "I saw some pictures. They have actual flooring, not just dirt. And furnishings. Neve might convince Claire they're on an adventure…"

He had to give it to her. The woman knew how to make lemonade out of lemons.

And he needed to get to work. "I've got enough specifics here, and with a topographic map, we'll at least be able to pinpoint some possibilities… Generally, the pump and dumps go straight up or horizontal. I'm guessing the diagonal angle of theirs means that there's rock face in the way. Which would most likely specify mountain terrain. And we want to stay within a couple of hours of Benson. Can't be too far out with the Fitzgeralds making frequent trips to Blue Larkspur."

"They could have stayed in motels. It's not like they chose to build to be close to Mark. They had no idea where he was."

"A simple assessors records search for his name could have shown them property owners in the state. And with probable dark-web access…"

"But you said credit cards hadn't shown any motel stays…"

He had said that. They could have paid cash. Or used assumed names. But since they hadn't been hiding their presence in Blue Larkspur, why would they do either? Most motels didn't even allow check-in without a credit card to pay for any damage done to the room.

"Okay, we'll narrow our start to within sixty miles of Benson. Obviously, they shop here. The ammunitions guy knew to watch for us. And keep us out."

He texted Dom. He'd failed to relay that information and wanted his brother on it.

Out of the text app and back to his search engine, he found a topographic map that allowed him to narrow down regions with specific geographic qualifications. No lake or stream nearby—the ground would be too vulnerable to flooding and caving. No underground utility lines, probably not a huge consideration out in the middle of nowhere. And probably not in a wooded area—trenching with trees would be a nightmare of roots. Mountain region...

"Do you know exactly what mountain Mark climbed?"

She nodded. Named a peak. And he narrowed his search to there. He could be wrong. Had to start somewhere. Typed in various coordinates, looking for areas that would fit trenching and diagonal dumping coordinates.

Theresa, sitting so close that her knee was touching his, worked her screen with a thumb that didn't quit. "You a speed reader?" he asked at one point, giving his eyes a rest from the small screen he had to work with.

"Yeah. I sing, too," she added, and he didn't know if she was being sarcastic or really had a good voice. He wanted to ask.

Specifically did not allow himself to do so.

He'd expect, with all of the specific guidelines narrowing his search, that there'd be one or two areas of interest to him. He had seven. In three different directions from where he sat. Could take three days to a week to get to them all.

He looked for roads into the regions. No way Eric Fitzgerald could haul a toilet system up a trail, even with determination and trolleys.

And it wasn't likely Claire and Neve were going to be up for serious climbing, either. Not without training.

"Did Mark ever say whether or not his parents were preparing right where they lived? Or was their bunker elsewhere?"

"He didn't specifically say..." She drew out the

word. "But he was claustrophobic. Not in any debilitating sense. But he didn't like to have the curtains closed in the house. And when we went to Disney World, he opted not to go on any of the rides that took us underground or in tunnels..." She looked at him, her gaze wide. "It makes sense, doesn't it, that he spent time in their bunker?"

"It sounds like they could have been living there, at least part-time, even then. Maybe they slept down there? I know some doomsdayers do that." He knew a veteran with PTSD who did. Granted, the bunker was more of a tented camping spot, but it was down an incline into a cave in Arizona. The bunker gave Dave peace. Highly unlikely that Mark Fitzgerald had had the same reaction.

And Ezra had thought he'd had it rough with a famous, revered father who turned out to be a lying, bribe-taking criminal, sending innocent people to live in dark cages.

But not Ezra. Ben Colton had only ever treated his children with love and respect.

An hour later, Ezra had a map with possible bunker locations, with road access, charted on it. They intended to head out at daybreak. If they got lucky, and were able to quickly eliminate places, they could get five narrowed down to one in a day.

And have the girls home before darkness fell a second time. One night of adventure might be fun. Two nights trapped underground, with no contact with their mother, could prove to be emotionally scarring.

"It's probably a good idea to order room service for breakfast," Theresa said, as he saved his map and went to plug in his phone. "The kitchen opens at five, and we can have it packed to go. Eat on the way." She'd already retrieved the padded brown in-room dining menu from the desk not far from his bed. Was perusing it while he made plans to sleep in his clothes on top of the bed serving as his bunk—something he'd done many times in his life.

"Oh," she said, looking over at him standing there looking at the daybed by the window.

"What?"

"Prickly pear."

"What about it?"

"They have prickly pear jelly on the menu. Mark hated prickly pear anything," she said. "We were in Arizona once before we were married, and some friends of his from college had told us we had to try these prickly pear margaritas, which I did, and they were fabulous, but Mark wouldn't even try it. Said he couldn't stand the stuff. I just figured he'd had it before and really had a distaste for it, but now...with you asking me about him, our backdoor way of learning about Eric and Jennifer...what if a memory from his childhood had something to do with his reaction?"

"Prickly pear grows in the Rockies, mostly lower elevations," Ezra said, moving over to join her by the desk. He stopped a good foot away, had almost grabbed her shoulders with hope as another thought occurred to him. "Say the Fitzgerald bunker has prickly pear growing nearby and Mark stepped back into it. Or walked into it in the dark. Maybe he never had a bad incident with it, but it was something he saw by the bunker entrance, so the thought of it just reminded him..."

"Maybe his parents made him drink juice from it

if the plant was growing in abundance on their land," Theresa joined in.

Her comment spurred another. "Now add a six-year-old compost fertilization on the surface within fifty yards of the bunker surface," he continued. "It stands to reason that vegetation would grow more profusely with fertilization…"

"So tomorrow, when we're driving, we look for areas with healthy prickly pear growth…" Her voice faded, but the light in her eyes did not. "Maybe it won't be the prickly pear. Maybe it's one of these other things we've homed in on. We're going to find them, Ezra."

It was a long shot.

A really long one.

Mammothly long.

But any kind of shot at all was better than none.

THEY HAD A PLAN, and they needed rest.

She needed some distance from the man who'd become a lifeline to her. A few hours of sleep to give her some perspective.

In the bathroom, Theresa went through her shopping bags, found the sweats she'd grabbed from an endcap, the gray, doomsday-appropriate T-shirt she'd snatched without even looking at the price because it had a unicorn on the front of it. Toothbrush, toothpaste… She'd done well, considering the state she'd been in when she'd been given ten minutes to shop.

It took her less than ten minutes to get ready for bed. Ezra headed into the bathroom right after she came out, giving her a chance to get into bed, snuggle the soft, fresh-smelling covers up to her chin, turn toward the wall—with her back to the daybed—and will herself to sleep.

She heard the water running. Heard him pee and flush, too, though she tried really hard not to listen. Heard water running again. And his bag rustling some more. She heard the turn of the doorknob. And the swish of his feet on the carpet as he passed by the end of her bed.

With a click, the light went out.

And…her nightmare started.

As though the light switch in the room also controlled a mechanism in her brain. As soon as darkness consumed the room, and the moment became officially designated as sleep time, Theresa's mind went from rational to worry mode, igniting a series of scenarios that scared her to death.

The girls trapped in the ground, in the dark, lost and clutching to each other as they cried for her.

Visions of bad things that could be happening lingered around every mental turn she tried to make.

Eric losing his temper with them as they failed to conform to his idea of who they should be.

Were they hiding someplace? Under something?

Had they eaten?

Claire was such a picky eater… Had Jennifer been patient with her as she tried to find something the little girl could eat without triggering her gag reflex?

Mark had never understood that one—always thinking that Claire just had to be taught to eat her food. She had to understand that even if she didn't like something, she just had to chew and swallow and make it gone.

Until the night he'd forced her to sit in her seat across

from him, put a spoonful of peas into her mouth, and chew and swallow them. She'd done so. She'd adored her daddy.

And as she'd swallowed, the peas had failed to make it past her throat. She'd gagged and spewed peas all over the table.

Neve's laughter had saved that day. After a moment of shock, Mark had laughed, too, and then Claire had.

Theresa had been cleaning up the mess…

Her stomach ached, muscles clutching against each other, and she pulled the bed's extra pillow down to apply soft pressure, hoping to ease the pain.

Had the girls been crying for hours? Were they dehydrated?

Had her babies learned how to hold guns? Had they been forced to aim and fire?

She moved again, trying to find comfort where there was none.

Oh my God. What would happen if one of them got sick? Or fell and broke an arm or cut themselves? It wasn't like their grandparents were just going to waltz them in to see a medical professional. They had no paperwork, no records, no insurance information.

And there was an Amber Alert out on the girls. Eric and Jennifer would know that. They'd avoid any chance of being recognized.

The Amber Alert had to be canceled. Immediately. Someone had to get one of the band of doomsdayers who all hung together to get word to Eric and Jennifer, letting them know that they'd be free to get medical treatment for the girls with no repercussions.

Tom Smith. They could make him do it. He owed them for shooting at them. And he'd want his compatriots to have the immunity she was offering. Should she get up and call him right then? If Neve or Claire got sick in the night, the morning could be too late.

She could use her burner phone. Text him…

Or call for a rideshare and go see him herself. That way she could sign whatever she'd have to sign saying that no charges would be pressed. He could hold her hostage in the event that someone tried to intervene and take Eric and Jennifer into custody.

Could the police charge them anyway, even if she said no, since there'd been a kidnapping?

Oh, God.

Her babies had no medical protection. They could already be hurt.

What if there'd been an accident during gun training?

Chance of that was huge. Six-year-olds with loaded guns?

And Neve…bless her…she didn't always listen the first time around. Her little mind spun with such great stories of her own that sometimes things just didn't sink in.

A vision of Neve calling out to her sister, telling her to look, and a little finger hitting a trigger…

Claire!

Neve would scream. There'd be blood…

Stop.

She could say the word. Fear, despair, dread…they didn't dissipate.

For the first time since her baby girls were born, she hadn't been there to kiss them good-night. To tell them to have sweet dreams.

Hope was gone as tears trickled out from tightly

squeezed lids. She couldn't cry. Her nose would run and then she'd either have to sniffle, which would be loud, or get a tissue, blow her nose, which would be louder.

With the hand clutching the comforter to her chin, she wiped at the tears.

Through all of Mark's illness, times when she'd had to work the night shift at the home, the time she was sick with the flu, she'd always kissed her babies' cheeks good-night—albeit with a face mask on when she was sick—and told them sweet dreams.

All the years of never missing, and her record was broken.

Tears spurted from the corners of her eyes, fell across her nose and to the pillowcase. Her nose ran. Burying her head, she tried to stifle her sniffle with the covers.

The girls were gone.

What if she never saw them again?

What if…?

Her mattress moved, sinking from weight on the edge of it. "Hey."

She knew the voice. Trusted it.

But there was nothing that it could say to help…

"Talk to me."

There was nothing to say. Nothing anyone could do that would…

"Help me," he said.

What? She stilled. Waiting. Of course she'd help. If someone needed her help, she'd… Ezra. She rolled to her back, looking for his face in the darkness. Could make out shadowy outlines of features. "What's wrong?" Lifting her arm, she touched his neck with the back of her hand, testing for skin warmth. Did he have a fever?

Mark had run them regularly there at the end.

"I don't know what to do here. How to help. I'm lying over there listening to your restlessness, hearing you cry and… Earlier, you were going to tell me how to help you, and then Dom called and… Help me help you, Theresa."

He sounded so pathetic. Seriously. He was lost, needy. A man like Ezra wouldn't sit well with an inability to accomplish what he'd set out to do.

Even as she had the thoughts, she recognized that they were still a bit inane, but there was some truth there, too.

He really wanted to help.

How could she tell such a strong, risk-his-life-for-the-good-of-others fighter that he was powerless?

"I'm so sorry this is happening to you," he said. "You've been through so much, and…"

"Stop," she said, supine in her unicorn T-shirt, covers up to shoulders, looking up at him. "Please, Ezra, the last thing I need right now is sympathy."

Her face felt stiff with drying tears. A reminder that she'd been lying there feeling sorry for herself.

"What *do* you need?" he asked, his tone softening.

And it dawned on her. He knew.

Did he know?

Maybe subconsciously?

Did he feel it, too?

The flow of emotion between them… It had been there before the girls had been taken.

She'd sworn to do whatever it took to keep herself

focused so that she'd be able to nurture her girls when she got them back.

Staying in that bed, alone in the dark, wasn't healthy for her.

"I need warmth," she said, shivering in spite of the covers.

"You want me to turn up the thermostat?"

"No." Her voice was dry. Husky. Filled with fear and exhaustion, tears and need. "I want arms around me," she told him honestly.

He didn't stand, move away. He didn't reach for her, either.

"I'm so tired, and know I need to sleep, but my head…lying here alone… I need hope. And you give me hope, Ezra."

The covers moved, the mattress dipped, and he was there, fully dressed, filling up the darkness as he pulled her against solid muscles that protected her from bad guys.

Chapter Seventeen

Shockingly, Ezra slept. Lying with Theresa snuggled up to his chest, breathing softly, evenly, he'd thought he'd give her a bit and then gently extricate himself to return to his own bunk.

The next thing he knew, daylight was peeking around the edges of the drapes he'd drawn the night before.

They'd never said a word. From the second he'd slid down on her sheets, there'd been not one attempt at conversation. She'd relaxed against him and within minutes had been out.

All the anguish she'd been putting herself through, and in his arms, she'd found peace.

You had to like a woman who knew what she needed and had the guts to ask for it.

Because he couldn't focus on the rest of it. Her peace. His arms. There was no future in it. So no permission to go there.

She awoke as he started to slide away from her. Pulled herself off his chest. Let him go. He didn't look back.

Or speak.

He just made a beeline for the shower. A cold one. To wake himself up. And to calm himself down, too.

And by the time he'd reentered the room, she'd been up and waiting for her turn in the bath. He already had breakfast there and waiting when she exited twenty minutes later, dressed in a pair of brown cotton pants, another long-sleeved lighter brown shirt and her boots. Breakfast in hand, they hit the road.

They discussed the omelets. The route they were on. Filling up with gas. And the clear skies. Neither mentioned the night they'd spent in each other's arms.

The first two locations on his map were a bust. One area was off from a single-lane dirt road that had been blocked for some time by two fallen trees that had clearly been the result of a lightning strike at least a year before. Vegetation had already grown and covered the spot. There was a scattering of prickly pear, though, and Ezra scouted the mostly flat, open area on foot anyway, with Theresa in the truck researching message boards and websites for information about doomsdayers. He'd found no sign of any kind of human presence, period.

They'd wasted a couple of hours.

Another single-lane dirt road, miles off from a county highway, led them to the second area. Badly rutted—to the point that Theresa was holding on as they bounced along—the road had clearly not been traveled on recently. Still, he persevered, and they spent an hour walking the flat land that met all bunker criteria, with no sign of footsteps, tamped-down vegetation from someone or something having gone through the space, and no sign of any kind of cover or cave opening.

"There's prickly pear, though," Theresa said as they

made their way back to the Jeep. They'd scared up rabbits, too, and had walked to the chorus of multiple birdcalls.

The sun was climbing steadily, and Ezra felt the tension start to build again. Within himself, but in his companion as well. Theresa's expressions were growing stiffer, her sentences less wordy.

Dom hadn't called yet that day.

They'd rushed out just after dawn and had gotten nowhere.

While time ticked and Claire and Neve experienced life unknown to them.

He needed a plan B. Didn't have one.

Every soldier knew you didn't enter the battlefield without a plan B.

"We're doing something," Theresa said as she climbed back in beside him. "If nothing else, we're narrowing down areas they might be by knowing where they aren't."

He and this woman were in sync. There was just no denying it.

He glanced her way. Smiled.

And she smiled back.

THERESA DIDN'T EVEN see the little store at first. Set back from the road—down a single-lane road, that continued past it up the mountain—its brown shingled siding and roof looked more like a dilapidated shack than a place of business. She frowned when Ezra slowed, then glanced over at him.

"We're going in there?" It was the first time they'd spoken in a while. She'd been busy reading a doomsday message board she'd landed upon. He'd been doing... whatever it was he did when he went into himself.

"Fresh tracks," he said, nodding off to his left. The mountain road was one lane in places, two in others, mostly paved, though badly so, and climbed slowly by going around the mountain, not straight up, with very little shoulder. They'd seen other vehicles, but sparingly. Mostly campers and trucks.

And had rounded bends with drop-offs that were straight down one hundred feet of rock or more. She'd done better reading on her phone, trying to get into the Fitzgeralds' mindset, than watching the road. If nothing else, when the girls got back, they were going to have heard things, and she needed to be prepared to refute them. With fact, not just motherly assurances.

A rudimentary, handmade painted wood sign hung over a wooden screened door. Miller's Deli and Market, it read. The screen was dirty, but she could see a couple through it—older-looking—sitting in chairs behind a counter. They both looked up as Ezra and Theresa entered.

The place might have been a deli at one point. Any hint of fresh meat and cheeses had long since departed. Dust covered...everything. Much more aware of what she might be walking into than she'd been a day before, Theresa looked around for any sign of guns and ammunition.

Found the latter stacked neatly on shelves along the back wall.

"You camping?" the old man asked. Up close, she'd guess him to be eighty, at least. "Camping supplies is along the far wall, middle set of shelves. And water's stacked in cases of four gallons to a case in the closet back there to the far right. You can't miss it. You'll have to help yourself with that. Can't lift the damned things like I used to."

"Chip, the guy who delivers them each month, has to do it," the woman offered.

Smiling at her, Theresa felt Ezra close to her side. But not nudging her like a warning or anything.

"We'd like a box of crackers and some peanut butter if you have it," he said to the couple. And was told to take a look around.

"There should be some out there somewhere," the man offered. "Water's in the closet in the far back right corner," he said and pointed again to the opposite corner of the store. "Comes in four gallons a case, but you'll have to lift it yourself if you want some."

"I think we will take a case." Ezra nodded, starting to walk around one of the two small center aisles of goods.

"I'm Nancy. This is Howard," the woman offered to Theresa while Ezra "shopped."

"I'm ninety-four years old."

Though she tried to school her features, her shock must have shown, as the woman laughed. "Howard's ninety-six," she added. "He robbed the cradle when he married me." She laughed again, and Howard chuckled, too.

Theresa couldn't smile with them. "I have a degree in senior health management," she said, "and I have to say… I'm impressed. Do you two live around here?"

She sure as heck couldn't picture them in the Sunshine Senior Home.

"Around that corner," Howard replied, pointing to a closed door behind the counter, off to the left.

"Been here five years," Nancy told her, rocking back with her hands crossed over a belly that was only slightly protruding beneath the rose-and-white housedress she wore. Pride rang through the elderly woman's words.

"I met a couple who said they live up this way," Theresa said then, not forgetting for even a second that her only purpose for being there was to find her daughters. She pulled up a picture on her phone. "You ever see them?"

The couple leaned forward together, Howard pushing his glasses up, and Nancy raising her head to look through bifocals that were as thick as any Theresa had ever seen.

"Yep," Howard said, as Nancy spoke over him with, "They're nice people. Just wanting a safe place to live."

Ezra moved farther along the opposite side of the shelf separating them. Theresa could still feel his energy coming her way. There'd been no plan for her to be in charge—ever—but the opportunity had presented itself, and...

A deep breath helped her steady her shaking limbs.

"You see them recently?" she asked then.

Nancy looked at Howard, who looked at Theresa and shook his head. "Not for a while, I don't think. But we don't open every day. Mostly all's that ever comes up here is campers, and they buy their stuff in town. Cheaper that way. We're just here for locals who don't like to go to town, and they know to knock hard on the door if it's locked."

"Locals?" Ezra came up beside her. "There's a settlement up here?"

"Just folks looking to live safe," Howard said. "Next

hundred miles or so, they're scattered about." And Theresa's stomach churned with roosts of butterflies. "We had a safe place up here ourselves, been here forty years, but it got hard to haul the water in."

"I'm ninety-four," Nancy piped in. "I told Howard, what we staying safe for anymore? I wanted some flowers and blue skies overhead. So we bought this place and sit and watch the birds and look at sunshine every day." She smiled again.

"And wait for the Good Lord to take us," Howard added. "There's water in that closet back there in the far corner. Comes in cases, four gallons to a case..."

Ezra pulled a couple of twenties out of his pocket and laid them on the counter, handing Theresa an older-looking unopened box of saltines and a dusty jar of peanut butter as he went to collect their water and head out. She followed him with a chorus of "Have a nice day" from the husband and wife.

Waited while Ezra pulled open the only closet in the place.

The skinny space behind the door was completely empty. No water in sight.

"Their memory issues were age-appropriate," Theresa said the second they were outside the store, hurrying across gravel in the hot sun. "That doesn't mean that they didn't really recognize Eric and Jennifer."

Heading to his side of the Jeep, Ezra climbed inside and had the engine going and the vehicle in gear by the time she'd fastened her seat belt beside him.

"Whether they recognized them or not, they just told us that the next hundred miles contains bunkers," he

said, feeling energized in a way he hadn't been since
he'd come home for his brother's wedding.

He was closing in on his target. "We've only got one
area on the map over the next hundred miles—about
halfway up this road to a turnoff that I'm going to assume is more of a dirt drive than an actual street." He
didn't want to get her hopes up.

But he wasn't going to lie to her, either.

The Fitzgeralds weren't going to give up those girls
easily.

And they were well armed.

He called his brother. Gave Dom the coordinates
of the area he'd be searching. The war wasn't won.
Hadn't even started.

The battle was still ahead.

But at least he had one to fight.

With only one troop out of his usual hundreds. Himself.

He had fifty miles to prepare her.

"They might see us before we know they're there,"
he said. "I can almost guarantee they will." Even if
they weren't on the run, doomsdayers would likely
have traps set to alert them if anyone got close to their
domicile. It was all part of protecting oneself.

"And when they do, they're going to come out fighting. At this point, not only do they stand to lose the
girls, but they'll be arrested, separated and sent to live
in a cage with criminals if they're caught."

Theresa broke in. "It would make more sense for
them to leave the girls, as a distraction—because they
know that Claire and Neve are who we want—and run.
They'll have an escape route, Ezra. From all the read-

ing I've been doing today, I'm sure they already have a secure plan in place in case we do find them."

He hoped to God the plan wasn't to take the girls with them, risking them getting killed, to keep them from suffering through the slow burn of a nuclear blast with their mother.

And knew he couldn't rely on hope alone. It was up to him to make sure that Eric and Jennifer Fitzgerald didn't detect them in time to take the twins and disappear off the grid forever.

He was the front line in the fight of his life.

With a very special untrained soldier at his back. He had to keep her there. Behind him. So he would take any hits that came their way. And be the only one to see if something horrible happened.

That was his plan.

It was weak.

Unfinished.

And it was all he had.

Chapter Eighteen

The mountain road climbed and then rounded and seemed to slope back down. She'd seen the map they were traveling. A half circle around Benson. Since Ezra had already mapped out the areas without underground utility lines, lakes or streams nearby, or a lot of trees, there wasn't much reason to keep her eyes peeled out the window during the interim miles.

The challenge then became keeping her mind occupied so that fear didn't take possession of it.

Because while she much preferred the scenario where Eric and Jennifer sent the girls running at them, as a distraction, while the couple bolted through some underground escape hatch that would lead to a vehicle aboveground somewhere—maybe even a garage only ten feet away with a ladder up to it—she knew that another, probably more likely, possibility existed.

They'd take the twins with them. Why not, if they believed their escape plan was viable? And then, if something went wrong, they could all die together…

And…*cut.* She blinked, stared at the phone screen in front of her—her own phone, because the burner was only for use if she had to assume Molly's persona again.

Molly and Jack. Yes. Molly and Jack. A lighter feeling entered her system for a second. Easing the panic that her mind had brought on once again.

Molly and Jack. Her and Ezra.

He'd held her. No questioning or warnings. Just a wordless sliding under the covers and pulling her into his arms.

And the weirdest part was...she'd laid her head on his chest, closed her eyes, listened to his heartbeat and fallen asleep.

She couldn't remember the last time she'd drifted off so quickly. Or slept so peacefully.

Was it wrong to want to do it again?

If thinking about it kept her emotions from spiraling into panic, then that was definitely okay. Conversation might have helped, too. About the night they'd spent, or anything else. But Ezra was... Ezra. He was on a mission, and there was no way she was going to interrupt his process.

No way she'd do anything to save herself if it meant putting her daughters further at risk.

Thinking back over the way he'd gotten them out of Tom Smith's place, the way he'd read the second that congeniality turned into danger, even the shooting at trees as a cover to get himself back to her...

It was like Charlie had known exactly what he was doing when he'd burst into Alice's room the afternoon Ezra had been visiting his great-aunt.

Ezra was only with them for the moment, but she'd spend the rest of her life being thankful for him. Maybe when the girls were home, and Ezra left for his next assignment, they could keep in touch...just a text or email now and then, letting her know he was okay.

He might want to know she and the twins were okay, too. Since he was risking his life right now to save theirs.

What if Eric and Jennifer really did see them coming and grab the kids? What if Ezra foiled their escape plan and they felt trapped and chose to die together rather than risk leaving them to suffer what they believed to be an unbearable fate?

Jerking her head in Ezra's direction, she said, "It's more important to me that you rescue those girls than watch over me," she said as they drew closer to the area where he suspected the girls were being held. He had his phone lying on the console. She could see the live map on his GPS. "I'll distract Eric and Jennifer while you get the girls."

So much for staying out of his process.

He glanced her way. Briefly. Frowned. Then said, "Let's see what the situation presents, first."

Of course. That was a given. But… "I'm just saying, if it comes down to protecting me or saving them, there's no question. It's them."

The words garnered her another serious look.

But no verbal response.

EZRA HAD NEVER felt so ill prepared.

As he pulled off the dilapidated paved road onto an even more unkempt dirt one, he had a bad feeling. If it weren't for the fact that every second could make a difference between saving those kids or losing them to off-the-grid nothingness, he'd pull back. Gather a team of trained professionals, study a map and discuss parameters.

Law enforcement was already doing just that. And

so far had much less than he did. There were only so many of them, and they couldn't spend an entire day driving in the wilderness on the off chance that the landscape might produce a lead.

The first part of the road was wooded, so he passed through it with only cursory glances for signs of recent habitation.

Saw newly trod tracks from large-sized wheels quite clearly. Determined to follow them as far as they led.

Took his gun out of his waistband, safety still on, and laid it on the console.

"I know you don't know how to shoot, but if you have to pull the trigger, do so." He explained how, with one quick move, she would need to turn the safety off.

He saw her peek down at the gun. Was looking at her as she then turned to look up at him.

The road grabbed his attention almost immediately.

Which was a good thing.

No way he could afford to drown in those expressive warm pools of her eyes. Not then.

Not ever.

"The bunker entrance might just be a flat piece on the ground like a trapdoor. Oftentimes with brush over it so you wouldn't ever know it's there," she said, drawing another quick glance from him. Her voice was a little shaky, but her thoughts seemed to be steady.

As was her gaze.

He didn't blame her for her fear. He'd been living with his own version of it all of his adult life.

She feared for the lives of her daughters. He did, too, in that moment.

Overall, his biggest fear was failure.

He wasn't going to be able to live with it. Didn't set himself up for it.

And yet there he was...driving into God knew what, with no idea what he would actually need to do to rescue those little girls.

"Some of the fancier ones have actual shed-sized structures with a front door that opens to steps down into the living space below."

Climbing a ladder ten feet underground to be home didn't appeal to him. Nor did sleeping under all those feet of earth. With an inner shudder, he tried not to think about what two innocent little kids would think.

Unless their grandparents had made a fairy tale out of it. Like the hobbits, or Alice, who passed through the looking glass.

And...there. Foot on the brake, Ezra brought the Jeep to a slow enough stop not to kick up a lot of dirt. The tracks turned onto a rudimentary road that was little more than two tire tracks of tamped-down earth. As though the road had formed from being driven on over and over, not by formal construction.

"I've been following recent tire tracks," he told Theresa. "They turn here."

"But it's wooded."

"Yeah, but look around. Trees at the edge of the road, but none on either side. And while they're alive, they aren't particularly thriving."

"You think they were purposely planted here? Like...as a cover?"

"I think it's possible. Or they're natural, but not predominant in the area."

He didn't like what he was going to say next in the

event that she argued with him, and he knew she would. But he saw no other option.

"I have to do the rest on foot," he told her. Which meant she'd be left on the open road alone. "Do you have phone service?"

She shook her head. He didn't, either. Hadn't since they'd turned onto the dirt road.

"I'm leaving the gun with you," he said. "I've got my knife." Pulling up his right jeans leg, he showed her the weapon.

"I'm not staying out here." Knowing the objection was coming didn't make it any easier to take.

"Theresa." He said her name firmly, not kindly. "I have no idea what I'm walking into, what kind of maneuver I might have to do…"

"Which is why you need your gun. And if it comes to you going into action, I can always lie flat on the ground and wait. And pray. It'd be a lot harder to hide sitting out here in the open in a Jeep."

She had a point.

"Besides, I might be able to help."

Looking at her, seeing the stubbornness, and knowing their time was wasting, that they could have already been discovered, he did what he did. Came up with a plan.

"You come with me as far as the edge of the trees. And then you wait. Your job is lookout. Do not come out of the woods for any reason. You get seen, you likely get dead. If you see the girls and they're in danger, you scream once and change your location within the trees immediately. If you're in danger, you scream twice. If I find the girls, and have to use myself as a distraction and can't escort them out, I'm sending them your way and you take them to the Jeep and then straight back to the main road to alert Dom. Got it?"

"What if I'm in danger and can't scream?"

That would mean she was either comatose, or someone was preventing her from opening her mouth or using her throat. "Then the mission failed," he said, not wanting to consider that option. "This isn't Blue Larkspur, Theresa. You're going to have to be aware every second…listen to every sound. Anything that doesn't fit, a crack of a twig, or birds suddenly squawking all at once…you pay attention." He handed her the gun, but she shook her head.

"Someone would be more likely to get it from me before I got a shot off," she said. "But I'll take the knife, if you don't mind. I've done a lot of carving of fowl in my lifetime. And right now, Eric and Jennifer are both about as foul as it gets."

If they hadn't been fighting the clock and walking into way too much danger with no backup, Ezra might have kissed her right then.

And regretted it later, too.

Because the mission wasn't going to fail.

There would be a tomorrow.

A next week.

And the day after that, when he got his assignment and left Blue Larkspur for the life he needed to live.

EZRA WALKED AND couldn't be heard. Very quickly he taught her how. "We're in a hurry, but to get in there without being discovered, we have to move slowly," he said. "Keeping all of your weight on your left foot, knee bent, put your right foot down, pinkie toe first, then slowly roll to the ball of your foot. And repeat. You can't walk standing upright or you'll have less control of your balance, and it's always weight on the standing foot while setting the walking foot down, pinkie toe, ball of foot."

She practiced once. "What do I do with my heel?"

"Lower it as you roll to the ball of your foot." She tried, and he tapped her knee and said, "Knees bent, Theresa. You lose your balance, you fall. That leaves you fallen prey."

His words struck her cold, and the skin of her thigh still burned from the touch of his strong, thick fingers through her pants.

The man was going to drive her wild.

But his weird magic over her was keeping her focused long enough to find her girls, and that meant more than life.

By the time they'd reached the edge of the woods, completely without incident or any sound other than an occasional bird or quiet breeze in the trees, she was confident in her ability to move as he'd taught her. Had an idea of what he'd meant about paying attention to the sounds around her as well, to notice sudden change.

Which, he'd told her, would denote foreign occupation. Could be the enemy, because she'd been discovered. Or it could be a bear or other wildlife.

She had her knife. Was ready to use it.

She *was* a bear. A mama bear protecting her cubs.

The wildlife didn't worry her nearly as much as the thought of an armed former father-in-law did.

Ezra stood so close their bodies were touching as he used the last cluster of tree trunks for cover and surveyed the land before him. At first glance, she saw peaceful meadow.

And then, off to the right, so far away she could barely make it out, she saw the van. An impeccably kept brown van. Nudging Ezra, with her elbow to his side, she pulled her forearm up to her chest and pointed, with one finger only. Big motion, just like big steps, could be more easily detected.

He'd already seen the van. She got that when he nodded, leaned down, his head nestled into her neck, and gave her succinct, softly whispered instructions. "Do as I said. And don't watch me. Watch your six."

Putting her lips to his neck, she replied, "There are two of them and two of us. We've got this." After which she kissed him.

Right there on the neck.

A promise that she'd follow orders. A thank-you.

And a sip at his well of strength, too.

No matter what happened, the man was in her soul for keeps.

Chapter Nineteen

Did she just kiss his neck? Ezra had no idea what to make of the possibility, and while the idea of it lingered, he couldn't hang on to it right then. Moving stealthily, he headed to the front corner of the woods, leaving Theresa behind him, and didn't look back. Not even once.

A glance could cost him a missed detail, and one detail could be the difference between life and death.

If he didn't hear her scream, she didn't need him.

At the edge of the trees, he dropped to his stomach, arms stretched out in front of him, gun in his hand, with his head up only enough to be able to see his path. He'd chosen the shortest angle between him and the van, which was the only visible sign of human habitation. But as he lifted his head from the ground, looking upward, the view was different.

He noticed the glint right off. A camera lens in a tree to the left of him, pointing toward the prairie land into which he was heading. Rolling over to his back, he studied the lens, and then returned to lying stomach side down. He'd detected three cameras on the front line of the trees, and could assume there were others, most likely on the ground, but all of them were facing approximately three feet aboveground. The cameras' owners were interested in large intruders.

Maybe bear or bobcats, but most likely those of the human variety.

So he became a snake, slithering in the foot-high grasses slowly enough not to be obvious, gaze peeled to the point of dry eye. Every blink could come with a price.

Oddly, as he moved, he came back home to himself. Was comfortable, at home, with the activity. And trusted his ability to complete the mission.

Nostrils filling with the slightly sharp scent of grasses and plant life mixed with the sour smell of mildew, he moved along slowly and steadily, the van in sight at all times. Earth scraped against his stomach as his shirt pulled from the waistband of his jeans. He knew. Didn't care.

Blades of various straw-like growths tipped at his cheeks. His nose. Accepting the itch without scratching, he watched for any sign of movement. Burning with one need in those moments—to see Claire and Neve. Once he had them on his radar, he could formulate the exact rescue plan.

They could be tied up. Or guarded by an armed grandparent.

More likely, they would be safely down in the bunker, which was going to make Ezra's job trickier. It wasn't like he could just pull open the hatch and trot downstairs.

Not if he wanted to make it without bullet holes in his legs and possibly torso.

He was going to have to get Eric and Jennifer Fitzgerald to vacate the bunker. To join him on the surface. The guards had to be dealt with before he could free the prisoners.

He'd looked the old man in the eye just four days before. Had seen the steely resentment at Ezra's presence around Eric's dead son's family. At his dead son's residence.

The grandfather wasn't going to give up.

He'd have to be taken.

Blue skies and sunshine shone a bright light over the land, and beat down on his neck, too. Gray and rainy would be better. Keep him in shadows rather than in a spotlight. And camouflage movement in the growth.

Cool him down, too.

And make sliding on his gut less onerous, as rain would make mud.

Weather was always part of the battle challenge. He'd slugged through snow and ice, for an entire night, with exposed skin. And had survived twelve hours in one-hundred-fifteen-degree desert heat without water.

Still several yards from the van, he popped his head up far enough to get a good look at his surroundings, another take on the same view he'd been studying throughout his half-hour trek. And…there it was. On the opposite side of the van from his approach, a piece of steel, set in a thick frame six inches off the ground, protruding with a locking handle on it.

Holy crap. He had eyes on the bunker.

His gaze shot sideways, first right, then left, looking for prickly pear, or any well-growing vegetation that would signify compost fertilization. Nothing stood out as any different from the rest of the landscape, but he didn't have a full three-hundred-sixty-degree view of the seventy-five or so feet that the angle of his diagram had projected.

Inching his way to the van, intending to use the vehicle for cover, allowing him a more thorough look around without alerting cameras to his presence, he contemplated various ways to get the Fitzgeralds out of the bunker, if this was theirs.

Considering their irrational fear of blasts, he knew an explosion wouldn't do it. A gunshot might not, either, as both were sign of attack, and the bunker was their protection from that. It would have to be a threat to the bunker itself.

A threat to the entrance. No way he was equipped to drill down ten feet to reach the steel-enclosed mini home itself.

Of course, someone, maybe even the girls, could be in the van. He checked, as he drew closer, to see if anyone was visible through the windshield from his position on the ground, and saw nothing, but maybe they were all in the back? Eating a late lunch?

Not at all likely.

If the girls were in that van, it was more likely that they were tied up. Pray to God not drugged. Didn't make sense that the Fitzgeralds would hurt the twins. Eric and Jennifer's goal was to save their granddaughters' lives.

But irrational people did irrational things...

Crack! He saw the earth a foot to the right of him puff up in a cloud of dust a second before he heard the shot. Freezing in place, flat on the ground, he waited for a very brief breath, and then, moving sideways, he slowly inched his way closer to the van. Needing the metal for bullet protection while he assessed his enemy's strengths against his own weaknesses.

The one shot didn't mean for sure that he'd been made. Could have just been reaction to the possibility of someone on the premises—maybe a movement in the grass that triggered suspicion. A flash of color.

Could be someone thought his movement had been created by a rabbit, and the human was only seeking dinner.

Could be that Theresa had heard the shot and was panicking, thinking her girls had been hurt. Or that he wasn't coming back and she'd have to save her children on her own.

If she came any closer, she'd likely be shot.

No way for him to tell her that.

Best-case scenario, she was already on her way back to the Jeep to drive to where there was cell service and get Dom's butt in there to help Ezra get the girls to safety.

A knife against a bullet, long-distance... The knife would lose every time. Didn't matter how many turkeys she'd carved.

Another shot fired. Also landing barely a foot to the right of him. And it hit him... There weren't just cameras. There were motion detectors. Set within however many feet of the bunker he'd just reached.

His best hope was that the van would block the sensors. So thinking, he sped his pace, figuring that if he'd been seen, he was already a sitting duck, and if he hadn't been, his best chance at remaining undetected was the lone brown vehicle to which he'd been headed.

A third shot fired, following his progress. If he continued on the same path, he was going to lead his attacker straight to the van. Which would most likely bring Eric out of the bunker, but he'd leave Jennifer down in safety with the girls.

Should Ezra take out the grandfather?

Was it his only hope of getting those kids safely home with their mother?

Backtracking a bit, he rolled and slithered, rolled and slithered, on no sensible course, but inching his way closer to the back side of the van, the driver's side, as it happened to be. If sensors were showing movement, it wasn't going to look human. That was the best he could do in the moment.

That and plan. His heart pounded, his body hurt, but he couldn't waste thoughts on either situation. Feelings didn't matter. Staying mentally alert and ahead of his enemy was the only way to stay alive.

All three shots had come from the same spot. As though the gun were stationary, not being carried by someone on the move.

And they'd been rifle blasts, not from a pistol or shotgun. He might not be able to distinguish one from the other in a battle of many shots—but one at a time, he'd get it right.

The bullets had each been a single shot. Not with pellets, like a shotgun would emit.

Scratched and sweaty, he made it to the van, taking cover behind the front wheel, surveying the area around the bunker door from beneath the vehicle.

And saw the rifle. Attached to a telescoping apparatus coming up from underground. The shooter was down in the bunker. Aiming and firing from there.

Fancy setup. Military style.

Had Eric Fitzgerald served?

Was he up against a brother in arms possibly suffering from PTSD?

The thought came—and went. Two defenseless little girls made the point moot.

Knowing the source of the gun, more particularly knowing that its location wasn't going to change, made his job less harrowing for the moment. As long as he kept the van between him and the barrel, he'd stay alive.

He had to stay alive. Theresa and her daughters were counting on him. There were no troops behind him, fighting beside him, no one else to back him up in that particular maneuver if he failed. And the Fitzgeralds would have time to move the girls, to sequester themselves and the twins, and they might never be found again.

With a quick lift of his body, he glanced inside the driver's-side window of the van, noting the mess on the floor—blankets, fast-food trash. And the lack of seats in the back.

Shots were fired again. Straight at his head. From a handgun, not the rifle. And based on the trajectory, the shooter was traveling—and could be using children as cover. At that point, with the older couple feeling cornered, who knew what they'd do? Would they rather the girls die with them than have to live through a nuclear blast?

Ezra couldn't shoot back unless he could make certain the girls weren't in the vicinity.

His gaze fell to the van's ignition. He knew how to hot-wire a vehicle, but couldn't do so just by... The keys were in the ignition.

Shots fired again, hitting the van's passenger window, and Ezra jumped in. Head down by the console, he turned the key, threw the vehicle in gear and pressed the gas pedal.

Another loud crack sounded, followed by a large thud to the van that shot him up in the air and back down. A tire had blown out. Sitting up enough to monitor his destination, Ezra kept going. Thumping over the ground, skidding and having to floor the gas when the blown tire got stuck in ruts, he continued toward the tracks leading back to the bunker, headed toward the road. There'd been no other vehicle in the area. His pursuer would be on foot.

And he prayed to God that if Theresa was still on the premises, she'd made a run for the Jeep.

If they were going to stay alive, they had to get the hell out of there.

SHAKING, HEART THUMPING so hard she wasn't sure how long it would last before giving out, Theresa sat behind the wheel of the Jeep, watching for any sign of human activity. Ezra, the girls, coming at her from any direction—she was ready to get them to safety.

She'd heard the first shot ring out, had never been able to figure out the source. Not even after the fifth had sounded. She'd seen a blur of movement by the far side of the van. Hoped it was Ezra, but didn't know that it was.

And she'd run for the Jeep.

Was Ezra lying shot and bleeding?

Would the Fitzgeralds be coming for her next?

Were the girls hurt?

Should she go for help or, if she left with the Jeep,

would she be taking Ezra and Claire and Neve's only chance at getting to safety?

They could need emergency attention. Should she drive toward the main road until she got service, call Dom and then head back?

If the Jeep was their only hope of safe refuge, and she took it, then what?

Ezra was good at what he did, the best, but he'd never dealt with children before. Any children. Normal, happy children.

He most certainly would be in over his head with a traumatized set of twin girls who'd already been through so much.

If any of them were injured, they wouldn't be able to travel far. Or quickly. Not on foot, at any rate.

Biting her lip, blinking back tears, she sat with the Jeep in gear, worried about having enough gas, afraid to turn off the engine, as it was the only source of escape, and keeping her gaze focused on the landscape around her. Both sides. Front and back, too.

Two days in a row of hearing shots fired had taught her quickly.

She searched for clothing, movement, any sign of Ezra or the girls. And for Eric Fitzgerald, too. If he'd killed Ezra, and was coming for her, he wasn't going to succeed. She'd gun the Jeep she'd already turned to face the way out, and get help back there, or die trying.

The Jeep rocked, and she screamed as she realized the passenger door was opening. Mouth open to scream again, she had her foot on the gas, ready to floor it, sending whoever was there to the ground, when she recognized Ezra's head as he catapulted in beside her.

"Go!"

One look at his dirty, disheveled body, and she asked no questions.

She just went.

Trembling with fear, nauseous, she sped up the dirt road, leaving a large cloud of dust behind them, afraid to death for her daughters.

Afraid to ask questions.

Afraid of the answers.

Was Ezra hurt? Bleeding? She didn't look. Didn't dare take her gaze from the road. Half a mile passed, she rounded a corner, and he said, "Okay, you can stop. I'll take over."

"But…"

"We're not being followed" was all he said, exiting as she pulled to a stop. He rushed around to the driver's door. She didn't want to get out or waste precious time. Climbing over the console, she dropped her butt in the passenger seat he'd just vacated, allowing him to shove in behind the wheel and get the Jeep back in motion.

She tried to keep silent, to let him concentrate and do what he did, but after a couple of minutes, her throat clogged with tears, she asked, "Did you see them?"

"No." He focused only on the road, except to keep close watch in the rearview and side mirrors.

If he hadn't seen her girls, it stood to reason that he didn't know how they were. She digested the news, accepted it as best she could, and watched her side mirror as well as her phone, waiting for service.

"Are you okay?" she asked.

She just needed basic facts.

"Fine."

He didn't look fine. Not only did the tight line of his jaw and the steely glaze over his eyes tell her he wasn't fine, but his clothes were filthy, and his shirt was ripped. She was pretty sure, when he moved and she caught a glimpse of his stomach through a rip, that she'd seen red.

His stomach was bleeding?

Horrified, she asked, "Were you hit?" She should never have let him drive.

"No." He glanced at her then, once, quickly, and for that second, his gaze softened. "I'm fine, Theresa— scraped up, maybe. Right now, we have to get word to Dom so they can get aerial surveillance out before the Fitzgeralds have a chance to lose us again. The van isn't drivable, but we have no idea what other plans they might have in place, maybe two-way radios that allow them to communicate with someone in a bunker close by. Some kind of signal they send. The technology back there was expensive."

That was why he kept looking behind them. And was racing to get off the road before someone else came at them, too?

They might not just be fighting one older couple. There could be a whole community behind the grandparents, believers in the cause, who'd help them in their fight to keep their granddaughters safe.

Sitting stiffly, feeling like she was dying an excruciating death one emotion at a time, she watched in all directions and imagined her face lying against warm T-shirt-covered chest muscle as she counted heartbeats.

Chapter Twenty

The second Theresa told him she had cell service, Ezra pushed a call into his brother, leaving the audio on the vehicle's speaker. He gave Dom the exact coordinates of the bunker, listed camera locations, the telescopic gun site, how many shots had been fired, and a moving shooter who was invisible to him. And noted that he wasn't sure it even belonged to the Fitzgeralds. He described the brown van, down to tire type, listing all of the bags he'd seen from various fast-food outlets so someone could check their security cameras.

"It's no longer drivable," he relayed. "Tire rim meeting rock took care of that. Broken axle guarantees it. Reconnaissance says you're going to have to go in aerial first," he finished.

"I'll get drones out immediately." Dom's tone held urgency, which calmed Ezra's a bit. A good soldier knew when to back off and trust the man with superior ability to get the job done.

"There's a scenic pull-off a quarter of a mile down the main road," he said then. "We'll wait there."

Ezra hung up before Dom could argue. Or advise.

If his brother had something pertinent to say, he'd call back.

"We're staying in the area?" Theresa's tone sounded much better than it had the last time she'd spoken.

"Of course. Strangers go in and get your daughters out, you need to be one of the first things they see." He might not be child-savvy, but he wasn't a moron.

She looked at him, and he had no excuse not to look back. He read the panic, the pain, coursing through her. Swallowed hard.

He couldn't tell her there was no reason to fear.

"What are the chances of getting them out unharmed?" Her gaze, more than her voice, demanded honesty.

He had a much easier time telling a platoon of soldiers that they might die than telling Theresa that her two little girls could end up with the same fate. Easier, but still, excruciatingly hard.

"Reason says to look at the motivation of the captor." He changed the word from *enemy* at the last moment. He was talking about her dead husband's parents. People who'd been devastated by the death of their only child. "They are motivated by love for those little girls. Their goal is to ensure that they're safe when the debilitating blast that they believe is coming actually hits. We aren't dealing with narcissistic psychopaths," he finished. "The Fitzgeralds love deeply. They have consciences."

And their minds were misguided. While the last bit of his thought remained unsaid, he knew Theresa was fully aware it was there.

And that the older couple's instability gave possibility to any scenario.

He also knew that he'd met the woman of a lifetime

in the person sitting upright next to him. She wasn't immune to her emotions. But she took them and still managed to present herself to the problem.

He admired the hell out of her.

The way she'd not only held up over the past two days but had managed to think and act in a rational, beneficial way, as good as many trained soldiers. He was…beyond impressed.

He'd recommend her for a Purple Heart if she was a soldier. Although she hadn't been physically wounded, the emotional wounds she was bearing while continuing to serve effectively weighed far more.

And he knew that though he'd be leaving her, he wouldn't do it until he'd brought her daughters home.

One way or another, he was going to be there.

THERESA MANAGED TO stay logical for about five minutes after they'd pulled into the lay-by, which was really a fancy word for gravel at the side of the road. The scenic view was across the street—looking out from the mountain down into the valley stretching all the way to Denver, not that they could see that far if they went over and took a peek. Glints from Benson were visible, cars moving, probably, like little stars on the ground, from where they sat, Jeep turned and pointed toward the road in the direction heading to the Fitzgerald homestead. Land with a door to the home underground.

From what Ezra had described, there was no way anyone was going to get those girls out. At least, not until Eric and Jennifer ran out of ammunition to shoot in the legs anyone who attempted to descend the ten feet down to them.

Unless the rescuer had head-to-toe body armor, and such a thing didn't exist.

Although, some military gear came close…

The Fitzgeralds likely had enough ammo to last through more law enforcement manpower than existed in the state of Colorado. They'd been stockpiling for decades.

And Claire and Neve would witness it…

You didn't ever forget something like that. Her sweet little ones, if they survived, would be emotionally scarred for life.

She couldn't fix that, no matter how much mother's intuition or love she poured into them.

And what was her other option? To leave them down in that bunker for the rest of their lives? They had to be rescued…

Sitting there contemplating options, she felt as trapped as they were. Flying out of her skin as she sat quietly within it.

Feeling the darkness closing in as it had the night before when she'd crawled into bed. Her stomach swarmed. With dread and fear-induced butterflies. Her mind careened to a place where emotion ruled and created thoughts.

Her precious little girls were being irreparably damaged, and there was nothing she could do about it and no way she'd ever be able to make them better. Were they already hurt physically? Restrained? Bruised? Or…

Ezra shifted in his seat, drawing her attention. Watching out the window, he seemed to be on the lookout every second. As though the Fitzgeralds might drive past them at any moment.

. Because…that was Ezra. Always aware. Always prepared.

Always focused.

Butterflies flitted away with that thought.

Focus dissipated them.

Thinking about Ezra wiped them out.

And the moment she tried to concentrate on the occasional car driving past, on whether or not the drones were in place yet, what images the powerful cameras might be portraying…she catapulted into darkness.

Was reminded of the night before…the despair.

If they didn't find the girls, she'd be right back there that night. Only eight or so hours in the future, she could be climbing back between the sheets of the bed she'd left back in Benson that morning.

She couldn't do it.

But she'd already done it.

So…if she had to…maybe she could…

"If we don't find the girls tonight, will you hold me again until I fall asleep?" The words blurted out of her, born of panic, pushed out by desperation.

"Of course."

The certainty, the rapidity, of his response reached deep within her. As did the promise within it. She glanced at the unusual, one-of-a-kind man at her side and knew that, no matter what, she'd survive another day.

So that she could be the mother she was meant to be.

DOM'S CALLER ID showed up before Ezra was expecting it to. Dread filled his gut as he grabbed his phone. The Jeep and thus its audio system were turned off, conserving gas. No reason for him to make it obvious that he wanted the call to be a private one. There hadn't been enough time for surveillance and then a successful extraction.

Even Dom wasn't that good.

But if the cameras showed death…

"Yeah."

"It's not them."

Feeling Theresa's gaze hot on him, Ezra said, "What's not?"

"The people in that bunker… It's a young guy and his pregnant wife."

He didn't say the string of words that ran through his mind, but he sat with them for a couple of seconds. Avoiding the woman seated to his right completely.

"You've trespassed and have been shot at twice now, bro."

Yeah. And he'd let Theresa down twice, too, which hurt far worse.

"Guy's claiming self-defense and is well within his rights to do so. He saw your gun. He wants reimbursement for the van you damaged. He agrees not to press theft charges against you, considering the circumstances, as long as he gets a new van."

"Fine." He could afford to buy a guy a van. Even without a financial wizard as a sibling, like Oliver looking after his investments for years.

"I get what you're doing, Ezra," Dom said then, sounding a bit like he needed a beer—and maybe a night alone with his fiancée. "I get why. But you're making me look bad here."

"Yeah."

"Don't call again until you've confirmed their location."

Dom had stopped short of ordering him to cease and desist. Ezra owed him one. "Yeah, okay."

"Caleb called," his triplet said then, the comment random enough that Ezra knew it was important.

"He's got verified intel that shows evidence of Ronald Spence smuggling, just like I suspected. In or very close to Blue Larkspur. Hitting us at home."

"Thumbing his nose at all of us." The idea made Ezra burn. As did the fact that he'd failed his older brother. He'd told Caleb he'd help look for evidence on the guy Caleb and Morgan had erroneously helped get out of prison, thinking he'd been one of their father's victims who'd been sent to prison for a crime he didn't commit.

Ezra couldn't remember a time when his family had needed him. Now Caleb had, and he hadn't been there for him.

The knowledge didn't sit well, not that Dom knew what Ezra had told Caleb. His brother was just filling him in on family business.

None of what Dom was telling him sat well.

"Hey." Dom's tone was firm. Like a slap upside the head.

"Yeah."

"Don't give up." Dead silence followed the words. Dom had ended the call.

Leaving Ezra alone with one of the strongest women he'd ever known. A woman who was hanging on by a thread that he was about to cut.

It was like she was in a free fall that just didn't stop.

"...a young couple..."

She heard Ezra's voice filling the Jeep sitting on the gravel lay-by. Only caught a few of the words that came after the ones that kept replaying themselves over and over in her mind.

It wasn't them.

Such innocuous words could mean anything. *Them* could mean anyone. It might mean that Eric and Jennifer weren't the ones shooting at Ezra, because they were down in the bunker playing the girls' favorite princess board game with them and a friend had been visiting and taken care of the intruder for them.

Or...or...it wasn't the Fitzgeralds there at all. What if the girls had been left in the care of a babysitter who'd been told to protect them at any cost, so she'd pushed the button that set off an electronically manipulated rifle to shoot at sensor movement?

It wasn't them.

A young couple...

"You were shot at...could have been killed...for nothing." The words fell from her lips, born from the depths of despair into which she'd fallen.

And she hadn't finished descending the downward trajectory inside of her. The longer she sat there, the deeper she went into a darkness that had no beginning and no damned end.

Starting the Jeep, Ezra pulled out onto the mostly deserted road. Drove without saying where he was taking them. She didn't ask.

Just sat frozen, watching trees go by, seeing mountainsides and distant vistas, and hearing *It wasn't them.*

A whole day had passed, and all of the law enforcement agencies looking for her daughters had made no progress. The Fitzgeralds had planned long and well. For a crime that had obviously been spurred on by their son's death. They were successfully completely off the grid. And might not ever be found.

With no power to change the circumstances, she had to face facts...

"It wasn't for nothing."

Ezra's words were a long time coming. So long, in fact, that the shock of hearing his voice again got her attention, and she heard every one of them.

"How can you say that?" What good could possibly have come of that afternoon's debacle? Of the wasted time? Darkness was going to be falling before they could make it to the next destination on the map.

She'd done the math. Unless some miracle happened and her daughters came walking up the road toward them, or showed up on law enforcement's radar, her wish for their sweet dreams was going to be delivered to them via angels again that night.

"We're on the right path, Theresa." The cadence of his voice flat, he didn't even glance her way. Whatever he was giving her, it was no pep rally. He wasn't trying to convince her. To build her spirits. He was giving her facts as he believed them.

So she didn't argue with him. She just sat there, arms crossed over her aching body, and wondered if he was hurting, too. The man had spent close to an hour dragging himself along on his stomach on her behalf.

Glancing over, she saw the tear in his shirt again. And felt something besides death inside.

She felt gratitude. Toward him.

And toward a world that held people who got up every day to risk their lives for others.

"The authorities can't go and search private property," he reminded her. "And today we proved that our theories are accurate. We found a bunker. Just not the right one. Yet."

Yet.

"We know they're out there. And we know enough to reasonably assume that their bunker is in the state and out there, too. It's just a matter of time until we find it."

Time was something he didn't have. A couple of weeks, maybe, was all he had left before he'd be off on assignment again.

Panic soared within her. Taking over mind and body.

"We have two more areas on our list," he continued, speaking without inflection. And yet somehow getting through to her. "We knocked off three today. Tomorrow, instead of heading west, we head north from the motel and hit both of them."

There were two more areas on their initial list.

There could be another list, too, expanding farther around the state. They had the recipe for bunker search parameters. They just had to stay in the kitchen until... until...

"I'm sorry."

Those words drew her gaze in a flash. "Sorry? For what?"

"I honestly have no idea. This is war. You make the most logical plan with the best chance of success, you go out, you fight like hell, and you keep doing it until the battle's won. I've just never had someone with personal investment in my platoon before. I've never fought for someone I knew personally, and it feels..."

He broke off midsentence.

And just like that, Theresa's panic-filled pity party

was gone for the moment. She was outside of herself, caring for someone else.

Ezra wasn't just a body on the job. He was a man, a person, with a good heart, a great heart, and…a friend with his own struggles.

"You might be out of your element, but you're doing far more for me than I would have thought anyone ever could, Ezra Colton, and I don't just mean finding bunkers and getting shot at."

He continued to stare straight ahead, but she saw his jaw tensing. Showing, to her, that he cared.

And she cared, too. Even if she hadn't…she'd never been one to make the world all about her. Doing things for others felt better. And Ezra, whether he knew it or not, had just given her a job to do. She had to be okay, to show him that she was holding up; she had to hold on to her hope, so that he could focus on getting his job done.

"What's your favorite food?" she asked him. Yeah, it was random, but feeding others was what she knew. Everyone had to eat—Maslow's lowest level on the hierarchy, food in the belly and roof over the head.

He glanced at her. Finally. Probably checking to see if she'd lost her mind. "Filet mignon."

"So before we head back to the hotel, how about we find the best steak house in this part of the state and have a decent meal?"

She might choke on it. She might not. She might not be able to keep it down. But she'd do everything she could to tend to him as he was tending to her.

"How about we find the best steak in Benson?" he asked then, the lines on his forehead and around his eyes finally fading a bit. "I need to change my shirt."

She looked at the torn cotton hanging over his flat belly. Worried again about the damage he might have done to himself.

He glanced at her again then, almost as though he could read her mind.

She smiled her gratitude, her regard for him. A smile she knew was tinged with the desperation and agony that hung in the air, but still a real expression.

And he smiled back.

The same way.

Chapter Twenty-One

Ezra almost welcomed the sting of the soap to his scraped skin as he stood beneath the shower, thinking about the day, replaying the information that had come at him, the way he'd processed it, the choices he'd made. He found he'd done all he could possibly have been expected to do given the circumstances.

Satisfied that he'd lived up to the ideal he'd once thought his father to be, to the best of his ability, he rinsed, determined that his stomach wasn't nearly as bad as he'd thought, the skin more surface-burned than actually pierced, and pulled on his last set of clean clothes.

Jeans and another long-sleeved T-shirt, this one in green. Balling up the dirties, he headed out to rejoin Theresa in the room they were sharing. She'd redone her bun. Was sitting at the table, scrolling on her phone.

"I need to make a stop at the washer and dryer before we go," he said, telling himself not to notice how incredibly beautiful she looked, sitting there so quietly, so still, while he knew emotions raged inside her. In some ways she was more like him than even his own brothers. The way she could be calm, collected, and raging inside at the same time. The way she could hurt, and yet wall herself off from the pain enough to get the job done.

"I was just thinking about that, too," she said. "Between the two of us, we've got a load. You mind throwing them in together?"

He shouldn't mind. Didn't mind, really.

Except that…he did.

From the time he was eighteen, his clothes had usually been washed on their own. By him…

"Of course," he said. "Fine…" He held out his spare arm. "Load me up."

"I'll do them," she replied, grabbing the clothes out of his grasp before he knew where she'd been headed. "Your others are here, right?" she asked, bending over to the shopping bag he'd used for a laundry basket. She had his skivvies there…

Grabbing her purse and a similarly filled shopping bag to his, she headed for the door. "Be right back," she said and walked out.

Ezra stood there, watching her go, hard as a rock.

Because a woman—Theresa—was doing his laundry.

As though it was all in a normal day. And then it hit him… Of course it was all in a normal day. She would have done laundry for three every time she did the chore. And had done it for four, too, back when her husband had been alive. As sick as he'd been at the end, there'd been no way Mark could have, or would have, gotten up to wash his own dirty clothes.

Ezra's growing erection shrank right up at the thought of her late spouse by the time Theresa returned. She let him know that the clerk at the front desk had just told her the best steak in town was right

next door, and out they went, to have their first dinner together while his underwear soaked back at the
motel with hers.

How sick was he to be jealous of his own skivvies?

DINNER WAS AS nice as a dinner could get when you
were a woman adrift with her children in danger in an
unknown location. As if by silent declaration, neither
she nor Ezra spoke about bunkers, their search or the
day they'd just had. They didn't talk about Mark, his
illness or how difficult the past year had been for her.
And they didn't discuss his family, or his father, either.

They talked about the movies they'd seen, some the
same, some not, held the same opinions on some, dis-
agreed on others. He'd listened to classic rock growing
up. She'd preferred the female pop singers of the time.
Their favorite vacation spots both included the beach.
He ordered a beer. She had a glass of wine.

She'd had a high school sweetheart. He hadn't. She
had a college degree. He didn't.

She'd been married. He'd never been in a long-term
serious relationship.

What they didn't do was expound on much of anything—except maybe the movies they'd seen. And by
the time the waitress brought them their check, Theresa was shocked to see that she'd almost emptied her
plate.

He paid for dinner, and then walked with her to
move the clean clothes to the dryer. She wasn't sure
whose idea it was to take a walk around town, just up
and down the main drag, but it did her good, seeing
normal people milling about, having normal lives. And
it made her incredibly lonely and antsy, too, because

everywhere she looked, she thought about the twins, what they'd like, where they'd want to go, what they'd be saying if they were with her.

The length of the walk was predicated by the dryer cycle, and Theresa wasn't at all ready to head back to reality as they stood side by side at the laundry table and, each grabbing their own things, folded and bagged separately.

They could have been strangers at a Laundromat, where bras and panties were handled in every city, every day, by tons of people without incident or undue thought.

Except that she'd had thoughts.

Of him taking an interest in her underthings. She'd noticed his, after all.

And when those thoughts raised such sorely needed good feelings inside her, she allowed more of them. Wondering if he'd like to see her wearing her underthings.

If he'd like to take them off her.

If he'd thought about undoing her bra and touching her breasts...

If he'd seen her panties there on the table with his underwear and thought about their respective body parts together...her crotch on top of his.

Then his phone rang.

His brother Dominic again.

An officer from Padillac, a small town just west of Benson—not far from the gas station where she and Ezra had stopped that first day—had found the Fitzgeralds' old blue truck nose-first in a river. There was no sign of any bodies.

But there'd been some blood inside.

Some. Not a lot.

Some.

Ezra stressed the word. Over and over.

There'd been no melted ice cream sandwiches in it, though.

And based on the water's rise and fall and the debris, the truck had been there less than a day. Which meant the nosedive happened after the brown van had been at the ice cream store.

Had the girls been hurt in the accident? Had they even been in the brown van? Did the Fitzgeralds have two vehicles?

Had a friend loaned them the van?

Maybe even the young couple who'd shot at Ezra earlier that day?

FBI forensics were going over the truck, lifting prints, and the blood would be tested. They wanted Theresa's permission to access her daughters' medical records for possible matches.

"To rule them out," Ezra said. More than once.

She listened. Gave permissions. But floated in and out of focus. And when it was time for bed, and Ezra crawled in beside her, wrapping her in his arms, Theresa allowed herself to rest her head on his chest and lose consciousness for a little while.

He ached. Hard as a rock. Needed release.

Movement on his chest. Fingers. Heading slowly downward.

Excruciatingly heightened sexual desire pounded Ezra, bringing him from sleep.

Not unusual. He was a healthy guy. And…

He wasn't alone. The weight against him…wasn't just in his sleep.

Full consciousness hit with a slam. Holy hell.

Theresa.

She was moving her fingers softly down to his penis. She palmed him there.

How was he going to get his body under control with her doing that?

Rubbing her face against his chest, she moaned, more like a hum, sounding pleased, and he lay there, trying to school himself into not reacting, but unable to stop her. Not that he wanted to.

She was obviously dreaming, thinking he was Mark, and if she woke her…

She had enough emotional crap to deal with. The day ahead was going to be rough, no matter what, and if she had to go into it with an embarrassingly awkward sexual component between them…

Her hand stilled, and he told himself it would only be a few minutes. Then he'd get himself back to size and quietly extricate himself from the bed.

No. No. Her fingers were on the move again. To his side…his other side…circling around his belly button area while his groin ached painfully.

He was going to have to stop her. Sorry for the embarrassment. But it would be much worse if he exploded right there.

Her hand slipped lower. Just an inch from the tip of him, and she lifted her head. Slid up to place her mouth on his, kissing him full-on.

His lips knew what to do. How to respond. They did it.

For her.

Surely that would be it. She'd lie back down and drift off, with no conscious memory of doing anything more than having a dream. She'd been so distraught. Bottling up more emotion than any one person could reasonably expect to keep contained.

Forcing her subconscious to seek an outlet in the only way...

Her lips came at his again. Open and soft, her tongue looking to tangle. And...oh, God...he tangled with her. Just for a second.

Because the incredible woman who he'd been wanting for days and couldn't have was sticking her tongue in his mouth.

Meaning him to be her husband, he figured.

With her lips still on his, she moved, throwing one leg over his, straddling his thigh, and rubbed her core on him.

Using every ounce of the rigid self-control he'd honed over the years, he lay still, prolonging the sweet torture as long as he could before being forced to wake her.

Maybe she'd stop. The dream would end as if it had never been. She'd wake in the morning with no knowledge of...

With her lips on his throat, sending delicious shards of desire through him, her hips moved upward on him, and her knee gently rubbed against his way-too-sensitive privates.

He almost embarrassed himself. Barely held it back. Took a second to let things simmer lest he move and explode, fully aware in that second that what he was doing was wrong.

He couldn't pretend to be another man even if he was doing it to help her. It wasn't right and,...

"Ezra?"

No trouble freezing everything then. He didn't move. Had no clue what to do.

"I just... I know you aren't much for words, but... I just need to know that you're okay with this. That I'm not taking advantage..."

Her body lay against his. Still, but for the heart that was beating hard against his chest.

"It's just for tonight," she whispered. "Just to get through the night...and only if you really want to do it with me, too."

He still didn't speak. The right words didn't come. But he rolled with her, arms supporting his weight on each side of her, cradling her. Gazing into her eyes, seeing himself reflected there amid her want, he lowered his lips to hers.

It's just for tonight. Even as she kissed Ezra, Theresa heard her own words again. Silently. A reminder.

She'd known, when she'd woken up with her leg thrown across Ezra and had felt his hard-on, that he hadn't been reacting to her specifically. His even, slightly raspy breathing had told her he'd still been asleep.

She'd carefully removed her leg, but continued to lie against him as she dozed off again. To dream about him.

Waking to see her fingers splayed on his chest.

And to find his entire body tensed. His breathing too rhythmically controlled.

Clearly awake.

The rest... There hadn't been thought. She'd just acted.

Him lying there awake beneath her, still hard... The surge of feeling had been so good, so energizing, she hadn't been able to resist.

There'd been no plan to seduce him. Or even to do more than explore the expanse of muscles and hard stomach she'd been finding irresistibly hot over the past week.

Thought returned briefly as she lay under him, looking up at his strong, gorgeous face. An acknowledgment that she was about to have sex with a man who was not her husband, for the first time since she and Mark had met.

Her heart knew...and was okay, too.

Her body needed Ezra Colton in a way she'd never craved a man in her life. The desire coursing through her was alive, an entity that was in control, demanding strong response.

Tenderness was there as well, but almost as an afterthought.

Urgency came first.

Feeling as much of him, taking as much of him, as she possibly could, the only goal. He was familiar and brand-new.

Exciting beyond recognition and safe.

His lips didn't just kiss hers. They consumed her, mingling tongues and breath into a taste that hadn't existed before that night.

One that was exclusive to them.

She loved it. Couldn't get enough.

When he sat up to pull his shirt over his head, she started to pull hers off, too. He reached out a hand and helped, tugging the material over her head and tossing it away.

Cool air hit her breasts, while his hot gaze warmed them. She liked sitting there for him, watching him enjoy the sight of her.

And that made her too hungry again. With her hands on his chest, she pushed him over, lying fully on top of him, moving her breasts and her hands over his chest, learning the feel of his springy hair, rubbing their nipples together.

With one arm around her back, he rolled them again, lifting himself up to slip out of his sweatpants, taking his underwear with them, and Theresa stared.

He was male perfection. Truly beautiful. Muscled and strong and so gorgeous.

And his penis was…clearly ready.

She went for the elastic waistband of her sweat bottoms, but his hands were there first, one on each hip. With his thumbs hooked in the waistband, he pulled down slowly.

Very slowly.

Revealing her mama hips, and what lay in between them, with a glow in his eyes that she'd never forget.

It had been a long time since Theresa had felt beautiful. Desirable.

Too long.

And that moment was hers.

All hers.

EZRA NEVER LOOKED away from Theresa as he left the bed only long enough, and only far enough, to grab his wallet and the condom he always carried, tossing it to the pillow as he lowered himself beside a woman like none other. Over the next while, he committed every inch of Theresa to memory. He touched every part of her, with the intention to give her as much pleasant feeling as he could, to offset the bad consuming her world. To create a good memory for her in the middle of hell.

It wasn't about him. He'd had sex before. He'd have it again.

It was always good.

And then she pushed him to his back on the mattress, straddled his stomach and started touching him. Every inch. Watching herself do it.

At one point she grabbed the condom. Ripped it open with her teeth, while her free hand teased his nipple, and then gave him a mouthwatering look at what he was going to feast on.

Turning, she sucked on his neck, kissed him long and wet and hard, and moved to his arms. Sliding her hands up and down them. Kissing them.

Her gaze was focused, and yet…ethereal, too. As though she was on another plane, being guided, knowing full well what she was doing to him and getting hot doing it.

He'd never had anything like that before.

She wasn't rough, but she wasn't gentle, either. And when she suddenly scooted lower, impaling herself with one movement, he hissed and almost came right then and there.

He held on, and thanked fate that he had when she started moving on him, eyes wide open, watching him, and bending to watch them coupling before looking him in the eye again.

If there'd been any doubt at all that the woman

knew who she was having sex with, even though he knew she was aware, it would have vanished. Her voice was loud and clear, telling him she knew that she was with Ezra.

And that was what made him come.

Chapter Twenty-Two

Theresa slept naked, still slick with sex, cuddled up to Ezra's chest. She was exhausted, satiated, mind blown, but more, she'd poured so much energy into him. Her emotional well was drained dry for the moment, allowing her the respite necessary to refill.

A few hours later, she woke before dawn, knew exactly where she was, what she'd done, and was glad she'd done it.

Slowly and gently removing herself from Ezra's body and the bed, she used her newly learned silent walk to get to the bathroom and closed the door before turning on the light.

The sight of her wild dark hair tangled and falling around her shoulders and breasts made her smile for a second.

The one second she gave to herself.

And then it was into the shower, taking care of her ablutions quickly and concisely, barely pausing over the sore parts of her that hadn't been used in too long. The tender nipples that she soaped just as she did every morning.

There was no lingering, no prolonging what was already over.

She would be ready for whatever the day needed from her the second Ezra said it was time to go.

There were also no regrets, she found, as she looked herself in the mirror while applying a light coat of makeup with sunscreen to her face.

She'd made a choice and didn't feel sorry about it.

Was it going to be harder to tell him goodbye when the time came for him to go?

Probably.

But it wasn't like it would have been a piece of cake to see him depart, even if she hadn't slept with him.

Was she going to ache to the bone for a bit after he left?

Obviously.

But she'd rather have been alive in a moment than let her libido lie dormant forever. The thought made a sad kind of sense to her, and with one last look in the mirror, she became only the mother who desperately wanted more than anything for her daughters to be returned safely to her care, and went to face the rest of her life.

EZRA HAD LEARNED at sixteen how to compartmentalize. More importantly, he'd perfected the talent of putting anything that made him feel emotionally vulnerable into one particular area. That part of him received and never opened enough to allow anything to escape.

That Thursday morning's dawn came with a major malfunction there, though. It was rejecting Theresa Fitzgerald. Wouldn't let him pack her away, emotionally speaking.

And, of course, it happened on a day when he didn't have the time or resources to deal with it. He couldn't head to the gym, take a long run or climb a mountain. He couldn't go to target practice or make a surprise visit to the nearest boot camp in his area to join the recruits in their training.

Those resources, and others like them, had helped seal away his emotions every single time.

Without them, he did the only thing left to him— carried on with baggage in tow. And he'd make damned certain that his growing feelings didn't slow him down or get in the way of successfully completing his mission.

While Theresa was in the shower, he went for breakfast, ordered it to go, ate his on the way back to the room and waited long enough for her to get out of the bathroom before he reentered the room. No listening to her shower or entertaining thoughts about being in there with her.

What was done was done.

She'd made clear the night before that what was between them was just for that evening.

By touching her back, he'd agreed to that stipulation.

Wanted it, even.

And so it was.

He went in only far enough to set her foam take-out container on the edge of the dresser. "Eat up while it's hot," he said, and without more than a glance in her direction, seeing that she was all put together, green pants and shirt again, hair in that perennially messy bun, he shut himself behind the bathroom door.

A cold shower and quick shave later, he gathered his things, left them in the bags on the counter as he'd done the day before—on the other side of the sink from her bags of things—and headed out to find her standing, purse on her shoulder, in the middle of the room.

Looking lost?

"Ready?" His tone was a little softer than normal. He'd work on it.

"Thanks for breakfast," she said as she left him to follow her. Her response was short and to the point. No words, just meeting him at the door and opening it before he could.

And so it went for most of the morning. They tended to the business at hand. Neither of them spoke of what they'd done in the darkness.

If she thought about it at all, it didn't show. No covert looks, chance glances or accidental touches.

As soon as he was on the road, he didn't notice as much. Keeping his mind on the job was second nature to him, and he settled into his skin gladly.

Traveling the other side of the U on their map that morning, they had all-new scenery to canvass as they passed. He noted more prickly pear than he'd seen the day before, but there were fewer of some of the other plants natural to the Colorado mountains.

Still, he took note, with a check mark in the positive instead of the negative column. Could be a sign they were finally on the right track.

"I widened my search while you were in the shower this morning," he told Theresa as the miles sped past and they drew closer to their first destination. Silence was fine, but he had to know that she was really okay— and up for whatever might lie ahead.

Partially because she was putting her own life at risk, as well as his and the kids', if she couldn't hold her own.

Or if she wasn't willing to follow orders.

He had no God complex, but the truth was, on any job, there could only be one boss. On that particular job, that particular day, the boss was him.

She wasn't jumping into the conversation. So he eventually told her, "I included old homesteads in the parameters. Maybe they happened upon an abandoned one in the mountains someplace, set up shop, and no one came along to question their right to be there."

The idea had occurred to him when they'd first gone to bed the night before. He'd had to keep his mind firmly on the case to keep it off her snuggled up against him.

"That would explain why they show up in no property searches," she said, her voice even. Her brow furrowed, more in consideration than displeasure, he figured from the brief glance he took, and he felt better.

She was with him. Holding up.

"For all we know, they could have raised Mark there," she added. And his gut clenched a little.

Was the reference merely because they were seeking her deceased husband's parents? Or did she have Mark on her mind? Were there deep regrets for what she'd done with Ezra, given Ezra, the night before?

He didn't blame her.

He was mostly all right with having been a probable substitute. He totally understood. Searched for a way to tell her that it was okay.

He didn't find one.

And didn't see that it mattered where Eric and Jennifer had raised their son. What mattered was finding where they were planning to raise their granddaughters.

But he and Theresa would be rescuing them.

Returning them, safe and sound, to their mother's arms, to their freshly painted little home with a dog named Charlie.

And then he would be getting the hell out of Blue Larkspur before he made any major blunders.

Like asking a grieving widow if he could sleep with her one more time for good luck before he set out.

THEY'D BEEN IN the Jeep a couple of hours, and Theresa was having a hard time keeping hope alive by the time Dominic's call came in.

She'd tried not to worry about that nose-dived blue truck, but she'd known from the second she heard about the accident that there was no good scenario for it.

When Ezra pushed to answer his brother's call and said, "Yeah," she almost covered her ears. She didn't want to know.

But she had to know. She couldn't help her children if she didn't know...

"Blood in the truck is no match," the FBI agent said right off.

"It's not Claire's or Neve's?" she called out to him. No room for misunderstanding on that one.

"Correct."

"Oh, thank God." Tears spurted and she looked away, sorry to appear like a weak link to the two strong men helping her so diligently.

Peripherally, she saw Ezra's head turn a few quick times, but she didn't so much as glance over. Didn't dare allow herself the chance to connect with him at the moment.

She'd had what she could have.

Because even if Ezra was aware of the powerful

feelings she had for him, even if he shared them, she'd never love him enough to be okay with his career. To the contrary, the more she fell in love, the more problematic his career would become.

And by all accounts, Ezra Colton was a soldier. To not be okay with that was to not be okay with him.

And even if she'd risk her own heart, there was no way she could put her daughters' hearts out there again. Not with such a strong chance that they could lose Ezra, after having already lost their father.

And, yes, she'd fallen for Ezra Colton. She was fairly certain she'd had no choice in the matter. It wasn't one she'd have willingly made. But she wasn't going to lie to herself about it, either.

She'd learned the hard way, with Mark's illness, that lying to oneself only hurt more in the end when you had to accept reality.

Dom's words flew in and out between her thoughts. The FBI had gotten no hits in the fingerprint database that matched the prints taken from the truck. And no DNA match off the blood, either, for the girls or their grandparents.

The area search produced no evidence of a struggle or recent footprints—but it didn't rule them out, either.

Personnel had combed the banks of the river for several miles both ways from the crash site. No sign of a body, or even clothes, had turned up.

"We did get one hit, though," Dom said. Theresa swung her gaze straight to the car's audio system, as though she could see the man on the screen that currently displayed his name. "Doesn't help us much today, but officers have been canvassing the area between that first little gas station you visited outside

Blue Larkspur and Benson, going door-to-door, which was a feat since places are so few and far between…"

"Today, Dom." Ezra's tone carried definite tension.

"Found a home security system. Got an older brown van, mint condition, heading from Benson, and later the blue truck heading toward Benson, coinciding perfectly with the time we catch it on the two cameras there from two days ago, and just a bit later, we get the brown van heading back toward Benson again."

"They switched vehicles someplace along the way."

"And if it really was them in the brown van, they headed back to Benson as we'd thought."

Maybe it wasn't much to people like Dominic and Ezra Colton, who fought bad guys every day and knew that two-day-old news wasn't going to help them find the girls that day. But to Theresa, who'd just had confirmation that it was *likely* that the Fitzgeralds really had been buying two cases of ice cream sandwiches, the news was a gift from heaven. You didn't buy perishables by the case unless you were planning to spoil the intended recipients for a long time.

To her, that ice cream symbolized hope that her daughters were being well cared for—to the extent that unstable conspiracy believers could administer good care.

"Good to have a piece fall into place," Ezra said, almost as though he'd read Theresa's thoughts.

"Doesn't bring 'em home." Dom clearly wasn't into sugarcoating. Ezra hadn't been, either, the two prior days they'd been on the road. If he was suddenly changing his tactics, thinking he needed to protect her…

"Nope, it's up to us to do that," Ezra replied and clicked off before Dominic said another word.

"I won't be coddled," she said, almost glad to have something to be angry with him about. "I prefer Dominic's honesty to false hope."

His jaw tightened. He stared straight ahead, both hands on the steering wheel. White-knuckled. Were they about to have their first fight?

Probably their only one?

Shoulders visibly relaxing, he gave her a quick glance. "Point taken. I apologize."

Good. She sat, staring out, watching ahead, and on both sides of the road, too, as had become habit. Glad that she'd set him straight.

So why, now that she'd made sure that Ezra wouldn't give her any special treatment, did that fact sadden her?

HE WASN'T TRYING to give her false hope. Ezra knew full well how damaging a fake sense of reality could be.

But *damn.*

When his brother started spouting off facts, without any regard as to how hard his words would hit Theresa...

He had to find the girls. Get them safely home.

And get his ass out of Blue Larkspur. New assignment or not.

He could spend a few days at the beach, drinking beer. Or take a side trip to Malaysia to shoot pool with Oliver.

Maybe even let him win.

"Ezra, stop!"

He hit the brakes gently. And then again. They'd been traveling for nearly forty miles on the same dirt road without slowing. Locations number four and five were both accessed by it, with fifty miles in between them. If she…

Theresa was out of the car before he'd even come to a complete stop. Thinking she was ill, he barely got the Jeep in Park before he rushed to join her.

She was bent over, but she wasn't heaving. Or peeing, either, which could have been another emergency necessitating a quick stop, he realized too late.

She was pointing toward the rock face that covered much of the ground around them. "Are those tire tracks?" she asked.

Following the point of her finger, he saw the black, almost grease-like markings on the mostly whitish rock, prepared to tell her kindly that she was seeing earth misplaced from a storm and cooked into the rock.

And then he noticed the glint…off to the right, several yards away, embedded in the mountainside that mostly lined the road. A camera.

"Get down," he said. He lowered himself to the ground, scooping her toward him, to make sure she landed on him, not the rock.

He rolled over immediately, keeping her under him, as he surveyed the area. It was all overkill, he was sure.

They were on the edge of private property. Fence line had been clearly marked by posts and flags on both sides of the rock face, which had made installing fence on that one spot impossible. And needless.

The flat ground she'd seen could be a gully or could lead back behind the rock face to something more. Entire towns could be erected back there, and from the road, it would look like nothing.

He knew there wasn't a settlement of some sort, though. His topographic map had told him so.

But he couldn't be sure there wasn't another hermit who'd shoot them off his property.

"Stay on your belly and get back to the Jeep." He bit out the words as he slid her his knife. "Stay low and get around to the driver's side and climb in the back. Get down on the floor." He moved off her. "Go."

Ezra waited until he heard the far side door close, and then he moved forward, inch by inch, to get a better look at the marks she'd seen.

Adrenaline kicked in when he got close enough to see that she'd been right.

The markings were tire tracks.

Recent ones.

He was still ten miles from the map's designation of the ideal location for the Fitzgeralds' bunker, but his quest wasn't science. Or exact.

And he could once again be on private property owned by an inhabitant, or inhabitants, who only wanted to be left alone.

He had no right to be there.

And absolutely did not want to put Dom in a tough situation at his job.

The visible track, a bit of mud mixed with tire tar, was on an angle. That told him the vehicle was headed away from them around the rock face, blocking his view from what might be beyond. And the tread was larger than a car's. Not as large as a work truck's. A van?

The tread was solid. The kid at the store in town had noted the van's tires being in good shape.

Was he so desperate to help the woman he'd had sex with, so desperate to find two little girls who'd shown him how cool being around children could be, that he was going to turn a mark on a rock into a reason to break the law again?

His life was about order.

And absolutely upholding what was right and just.

He would not be his father.

Peering carefully at every inch of the rock face upon which he lay, smelling dirt and fresh air, listening for anything, Ezra questioned himself as he never had before.

His number one rule of engagement? Don't hesitate.

Sliding forward, he tried to get a glimpse of where the vehicle might have gone, without compromising any potential landowner's privacy. Twelve inches at a time. Then another foot.

What was he doing?

What kind of real evidence did he have?

Had he been so desperate to help Theresa Fitzgerald, to fight her fight with her, that he'd been leading them on wild-goose chases all along?

And why?

Why did he think he could do any more to find those little kids than all of the law enforcement agencies in the state? Like he was better than the entire FBI, which was taxed with kidnapping cases all the time?

He knew nothing about kidnappers.

Or kids, either, for that matter.

He knew about fighting terrorists and cartels in Afghanistan.

Why in the hell was he lying on a rock face in the middle of nowhere?

Because Theresa had intrigued him?

Because he'd wanted to ask her out on a date, even though he knew that it could lead nowhere?

With the new van he'd be paying for, he had to admit he was certainly on the most expensive outing he'd ever taken with a woman.

Strange, though, that the same kind of camera as at the first homestead, set at about the same angle, had been protruding out of a cliff face.

Maybe it was because those who lived off the grid were a kind of community of themselves, buying their supplies from those who were like them.

Continuing to mountain climb the flat surface on his belly, bending one leg to push him along, and then the other, he just needed a glimpse of where the vehicle had been headed. If it had been headed anywhere.

The driver could have just pulled off to take a leak. A nap. A photo.

Could have been turning around.

But just the one tire track. At that angle…

One more push and more mountain wall…with a breakaway, flatter surface that led farther into the mountain range. And there at the bend was a healthy bed of prickly pear cactus.

It was too much. Too coincidental.

Unless he'd been spot-on from the beginning of the day, and the Fitzgeralds *were* here after all. Heart pounding, he moved forward. He had good tracking skills. Knew to look at the basic things others missed. Like healthy growth at the site of a compost dump that turned into fertilization. Lusher vegetation than the rest of the landscape around him.

It was a stretch. He got that. And trusting his instincts had saved a lot of lives. Including his own a few times.

He had to make sure, though.

He crawled farther forward. Saw nothing but more flat rock running through hills like a path. Curving so that he could only see a few feet at a time.

Reminding him of a remote village he'd once stumbled upon in a foreign desert, a valley completely protected by three-hundred-sixty-degree mountain ranges.

And there was another tire print. He couldn't sit up, couldn't take a chance on other cameras being strategically hidden in the rocks towering above him. But he managed to pull his gun from his waistband and his phone from his pocket. They'd still had service on the road—the result of some satellite system.

He had to call Dom. To get drone surveillance out there. The tire prints would have to be evidence enough…

And he had no service.

He also had to turn around and go back, to make the call, and do things right this time. But as he made one slide to the side, he heard the loud crack of a gunshot.

Rocks crumbled not far from where his head had been, falling down on his hand, but he barely registered them. His ears were ringing, his brain was ringing, his heart was pounding…with the sound of a little girl's scream that had sounded right after a bullet flew.

Chapter Twenty-Three

With the sudden cry repeating like a discharging rifle in his brain, Ezra wasted no time. The shriek had carried bloodcurdling fear. No way would he turn his back on it.

Hugging the mountainside, his forearms pulled into his chest, holding his gun in front of his face, he used his elbows and his feet to propel himself quickly along the flat rock. The bullet had hit high, maybe a couple of feet above him. If he was lucky, it had come from a stationary gun with limited aim, and the ground would be out of range. He didn't need to tread slowly. He'd already been discovered.

The only thing that mattered was getting to that child before she was hidden away.

Or worse.

He'd heard only one scream.

Had no idea if Claire and Neve were even there. Could have been another little girl entirely.

Didn't much matter to him at that point.

The chilling terror in that scream required action. Two minutes later, he rounded a small bend and was transported to another world. A grassy clearing, several acres' worth. A private little valley in the mountains. An old farmhouse.

And...two little dark-haired people holding on to each other, and a tree, while a woman pulled at both of them.

Claire and Neve. Had to be.

And Jennifer?

Pulling his gaze from the children, he searched for Eric.

Stiffened at the loud crack of a shotgun being fired. Heard a bullet hit above and behind him, coming from the direction of what he was guessing was the trapdoor of a bunker. Eric was likely in the bunker using a telescoping rifle.

Another scream rang out, echoing across the valley. So closely surrounded by mountains as the area was, sounds would reverberate. Which was probably why Ezra had heard the sound at all.

His mind cataloged. Calculated. Possible positions of people. Sounds. The young girls he'd grown to care about in such a short time. Continuing extra carefully, aware that any small noise would travel, he rounded the side of the mountain and moved into the grassy clearing.

Those girls weren't going to be able to hold out much longer, and if the woman got them down in that bunker, trying to rescue them could push the unstable older couple to drastic measures.

They could also have an escape tunnel, with an unknown outlet, and a vehicle waiting to take them further off the grid.

He didn't see the brown van. Or any other vehicle.

One of the twins—Claire, based on the braided

hair—lost her grip on the tree. Another scream pealed, and the woman gained ground, pulling the pair backward. Neve held on to the tree, Claire grasping her twin. And Ezra shot his gun on an angle, into the air.

A warning. A distraction. Hard to tell where it came from.

As he'd hoped, Jennifer—it had to be—loosened her grip on the twins just long enough for them to break free and run. Eric came around the trapdoor of the bunker, a rifle in one hand and a pistol in the other.

Jennifer also had a gun out, pointed, as she circled in place and then dashed behind a tree.

Ezra, aware of both of them, gave most of his attention to two pairs of the fastest running legs he'd ever seen. The children were heading for the house.

Pride filled him. As though he'd taught them himself. Keeping himself down was one of the hardest things he'd ever done, but he stayed in the prairie grass, working his way toward the old farmhouse, twisting his gun around and shooting upward and behind him.

His extended magazine held thirty bullets. He'd used up two. He was so far outgunned he'd be a dead man if he didn't think of some other way to get those children out of there.

And just like that, it came to him. *He* was their way out.

He had twenty-eight bullets to keep the Fitzgeralds more worried about intruders than about the kids. He had to make the grandparents feel as though they were surrounded. Keep them turning circles, while he got the twins' attention and sent them out to their mother.

And plan B—surrender himself to give the girls

time to get out to their mother. Take whatever the Fitzgeralds handed out to him.

He'd risked his life many times for people he didn't even know.

He'd give it up in a heartbeat for Claire, Neve and Theresa Fitzgerald.

Clear plan.

EZRA MOVED, SHOT, moved more, shot again. His bullets flew from different trajectories to various parts of the compound, staying clear of the homestead. He was praying that the twins would run to the front of the house, keeping them out of view of their grandparents.

Ezra continued to shoot bullets that ricocheted off to the side of the structure. Carefully choosing his times, with pauses in between. He caught glimpses of the older couple, both with their backs to the house, watching their perimeter, keeping cover with trees that he realized had been strategically placed.

They'd planned for years. Had clearly practiced. Long before they'd even known the twins existed.

Above all else, they protected their safe space. Were focused and on task.

Reminded him of armies he'd fought.

And had fought in.

A semiautomatic unloaded into a mountainside.

Shots fired into the other side of the clearing.

They were gunning for him.

And if they thought the girls were safe for the moment, in the farmhouse, his plan would work.

If they even thought about the children at all. They'd let their son go rather than let go of the belief that they had to protect themselves from a nuclear blast at all cost...

He saw a flash of color near a small porch on the side of the house. Yellow. The twins had been wearing yellow shirts. Positioning himself behind a boulder in the yard, he grabbed a smaller rock and threw it toward the porch. Arched back, took a shot at the other side of the homestead perimeter and then threw another stone.

Ripped a piece of his shirt, tied it around one more rock and threw that. Letting the girls know that someone besides their grandparents was there. Hoping to God they'd peek to see who it was.

He was down to eleven bullets. And...

Neve peeked her head out.

He wasn't going to get another chance. Staying low, Ezra lifted his head, and one hand, above the grass. Saw Claire pop her head out, too. He motioned to the rock face that wound around the mountain and out to the road not far beyond.

Held up three fingers.

Counted them down and threw his hand in the direction he'd pointed. As both girls took off, Ezra stood up, running toward the house, and started shooting. One bullet headed toward Jennifer, a second later, one toward Eric, and then back toward Jennifer.

He shot until he ran out of bullets.

And then heard shots ring out toward him.

WHEN THE FIRST bullets had been fired, Theresa had crawled from the back seat of the Jeep to the driver's side. Ezra had told her the day before to drive until she had cell service and call for help if she heard gunshots.

But if she left, and he came running back, needing a getaway, and she was gone...

Or if he sent the girls out to her...

She'd made a choice.

She'd stayed put.

And when the gunshots started to ring out in quick succession, and rapid fire joined in, she trembled, her heart thudding, and feared she'd made a gross, severely negligent error. She started the Jeep, but didn't move it.

Turned it off and jumped out.

She couldn't just sit there while someone killed the man she loved.

There was no long-term thought process on that one. Just a knowledge that prompted action. Seconds later, she was already at the first tire track when she heard footsteps.

Coming rapidly.

Frantically diving for an alcove in the mountainside, she stood, panting, hardly able to breathe, knife in hand, and waited.

The noise came closer. More than one pair of feet.

Homesteaders protecting their territory? Thinking they were under attack?

Or...

Blood drained from her face, and she dropped the blade. Weak, thinking she was hallucinating, she watched first one dear little face come around the bend, and then the other.

"Neve! Claire!" She heard her joyful cry. Opened her arms.

But it wasn't until two trembling, crying little bodies plastered themselves against her, and four arms wrapped with strangulating strength around her neck, that she knew she wasn't dreaming.

"Are you two okay?" she asked, pulling back far enough to study both of them in rapid succession.

"I got gum in my hair," Neve said.

"It wasn't her fault, Mom," Claire added, her gaze wide and solemn, though her eyes were still wet with tears. "Grammy made her go to bed with it so she'd chew and not cry."

Theresa's stomach knotted, her heart ached, but... "But you aren't hurt?"

They both shook their heads, and she hugged them to her, never wanting to let go.

Ezra had done what he'd said he would do.

He'd sent her girls out to her.

Theresa barely managed to stay on her feet as she gathered those little bodies close, holding them as tightly as they held her. Her face wet, she buried it against dirty brown hair for one brief second. Then, shielding the children's bodies with her own, she quickly ushered the girls to the far side of the Jeep. Opening the back door, she helped them inside.

"Down on the floor and don't get up," she said. And then added, "I love you so much," before shutting the door after them.

"Wait!" Neve cried out, popping right back up and pulling on the door handle. Her sweet face wet with tears, she said, "You have to get Mr. Giant! They're going to hurt him!"

"Neve, get down here," Claire yelled. Theresa saw Neve's little body jerk downward, as though her twin had given her a huge pull.

God, she loved those kids.

Standing there at the Jeep, she glanced toward the flat rock face, not knowing what she'd see if she followed it. Looked at the driver's seat of the Jeep.

But in the split second, a sound—sirens—came from the distance. Approaching rapidly.

Looking up, she could hardly believe it when she saw several law enforcement vehicles, different colors from different agencies, converging upon them. Taking over the road, the cars parked all around and across from the Jeep.

Weak with relief, before she could fully process the fact that help had somehow arrived, she saw Dominic jumping out of a vehicle and running up to her.

"I've got the girls," she said. "Ezra's still in there. Lots of shots fired. Rapid-fire ones, too…"

He didn't say a word, didn't wait to hear any more, either.

He was gone before she could blink.

Theresa climbed into the back seat. Asked the girls to stay down, just in case, for a little bit. Not sure what, or who, Dom and his army of officers would be bringing out of the mountain. Not sure the state any of them would be in.

No matter what happened from there, she and her daughters were going to talk about Ezra for the rest of their lives, say continual thanks for him. None of them would ever forget who he was and what he'd done for them.

As if they could read her thoughts, the twins hugged her legs. Both girls were silent for once. They'd need to talk about what had happened, what they'd just seen, too, but not yet. With a hand on each of her very-much-alive daughters' backs, rubbing slowly, Theresa blinked back tears.

Uttering prayers for Ezra that hadn't been answered when Mark had been sick.

And waited.

SHE DIDN'T HAVE long to wait. Within minutes of disappearing around the rock face, officers were back with Jennifer and Eric Fitzgerald, the latter with a tourniquet tied around his hand, in custody. Looking for Ezra behind them, not seeing him, she felt her heart stop.

"Stay here and stay down," she told the girls. And then tapped Neve lightly on the shoulder and said, "I mean it. I'll be angrier at you than I've ever been if you so much as pop your head up, got it?"

The messy little head nodded, and as Theresa exited the vehicle, she saw the two six-year-olds holding hands.

"Paramedics are almost here." A female officer came up to her. "We can have them take a look at the girls…"

Theresa shook her head, not wanting the girls to face any more trauma. "Not now," she said. She'd have them checked, just to be safe, by the doctor they knew and liked back home.

At the moment, she needed to see Ezra come walking around that bend.

A few long seconds later, Dominic came forward, glancing back, and then stepping aside to let officers through carrying a long board by the corners. A makeshift stretcher.

With Ezra, blood covering his shirt, lying unconscious on top of it.

Chapter Twenty-Four

Antiseptic smell. Rhythmic swishing. Beep. Beep. Beep.

He'd rather sleep than deal with the noise. Ezra meant to drift off again, but couldn't quite let go. He had to know…

Had to know.

His eyes popped open. Claire and Neve.

With a swift glance around the room, he knew immediately that he was in the hospital. And that he was alone.

He remembered going into the valley compound. Telling the girls to run.

Running toward the old farmhouse as a distraction…

And then…nothing.

He fell asleep again and woke up sometime later. A look at the window told him it was daytime. The clock on the wall said seven.

Seven in the morning?

He'd been out overnight?

He tried to sit up, felt the immediate jabs of pain in his gut and lay back down.

Obviously he'd been hit.

How bad?

And most importantly…the girls.

Reaching for the call button hanging over the side of the bed, he saw his cell phone on the table beside him. Grabbed it.

Pushed speed dial.

"'Bout time you woke up," Dom answered on the first ring. "I sit there all night, leave for ten minutes to get a cup of coffee with Sami, and you call me," his brother continued, and as he spoke, Ezra could hear Dom's voice both over the phone and coming down the hall.

He'd said he was with Sami, but he came in the room alone, his expression serious, in spite of his tone, as he studied Ezra.

"What the hell, bro?" Dom said, shoving his phone in his pocket. "Coulda done without the scare…"

He shrugged. It hurt, but whatever. "Neve and Claire…"

"Are fine." Setting a foam coffee cup down on Ezra's table, Dom pulled up the only chair in the small, private room, where he'd obviously spent the night. "They've been checked out by their doctor and, other than understandable trauma from the unexpected separation from their mother, are doing well. They were glad to be home. Won't let Theresa out of their sight. Insisted on sleeping with her last night, I was told when she called to check on you, but overall…you saved the day."

Good. He was ready for that nap, then.

Turned his head, and when he woke again, Dom was still sitting there, scrolling on his phone. Clock said seven thirty. Still light outside. But nighttime?

"How bad am I?"

Glancing up, his brother said, "You'll live."

And when Ezra stared silently, Dom said, "You lost your spleen. Doc says four to eight weeks and you can get back to duty. I've already looked up army regulations and they allow for splenectomy when it's caused by trauma."

Relief flooded him, and he pushed the button on the bed to get himself more upright. He was still army.

Still capable.

And the better he followed orders, the sooner he'd be back with his troops.

"What about Eric and Jennifer Fitzgerald?"

"Ultimately it's up to the judge." Dom shrugged. "But Rachel is talking about recommending long-term mandatory psych admission for both of them, separately, with the possibility, sometime in the distant future, of supervised visitation, at the institution where they're locked up, with Claire and Neve if it's deemed to be a healthy choice for the twins."

He swallowed. Would have maybe taken the news in a more congenial manner if he hadn't been lying there without a spleen because of the older couple. From blood loss alone, he could have died. Because of them.

"Neither of them shot you," Dom said then.

And it occurred to Ezra to wonder, "How did it go down?" Had Theresa gotten him and the girls out of there? Had he stumbled out? Did she leave and go for help when she'd heard the first shot?

His lack of memory was pissing him off.

Theresa. The thought of her made him swallow. Hard.

"Funny thing," Dom said. "We had no idea you were

there. We were following up on a lead… We took the van you messed up, ran forensics and found evidence that the Fitzgerald twins had been inside. And that it was registered to a guy who's been dead for thirty years. He had an old homestead on file, coordinates, not an address. Turns out the guy's son, Steve, is Eric's half brother, through their mother. But it was from Steve's father, who never married Eric's mother, that Eric was first turned on to doomsdaying when he was a young teen. And it was Steve's son, Jamison, Eric's half nephew, whose bunker you found yesterday. Jamison told us exactly where to find the old homestead when we hauled him in for withholding information in a kidnapping investigation. Steve is the one who shot you. The bullet was from his gun."

Wow. "Talk about all in the family…"

Dom nodded, gave Ezra a noncomedic half grin. "Guess we don't have a lot of room to talk, huh?"

Maybe. He hadn't been around enough to be all that close with his family in recent years. But when he came home, they certainly acted like he was one of them.

And…maybe he liked it.

Though a couple of hours later, he wasn't so sure about that. There were only so many visitors a guy could take, only so much mothering. Most particularly when there was only one woman he really needed to see right then.

And she wasn't there.

THERESA HAD TO see Ezra. To assure herself that Dom had been telling her the truth that his triplet was going to be fine. But she couldn't leave her girls.

Claire and Neve were eating well. They'd slept well.

They were playing, but the second she left the room, they stopped what they were doing and followed her.

Their first therapist appointment was already set for later in the week, but she knew there would be no quick or easy fix.

They'd been terrorized.

She got it.

Was up for it, for however long it took, to help them feel safe and secure again. When her children truly needed her, she was a mother first, a woman second. Her choice. In her world, the right choice.

And every second that passed that she wasn't at Ezra's side, she died a little inside, too.

When Isa showed up at a little past ten in the morning, two days after the shooting, pulling up to Theresa's little house, freshly painted but still in need of work, Theresa automatically assumed the worst. Met Isa on the front porch, with the door open and in full sight of the girls, but hopefully out of earshot.

"What happened?" she asked. "Is Ezra okay?"

Isadora Colton smiled, her beautifully elegant face showing genuine compassion, and maybe a bit of... pleasure as she sized up Theresa, who was standing there in an old cotton spaghetti-strap sundress that had aged about as gracefully as her house. "He's fine, dear," Isadora said. "A bit grumpy for my taste, but that's Ezra when he's feeling caged in. I think he'd like to see you, which is why I'm here. I know your sweet babies have been through a lot—Dom told me about them refusing to go to bed in their own room again last night. Certainly a hospital surgical ward is no place for them to be right now. I was thinking... They took such pleasure in being out at the Gemini, playing in the kids' hut and spending time with the horses, and if you wouldn't mind, I'd love to take them out for a visit while you go see my son."

Heart leaping into her throat, Theresa just had one thought… "Ezra said he wanted to see me?"

"No." Isadora shook her head. "You really think he'd come out and admit something like that?"

The question was rhetorical, but Theresa smiled then—a genuine, toe-to-scalp feeling of happiness—and said, "No, of course he wouldn't. And thank you. As long as the girls are comfortable with going…"

"Yes! Yes! Yes!" Claire and Neve jumped up in unison. Running to the door.

So much for out of earshot.

Half an hour later, Theresa stood outside Ezra's cracked-open hospital room door, shaking hard. She knocked, and blinked back tears when she heard his voice call, "Come in."

She couldn't stop tears from falling, though, when she saw her big, strong hero dressed in a tied-on hospital gown, propped up by pillows, with tubes taped to his skin.

"Looks worse than it is," he said, holding up his left arm and gesturing toward the IV bag. "This is done, just hanging around for another hour or so until they're convinced I don't need the pain meds they've been pumping through it. Switched to saline a couple of hours ago."

"Oh, Ezra…" She smiled, dropped to the edge of the one chair in the room, wanted so badly to touch him, hug him, kiss him, hold his hand. Instead, she held her own hands in her lap. "I just…"

Couldn't say most of what needed to have come

tumbling out of her. Love meant thinking of those you loved as much as yourself. "I will never, ever be able to thank you…" She broke off. For saving her girls, first and foremost.

But for saving her, too. The days with him…making love with him. He'd shown her that while a part of her had died with Mark—the part that had seen them together forever—she'd become a different woman.

And that woman was still very much alive.

"Just doing my job, ma'am," he said with a shrug.

And while she knew she had to let him go, knew that he was a soldier who had to go out into the world and fight, she'd become a fighter, too.

"Technically, it was the FBI's job," she said. "And about a gazillion other law enforcement officials…" She let her voice trail off. Looked him in the eye, and when he looked back like he did, she couldn't turn away.

And knew she had to. But— "I just…would very much like it if maybe it would be possible for us to stay in touch," she said. "Even just a text now and then. Just to let me know you're safe."

"Sure." He smiled, though his expression seemed a bit cloudy. Medication, maybe. Or the pain.

"If you need anything," she said, "please call, this week, next, whenever…"

He nodded. The polite kind that said he would, but he never would. And then asked, "How are the girls? All I get out of Dom is 'fine.'"

She smiled then, spent the next five minutes telling him about the past forty-eight or so hours since he'd sent her back to the Jeep and left her there to rescue her children.

She'd heard bits and pieces of what had gone on at the homestead in that little mountain valley and hoped some of the details she'd heard through her six-year-olds' perspectives were largely exaggerated, but feared they were not. Ezra neither denied nor confirmed the details. But he grinned from ear to ear when she told him about his mother taking the twins to the Gemini.

"Great idea," he said. "Should have thought of it myself."

As if he hadn't already done enough for them.

Silence fell. She feared she was outstaying her welcome and stood. She had to touch him, knowing that she might never see him again. Leaning down, she kissed his forehead. And then, because it would have seemed wrong not to, brushed her lips across his, too. "Thank you, Ezra. You gave me back my life and will always hold an honored place in my heart."

With that, she turned and walked out the door.

Before she broke and begged him to let her stay.

Ezra watched her go. Stared at the door after she left, too, because there was nothing else in the room that he wanted. Why Theresa Fitzgerald had impacted his head and heart so strongly, he had no idea. He'd have bet every dime of his investments that he'd never fall for one particular woman. But then, he'd have bet against Dom ever doing so, too, and he'd have lost his shirt on that one.

Not that Theresa was Ezra's Sami. There was no happy ending for the two of them, and one seemed pretty much a given with Dom and Sami. They weren't just in love, both of them, with each other; their lives also fit together, in spite of the fact that Dom had been trying to take down Sami's father, and Sami's dad had died in the process. Sami loved Dom.

Theresa wasn't in love with him. She'd given him a place in her heart because of what he'd done for her girls. He'd take what she could give, remember her with fondness and get on with his life. Because while it had become clear over the past hours that Theresa and her daughters had a much more powerful pull on him than any need to travel the world, and while it had become clear that he felt much more strongly about being around to fight their battles with them rather than fighting for strangers, there was no way in hell he was putting her on the spot or misreading her gratitude. No way he'd make her feel bad by asking her for more than she had to give.

Her true love was a man who had died.

He'd known that going in.

And still…he'd gone.

He wasn't sorry about that.

Not even minus a spleen.

At that point in his thought process, he'd usually get up and go to the gym. Or paint a house. Strapped to the bed by the damned tube he no longer needed, Ezra reached for the call button, ready to tell someone, anyone, that if they didn't get the IV out of him, he'd remove it himself, but answered his phone when it rang instead.

Rachel. The one sister who hadn't already been in to see him. The next closest to him and Oliver and Dom in age. One of the few single births Isadora had carried. And the district attorney of Lark's County. Her schedule was intense.

"Hey, little sis, what's up?"

"First, I just wanted to hear for myself that you're as fine as Dom claimed you were."

"Unfortunately, I have to disagree with him there," he said, but he was doing it as much to be contrary as anything. "I'll be fine as soon as someone comes in here and gets this damned tube off my arm so I can go pee in peace. You're the DA—you got any pull here?"

"Yep, you're fine." She chuckled. Asked her version of the same questions he'd been fielding from family members all morning, and then said, "I've already talked to Dom, and will be calling Oliver next, but I wanted to let you know… You remember Clay Houseman?"

"The guy who confessed to the crimes Dad put Ronald Spence away for," Ezra said. He might have kept his distance from the family, but he knew every pertinent detail when it came to what mattered most.

"Yeah."

"What about him?"

"He was killed in a prison fight. Thing is, the guy he was fighting was also killed…"

Ezra's instincts barged full speed ahead. "That's not suspicious," he said with full-on sarcasm. "You think Spence had him killed to stop him from admitting that he paid Houseman to confess and take the fall for him?"

"Some of the others think so. And, yeah, I do, too. At least, I think it's absolutely a possibility that needs to stay on the table."

"This Spence guy. He's close. Right here in town, from what I hear. You be careful, Rach."

"Always."

His sister rang off with her usual "love you" to him,

but this time, when he said it back, he wasn't just spouting words he'd been saying all his life.

He was thinking about what they meant.

He loved his family.

And, whether he liked it or not, he needed them, too. He'd let himself think for years that he didn't. They'd never seemed to require much from him, either.

Or maybe he'd just been a scared ass who'd refused to love so deeply that you could hurt until you wished you'd never been born.

He'd been in town a couple of weeks, and aside from the past few days hunting down Theresa's children, he could have been using his backdoor skills to see what he could find on Spence. He hadn't done so.

But he wasn't going to let his family down again. From what he'd been told by the doctor who'd stopped in to see him earlier, and others, too, it would be eight weeks before he'd be released to go back into the field. That gave him eight weeks to see what he could find on Ronald Spence.

The man had better watch out.

He was soon to have a very determined, very frustrated hunter on his trail.

THERESA TOOK AN extra few minutes for herself, stopping for an iced coffee, before heading out to the Gemini to pick up the girls. While she was edgy being away from them, she knew that their path to security and mental health was through her.

She couldn't overprotect them or she'd make them fearful of being out of her sight. The Fitzgeralds hadn't wanted to hurt the twins, not that she'd been to see them or spoken to them since their arrest. But by all accounts, they'd wanted to protect Claire and Neve. And too much of anything could be bad.

But maybe, if they were committed to a psychiatric facility rather than prosecuted and put in jail, they'd get to the point where the girls could visit them. When Claire and Neve were old enough to better understand the nuances of what had happened to them. Hopefully Claire and Neve would then be able to further put to rest the horror of the past few days.

Antsy about leaving them for too long lest they start to lose interest in the horses and start to fret without her, she dumped the rest of her coffee and barely managed to keep her old van down to the speed limit as she headed out to the ranch.

The twins weren't waiting for her. In fact, their faces fell when they saw her and realized it was time to leave. "We were going to have another ride on the horses," Neve said, but the little girl was clinging to Theresa's arm like she never wanted to let her go.

Claire, always the practical one, but also clinging to Theresa, looked up at Isa and asked, "May we have that second ride at a different time, Mrs. Isa?"

"Mrs. Isa?" Theresa glanced at the blonde who was smiling, so clearly enjoying herself that she let the name go.

"Of course," Isa said. "As long as your mom says it's okay?"

"Can we? Can we?" the girls said in unison, and looking into those uplifted little faces—one freckled, one not—reading the happiness in their eyes at the prospect of another trip to the ranch, there was no way Theresa could refuse them.

"Yay!" they both cried out, and then ran to get the

swimsuits they'd brought with them in case the sun came out and they could get in the pool.

Claire carried the bag Theresa had hurriedly packed for the girls earlier. Neve had a big envelope in her hand. Sealed, she showed Theresa when she walked up. "We made it for Ezra," she said, and the second the three of them were belted into the van, both children started begging to stop by the hospital to give Ezra his card before they went home.

"He did save our lives, Mom," Claire said, quite solemnly. "And Mrs. Isa said he gets visitors, 'cept we can't bring Charlie like we do when we visit rooms on Tuesdays."

And, as Claire had so deftly pointed out without actually doing so, her daughters were no strangers to rooms with frail human bodies. They were no strangers to illness, period.

"All right," she told them, partially because she couldn't find the wherewithal to tell them no. And partly, she knew, because it gave her a legitimate opportunity to see Ezra one more time.

EZRA, IN SWEATPANTS and that hospital gown, was sitting in the chair by his bed. He was planning his own hospital breakout—seriously, one more night and he was gone—when he heard a bump against his door, followed by whispering.

"Can we come in?" Theresa's voice.

"Hell, yes" turned into "Hellyes—oh" as he saw the two faces peeking around the door at him. When he smiled, they pushed through, practically marching toward him, their mother lagging behind.

Neve carried a card, a get-well wish from their family, he surmised. But when Claire said, "Neve," both stopped a couple of feet in front of him, and Neve gave the envelope to Claire.

"I'm sorry for the intrusion," Theresa said, as Ezra, brows raised, watched the scene unfold. "They insisted..."

He didn't want an apology. Or for her to feel one was even necessary.

"Hey, you two," he said. He kept his face serious as they looked in his direction, recognizing that the rush of emotion he was experiencing was a new kind of love to him. A protective, die-for-you, paternal kind of love. "You know what Purple Hearts are?" he asked, spouting out something he'd thought of earlier.

Theresa stopped halfway into the room, standing a few feet behind her daughters. He saw her, was inordinately pleased to have her back, but mostly was engrossed by the two sets of wide brown eyes as the twins slowly shook their heads.

"It's a medal only the bravest and strongest soldiers earn. And as a sergeant, I decide sometimes who gets one. While I can't give you an army one, because, well, you aren't in the army, I've decided, as sergeant, to give you my very own Colton Purple Hearts for what you did the other day."

The girls looked at each other, and then turned around, in tandem, and looked toward their mother. Her eyes brimmed with tears, but she smiled hugely, too, and they turned back to Ezra.

"What you two did, following my clues when I threw the rocks, and then following my signals and running so fast without stopping...that makes you both the bravest, strongest six-year-olds ever, and I don't ever want you to forget that. That's why, when I get out of here, I'm going to bring you your medals."

He'd get to see them all one more time. Which was great, too.

But... "That way, whenever you remember what happened, and some of the kind of scary stuff, you can always look at your medals and remember what you did and how great that was. You can remember that you're strong and brave and that's why you don't have any reason to be afraid. Deal?"

They nodded. Neve nudged Claire, and Theresa's so-serious daughter took one step forward, handing him the envelope she held.

The envelope she'd insisted that Neve give her.

"It's from both of us." Neve stepped up next to her sister. "We made it."

"Shhh, Neve, don't give it away," Claire told her.

"Open it, Mr. Giant!" Neve said then, shifting from one little tennis-shoed foot to the other. "We were at your ranch today and rode the horses again because Mrs. Isa took us and that's why we had to wear jeans," the girl said.

"And that's where we made the card," Claire added.

He was taking his time with opening the envelope. Making a production out it for their sake, but also because he didn't want to rip it. Didn't matter to him what was inside. The twins had made it for him, so it would be sacred. Would travel with him from land to land, a memento to hang next to his bunk. A lot of guys had them: pictures of families or girlfriends, mostly, sometimes a card.

The twins' card would be his first.

He pulled it out slowly. Also for production. Sort

of. Mostly because when he caught sight of the display inside, the hearts and stars, all traced and colored, surrounding four slightly crooked handwritten words, he had to choke back his own tears.

"It's the Best Second Daddy Award!" Neve blurted, as though he couldn't read what she'd written.

"Because you were like our daddy, coming to save us," Claire said then. And Ezra had no choice but to hold out his arms and catch the kids who hurled themselves against his stitched midsection.

The pain didn't faze him.

The idea of leaving those two girls, of not being some part of their lives, hurt worse than the bullet that had seared his gut.

THERESA NEEDED A HUG, too. Ezra knew from the look he glimpsed over her daughters' shoulders. Grabbing the bag of handheld video games Naomi had brought him earlier that day, he gave them to Neve and Claire. And they were soon huddled in a corner of the room, consumed by the sack's contents.

He heard their voices. Heard Neve exclaiming and then asking questions, which Claire patiently answered. But his focus was on Theresa. She'd come to pick up the card her daughters had made. Was studying it with tears in her eyes.

"I take it you hadn't seen it?" he asked as she settled back to the side of his bed.

She shook her head, was still looking at the paper, not at him, and he had to say, "I'll always be there for you and the girls." Even as he heard the words, he knew they weren't right. And weren't enough. "I'll always have their backs," he added. "All you have to do is call." He'd take leave, do whatever he had to, to help. "I know I'm not the man you all want most, but I've come to realize that being second best is still a win. And it's far better than not placing at all."

Instead of Theresa smiling, thanking him, her chin trembled, and tears dripped down her cheeks. "I loved Mark," she told. "I still love his memory. But I'm no longer the woman he married. I'm no longer his wife. That part of me died with him, and…his illness, his death, raising the girls alone…this past year… It's all made me a new woman. A changed woman. And…" She drew a shuddering breath. Let it out and said, "I know you have to go, Ezra, but please know that, with me, with the woman I am now, you will never come second. Not ever."

He couldn't be sure he was understanding her right. And couldn't blame his confusion on pain meds, because he hadn't had any since early morning. He stared up into her gaze and remembered the way she'd said his name right before she'd shown him that sex was far, far more than mere physical pleasure.

"I might be out of line here, but…what if I didn't have to go?"

He wasn't sure what he was saying. And yet when he voiced the words, they weren't a shock to him.

"Of course you have to go. There's no battle here, no army, no…" She stopped talking. Stared at him.

"I'm thinking that I've been running long enough. Frankly, that I've been running from what I most wanted—the family life I'd believed I had until I was sixteen. A life that's probably always been here. I just cut out when times got tough. But I think I'm done cutting out…"

Dropping to her knees at his feet, taking his hands, Theresa looked up at him, eyes wide open and serious. "Don't do this for me, Ezra," she said. "Seriously, I'll be here. I'll wait. I'll marry you or not. I'll deal with the fear of you being gone if it means that, when you can, you'll be back. Like you, I don't want to spend my life running from the fear of being hurt."

Ezra knew how to defeat enemies. But he had no idea how to deal with the intense emotions love caused in him, how to let himself just experience or express them.

"I might need a place to stay while I recover." He blurted the best version he could communicate of what he was feeling. "I can always go to Mom's, but…"

He was unprepared for the face that launched up at him, but when his lips were overtaken by Theresa's, he knew exactly what to do.

There were things that had to be worked out. Details to handle. Conversations to have. And adjustments to make.

But he didn't have a single doubt that, with him and Theresa working together as a team, they'd get it all done.

And maybe even, someday, add a set of triplets or two to their own branch of the Colton family.

* * * * *

COMING SOON!

We really hope you enjoyed reading this book.
If you're looking for more romance, be sure to
head to the shops when new books are
available on

Thursday 7th
July

To see which titles are coming soon, please visit

millsandboon.co.uk/nextmonth

MILLS & BOON

THE HEART OF ROMANCE

A ROMANCE FOR EVERY READER

MODERN

Prepare to be swept off your feet by sophisticated, sexy and seductive heroes, in some of the world's most glamourous and romantic locations, where power and passion collide.

HISTORICAL

Escape with historical heroes from time gone by. Whether your passion is for wicked Regency Rakes, muscled Vikings or rugged Highlanders, awake the romance of the past.

MEDICAL

Set your pulse racing with dedicated, delectable doctors in the high-pressure world of medicine, where emotions run high and passion, comfort and love are the best medicine.

True Love

Celebrate true love with tender stories of heartfelt romance, from the rush of falling in love to the joy a new baby can bring, and a focus on the emotional heart of a relationship.

Desire

Indulge in secrets and scandal, intense drama and plenty of sizzling hot action with powerful and passionate heroes who have it all: wealth, status, good looks…everything but the right woman.

HEROES

Experience all the excitement of a gripping thriller, with an intense romance at its heart. Resourceful, true-to-life women and strong, fearless men face danger and desire - a killer combination!

To see which titles are coming soon, please visit

millsandboon.co.uk/nextmonth

GET YOUR ROMANCE FIX!

MILLS & BOON
— *blog* —

Get the latest romance news, exclusive author
interviews, story extracts and much more!

MILLS & BOON
Desire

Indulge in secrets and scandal, intense drama and plenty of sizzling hot action with powerful and passionate heroes who have it all: wealth, status, good looks…everything but the right woman.

MILLS & BOON
MODERN
Power and Passion

Prepare to be swept off your feet by sophisticated, sexy and seductive heroes, in some of the world's most glamourous and romantic locations, where power and passion collide.

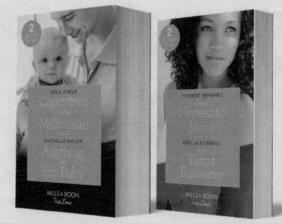